BOUND TO YOU

VOLUMES 1-3

VANESSA BOOKE

Edited by
ROGENA MITCHELL JONES

Illustrated by
KASMIT COVERS

VANESSA BOOKE

NEWSLETTER SIGN UP

Sign up to get notifications when I have a new release:
MAILING LIST SIGN UP

Edited by: Rogena Mitchell-Jones

This one is for all the curvy girls out there.

ACKNOWLEDGEMENTS

To my beloved husband, I'm grateful that every day I get to wake up next to you. If it weren't for your unyielding support, writing a book would still be just a dream for me. Thank you, baby. Xx

"I ask you to pass through life at my side—to be my second self, and best earthly companion."
— Charlotte Brontë, *Jane Eyre*

"Our scars make us know that our past was for real"
— Jane Austen, *Pride and Prejudice*

"We are all fools in love"
— Jane Austen, *Pride and Prejudice*

"It is a truth universally acknowledged, that a single man in possession of a good fortune, must be in want of a wife."
— Jane Austen, *Pride & Prejudice*

"I have for the first time found what I can truly love–I have found you. You are my sympathy–my better self–my good angel–I am bound to you with a

strong attachment. I think you good, gifted, lovely: a fervent, a solemn passion is conceived in my heart; it leans to you, draws you to my centre and spring of life, wrap my existence about you—and, kindling in pure, powerful flame, fuses you and me in one."

— Charlotte Brontë, *Jane Eyre*

PART I

PROLOGUE

He's cheating on me with her? My hand burns as I slug the tall blonde in front of me right across her collagen-injected face. A smile of satisfaction spreads across my mine as blood gushes from her nose like a busted faucet. She leaps back, falling as she clutches for the bed behind her. Her almost too symmetrical tits bounce as she lands with a loud thud on her ass. Adrenaline pumps through my veins as she leans against the bed, clutching her nose. I'm shaking, but I'm ready for more. A furnace of rage burns through me as she sneers at me and mutters the word *bitch* under her breath. I'm usually not in the habit of punching people I don't know, but I'm ready to do it again.

"Rebecca, stop!" Miles scrambles toward me as he pulls his pants up as if the floor is on fire. His honey-colored eyes stare back at me in disbelief as he assesses the carnage that's ensued. It was only an hour ago that I was on my way to his apartment to celebrate our anniversary together. The last thing I expected was to find him here with another woman.

"Who is she?" I snap. I can't stand to look at him, and at the same time, I can't look away. His usually silky brown hair is disheveled into a messy flop of fuck-me hair. The overpowering amount of evidence sends a wave of nausea right through me. *You're disgusting.*

"She's my co-worker on the show." The realization of who she is hits me as I look down at her petite frame leaning against the bed. She plays his love interest on the show *Future Outlaw*. It's the TV series Miles has been working on. He's described it as a fictional reimagining of Jesse James with time traveling cowboys fighting off the Italian Mafia. I've only been able to watch a couple of episodes because I've been so busy filling out grad school applications, but I'm shocked I didn't immediately recognize her. Apparently, the lines of reality and make believe have been blurred, because a minute ago, I walked in on the two of them fucking like cats in heat.

"Becca, are you okay?" His voice is full of concern but it's meaningless.

Miles steps closer, snapping me back to reality. I don't want him anywhere near me. The truth of his betrayal confounds me. It didn't take me long to realize something was terribly and utterly wrong from the moment I stepped into the apartment. There were rose petals meshed against the carpet leading to the bedroom, a bottle of wine sitting on the dining room table, and a note sitting on the stand in the hallway. I was surprised by Miles's overly romantic gesture. It's not his style. He's simplistic and so unromantic. He's never bought me flowers, and I've always been stupid enough to tell him that I don't care for them, when the truth is I love them. I was enjoying my ignorant bliss up until the point where I heard a sensual giggle echo behind the double doors of Miles's bedroom.

"Rebecca, it just happened," Miles starts to say. *Just happened?*

"So your dick just happened to fall into her?" I ask.

"He's been fucking me for a while," Scarlett says, standing back up. "He said he was tired of fucking you. Too much baggage." She smirks as she gives me a once over. "You're a lot bigger than I imagined. He said you were curvy," she says with a smile. "But I think he was just trying to be nice…"

1

REBECCA

I t's been three weeks—twenty-one days and five-hundred-four hours since I last saw and spoke with my cheating ex-fiancé, Miles. Since the brutal encounter with Scarlett and him, I've been seeing two new men in my life. The first is Ben and the second is Jerry. They're sweet, dependable, and they know just the right spots to hit. The sad part is they're not real. Nope, I've been having a three-week affair with several different pints of ice cream. *I know. The scandal!* Everything from Americone Dream to Milk and Cookies. The only thing to break me out of this endless loop of misery is an e-mail that I received yesterday.

To: Rebecca Gellar

From: HR@SHPublishing.com

Subject: Interview Invitation

"Ms. Gellar,

It is with great pleasure that we invite you to come in for an interview for a position at StoneHaven Publishing Co..."

I re-read the email over and over, letting reality set in a little more each time. The obsessive part of me has compulsively checked my inbox every five minutes, deathly afraid that the email will magically disappear. I've even forwarded it to two different emails, just to make sure I'm not dreaming it up. Everything is going exactly how I had hoped. I'm moving to New York and now I have an interview for my dream job. *This is really happening.* The past four years of working my ass off has finally paid off.

StoneHaven Publishing Co. is one of New York's oldest and most respected independent publishers. They're well-known for their debut authors, and I haven't seen one that hasn't become a bestseller on any of the major lists – *NY Times, USA Today*, and *Publisher's Weekly*. The thought of potentially working with one of them sends a warm rush of excitement through me. I have to admit I love the written word. There's just something about reading a story that makes me happier than anything else in the world. Even chocolate. And for me that says a lot, because I love my chocolate. My hips even agree.

The timing of this email literally couldn't be more perfect. In less than two days, I'll be on my way to the *Big Apple*. Carol Livingston, my best friend and college roommate, whom I haven't seen in over two years, will be picking me up at the airport, and then my new life begins.

"You know, you don't really have to move all the way to New York City," Mom says, slowly unzipping my hideous pink suitcase covered in glittered Hello Kitty stickers. As much as I want to, I can't get rid of the bag—my grandmother gave it to me. She has a thing for cats and the color pink, and the fusion of them together equaled my college graduation gift.

My mother isn't the sort of woman to be in her pajamas all day. She's always quick to get dolled up, even if it's just her and me in the house, so I'm pretty sure this current choice of outfit is an open protest to me going to New York. It's one o'clock in the afternoon and she's still wearing her overnight pajamas, fluffy pink slippers, and her baby blue curlers. It's the twenty-first century, but I still can't convince her to use an actual curling iron for her hair.

I've been trying to avoid the 'goodbye' conversation for the past week. I sort of sprang moving across the country on Mom and she's still upset with me. Despite the fact that I'm twenty-four, she still acts like an overprotective mother bear. I'm pretty sure the only reason she hasn't locked me in my room is because my father convinced her to be civil with me while he's away. He's a truck driver, and most weeks he's driving up to Northern California, delivering barrels of wine to local restaurants.

For the past week, my mother's been trying to convince me not to leave Los Angeles. She's told, asked, and even pleaded with me to stay. There's no convincing her that this is the right move, and there's no convincing me that it isn't. Dad always tells me that I got my stubbornness from her. I think he might be right. We're both relentless in our nature.

"I know you're worried," I say, grabbing the last pile of outfits off my bed and stuffing my phone back into my pocket. There isn't enough time in the world to try to explain to her why I needed to leave California ASAP.

"Of course, I am. I don't understand why you're moving across the world."

"Don't exaggerate."

"I'm not, I think you should stay and find work here. You won't like it in New York."

"This is a great opportunity. I'm surprised you're against it, you always told me to go for my dreams," I say. "And you were always the one saying how living in New York was such a big deal for you when you were my age."

"I think it's great you're going after your dreams, Rebecca, but I just wish that meant you living in Los Angeles. How do you know if you'll even like New York?"

It's true. I've never been to New York City. I've only seen it in pictures, movies, my mother's old postcards, and reruns of *Sex and the City*. But the thought of going somewhere new is exciting. I need it. Staying in California means facing reality, and my reality is I'm recently single, because my boyfriend of three years cheated on me with his TV co-star. I've permanently set Miles's ringtone to Puddle of Mudd's *She Hates Me*.

It doesn't help that every inch of this state reminds me of him. From the concert at the Roxy in West Hollywood where we had our first date to the Getty Museum where he asked me to be his girlfriend to Malibu Beach where he proposed. There's no getting around him. And the worst part is—I miss him.

"Carol is offering me a couch to crash on until I find work. Her cousin Ken gave me a great reference at StoneHaven Publishing. He's an Associate Editor there."

"Carol Livingston?" she asks.

"Yes, you remember her, right? She was my college roommate at UCLA."

"What is she doing in New York?"

"She does freelance public relations. She works with a lot of big name clients."

Carol graduated two years before me and she moved to New York right away. It didn't take long for her to find her niche. She's great at what she does, and now she's making the big bucks. After she left, we never lost touch. She kept inviting me to come to New York, but I could never make it because of school. Despite the thousands of miles between us, we stayed best friends. I called her for advice on moving to NY. She didn't hesitate for a second. Within a few minutes, I received a text confirming a booking for a flight from LAX to the JFK airport. She had paid for my airfare.

"What about graduate school?" my mother says, pulling out my acceptance letter from my dresser.

"I've been meaning to talk to you about that." I grab the letter from her and stuff it back inside. "I don't know if I'm still going."

"Is this because of Miles?"

Just hearing his name sends my heart flip-flopping. It's hard keeping things from my mother. She's good at reading me—too good. I hadn't explained my fiancé's absence, but there's never a good way of telling someone that the person you were planning to marry cheated on you—get ready for the fire and pitchforks.

The sound of buzzing echoes from the front door all the way to the back of the house. *I'm not expecting anyone...* I look up at my mother, and the slight smirk on her face gives me the feeling that she is.

"I wonder who that is," she says nonchalantly.

"Mother, who did you invite over?"

"Just a friend," she says as she quickly slips away.

I watch her hurry down the stairs, half running. She hates keeping visitors waiting. As I step down the stairs, I spot a headful of brown hair peeking through the side of the doorway. The voice at the door is low, almost a whisper. Who the hell is my mother talking to?

"I'm so glad you came," my mother gushes. "Rebecca will be so happy to see you. I haven't seen you around very much."

My heart stops at the sight of Miles standing on our front porch. From the look of his outfit, he must be on his way to the set for *Future Outlaw*. He's wearing jeans, cowboy boots, and a green plaid shirt.

What the hell is he doing here?

He looks good, too good. It's hard not to take notice of his tan skin and hazel eyes. They remind me of honey. Deep down inside I was hoping he looked as shitty as I feel, but I'm S.O.L. His eyes catch mine as I make my way down the stairs.

"Becca, it's good to see you." The warmth in his voice sends chills down my skin as it washes over me. My heart hammers in my chest with a chaotic beat. It's hard to pretend like everything's okay. The scent of cedar and aftershave tickles my nose as he steps closer.

"I'll leave you two alone," my mother says, scurrying off into the kitchen.

"Mrs. Gellar, it was nice to see you," he says, taking his hat off and bowing. It's as if I'm transported back in time. I hate the way he charms women—even my mother isn't immune to his ways. Miles takes my hand and pulls me to the door. The gesture sends a shock through me and I pull back instantly. We haven't touched since the day I found him in bed with Scarlett Jones, Hollywood's sexiest starlet. On my way home the other day, I saw that she had made this month's cover of *Maxim*. It took every amount of strength I had not to fling the stack of magazines off the grocery rack. *I was so close.*

"What do you want, Miles?" I try my best to sound apathetic. I don't want him to know I care. I want him to think I've moved on because I have. *Or at least that's what I keep telling myself.*

"Becca, can we talk? Alone?" he says with pleading eyes. I hate when uses his sad-puppy-dog-eyes on me. It would be so much easier to hate him if he wasn't so good looking. Not that looks are everything, but Miles is blessed with abundance. It's like God puts men like him on this earth to taunt me.

"I really don't think there's anything for you to say." Miles smirks as I put my hand on my hip. He used to say that I was sexy when I was mad.

"Would you just give me a chance to at least talk to you?" I step back as he tries to close the space between us. His presence is overwhelming. I hold back tears as a rush of sadness washes over me. We've known each other for so many years. How do you just cut someone like that from your life? Being alone with my ex-fiancé is probably not a good idea, but my curiosity always gets the best of me.

"Are you going to tell me how you didn't mean to fuck her?" I can taste the bitterness of my words, but I don't care if I hurt him. I want him to hurt.

"Becca..."

"Fine, let's go outside. My mom doesn't know what's going on."

"You still haven't told her?" he says in a hopeful tone.

Miles and I sit inside his red Ford pickup truck staring out over the view of downtown Los Angeles. The sky is surprisingly clear of smog. It's a rarity out here. My parents' house is situated on a hill that has a beautiful view of the city. It reminds me of the view from Mulholland Drive. We used to love going up there. We'd drive up, pull off on the side of the road, and mess around. The few times I've driven up since we broke up have been heartbreaking. The scenery no longer brings me happy memories. Only tears.

"I heard you were leaving," Miles says, frowning.

I reposition my body against the door, trying to distance myself from him. There isn't much room between us, and each time he moves his hand, it brushes my leg.

"I am."

"Why? Because of what happened?"

He makes it sound like 'what happened' isn't a big deal. I don't need to explain myself to him. Apparently, I haven't made it clear enough that I'm not his anymore.

"Not everything revolves around you."

"Then why?" Miles says, putting his arm around the top of my seat. "Why haven't you returned my calls, Becca?"

The past few weeks have been difficult to say the least. I miss him —as much as I don't want to. I know it would be so much easier to just slip back into his arms. To pretend like nothing happened, but my pride won't let me.

"Miles, I can't forgive you for sleeping with her."

"It isn't what you think."

"Oh, really, tell me then..."

"Becca, we're co-stars. We're doing the TV show together. That's it."

"I caught you two together in our bed! You're just sorry you got caught." *Be strong.* My voice nearly breaks. "You're lucky my mother doesn't watch cable or she would've thrown you out of the house the moment you tried stepping inside."

"Scarlett doesn't mean anything to me."

Scarlett. Just hearing the name makes my head want to explode. She's some famous Australian blonde beauty that has everything going for her—including huge assets.

"There's only you," he says, nuzzling his nose into my hair. "I've missed you."

"Stop," I whisper.

"I know you still love me," he says, brushing back a strand of hair.

"I do, I mean, I did."

He traces his finger down my arm. He's too close. I can't trust myself around him. He doesn't wait for my response. It happens so fast, there isn't enough time to react. He crushes his lips against mine, pulling me to him. I used to love the way Miles would kiss me. It was gentle, slow, and sensual, but this was different. His hand creeps up my shirt, finding its way to my nipple and pinching it slightly.

"Miles... no."

"Becca, it's not my fault. My agent said I would get more camera time if I started seeing Scarlett. It's for the show! She doesn't mean anything to me. He didn't think it would be a good idea for me to be seen..."

"Seen with what? A normal woman? Or do you mean someone

my size?" I have to admit I threw in that last part just for the hell of it. I can't help but feel a little self-conscious when Miles went from sleeping with someone like me to sleeping with Ms. Double Ds.

"It's not like that, Becca. Please let me show you how much I've missed you." His hand slides up my dress, pushing apart my legs. "I've thought about this every night."

"No." I slap his hand away. "You can't just pretend like we're okay and go back to how it used to be."

"Becca, please. Let's try again."

"I gave you everything, Miles, but you ripped it all away. You chose her instead of me." *You chose someone you barely know over me.*

"But I love you."

I don't say anything. I can't. The words I want to say are on the tip of my tongue, and just knowing that tears my insides. *I love you, too.* I can't show him any weakness. I need to go. Miles stares at me in confusion as I open the car and jump out of the truck.

"At least let me walk you inside," he says, calling after me.

I don't stop walking until I'm in the house. I don't bother telling my mother that Miles is gone. She would only start an inquisition if she saw me crying. At this moment, nothing else matters—only the pain.

2

REBECCA

"Can I get you anything else, miss?" the dainty brunette stewardess asks as she hands me a glass of champagne and a napkin.

"No, thank you. The champagne is lovely." My nerves are on high alert. I can feel a knot forming in my shoulders every time we hit a bump of turbulence. I grasp the arms of my chair with my clammy hands and fight back the building need to spew all over the seat in front of me. The older man sitting next to me leans back, eyeing me with caution. There isn't much room between us. I'm sure he's kicking himself for being seated next to this train wreck. If I throw up, he's definitely in the splash zone. My stomach turns again as the plane rattles. *Don't puke. Don't puke. Don't puke.* I pinch my nose as I silently count to ten, hoping that it will calm me. The last thing I need right now is to show up in a new city with vomit all over me.

God, I hate flying.

When I called Carol to let her know my flight was leaving, she offered to upgrade my ticket to first class so I wouldn't be *sausaged* beside someone for the next four hours. As tempting as the offer was, she's already done enough for me. I even thought about booking a train from California to New York, but it would've taken too long. My interview with StoneHaven Publishing is on Monday—only three days away. I need time to prepare for it. As confident as I am that I would make a great fit, there's still the possibility of not getting the job. I'm sure my mother would love to hear that I'm coming back home. She wants me to follow my dreams, but only if that includes catching a husband and staying in California.

Saying goodbye to my mother was painful. Each time I carried one of my luggage bags outside, she made a face as if I had just killed one of her non-existent grandbabies. I didn't have the heart to tell her that Miles is a really big douche and that we're done. I may have told her a little white lie. She asked me if we we're on a break, and I kind of nodded my head yes. I'm not sure if lying to her about it is any better, but I wasn't in the mood to hear her complain that I'm never going to get married. She loves to remind me that I'll probably die a spinster. At the current moment, that doesn't sound too bad. I can almost see my name in the papers. *Rebecca Gellar, spinster with five cats, dies after Hollywood breakup.* Speaking of Hollywood, I definitely need a welcomed distraction from this plane ride, so catching up on my latest celebrity gossip sounds like heaven. Reading the celebrity magazine STARS is my newest guilty pleasure.

I flip through the latest issue and cringe at the sight of a paparazzi photo of Miles and Scarlett cuddling close together at our favorite pastry & coffee shop on Melrose. They seem to be Hollywood's latest *IT* couple. I know I'm better off without Miles's cheating ass, but it still hurts to see them together. As I scan down to the picture of Scarlett and Miles to read the article beside it, my heart jolts at the bolded word: ENGAGED. We're nearly forty-thousand feet in the air, but I can still feel my whole world plummet as I read over the details of the article. 'Hollywood TV star Miles Storm and co-star Scarlett Jones are engaged.' My eyes begin to water at the zoomed in picture of Scarlett's ring.

The real zinger is the fact that Miles gave her a ring. We were engaged almost six months and he had been dragging his feet to buy me an engagement ring. I guess our relationship was never really meant to last. I can't believe he tried to feed me his bullshit about how Scarlett didn't mean anything to him. Apparently, she meant a lot more than I did.

The voice of the airplane's captain comes in muffled over the intercom, drawing me from my thoughts. I strain to hear him over the general noise of the plane and only manage to catch three words: STORM and STRONG WINDS. My hand immediately goes to my seatbelt just in time to fasten it, as the plane hits a major gust of wind. The whole body of the airplane shakes causing my glass of champagne to teeter and spill over. The dip of the plane sends a familiar but strange sensation through my stomach. It's like free-falling on a rollercoaster decline.

The fasten seatbelt sign lights up as I spot the stewardesses coming down the rows checking each seat. I push up my tray, down what's left of the spilled glass, and grab ahold of my purse. I need to calm my nerves and my stomach. My imagination starts to drift, and I can feel the cold sliver of anxiety creep into my chest. I need to get off. *This is the last way I want to die.* God, if it weren't for Miles, I wouldn't even be on this stupid plane flying in this disastrous weather. I've never hated him as much as I do right now! I fight my every desire to run down the aisle like a raving mad woman. We hit another air pocket and my body goes flying up, along with my purse. My bag flips over, sliding into first class, along with my wallet and motion sickness pills inside. Shit. I should just leave it there until the storm settles. I'll be fine. *I'm fine. I'm fine. I'm fine.* The plane jostles us again. *Oh, god, I'm not fine.* I start to hyperventilate in my seat. I need a bag. I pull out the brown paper bag wedged between the seat pockets in front of me.

Everything I've seen on TV tells me that this will help, but as soon as I slip the brown bag over my nose and mouth, I feel worse. I need my pills. I need to take some more. I click off my seatbelt and scramble down the row, running into seats as the airplane sways. A shrill voice of a flight attendant stops me as I make it to the curtain dividing first class from economy. I know I don't have much time to run and grab my purse.

"Ma'am! Please, get back to your seat immediately."

I turn slightly, my body shaking from anxiety and dread. I don't wait for her to stop me from entering first class. The first thing I notice is the stark contrast between the seat spacing. In economy, you're cramped with little-to-no legroom. For the past two hours, I've been fighting with the gentleman next to me over the armrest. I can't help but frown at the disparity between first class and economy. Each row has enough space to recline back and fall asleep. The lights are dimmed throughout the section, and the general atmosphere seems a lot more relaxed. In fact, many of the passengers seem to be sleeping —all but one, a beautiful blonde stranger staring at the bright screen of his tablet. The luminous light gives his face an almost angelic appearance with the exception of his brows, which seem shrouded in deep thought. The plane sways to the side, tossing me against the chair of a nearby female passenger. She stirs and looks up at me with a mixture of annoyance and sleep.

"Sorry," I whisper.

The beautiful stranger a few rows ahead seems undisturbed by my presence. The leather seat chairs to his right and left are completely empty, and it takes me a moment to realize that he probably purchased all of them. I can only imagine how much it is to buy *one* first class seat, not to mention six. I know Carol spent entirely too much money on my ticket and I'm not even up here.

I scan the floor for my belongings and notice my purse clinging for life only a few feet away from the stranger's seat. Before I have a chance to move, I notice the prissy flight attendant staring me down from the opening of the curtain divider. *Geez, lady.*

"Ma'am, please return to your seat. Coach passengers are not allowed up here." Despite her calmness, I sense a thread of disdain in her voice. Perhaps this isn't the first time a passenger made their way up here. She probably thinks I'm trying to switch my seat. As much as I would love not to be stuck in a seat with barely any legroom, I'm more worried about puking everywhere. *I need my purse.* A wave of nausea flows over me. I can feel beads of sweat breaking out on my neck and forehead.

"I'm just getting my purse..." I manage to squeak.

"Ma'am, the fasten seatbelt sign is still on," she says, pointing to the drawing of two hands buckling a seatbelt. "We cannot have anyone walking around at this time."

I shrug off her awkward stare and scramble over to my purse. The blond stranger doesn't notice me at first as I kneel to search beneath his seat. It isn't until I pull the strap of my purse that he senses my presence. I yank hard to release my purse, but my wallet goes flying, along with my pills. *Fuck.* A sigh of frustration escapes me as I grab for them. A flash of light cascades over me as a warm hand encloses around my wrist, stopping me midway.

"Excuse me, miss, what are you doing down there?" I'm immediately taken aback by the closeness of his face. Two blue eyes stare at me impassively. They somehow perfectly match his nose and striking cheekbones. If it weren't for the slight smirk on his lips, you'd think he was angry. But it's worse. He's laughing at me. He must find this all so very amusing. A streak of anger rushes to my cheeks, setting them on fire.

"Are you laughing at me?" I ask, clenching back my irritation.

He eyes me with curiosity as he slowly studies me. He's a playboy I'm sure. Handsome men like him are trouble. I'm sure he's used to women throwing themselves at his feet. I silently admire the light beard he sports. It makes him look like a bit of a rogue in his grey tailored suit. His facial hair reminds me of the way Miles used to wear his. He used to run his chin across my bare skin in the morning. It was his way of waking me up. I loved the way it felt on me when we made love. The way it *used* to feel before he went and smashed my whole world into tiny little pieces.

My eyes stray to his hand and a mixture of lustful emotions cling to me, warming my insides. I'm strangely relieved to see no ring on his finger. *That doesn't mean he's not married. He totally could be.* I find myself unknowingly leaning into him and his alluring scent of spicy cinnamon and fresh mint leaves. It reminds me of my favorite home-made tea back in Cali.

"Can I help you find something?" he asks, grazing over my comment.

"I dropped my purse." His hand never leaves my wrist as he gently helps me up. My legs are unstable. I wobble to a stand.

"Let me help," he says with another smile.

"It's caught on your chair," I say.

The stewardess lingering in the back clears her throat, directing our attention back toward her. She waits in front of our aisle looking extremely nervous. "I apologize, sir, would you like me to escort this young lady back to her seat?" I turn, glancing from him to her. I've never seen anyone so worried. *Who is this guy? Maybe he's some rich hot shot.* It doesn't matter. I should mind my own business and get back to my seat.

"Melissa, it's fine. She isn't bothering me," he says without looking up. I don't think I've ever heard anyone address a stewardess by their first name, not unless they were purposely trying to be snarky, but reading his tone, it's more irritation than anything else. He seems like someone who's used to bossing people around. Or maybe he just flies this airline often.

"I apologize, Mr. St —"

"That will be all, thank you." He waves her off like an annoying fly. She scurries off back to the back of the plane without looking back. Part of me feels sorry for her. She was just doing her job even if she was kind of bitchy. I'm sure I would've done the same thing.

"Is this it?" he says, handing me my purse and wallet. Somehow, even my gigantic bag seems so small in his hands. His hand grazes mine, sending a tingling vibration up my arm. I try my best not to stare at his fingers, but I can't stop myself. I have a thing for hands, and his are the type you don't mind wrapping around you or inside of you.

I blush instantly as he clears his throat, indicating that I've lingered in his presence for much too long. Ironically, my motion sickness pills are still under his chair, but I don't even bother mentioning it. I need to get out of here. The same out-of-breath feeling I felt a moment ago in my seat has returned. I don't need to be embarrassed more than once this week.

"Yes, thank you. Excuse me." I try to go, but the warmth of his touch returns as he captures my hand.

"Your name, you didn't tell me it." He's smiling again. I blush as his touch sends goose bumps up my skin. The air grows warmer by the minute as his fingers rub circular motions across the skin of my wrist. I've never felt anything quite as erotic as this, and my clothes aren't even off. I'm almost too willing to jump into his lap. My blush deepens at the thought of what he might feel like on top of me. *Since when did I become so horny?* I have to admit, sex has been the last thing on my mind since the disaster with Miles. I haven't had the urge to be with anyone. Yet, right now, I can almost feel the sexual energy radiating off him. There are just some men who scream sex, and he's definitely one of them.

"My name is Rebecca," I respond, nearly breathless.

"It's lovely to meet you, Becca," he says, kissing my hand. "I'm Nicholas." His lips feel cool like ice water against my skin, and I smile at the way he's shortened my name. I don't typically let anyone call me Becca, but I'm inclined to let this handsome stranger call me whatever he wants as long as he keeps touching me.

I cling to his chair as a sudden shift in the plane throws me off balance. The cabin rings signaling the plane's stewardesses to check each passenger's seatbelt. *I should've gone back to my seat.* I sway backwards almost losing my balance, but Nicholas grips my hand, pulling me back. I'm almost steady until the plane dips, pushing me straight into his lap. The sudden force of my body colliding into his sends his tablet flying onto the floor with a thud. He catches me by the waist, his fingers sliding down to my bottom. I know it isn't intentional, but his touch is undeniably sensual.

"Are you all right?" he asks. A quiet concern shrouds his face. He doesn't immediately let me go. He simply moves his hand to brush back a loose tendril from my face. The touch of his fingertips heats my skin like liquid fire. It spreads in a rapid rush of heat down my body, exposing me beneath his unrelenting stare. His grasp tightens around my waist, and for a moment, I feel something hard poking me beneath my jeans. *Is that? Oh, my.*

"I should get back to my seat before that stewardess has a heart attack," I whisper. The sentence sounds more like a question than a statement.

"Stay." His husky voice draws me in. There's a slight accent to his voice, but I can't quite place it. I've never been a snob about the guys I've dated, but there's something about an accent that just makes women's panties drop. It's probably not the only thing about him that would turn me on. His eyes linger over me, watching me closely. If I knew I was going to meet the living Adonis on an airplane, I probably wouldn't have been so afraid to fly. No, that's probably a lie. I still would've been scared, but I definitely would've picked a cuter outfit.

Now, this beautiful Greek god has his hands on me, and I can't stop thinking about what it would feel like to have them inside me. I reach up and stroke the hair that trails below his bottom lip. I want to know what it feels like to kiss him. It isn't until I hear almost a low growl in his throat that I realize what I'm doing. *Jesus, Rebecca. You're fondling a complete stranger.* I pull back my hand, but he immediately brings it back to his lips. He takes my fingers and slowly kisses them. I inhale sharply as he runs his beard on the inside of my wrist. For some reason, it feels unexpectedly intimate, as if we're old lovers, and despite the cloistered space around us, it feels like the whole world is watching.

He stops and looks up at me before leaning in. His mouth captures mine in a heated kiss. I'm hesitant as he starts to slowly nibble my bottom lip, gently making his way to the top one. The sensation of his hands grazing my breast causes me to moan. He traces his thumb along my neckline and I give in to his kiss. A whirlwind of lust passes through my body, and I instantly grow wet. He pulls me closer, and soon, I'm so enraptured by the feeling of his mouth on me that I forget what it feels like to breathe. A strange electric charge dissipates as we pull apart. I smile inwardly at the realization that he's panting almost as much as I am.

"What are you thinking about?" he asks, staring down at me.

His question makes me uneasy. Not because it's too personal, but because what I'm thinking about involves him undressing me. He's a stranger. Someone I'll never see again, and right now, I'm not sure if that's a good or bad thing. Maybe part of moving on means doing things you wouldn't normally do. Like hooking up with handsome strangers forty-thousand feet in the air or maybe I'm just trying to numb my pain. It's time to stop living in a fantasy.

"It was nice meeting you, but I do need to get back to my seat," I whisper, unwinding myself from him.

"If you insist," he says with a polite smile. I want to tell him thank you, but telling him thank you for the kiss sounds way too awkward in my head. I can only imagine what it would sound like if I actually said it.

"I hope to see you around," he says.

"Me, too."

I'll never see him again, and while I really wish I could spend the rest of the plane ride with him up here, it would be a mistake. It's been less than a month since Miles. I don't need to go chasing someone else. I just need to be alone. I don't want to be one of those girls who always need a guy on her arm to feel complete. I don't want prince charming to come save me and fix everything. I want to save myself.

I leave without asking for his number, and he doesn't stop me to ask for mine. Disappointment creeps into the back of my mind. I'm not sure what I was hoping for. This isn't some romantic comedy where the gorgeous playboy falls in love with the shy curvy girl. My grandmother used to have a saying—*what's yours, no one else can take.* I guess if it's meant to be, maybe I'll meet him again one day, but for now, I'm happy with the calmness that he's enveloped me in. I hold onto it as I make my way back to my seat and fall asleep for the rest of the trip.

I don't wake again until I hear the sound of the captain announcing that we will be landing at the JFK airport in less than fifteen minutes. After flying over three-thousand miles in a cramped, overbooked airplane, I'm more than anxious to be on the ground again. Four hours of flying is exhausting, and I am definitely mentally drained. I keep reminding myself that it's all worth it. Soon, I'll be in the big city and thus begins my journey of trying to land a job at StoneHaven Publishing. With a little luck, by this time next month, I'll be working and living in my own apartment. New York, here I come.

3

REBECCA

The airport is buzzing as I make my way over to the baggage claim area. I'm glad I didn't listen to my mom when she suggested that I take a later flight. With the unpredictable East Coast weather, I've already lost more than a day stuck at the Dallas airport in Texas. To my dismay, I did not see Mr. Tall, Blond, and Sexy as I exited the plane, but that's probably a good thing.

"Rebecca!"

I spot Carol standing near the drop-off section just outside of the JFK airport. Her short, blonde pixie cut from college is replaced with long strands of brown hair pulled into a perfectly set bun. I smile as she pushes up her stylish glasses and heads my way. I have to admit she looks stunning. She makes wearing a bun look like fashion chic. I think I've always been jealous of the way confidence just seems to ooze out of her. I peek down at my raggedy jeans, Chuck Taylors, and my ten-dollar T-shirt, slightly embarrassed at just how plain I look.

Finding fancy clothes is difficult with my size. I hate the term 'plus size,' yet that's what the world insists on labeling me as. If I've gained weight since college, Carol doesn't mention it. I grab my suitcase and haul it across the sidewalk trying my best not to get run over as I make my way toward Carol. "Oh, my god. Becca, it's so amazing to see you!" She hugs me, and the memories of our late night study sessions, frat parties, and college heartaches come rushing back to me. I didn't even realize how much I've really missed her until right now. Carol is like the sister I never had. Sometimes being an only child sucks. Not to mention I don't have any younger or older sisters for my mother to marry off.

"You look great, Carol. New York has done you good."

"Thanks, girly. It's a crazy world over here, but you're going to love it! I can't wait to get back to my apartment. I have so many plans for tonight!"

"I'm excited to be here. Thanks for letting me crash with you." Excited wasn't even close to how I really felt. *Scared. Anxious. Ecstatic. Pumped.* I feel invincible—ready to take on the world.

"It's not a problem, really. I would've been terribly offended if you hadn't have asked."

She hooks her arm through mine as she tugs me toward a sleek, black Lexus. It's as if we're teenagers again, off on an adventure. Taxicabs flood the airport, pulling in and out every few seconds. It's a miracle anyone can get out of here. My attention is drawn to a handsome older man stepping out of Carol's car.

"Ms. Gellar," he says, quickly bending down to grab my suitcase. His movements are so swift that my suitcase is settled into the trunk of the car in what seems like a blur. He walks over and opens the back passenger side of the Lexus. If he didn't look at least twenty-years my senior, I would say he's pretty sexy.

"Oh, I almost forgot, this is my driver, Steven," Carol says, grinning. Whoa, she has a chauffeur?

"He's fantastic. If you need anything—he'll get it. Even tampons and stuff." The thought of Steven, who coincidentally reminds me of Liam Neeson from *Taken*, picking up tampons for me makes my cheeks burn.

"That's okay, I'll be good."

Steven chuckles, obviously amused at my shyness. "It would be my pleasure picking up anything you may require, Ms. Gellar."

"Please, call me Rebecca." The only people who call me by my last name are my professors and the occasional telemarketer. Gosh, I hate telemarketers. I always feel bad when they call because you know half the time they're just as miserable as you are.

"Steven, on our way home let's stop by Cheri's place." Carol's PR business must be skyrocketing if she can afford her own chauffeur. I can only wish to have half the success Carol's had.

"Who's Cheri?" I ask.

"She's one of my clients. She runs her own fashion line, Retro Thrift. She does a lot of affordable pinup styles and some great formal dresses that look like they're from the nineteen-thirties," Carol says, digging through her black leather purse and pulling out her phone. "Here, check it out." Carol pulls up Cheri's online web store. It's like looking at old photographs. The dresses on Cheri's site are absolutely gorgeous. I have no idea how she's managed to make them affordable. Unless thrift is a new word for overpriced vintage clothes.

"Wow, I wish I could wear all of them." I'm such a nerd for vintage fashion. My mother is always rolling her eyes at me when I find vintage outfits at the Salvation Army. She can't understand why people want to dress like they're from the past.

"Yeah, I just need to pick up a few outfits for a photo shoot we're doing tomorrow," Carol says, throwing her phone back inside her purse. A loud buzzing sound draws her attention back to her phone as she scoops it out of her bag. Carol bursts into laughter, shoving her cell in my hands.

Carol,

Take care of Becca. Please.

Love,

Mrs. G

I am mortified that my mother has Carol's cell phone number. I didn't give it to her, which means she probably copied it out of my phone contacts. She's too sneaky for her own good.

"Becca, I have to warn you, this isn't the first time your mom has called me. She called before I came to pick you up." I turn to Carol, covering the red blazing on my cheeks. "And she called again about an hour ago."

"Oh, god." It was like I was back in freshmen year of college spending my first night away from home. I can still remember the way the other college girls in our dorm stared at me when my RA came in, saying that my mother had called to ask if I was doing all right on my first night away from home. Can you say utterly embarrassing? Yup. That's her.

"She said she's worried about you." Carol eyes me with curiosity. Yeah, she would be, but I actually think she's more concerned that I've totally blown it with Miles.

Not that I would count that as a bad thing.

"I think she's worried that I might've ruined her shot at grandbabies."

"What?" Carol laughs, playfully shoving me. "Are you pregnant?"

"Gosh, no!" That would be a serious problem. Not just because I'm totally not ready for babies, but if I were, Miles would definitely be the wrong guy.

"Miles came to see me before I left," I admit, avoiding Carol's stare. She can see through anything. It's like she has x-ray vision of the mind.

"What? Seriously?"

"Yeah, he wanted to get back together."

"Is that a good thing?"

"No, definitely not."

"You know, you never really explained what he did to mess up. You promised to explain it to me in person. Are you ready to tell me now?"

Somehow, when I really think about it, Miles's betrayal feels partly my fault. Maybe I wasn't a good enough girlfriend. Maybe I made him stray. Our physical relationship seemed a lot more important to him than anything else. It's not that I'm a prude about sex, but the fact that Miles made me feel incompetent on the subject. He has a nasty habit of trying to tell me what he wanted by bringing up old girlfriends used to do. From there, the chemistry between us began to flicker out. I wanted to work on 'us,' but unfortunately, Miles didn't seem to share the same sentiment. I guess it was easier to go fuck someone else.

"He cheated on me with his co-star."

"Ew, you mean the blonde in *Future Outlaw*?"

"Yeah, she's the one who plays his love interest on the show."

"Lovely," Carol huffs. "The little slut."

"She is lovely. She has legs for miles and she's thin. According to the latest gossip, Miles had dumped his no-name girlfriend, me, for his thinner, with an emphasis on thinner, girlfriend. What's worse is I just found out through STARS magazine that they're engaged."

"What a douche! He doesn't deserve you." Carol grabs my hand, giving it a quick squeeze. "He really doesn't. And please don't listen to the stupid TV or any of those gossip magazines. You're beautiful. Who wouldn't want you? I mean, I do, and I'm not even into girls," she says.

"Thanks, girly."

Carol playfully nudges me with her shoulder. "I know you'll be okay, but is there anything I can do? I mean, I do know some people," she says, giving me a knowing look.

I miss having someone to talk to, at least someone other than my mother. It feels great knowing that Carol has my back. It makes this trip out here a little easier. I hope the transition is just as smooth.

"I'm okay. A little shaky, but okay." I smile.

"Well, fuck him."

"I just wish I could forget we were ever together."

"Cheri has just the thing for that!" Carol says, excitement coursing through her. "C'mon, let's pick up the outfits I need from her, an extra something for you, and get back to my pad. We have to get ready for your date tonight," Carol says, winking.

"Date? How the hell do I have a date?" I really hoped Carol doesn't plan to hook me up with a friend of hers. I hate blind dates.

"It's complicated. In short, I'm meeting Tristan Knight, another client of mine at a club opening. It's tonight. He wants to talk over some plans for getting publicity for the new art gallery he's thinking of opening. I only agreed to meet tonight because he said he didn't mind if I brought a friend along who just moved here. He actually said that he would bring a friend, too."

"Oh, gosh, Carol. I'm really not up to meeting anyone tonight. I need to catch up on sleep. I have jetlag." I think I've filled my quota for meeting beautiful men today. After Nicholas, I don't think I can handle another. It's like sensory overload waiting to happen.

"Sweetheart, nobody gets jetlag from California to New York. It's only four hours, tops."

Part of me wants to whine and complain that I don't want to meet some rich, stuffy guy, but Carol definitely is what I would consider wealthy, and she isn't stuffy. Not one bit.

Carol's apartment is on the Upper West Side of Manhattan. I remember reading about the area online. Or rather, drooling about it. The neighborhood is known for its history of artistic workers and its wealthy community. I'm not surprised that she wanted to live in an artsy neighborhood. Even when we were living in Los Angeles, Carol always talked about moving near the art center of Los Angeles. But I have to say, LA doesn't have anything on the Upper West Side of Manhattan.

The inside of Carol's apartment is just as extravagant as the outside. Wood flooring leads to a kitchen with marble floors and granite countertops. The kitchen is probably as big as Gordon Ramsay's *Hell's Kitchen*. I wonder if she has a pantry with every ingredient that you could ever think of, too. This must be what heaven looks like for foodies, aka food lovers.

Carol leads me into the bedroom where she sets the five outfits for tomorrow's photo shoot down on the bed, plus one little black dress for me. Apparently, the wondrous fashion designer, Cheri Coy, has plenty of dresses in my size. I was afraid she only made supermodel sizes, but her line actually caters to curvy women. The dress she graciously lent me isn't just any ordinary cocktail dress. It hugs my waist in just the right way, giving me an hourglass figure, instead of a muffin top. The back slits up, almost like a pencil skirt, and the front dips low in heart shapes on my breasts. If it weren't for my fifteen-dollar dress shoes, I'd say I could pass for someone in the VIP lounge.

"Whoa, look at you!" Carol takes a turn around me to get the full effect of the dress. "You... look... amazing."

"Thank you." I blush. It's always been hard taking compliments. Being the center of attention usually isn't my style, but tonight it is.

"Seriously, you'd give Joan Holloway a run for her money," she says, grinning. Carol knows exactly what to say to make me feel like a million bucks. Joan Holloway is my favorite character from the period drama *Mad Men*.

"I think you should borrow some of my shoes. I have some great Mary Jane's that would complete your look." Carol walks over to her closet and pulls out a pair of sleek, black shoes with white accents. I stand in awe at the monstrosity she calls a closet. The thing is bigger than my bedroom back home.

"You like that?" Carol asks, winking. "You should see my view." She pulls me toward the living room just as Steven pulls back the curtains from the panoramic windows. My breath catches at the sight of the New York City skyline. The best part about the apartment is definitely the view. I stare out the window at the beautiful chaos of the city below us. How the hell does anyone afford this?

"Do you have a sugar daddy or something?" I blurt. Carol winces slightly.

"Hey, I'm not someone's baby girl," she says.

"Sorry, it's just... I don't know how people afford to live in extravagant apartments like this," I confess.

"The apartment is on loan to me," Carol gushes. "One of my clients offered me the apartment in exchange for some help on a publicity campaign."

"Wow! That's amazing. I'm sort of jealous," I confess.

"Well, you get to enjoy this AMAZING place with me," she says, smiling. "Are you ready to live it up?"

I laugh in spite of the nerves eating away at me. "So ready."

"Let's get you looking drop dead gorgeous for tonight."

"So do you even know who your client's friend is? He could be a creeper."

"I'm not sure, but he's not a creeper. Mr. Knight is a reputable person, and knowing the people he keeps company with, I'm sure his friend is a big fish."

"I'm not looking to catch anyone," I say, laughing.

"You never know. Maybe you'll meet Mr. Right," Carol says, winking. Hah. I'm starting to think either Mr. Right is trapped in another dimension or he just doesn't exist. Either way, I'm single for life.

The memory of Nicholas' kiss still sears my thoughts. *I wonder if I'll ever see him again.*

4

NICHOLAS

This weekend would've been hell if it weren't for the redhead I met on the plane. My cock stirs at the thought of her round little ass pressed up against me. It doesn't matter that she was wearing jeans. I knew she could feel me growing hard underneath her. It took all of my strength not to take her into one of the lavatories and fuck her until she begged me to stop. Her lips were a tease for something even more delicious. I bet she tastes like peaches.

"Good morning, Mr. StoneHaven." Mary, our building receptionist breaks me from my thoughts as she hands me a manila envelope. Mary Striver has been with our company for over thirty years. I feel strangely close to her, although she doesn't usually say any more than hello or goodbye to me. I do have to admit, she does have a quirky character. Sometimes I refer to her as Mona Lisa because she always seems like she's hiding something funny.

"Good morning, Mary. What's this?"

"It's the folder of resumes your father wanted you to look over before Monday. He's looking to hire a new personal assistant for you."

"This has to be the fifth assistant this year." PAs don't seem to last too long with me. It's partly my fault. Most of them end up in my bed and they don't stay there long, which means they don't stay here long.

"Yes, it is," Mary says, half smiling to herself. "Your father is expecting you upstairs."

"Thank you, Mary. Don't go home too late."

"Of course, sir. Goodnight."

I swallow the irritation nipping at my heels as I make my way up the elevator to the thirtieth floor. The sight of the familiar marble flooring and gunmetal windows eases my nerves somewhat. *I'm home.* StoneHaven Publishing has been my home for as long as I can remember. It's filled with countless memories of summers spent helping my father as he built this company piece by piece. Every summer, I watched him labor over it for hours upon hours. I'm pretty sure this company is and will always be my father's baby. No, I'm damn sure.

After a four-hour flight, and two hours spent trying to get through the city, I'm exhausted. This past week has been grueling. I thought Los Angeles would be a nice break from the hectic New York scenery, but LA was just one of my father's distractions. He had me meeting with potential investors almost every day. I thought he was looking to expand and open up an office in California. I should've known better. He agreed too easily to send me to California. While I was working, he was planning an engagement.

As of this morning, I am supposed to announce my engagement to Alison Price, the daughter of one of my father's investors. It isn't as if I actually asked Alison to marry me. No, my father bartered with Grayson Price and this is the deal they came to. This is the twenty-first century, and yet somehow this feels archaic. The roles have reversed over these past centuries. Now, I'm being put up for auction. My father has a new mission for me—marriage. Just the thought of it sends my stomach turning. Married to one woman for the rest of my life is insanity. And it isn't even one I particularly like.

I thought we settled this argument before I flew to Los Angeles. Apparently, our conversation was moot because I received a text message from a fellow colleague congratulating me on my upcoming nuptials. The part that had me confused was why I was supposedly getting married in the first place. I thought it was some cruel joke. *But I was so wrong.*

My father's office sits in the furthest corner of the floor. Much like his egotistical self, he demanded the office with the best view overlooking the city below. I'm not sure why he wonders who I get my traits from. It's obvious. The floor is clear of employees, with the exception of security doing their nightly rounds of each floor. Sometimes I wonder if we need so many people clearing all of the floors.

I find Father sitting at his desk reading over a slew of documents. He doesn't bother looking up as I enter the room. He's wearing his bifocal glasses again. Emily, my little sister, is always teasing him by telling him that he looks like Benjamin Franklin with them on. If only she could see him right now. Father mutters something, which as far as I can guess, is him telling me to sit down.

"Good evening, I'm glad to see you finally made it in," he says, taking his glasses off and rubbing the dark circles under his eyes.

"Father, I need to speak with you about this impending marriage you seem to think is happening."

He looks up with a smirk of amusement. I know all too well that he's up to no good. If I could stare daggers at him right now, I would. I don't understand why he wants to micromanage everything, including my life. He places the stack of documents in his desk and leans back in his chair. His composure reminds me of when I was in high school and we would talk about the importance of studying. Father hated that I wanted to play sports in school. He'd rather me read all day. He finds greater value in the mind than in the body. I beg to differ. I think there's plenty of value in the body, especially when it comes to women.

"Yes, I think now is a good time to discuss your upcoming marriage, but first, I would like to discuss this issue of getting you a new personal assistant. I went ahead and had HR post a temporary position up on the site. We have several candidates lined up. Interviews will be held Monday morning. If you'd like, you can be there, but if not, I think I can manage on my own."

"Father, I don't need another assistant," I say with annoyance.

"You're right, son," he says, throwing his hands up in exasperation. "What you really need is a babysitter."

"What?" *A babysitter?* "I'm twenty-eight, not ten."

"You haven't proved that to me yet."

"I spent this past weekend speaking with investors under the impression that we were looking to open another office in California."

"I'm just glad to see you finally taking an interest in the family business," Father says.

It's difficult to appreciate something that's nearly destroyed our family. But I've learned to love this business.

"I don't have to sit here and listen to this." I begin to stand, but my father's words stop me.

"That's where you're wrong," he says, turning in his chair. "You forget your income comes from this company. You were born into wealth. You haven't really worked a day in your life. I've been trying to teach you to be responsible, because one day, you're going to inherit this company and with that, comes certain expectations."

"Yes, and marrying me off to one of your investors' daughters isn't enough to show my commitment to this company, and to this family?"

"No, Alison Price's money may save this company, but if you don't handle things properly, you can still run it straight into the ground."

"I refuse to marry someone I don't even like."

"When I married your mother, I wasn't in love with her. The love came later on. Sometimes it's better that way."

"Yes, because you and Mom are a perfect example of a lasting relationship." The words come out more bitter than I intend, but I can't help the anger rising in my chest. My mother isn't an easy topic for either of us. She married my father because of his wealth and she left us when we were at our lowest. She was everything to my father, to my brother, to me, and my sister Emily. *Was* being the keyword.

"You understand you're making my life a living hell, right?" I ask.

Father chuckles softly. "Since when is living in luxury hell?"

"You know I'm not going to make this easy," I warn.

"Of course not," he says, smiling. "I wouldn't expect anything less. Nicholas, just give Alison Price a chance. I need you to behave while we're in negotiations with her father. You'll see. At the end of all of this, you'll understand why I'm doing what I'm doing."

I highly doubt it.

"Keep her happy," he says, eyeing me. "Our relationship with her family is critical. At this time, they're one of our biggest investors. I hope I don't have to remind you that any ties you have with other women need to end. Now."

"Like I have a choice," I mutter. My father looks up at me with a smirk. He doesn't have to say it. I know the answer.

"Perfect, I understand."

"I want you to know that this was all Alison's father's idea. Apparently, she has a strong attachment to you. With good reason, I'm assuming."

It was one night. One big mistake. I should've known Alison couldn't see it as a one-time thing.

"It meant nothing."

"I was afraid you might say that. I think you should seriously consider spending more time with Alison. You may find that she grows on you." Father drums his fingers at my silence. "Perhaps, at some point, you may find the idea of her becoming your wife a pleasant thing. She'll make you a great wife."

Yes, like mother? The idea of having a wife gives me a headache.

"Are we done here?" I ask, bored.

"One more thing. You will have a personal assistant. He or she will be here to keep an eye on you and keep you out of trouble. You're a public figure for this company, and I can't have your face splashed all over the tabloids because of your 'extracurricular activities.'"

His words sting with each emphasis. We couldn't be more different. My father doesn't seem to remember the importance of mingling at social events or parties with other New York powerhouses. He thinks all I do is sleep around while he spends his time buried away in his office. He wasn't always so cold or hard with me. He changed when my mother left. The memory of her still leaves a bitter taste in my mouth.

"I guess there's nothing else to discuss."

"Good, then will I see you Monday for the interviews?"

"Yes."

I leave my father's office without another word. Although I'm fuming inside, I can't but hope that this mess will somehow fix itself. Maybe if I speak with Alison, I can make her understand how marrying me would be a mistake—for both of us.

———

O n my way home, I get a call from Tristan Knight, my childhood best friend. I haven't heard from his mug for several weeks now. He's been working on some top-secret project and he's pretty much kept me out of the loop. All I know is it has something to do with his art.

"Nick! How have you been, buddy?" From the blaring sound of the music blasting from the other end, I know Tristan's out somewhere, probably starting his weekend early.

"Tired. I just flew back in town," I grumble.

"Aw, but not too tired for drinks with some lovely ladies, right?"

"Tristan, I refuse to get pulled into one of your double date fiascos again. Plus, there's probably something I should tell you."

"Look, just get down here. I have some big news and it sounds like you do, too. I want you to be here."

Big news? Tristan doesn't throw around those two words lightly, so I'm genuinely intrigued. I guess I won't be staying home and catching up on some much needed sleep. I do need to stop by my apartment to change. I can still smell the sweat from sitting for four hours on the plane.

"All right, where do I meet you?"

"You're going to like this place. It's called *Riptide*. It's over in Chelsea."

5

REBECCA

The city of New York is a fearsome thing to behold. The city lights shine down on the club, lighting it up like a Hollywood stage. My body hums with excitement as Carol and I step out of her black Escalade and onto a red carpet swarming with paparazzi. Apparently, this is the place to be. Carol warned me about the press being at club openings, but I don't think I'm ready for this many people.

"Just follow me. The doorman knows we're on the list," she says, straightening her wistful strands of mocha brown.

I pull at the hem of my dress, conscious of the way it slips up, revealing a little too much of my thunder thighs as we make our way down the red carpet. A few cameramen snap pictures of us, whistling as we walk up. *I wonder if we'll be in tomorrow's paper.* I'm suddenly grateful that I'm wearing a black cocktail dress. At least with the black, my unwanted love handles are hidden. I hope that if my picture somehow finds it way on the Internet that Miles sees it. Nothing right now would give me more satisfaction than for him to know I'm doing wonderfully without him.

Hundreds of people gawk at us as they wait in line to go into the club. I've always wondered what it would feel like to walk to the front of a club line, drop a name, and then be escorted inside. Usually, I'm the one waiting in line, watching the bouncer admit all of the super-model twigs into the club.

"You're going to love this place," Carol says, grinning.

The front doorman to the club looks up with a smirk as he spots us. The mischievous look behind his eyes tells me he knows Carol well. He reminds me of a sexier version of Russell Crowe. Silvery grey hairs run through his short, brown hair and goatee, and his eyes crinkle slightly when he smiles.

"Ms. Livingston, it's nice to see you again." His British accent is thick. I can almost see him in some nineteenth century gothic story, walking across the moors of Northern England in his riding coat, searching for his long lost love. His eyes wash over the both of us with interest. Carol must be a lot bigger of a name in NYC than she let on.

"Hi, Derrick," she says, winking. "We're finally here, sorry to hold up the party," she says, smiling.

What a flirt.

Something tells me Carol has a lot of confessing to do later. His eyes dip to Carol's neckline. There's intensity behind them as they trail back up to her almost-innocent smile.

She knows the effect she has on him.

I can't help but laugh.

"Right this way," he says, holding open the front door of the club and never taking his eyes off her backside. "Welcome to *Riptide*."

"Carol, what the hell was that?"

"What was what?" she says coyly.

"The doorman and you. You guys were eye-fucking each other."

"Oh that," she says dismissively. "We just made out once in his car."

"Just made out?"

"Well, it started as just making out."

"Unbelievable," I say, laughing.

The inside of *Riptide* is phenomenal. The club's beach theme is present within each detail of the décor, from the blue lights spinning across the dance floor engulfing the room with rippling waves to the faint scent of citrus and the ocean breeze wafting in the air. Even though it makes me miss the weather in California, it's nice to have a piece of it here in New York.

"They really like giving you the whole experience here," Carol says, squeezing my hand. "Do you mind getting us a drink? I'm going to run to the ladies room."

"Sure, no problem."

"We'll look for my client as soon as I get back."

6

NICHOLAS

"I think you're being much too harsh, Nicholas. Alison Price can't be the worst woman to marry," Tristan says, giving me an incredulous look. Somehow, Tristan convinced me that coming down to Chelsea wasn't going to be a waste of my time. For the past hour, we've been talking nonstop about my father's overbearing expectations for my life, which eventually led to talking about Alison Price. My future wife.

"You have absolutely no idea how annoying she is."

"Annoying enough to not have sex with?" Tristan asks. I can almost see the sarcasm dripping from his lips.

"It was one time." I toss back my glass of whiskey. The liquid burns down my throat, creating a warm pool in the pit of my stomach.

"When is it not?"

It's true. Even my closest friends know that I pick up women for sex, but most of these women know my reputation. It's no secret around town—the tabloids do their hardest to keep it that way, too. I don't romance women; I fuck them. The problem is that I fucked the wrong one. Alison had other ideas about us when I met her this past summer.

"How did you meet her again?"

"We were at the black tie event at the museum. Remember, you donated the painting I told you I wanted."

"Ah, now I remember."

The night started like most, guests getting drunk on champagne and having fun, throwing away thousands of dollars in the live auction. As for me, well, I appreciated a more discreet way of spending my money—the silent auction table. Alison and I got into a bidding war over one of Tristan's paintings. She kept watching the auction table, waiting to pounce as I left. We went back forth for most of the night, trying to outbid the other. I wasn't about to lose. I wanted the painting. After a while, I had a feeling she wasn't interested in the painting any longer. I tested my theory, and she finally gave in when I wrote my cell number next to my bid. I guess I can technically blame Tristan for all of this. At the time, I had no idea she was the daughter of any of my father's friends.

"C'mon, let's have another drink and get you out of this funk. There are plenty of beautiful women here to take your mind off things," Tristan says, grinning as he raises his glass of wine.

Funk isn't even close to how I would describe my mood. More like steaming mad. I can't shake the irritation from earlier in the day. My father has managed to ruin everything. I'm being forced into an engagement to an insufferable woman, and now there are also plans for a wedding. A club is the last place I need to be, no matter how beautiful the women are, but I can't back out on a promise to a friend.

"Speaking of women, did you meet any beauties in Los Angeles?" Tristan inquires. "Is it true that most of them have plastic tits?"

"I met a few. Some had plastic tits, but not all of them." I laugh. "There was one in particular that I can't get off my mind."

"Wait, what did you say? Nicholas StoneHaven is smitten with a woman?"

"Smitten? No."

"So tell me about her. She must be something to behold if you can't get her off your mind."

"She's different than most of the women I date. Younger, curvy, fiery hair, and lips that made me want to fuck her forty-thousand feet up in the air."

"Ah, so you met her on the plane?"

"Yes."

"So what happened?"

"Nothing. We kissed. That was all."

"How very old school of you."

"I'm surprised, Nicholas."

"Believe me, I wanted to fuck her. But being arrested by a U.S. Air Marshal wasn't an option. My face would've been splashed all over the papers."

Meeting Rebecca was definitely the highlight of my trip. I could kick myself for not getting her number. Having her body meshed against me while I kissed her pouty lips made me feel like a high school boy going through puberty. I was pretty sure at one point I almost came just having her brush up against me.

"So when are you going to tell me about the big news you mentioned over the phone?" I ask, pushing away my lust driven thoughts. The crowded room around us is stifling with plastic smiles and glazed eyes.

"Well, I wanted to wait until she got here..."

"She? Are you dating someone I don't know about?"

Tristan breaks out into laughter. "No, of course not."

"Good."

"Am I really that horrible that I shouldn't even be in a relationship?"

"No, I'm merely saving you from having to make the same horrible mistake I'm being forced to make."

"I'm meeting a prospective PR specialist who I'd like to hire for the opening of my new art gallery, *Trinity*. She's the one who put together this event," Tristan says with a contagious grin.

"Art gallery? You mean you're actually taking my advice and selling your art instead of giving it all away?"

"All right, you can't take credit for the whole idea, but yes. I think it's time." Art was Tristan Knight's baby. As a connoisseur of it, opening a new art gallery was a pretty damn big deal.

"Congratulations. I don't know what to say, other than I know it'll be amazing. Your work is amazing."

"Thanks, Nick. You know that means a lot to me."

"Emily will be pleased to hear you're pursuing your art."

Tristan tenses slightly at the mention of my sister's name.

"How is Em?" he asks hesitantly. Something tells me that there's been something going on between my sister and my best friend lately. While it grinds my gears to know guys are looking at my twenty-two-year-old sister in *that way*, who better to take care of her than Tristan Knight? At least for now, that's all he better be doing.

"She's fine. She should be back any day now. She was vacationing in Florida with a few friends."

The awkwardness between them started this past summer when we vacationed in Southampton for Emily's birthday. She stormed off the beach when she saw Tristan and me speaking with some models vacationing a few houses down. At first, I thought she was mad because we were ignoring her. Now, I'm starting to get the feeling that she was mad because Tristan was ignoring her. Funny enough, Tristan didn't take either of the two models back to his room, but I did.

"Right, well, I'm going to make a call and grab another drink from the bar," he says, walking away. Yeah, something is definitely going on with him. I'll have to squeeze it out of Emily when I see her tomorrow.

My leg vibrates, telling me I must be receiving a call. When I pull it out, a single name flashes across the screen that sends my mood plummeting. Alison Price. I debate on whether to pick it up, but a tiny voice inside me reminds me that I have specific obligations now. Whether I want to or not, I'm stuck with her. So it's probably in my best interest if I make an effort to try to have a functional relationship with her. Then again, this is my night to relax. I pocket the phone and take another swig of my brandy. I need to avoid Alison as long as possible.

When Tristan returns with an extra drink, he has a sour look of irritation on his face. I don't often see him upset. He has the wonderful gift of always being able to muster a friendly smile. Whereas, I've been often told that I scowl.

"Is everything all right?" I ask.

"Yes, fine."

"Are you sure?"

"It's nothing."

"Good. When did this PR specialist say she would be here?"

"I'm sure she'll be here soon."

"Nicholas!" I recognize the voice before I even turn. Alison Price walks toward me wearing a short nude dress. Her hair looks different from the way she usually wears it. Now, instead of limp strands of blonde, her hair curls in tight ringlets. The look on her face is predatory. Most people wouldn't notice it, but I do. It's the same look I have when I see something I want. It's animalistic, I know, but it's also a natural part of me. She wants me. It should turn me on, but when it comes to Alison, I'm just the shiny new toy, for now.

"Sweetheart, I tried calling you. Your father said you were down here, so I thought I would join you."

The translation of that is my father called her father and struck a deal. No doubt, my father told Alison I would be down here. He doesn't want to give me time to acclimate to the idea of being forced to marry someone. He just wants me to do what I'm told.

"I'm sorry, it's hard to hear anything in here," I say, leaning in to kiss her cheek.

"Tristan, it's wonderful to see you again," Alison says, turning to give Tristan a once over as she extends her hand.

"Thank you, Alison. I'm glad you could make it out."

"Would you like a drink?" *I need to get away from this woman.*

"I would love one. A Long Island Iced Tea would be great." Alison slips her hand over my arm, squeezing it possessively.

"I'll be back."

The bar is overcrowded with groups of people waiting to order drinks, but I manage to find an all too willing waitress to take my order. She slips me her number, along with my receipt. I turn back to where Tristan and Alison are standing and spot a tall, slender brunette extending her hand to Tristan. This must be the PR woman he wants to hire. She looks sharp in her short, grey dress with black sequins. From her body language, I can tell she's an astute woman. She must know her stuff if she was able to pull off this party.

A flash of red catches my attention as a curvy young woman walks up to her and Tristan. The girl standing in front of them is young, and in her early twenties. I watch as Tristan greets her with a handshake. His eyes quickly trail over her with interest. Among the sea of bodies, she stands out in her black dress and red heels. I watch, mesmerized by her hair, long legs, and sun-kissed skin. She's doesn't look like your average New Yorker visiting a club, but there's something familiar about her. My breath hitches as she turns toward my direction. Her green eyes crowned by long black eyelashes widen at me. The expression on her angelic face reminds me of the porcelain dolls my sister used to collect when she was little. It's a mixed look of wonder and amazement. Her lips part just enough to send a streak of desire through me. *Fuck, I know her.* She's the young woman from the airplane.

7

REBECCA

The sight of him sends my heart into palpitations. *It's him.* I'm not sure how someone can be so good looking without a flock of women surrounding him. I'm pretty sure the gods put men like him on this earth to taunt me. His stormy blue eyes narrow in on the dip of my black dress. Thanks to Carol, my tits are on display like a Christmas light show, and if I knew any better, I would say he's unwrapping me with his mind. A slow smile slides across his mouth. Part of me wants to go to him and throw myself at his mercy. And by mercy, I mean his Greek god-like rock hard body. It's been several hours since I last saw him, but I can still taste him on my lips.

He slowly moves through the crowd of people brushing up against him. What I wouldn't give to be the fabric on the clothes rubbing against his skin. He's shaved since I last saw him on the plane. While a five o'clock shadow looks good on him, I love the way his bare skin accentuates his strong chin and cheekbones. He's in front of me before I can turn back to clue Carol in.

"Hello, it's wonderful to see you again." His voice is like warm liquid pouring over me. It's refreshing and yet, it sends my nerves spinning.

"Do you know him?" Carol whispers over her shoulder.

"Nicholas, you're back. Wonderful. I would like you to meet Ms. Livingston and her friend..."

"Rebecca," I offer. "Rebecca Gellar."

A ghost of a smile passes between us. Carol eyes me with curiosity. I know she'll be asking questions later. There isn't much to tell, sadly. I met a gorgeous man on an airplane. We kissed, touched, but we never exchanged any kind of contact information, and yet somehow, here he is. I'm not sure if fate is trying to tell me something, or it's just in my cards to meet gorgeous men who aren't for me.

The woman standing near Tristan takes a step forward, and wraps her hand through Nicholas' arm. She tugs on it, drawing his attention to her. His smile immediately vanishes. My heart squeezes as she leans into him. There's no mistaking it. The woman who I assumed was with Tristan is actually with my *beautiful stranger*.

"This is my fiancé, Nicholas," she purrs. I watch him hand her a drink. Anger pulsates through my veins at the realization of what this means. He was engaged when he kissed me on the plane. *How stupid can I be?* I watch the two as they stand side by side. Physically, they make the ideal couple. *Why didn't I see this coming?* Alison is beautiful, but her expression is cold. She stands silently assessing me. Her long legs are effortlessly toned. *What I wouldn't give to have her legs.*

Nicholas doesn't lean into Alison or even look at her as she slides her hand down his back. No, he keeps his eyes directly on me. I can't tell what he's thinking, but I honestly wish I knew. The situation is more than awkward. I have to pretend like this is our first time meeting. Images of his thumb grazing against my neck sends chills down my back. I shiver. The impression of his lips on mine still hasn't left me.

"Are you cold?" Carol asks.

"I'm fine," I squeak.

He's not yours. His expression tightens as he shakes my hand and then Carol's. He probably thinks I'm going to rat him out.

"Tristan, why don't we discuss some of your ideas for opening?" Carol says, piping in. I have no doubt she'll get this account. She can be very convincing.

"I was thinking of keeping it to a very intimate setting. Nowhere near this many people," he says, scanning the crowd.

"Perfect. Do you have a date in mind?"

"I was actually thinking about having the opening on New Year's Eve."

"Oh, that's very short notice..."

"Can you pull it off?" he asks, as if testing her.

Carol smirks. "Mr. Knight, I pulled together *Riptide's* opening in the same amount of time. What do you think?"

I smile at Carol's sassy but confident attitude. Despite how much I just want to escape, I can't. *God, I hope this night doesn't turn into a disaster.* Carol mentioned that the meeting wouldn't last too long. Maybe stepping outside for some air might be nice. I excuse myself from the group and head toward the back of the building. I sense Nicholas still watching me as I leave, but I dismiss the thoughts of him that filter through my mind. I can't stop myself from being attracted to him, but I sure as hell can control the filth in my head.

The back of the club is almost as crowded as the front. I spot a door that leads to an outside patio for guests who want to smoke. As tempting as it is to be outside, I can't stand the smell of the heavy smoke. I linger just in front of the door hoping to catch a passing breeze, but the night air is still. *This isn't helping. Maybe I should just go back to Carol's apartment.*

On my way back from the women's restroom, a pair of hands thrust me back against a dark corner. I nearly scream, but stop myself as Nicholas steps forward out of the shadows. The look he gives me melts away the words I have. He doesn't wait for me to question him. He simply takes. His lips crush into mine with full force, almost knocking me backward. The wall is the only thing that stops us from crashing. A million things race through my head, but the one thing that hits home is the knowledge that somewhere, his fiancée is waiting for him. I don't want to be like Scarlett. I'm not someone who goes around taking someone else's man.

"What are you doing?" I ask. It's more of an accusation than a question.

"Doing what I should've done forty-thousand feet in the air." He crosses my wrists and pushes them above me. I fight the urge to grab a fistful of his hair and kiss him.

"No, I can't."

The phrase *resistance is futile* has a whole new meaning. He pushes open my legs and strokes his hand up and down my center. As much as I want him to stop, I can't seem to verbalize my plea. My hips meet his hand and he continues the friction of fingers. He pauses to slide up my dress baring the bottom of me. I've never been the type to want to have sex in public, but god, does he make me want to. He skims his tongue across my neck and the act nearly sends my body into spasms. He finds his way inside my lace underwear.

"I want you." His words set my nerves on fire. He slowly parts me, slipping his fingers inside me. His fingers rock back and forth against me as he delves deeper inside. I'm lost in oblivion, falling farther and farther down the rabbit hole and I can't seem to stop myself. He presses against my clit and I nearly lose it. He growls lightly against my ear as he plants his lips below it. The sensation sends my head spinning. *I need to stop.*

Nicholas loosens his grip of my wrists and reaches down toward my breasts with his free hand. His thumb circles my right nipple and it grows hard beneath his finger. He leans forward and places it in his mouth, leaving a damp warm spot on my dress.

"I want you to come for me, baby."

The words aren't said with a silent plea. No, the way he says it is more of a command. I honestly haven't felt wanted like this since Miles. He wasn't always a caring lover. A lot of the time, he was just selfish. The thought of him sends a pang to my chest. Cheating on me was the most selfish thing he ever did. But how am I any better? Here I am, letting Nicholas touch me.

"Where'd you go, sweetheart?" Nicholas asks, breathing heavily. He caresses my cheek drawing my attention back to him.

"Stop," I whisper. *I can't give myself up like this.* He doesn't get to see that part of me. He doesn't get to unravel me just to watch me break. It frightens me to want him. It frightens me that someone like him could make me forget everything. Including myself.

"Wait," he says, grabbing my waist, but I don't. I push his hands off and yank my dress down. I don't look back. I just push past him and run out of there as fast as I can. In the distance, I can hear him calling after me. I don't think anyone's ever told him no, but he'll get over it. I'm just another girl to him. Someone he thinks he can have without any conditions.

I find Carol at the bar ordering a drink. The distress on my face must be obvious because she immediately asks me what's wrong. I don't tell her about Nicholas. I can't. Part of me is ashamed that it went so far. She doesn't poke or prod me to explain my sudden need to leave. She simply gives me a hug and calls Steven to pick me up.

"Steven is coming to take you home. Are you sure you don't want me to come with you, though?"

"No, Carol. Stay and mingle. You need this account." I smile, trying my best to reassure her that I mean it.

"Oh, don't worry about that. It's in the bag," she says, winking

"Thank you for taking me out."

"No problem. Make yourself at home back at my place."

"Thanks, I will."

It doesn't take long for Steven to arrive, and it takes even less time for us to get back to Carol's apartment. Somehow, Steven knows just what streets to avoid on our way back. He walks me all the way to Carol's door and shows me where to find the spare key.

As much as I want to sleep, I wait up for Carol to get home. She doesn't get back to the apartment until four a.m.

"Hey, you waited up?" she asks, whispering as she crawls into bed next to me. "And made yourself at home in my bed?"

"Yeah, I wanted to wait up and you said to make myself comfortable." I giggle as Carol swats me with her pillow. It's like we're in junior high having a sleepover. She slips off her shoes and jumps into bed.

"You totally didn't have to wait up, but thank you. I had to stay late to make sure the cleanup and breakdown crews were doing their jobs."

"It's a lot of work being a mega PR person."

"Yeah, but most of the time, I end up being more of an event planner. By the way, I got the account with Tristan Knight," she squeals.

"That's fantastic! I'm so happy for you," I say, hugging her.

"Thanks. Oh, yeah, I wanted to tell you, I think your blue-eyed friend was looking for you." She doesn't have to mention his name. I know she means Nicholas.

"He's not my friend."

"Why do I get the feeling there's something you're not telling me?" Carol says with a motherly tone. "Is he the reason why you left so early?"

"I'll explain tomorrow," I say, forcing a smile.

"Promise?"

"Sure."

Carol turns and shuts off the lamp beside her nightstand. The room is quickly engulfed in darkness with the exception of the glittering city outside our window. It sits shining beneath the moonlight and the stars.

"By the way..." Carol starts to say. "He was totally looking for you. He didn't say your name, but when I came back without you... the look on his face was like someone had killed his puppy."

As I close my eyes and let the darkness overtake my senses, the last thing I see is the image of Nicholas' stark blue eyes staring down at me, burning with need and desire.

8

NICHOLAS

Monday morning arrives far too quickly. The weekend was anything but restful. It was more like a painful and arduous process of replaying Friday's events over and over in my mind. To make things worse, I've been daydreaming about *her* for the past two hours. Her, as in Rebecca Gellar, the vivacious redhead I met on my flight back home with her sharp green eyes that sized me up from the get-go. It's stupid of me to let her get inside my head, but I can't stop the chain reaction she's started. *I want her.*

The events of the Friday night seem so serendipitous that it's hard to believe it actually happened. Out of all of the clubs in this city, she was at *Riptide*. When I saw her, I wanted to peel off her dress and kiss every inch of her. I can still taste those sweet lips on mine. One minute she was unraveling in my arms, moaning beneath my touch and the next, she was gone. I haven't stopped thinking about the way she felt. God, she was so wet. I remember my fingers sliding inside her with ease... my cock still twitches at the memory of her soft gasps. She shifted my world upside down, turning it on its axis with one simple kiss. Unfortunately, Alison ruined everything when she decided to just show up unannounced.

Rebecca's eyes opened up like saucers when she heard her introduce herself as my fiancée. I can only imagine what thoughts were going through Rebecca's head. From the tightlipped grimace on her face, she was pissed. She had every right to blurt out about our kiss on the airplane, but she didn't, and while I would've been more than happy to get rid of Alison, it would've royally fucked things up for the company.

I didn't want to chase Rebecca away, but it's probably better that I did. *I'm engaged.* Engaged... I'm still trying to sort out the ramifications of this reality in my head. I don't even do long-term relationships, but this is as permanent as one can get. Rebecca's face flashes in my mind. She must think the worse of me. I know she shouldn't mean anything. She's just another number in a city that's overflowing with women begging to be fucked, but all I can think about is finding her and punishing her for leaving me with blue balls.

I've been stroking myself for the past thirty minutes, but each time I get close to peaking, I lose the image of fucking her mouth. It's like she's cursed me. That fiery siren is my impending death by no release. Perhaps I should've taken Alison's offer for sex last night. She was all too willing. I'm surprised she didn't cup me in public by the way she was marking her territory. It didn't take much to notice the angry and jealous glances at Rebecca. *Rebecca.* Her name will forever be ingrained in my mind.

I begin stroking myself again, trying to imagine her face as I touched her soft folds. I grab a towel, as I get closer and closer to my release. *I'm almost there.*

"I'm home!" a familiar voice shouts from across my living room, instantly stopping me. Before I have time to throw my towel on the floor, Emily, my little sister, walks straight into my bedroom. Her eyes widen as she spots the towel in one hand, and my other hand underneath the sheets. Her cheeks flame bright red against her fair skin. *This is awkward.*

"Whoa! God, what are you, twelve?" she screams in disgust. "You should've locked your door if you're doing stuff like that."

"Why the hell don't you knock like a normal person?" I yell, irritated as fuck. *How the hell did she get into my apartment anyway?*

"I didn't think I would walk in on you yanking your chain."

"Just get out! I need to get dressed." *Frustration is how I will sum up today, and it's just gotten started.*

As I exit my room dressed in a fresh suit, I find Emily sitting on the couch, holding a sign that reads 'CONGRATULATIONS!' Written underneath are Alison's and my names. It seems news of my engagement has traveled fast.

"I'm so excited for you! When is the wedding?" she asks, pushing back a blonde wisp of hair from her face. She reminds me so much of our mother that it's painful at times. It's like looking at an old photograph. She has the same fair skin and long wavy hair. My brother and I were the ones who came out more like our father.

"Hopefully, never," I mutter.

Her face drops. "I thought this was happy news?" She eyes me suspiciously, as I begin to set my tie in place.

"It's not. I'm being forced into marriage."

"How medieval," she says, smirking. "I guess I should've known better."

"What's that supposed to mean?" I ask, pretending to be offended.

"Nothing, you just don't keep your girlfriends around for very long."

It's because most of them are gold diggers, like our mother. "You better watch out, you're next," I tease. "You know Father. If it's for the good of the family, he'll ship you off." Emily follows me as I walk to the kitchen and pour myself a glass of orange juice. She's dressed in a light yellow dress and red heels. Something tells me she's still on vacation. That or she's ditching class.

"Aren't you supposed to be at school?" I ask. "Isn't New York University back in session yet?"

"Not today, I go back tomorrow," she says with a mischievous grin. Although almost six years her senior, I've often wondered whether Emily isn't the older of us two. It's only when she grins that I'm reminded she's only twenty-two. Something about her smile screams youthful innocence.

"So, I thought you liked Alison?" she asks. "You dated her for a while, right?"

"You could call it that."

"Yuck, please don't tell me anymore."

I chuckle. The alarm on my phone starts to go off, reminding me that it's seven a.m. *Time to go.* My apartment is far enough from the office that it doesn't feel like I live at work, but close enough that it takes less than twenty minutes to get there. It's convenient and easy, but it also means that I have no excuses for being late.

"Can we talk about this later? I'm already running late," I say.

"Okay, are we still planning to take a trip to the French Riviera this January?"

"Of course," I say, kissing the top of her head as I grab my work case. "I gotta jet. Let yourself out, okay?"

"Will do," she says, grabbing the remote control and turning on my flat screen. Something tells me she's going to be here for a while. As I head out the door, I'm reminded of Tristan's odd behavior at the mere mention of Emily's name.

"Hey, you need to let me know what's going on between you and Tristan. Not right now, but later," I say.

Emily turns to me with a blank look. Her face flushes pink as she stutters to make a coherent sentence. "Um, I..."

"I can't help but get the feeling that you two are mad at each other," I say, cutting her off, "which is weird because you grew up together and I know he loves you like his little sister. I really hope whatever it is, you both will stop fighting."

"Okay," she manages to whisper.

"Great, we'll talk later."

———

By the time I reach StoneHaven Publishing, the lobby is busy with employees and visitors bustling about. Mary is tending to our festive holiday decorations as she places a wreath in front of the reception area. I always found it interesting that we tend to get many tourists coming around the holidays. Everyone seems to want to be in New York during Thanksgiving, and it's less than a month away.

"Good morning, Mr. StoneHaven," Mary says, greeting me with a meek smile.

"Good morning, Mary."

"Mr. StoneHaven, your father has called you multiple times. He said to tell you to go straight to his office when you got here."

"I'm sure he did. He probably can't wait to hire my new assistant."

Mary smiles as she hands me a note with my missed calls for the morning.

"I don't suppose you saw this woman? Is she old? Young?" I ask.

"She's young," Mary says, divulging nothing more. "Your father wanted me to print her resume for you." She hands me a single sheet of paper, and as I gaze down, my jaw drops at the name printed in size 12 Times New Roman font.

Rebecca Gellar.

I'm cursed. There's no better explanation as to why this is happening to me.

"Mary, are you sure this is who we're interviewing?" I ask. My heart accelerates in a chaotic rhythm.

"Yes," she says, smiling. "I'm positive."

———

The smell of faint jasmine is the first thing that hits me as I enter my father's office. It's intoxicating to my senses, seductive even. I find myself openly staring at the short, curvy redhead in front of me wearing a fitted blue dress. Rebecca sits sideways in one of the chairs with her back facing me. My eyes are drawn to the soft curve of her neckline. The taste of her skin is still on my lips even after days. She's wearing her hair up, and I can't help but think she looks like a 1950's sexy librarian. I stop short as she turns and focuses her piercing green eyes on me. Her shock and annoyance is evident on her face. She wasn't expecting to see me here. I wasn't expecting to see her ever again. *Not after Friday night.*

From her tight-lipped expression, I can tell she doesn't want me openly staring at her, but I can't stop. Her eyes glance everywhere but at me. I take a seat in the chair adjacent to hers. The air between us is electric. I can almost feel her disapproval for me. It's probably *pervish* of me to say that it turns me on. *It definitely turns me on.*

"You? What are you doing here?" she says, barely above a whisper. I can sense the bitterness in her words.

"I work here." I try my best to erase my emotions. A part of me is still angry that she left the club. I wanted her. No, I needed her. I know it's shitty of me, but I didn't care if Alison found out. I didn't care if people saw us. I wanted to be reckless because of her. *For her.* At that moment, I didn't even care if the paparazzi happened to see us. Nothing else mattered.

"Funny, you didn't mention that the other night," she remarks. "But I guess you have a lot of secrets. So you are Nicholas *Stone-Haven.*" Her insinuation of secrets sets off a trigger inside me.

"I don't tell random women that I meet where I work. What are you doing here?" I retort. Father comes waltzing back into the room before Rebecca has a chance to say anything else. He takes a moment to look from me to Rebecca. Sometimes I swear he has a sixth sense. He has a way of picking up on unspoken conversations.

"Do you know each other?" he asks.

"No," Rebecca says nervously as she turns back to me. "I was just introducing myself to your son." Rebecca turns to me. "I'm your new assistant." She flushes as I take her hand in mine, and even though the moment is brief, I can feel her tremble beneath my touch. As soon as father turns, she quickly breaks eye contact and snatches her hand away.

"I'm glad you could make it in, Nicholas. Although you're well over an hour late," Father says.

"I apologize. I had some other business to tend to, and I thought you received my message."

"Well, since you missed most of the interview, you'll be happy to know that we will be hiring Ms. Gellar. She will be your personal assistant for six months on a trial basis. From there, depending on her performance, she may be transferred as a full-time staff member."

My father stands, turning to Rebecca. "Ms. Gellar, if you can take this paperwork with you and return it tomorrow morning to HR that should be all we need."

"Thank you, Mr. StoneHaven," she says.

As she stands, the hem of her dress suit hikes up just above her knee. The mere sight of her naked leg stirs something inside me. She's stunning. As much as I don't want to admit it, I still want her. I've wanted her since I first saw her. *This is bad.* I can't have her working near me, let alone as my assistant.

"It was a pleasure to meet you," she says to me, but her eyes say differently. I can still see the radiant flecks of gold in her green eyes. Green... like my mother's eyes. My chest tightens at the realization.

"Nicholas, please show Rebecca around the building. I need to finish drawing up some documents."

"Of course," I say, gesturing for Rebecca to follow me out.

Father escorts us out of his office, and before I have a chance to speak, Rebecca heads for the elevator. She pushes the downstairs arrow over and over as if expecting it to pop right open. I'm sure she's hoping it will get here faster. I'm starting to get the feeling she can't stand to be around me. I follow her, standing a few inches away from her.

"You can't work here," I whisper.

She turns to me in shock. "I'm not any happier about this situation," she says. "But you're stuck with me for at least the next six months."

"Why didn't you tell me you were applying to work here?" I ask.

"I had no idea that you were the owner's son. You never mentioned your last name," she says accusingly.

"I'm sorry about Friday night," I blurt.

"Sorry? You mean you're sorry for coming on to me even though you're engaged?" Her tone is full of accusations.

"I wasn't engaged when I first met you."

"Oh, sure," she says, obviously not amused.

"I wasn't. I came back and found out about my engagement. I don't even want to marry her."

"How romantic," she says, unconvinced. "That really doesn't make it any better."

"Rebecca, I'll find you another position somewhere else," I begin to say.

"If you think you're going to scare me off, you're wrong," she says, whirling around on me.

The elevator pings open and Rebecca rushes in. The elevator isn't fast enough for her to lock me out, although it doesn't stop her from trying. The doors close behind us, leaving the two of us alone. Rebecca steps back against the wall, trying to keep her distance from me. It's useless. The smell of her jasmine perfume only drives me crazy. I need to scare her off. I need to make her regret coming to StoneHaven Publishing. I can't have her around my life if I can't have her in my bed. I'd like to think I'm strong enough, but I'm not. Having her here would only make things more complicated.

"Is it true what they say about California girls?" I ask, leaning against the elevator wall. She looks up at me with interest.

"I don't know. What do they say?"

"That you're all just begging for a good fuck." Her eyes widen. The crimson blush across her cheeks only encourages me. "Tell me, Rebecca, do the drapes match the carpet?"

"Your father warned me about you." Her voice is low, but her breathing is rapid. I trail a line with my finger down her arm, all the way to her waist.

"Did he?" I smile. "I think you came here for another reason."

"And what would that be?" she asks innocently.

"I think you wanted me to finish what I started in the club."

She doesn't move as I slide my hands down her ass. I'm instantly aroused. She feels too good against me. I push up against her, but she doesn't back down. She moves closer. I'm not sure if it's my imagination or what, but her hips grind into mine. It takes every part of my fiber to stop myself from pushing her skirt up and fucking her right there. I want to taste her and fuck her until she remembers only my name.

"You know what else they say about California girls," she whispers, running a hand up my chest. *She's a fucking minx.* She wants me just as much as I want her.

"What?"

"We have good aim." Her knee makes contact with my groin.

"Fuck!" My stomach instantly feels like it's ready to drop out of my body. Nausea hits me like a fucking tidal wave. I instinctively kneel to the ground, clutching myself.

"Don't worry. I'll find my own way around," she says over her shoulder. The elevator pings open, and in an instant, she walks out, leaving me disabled and cradling my balls. *Sorry, boys, today is just not your lucky day.* I look up to see a group of StoneHaven employees waiting by the elevator doors, shocked as they watch the scene unravel before them. This is one hell of a way to teach me a lesson.

Deep inside, I know it won't be the last time Rebecca gives me an erection and a kick in the balls within the same five minutes.

"Crazy redhead." *I don't stand a chance.*

9

REBECCA

That's it. I'm making a mental list.

The *Run-Like-Hell* **List**: *I, Rebecca Gellar, vow that under no circumstances will I ~~fuck~~ sleep with any man ~~especially Nicholas~~ who falls under these:*

1. Arrogant.
2. Dangerously handsome.
3. Brooding.
4. Domineering.
5. Possessive.
6. Playboy.

PART II

PROLOGUE

NICHOLAS

5 Years Ago

The sound of his heart monitor slowing down sends a sharp static pain through me. His chest rises and falls. My eyes will him to breathe, and each time his chest swells back up, I release the air I've been anxiously holding. I move closer and wrap my hand around his. His skin is cool beneath my fingers. I can barely make out a pulse as I press against his wrist. *Hold on.* My world is crashing all around me. *Please wake up, Alex.* I hear soft whimpers in the background coming from my sister, Emily. She sits in the corner of the room, detached from the rest of the world as she curls herself in a ball on the chair.

"He's gone, Nick," she cries. *No.* I refuse to believe that the only real thing keeping him here with me is this respirator. The world seems like fragmented pieces of film playing inside of my head. It was only hours ago that we were at the river. I can't think of a time when we were happier. Things like this don't just happen. *This is all my fault.* I shouldn't have pushed him to do it. I knew the cliff was way too high. He would still be here if I hadn't dared him to jump. He was just trying to impress everyone.

"Nick, Dad's on his way," Emily says, clutching her phone. I hear her get up from the chair. She wraps her arms around me and cries into my shoulder, sobbing my brother's name over and over.

"Nick, say something," she whispers.

I can't say goodbye. I won't. Not today. Not ever.

———

*A*lexander StoneHaven, heir to the publishing empire, dies in cliff jumping accident. Drugs likely involved.

I slam my fist into the wall dividing my bathroom from my bedroom. A part of it breaks almost instantly beneath my heated grip. Particles of dust fly off my knuckles like ash. *Lies. Bullshit.* I can't believe she would do this to our family. I pull my bloodied fist from the wall. The pain is excruciating. Good. If only I could forget the pain that she has caused this family with her lies.

I crush the newspaper in my hands and fling it across my bedroom. My mother spun her lies and sold my brother's death to the papers. I can't think of a single human being that would actually do that. *She's a fucking monster.*

My father was so blind.

10

NICHOLAS

R*ebecca Elizabeth Gellar.* On paper, she's every employer's wet dream. My cock twitches at the sight of her name. It sits there taunting me. As much as I would like to pretend seeing it has no effect, it does. Rebecca's HR file is still sitting on my desk. I've been looking it over trying to find a way into Gellar's head. Her letters of recommendation only confirm my assumptions about her work ethic. Letter after letter praises her professionalism, attention to detail, and her adaptability to any situation. There's not a single thing that will help get rid of her, and she's all too willing to fight me on this.

I know she's just as attracted to me as I am to her. Call me a cocky motherfucker, but I know it's not all in my head. Rebecca might have a tough exterior, but she's shy on the inside. I'm not sure why, but I get the feeling she isn't used to men eye-fucking her. The incident in the elevator was confirmation of just how easy it is to push her buttons. If I really wanted, I could scare her off, but I know she'll be a valuable employee to my father's company. I just can't have her around me, because whether I like it or not, Rebecca makes me feel like a caveman. She makes me feel like the only thing I need to survive this cruel fucking world is the thought of being inside her, and right now, that's a dangerous mindset.

My breath hitches as I slide Rebecca's picture out from a second manila folder delivered to me an hour ago. The sight of her face looking back at me from her photocopied driver's license sends electric waves down my body. There's a certain gleam in her eye. I've seen it once before. It's the same self-satisfied look she gave me right before she kneed me in the balls only hours ago. I shift in my chair, readjusting myself. My cock throbs beneath the soft fabric of my pants. I hold back a moan as it grazes against my pants. *Blue balls* are an understatement to how I really feel. The image of Rebecca walking away from me still makes me crazy. If I had the ability to actually get up within those thirty seconds, I would've thrown her over my knee and spanked the living hell out of her. Never in my twenty-eight years of existence has a woman ever done that to me. The funny part is, if she were trying to drive me away, it only made me want her more. I know it's stupid to want her. *Really stupid.* But I can't seem to stop.

If I didn't know any better, I'd say she's out of that crazy, beautiful head of hers... or maybe she's the smartest little fireball I've ever met. Rebecca is definitely a mystery. There's plenty about her that I don't know. I shouldn't need to know, but I want to.

This needs to stop. In less than five months, I'll be married to Alison. The thought of being chained to her for the rest of my life is so fucking depressing.

"Nick, you asked to see me?"

I look up, startled to find Striker, one of my father's employees, standing at the office door. It's almost seven o'clock at night. I'm surprised that he's even still here. Striker has been with StoneHaven Publishing since I was twenty-three. He used to be a security agent for an international organization that provides security detail for the rich and famous. He's also my father's best friend. My father happily recruited him out of retirement when my mother started sending my father threatening letters.

"Is everything here?" I ask as he stalks over and takes a seat across from my desk. The chair squeaks under the weight of his stocky frame. He casually sits back, fiddling with the knob on his watch, as if he has all of the time in the world. After the incident on the elevator, I phoned Striker, who was quick to get me information on Rebecca. I'm not usually the one asking him for favors, but I have a feeling Rebecca won't answer any of my questions willingly.

"Yes, you'll find everything from her bank statements to her phone records. I also looked into her family's background," he says, hesitating.

"And?"

"Nothing, they're clean."

"Thank you. If anything else comes in, send it my way."

"Sure."

"And Striker, I would prefer if my father didn't know about this."

He flashes me a smile. "Why do you need such detailed information on your assistant, Nick? The company does routine background checks."

"I'm not looking for basic information," I confess.

A smug smile spreads across Striker's face. "You like this one, don't you?"

"This one?" I ask, ignoring his smirk.

"The redhead. She's cute. A little spunky, but cute."

"You've met her?"

"The elevator camera, Nick."

"So you saw her knee me in the balls? And you did nothing?" I ask, surprised.

"You looked like you were handling it just fine," he says, letting out a low chuckle.

"Right, what do I pay you for?" I ask, laughing.

"You don't. Your dad does."

"Of course, how could I forget?"

Striker is all too familiar with my MO with women. I do one thing and one thing only—I fuck them. I'm sure he gets a kick out of watching me salivate over Rebecca. He's well aware of the number of assistants I've gone through. I think most people are. He's not really one to judge me, but this is the first time I've heard him verbalize that he actually likes one of my assistants.

If only liking my assistant didn't mean there would be hell to pay later. I should be in control of the situation, yet Rebecca makes me feel anything *but* in control. There's a part that scares me, and then there's the haunting fact that every time I see her, I'm heartbreakingly reminded of the one woman who ruined my confidence in all women. *My mother.* Father made the mistake of not knowing who she really was. *My mother destroyed our family.*

"Thank you for your help," I say.

Striker nods, leaving me to rifle through the layer of documents on my desk. I settle back in my chair and pull open Rebecca's file. It seems most of the information that Striker has gathered is just fragmented pieces of Rebecca's life. Toward the back of the folder, I spot an article clipped from a gossip magazine. I'm surprised to even see it in the folder. *Why would she be in a tabloid?*

My eyes zoom in on the photograph of Rebecca in an embrace with another man. She's smiling as *he* leans in to kiss her. A strange sensation fills my chest as I scan the photo. Beneath it is a caption that reads '*Just as this article went to press, Miles Storm broke off his engagement with his longtime college girlfriend, Rebecca Gellar. He is now dating his co-star, Scarlett Jones.*' I clench my teeth. *Shit. Who is this fucker?*

I pull my tablet out of my briefcase and type the names 'Scarlett Jones' and 'Miles Storm' into my browser. A dozen or so pictures of Rebecca's ex-fiancé and his co-star bombard my search result. Each one reveals a little more than the last. I've learned in my experience that there is always a story behind a photo. In this case, the paparazzi are the ones telling it. To my surprise, Scarlett isn't as beautiful as I was anticipating. Sure, she has nice tits and a big ass, and she's probably what most men would think of when you say the word beautiful, but she's nothing like Rebecca. I've seen plenty of both to know she's more.

Miles Storm. The name looks familiar. It takes me a moment to place him from the photos. I scroll through a gallery from a TV studio set that I recognize. The photos are scenes from a show my sister Emily watches. *I've seen him before. I know his character.* He's the guy Emily is always pining over when she watches *Future Outlaw*. As I scroll through another pair of photos, I realize there's an article attached to one of them. I click it and the headline that pops up sends my head spinning. *Miles Storm Cheats on Fiancée with Co-star.*

Fuck. This man broke Rebecca's heart. I've never been one to believe tabloids or celebrity gossip sites, but I have feeling this time they got something right. *That piece of shit.* Anger erupts through my veins as I read the gritty details of the article. He didn't even have the decency to break it off with Rebecca before fucking another woman. This is why Rebecca instantly hated me. This is why she pushed me away. It all makes perfect sense.

I force myself to unclench my hands, aching from being fisted into angry balls. *What I wouldn't give to end this motherfucker.* For the first time in my life, I actually feel like the asshole most women make me out to be.

11

REBECCA

ONE WEEK LATER…

"I totally get it, Becca. You want him to fuck your brains out," Carol says, throwing me one of her *you-know-it's-fucking-true* looks. I roll my eyes at her as she stands at the doorway of the guest bathroom analyzing the teal dress I've put on and my nude colored pumps. It's been a week since I've seen Nicholas StoneHaven, aka my overly vain, but gorgeous boss. I thought I would be starting work the same week of my interview, but I was scheduled to come in the following Monday. I think it's in my best interest that it worked out that way. Kneeing my boss in the balls was probably not a good idea, but watching the expression on Nicholas's arrogant face when I did it was priceless. I don't regret a single moment of it, and I particularly don't regret the feeling of his eyes watching me as I left him clutching his precious 'jewels.' I know it was beyond stupid to hurt him. He's the owner's son. In reality, I'm surprised I still have a job. *At least I hope do.* Call it pride, but Nicholas StoneHaven is not going to scare me off that easily. He can smirk at me all he wants. I'm staying.

Stefan, Nicholas's father, warned me his son would challenge him when it came to having another assistant, but he promised if I could stick it out then he would hire me permanently, in my department of choice. We'll see if I change my mind after a few months, but I'm leaning toward a job in publicity. I think it would be exciting to work with authors to promote their books. That's all I want. I want to work my dream job without having some playboy paw at me every time I see him. *Is that too much to ask for? Probably.* It doesn't matter. I'm not letting anyone ruin this opportunity for me.

I look up to find Carol peering at me with amusement. I've been quiet for too long. I'm sure the wheels of imagination are just churning in her head. She's like my mother. I'm almost certain she was a mind reader in another life. She knows me far too well, which means it's hard to keep secrets from her, and even harder to lie through my teeth.

"I do not want him to fuck my brains out," I mutter.

Carol lets out a laugh as she mocks me with her infectious smile. "Maybe not your brains," she begins to say, as she walks over and plucks a few stray hairs off my shoulder "But definitely something else. I think that's why you're so worked up about this."

I bite back a smile as she raises one perfectly plucked eyebrow at me. *Damn her.* I shouldn't have told her anything. As much as I hate to admit it, in a way, she's right. I've been dreaming about *his* mouth ever since that night. It's embarrassing, but twice I've woken up panting from dreams of Nicholas's head between my thighs. Each time I revel in the thought of pulling his hair, crushing his lips against me, and riding his face. As if waking up panting in your best friend's apartment isn't embarrassing enough. *Damn, I need to stop thinking about him. Get a grip, Rebecca. He's engaged...*

"I need to steer clear of him, Carol. I told you, Alison is his fiancée. We both met her at *Riptide, remember?*"

"He obviously doesn't want to be with her," Carol says, cutting me off. "He couldn't keep his eyes off you."

"It doesn't matter. He's engaged. I can't stoop to Miles's level. He cheated on me with another woman. If I sleep with Nicholas, how am I any better?"

I was stupid to think someone like Nicholas could be a good guy. No, men like him just want to fuck you, use you, and then leave you. I'm not going to be that woman anymore—the one who's naïve enough to think that she can change a man with a bat of her eyelashes. *Fuck that.*

"You're not anything like Miles," she says, grabbing my hand. "Seriously, nothing."

I clear my throat hinting that it's time for a change of subject. I can feel tears threatening to escape. Carol pulls a pair of earrings from her jewelry case and holds them up to my ears.

"You should wear these." The aquamarine earrings look more expensive than all of the jewelry I own put together. They're beautiful.

"I can't," I say, wrapping my hand around hers. "If I lost them, I could never replace them." It seems like I'll be borrowing many things from now on. Even my current outfit is on loan to me by Cheri, Carol's client who runs the fashion line *Retro Thrift.*

Unfortunately, the clothes that I brought from home are currently having cat pee dry-cleaned out of them. Carol forgot to mention that the client lending his apartment to her also designated Carol as his cat sitter. 'Sprinkles,' as he's adorably called, is a longhaired cat that's a tad too feisty. I've been on the wrong side of his wrath. He doesn't just claw the hell out of you. He pisses on people he doesn't like. It's disgusting, but Carol seems to think it's one of Sprinkles' most charming qualities. At first, I thought he was named Sprinkles because he's sweet, but I quickly came to realize that it's because he likes to 'sprinkle' all over your stuff. In my case, it means all over my luggage. So for now, I'm borrowing clothes until I can afford to buy my own.

"I'm glad Cheri had a dress coat for you. It's snowing outside," Carol says, handing it to me. "Let me call Steven to drive you."

"That's all right, I'll take the subway." I'm overdue for a bit of sightseeing. I haven't really gotten to explore since I've arrived, and seeing New York is definitely at the top of my to-do list. Maybe the fresh air will also help me clear my head. If I'm going to work with Nicholas for the next sixth months, then I need to find a way to ignore his irritating qualities.

"Are you sure you won't get lost trying to find the subway?" Carol asks in a motherly tone.

"That's why I'm leaving early. I'll be fine," I say. "I checked the subway route online."

"Okay. Well, have a great first day of work." Carol hugs me and then heads for the front door.

"Thanks, I'll see you for dinner."

"Becca?" I turn to find Carol staring at me. "A word of advice. Try not to get fired today, okay?"

"Never," I answer, laughing.

12

REBECCA

I stick out my tongue to catch the puffs of white floating down toward me. I've never seen snow. The closest I've come to seeing it is having hail rain down on me, and that's nowhere near as fun, especially when the hail's the size of ping pong balls. The snow-plows didn't clear the streets in time for the morning rush. I've trudged through it for what seems like three miles now and I'm already out of breath.

I stop to stare up at the sleek grey building before me. Crisp white letters read STONEHAVEN. It pops against the steel and glass skyscrapers surrounding its magnificent presence. I shiver at the memory of my last visit. I didn't exactly leave here on the best of terms. I glance up to the top of the building, unable to stop myself from wondering if Nicholas is staring down at me from his office.

The glass-like structure has a clean, contemporary look. The kind you mostly see in art districts. The company's hub is located on 6th Avenue, which mostly seems taken up by commercial businesses. The streets are inundated with tourists, employees, and what I can only assume are Wall Street bankers on their way to work. Getting here wasn't as easy as I hoped it would be. It's strange to think how similar and yet drastically different Los Angeles and New York are. The city of Los Angeles is lively and full of color, whereas in New

York, everything seems to be a different shade of grey. There's also a metro rail system in Los Angeles but it's nowhere near as crazy as the subway here. For a moment, I had considered Carol's offer of having Steven give me a ride to work this morning, but I instead chose to brave the gritty streets of NY and here I am. *Still alive. So far at least.*

Coincidentally, Carol warned me about the mugging rate out here. I guess it's common for people to run up and snatch your purse. I can't say I carry many valuables on me, but I'm definitely keeping a close watch on my bag. I can't afford to lose that, too. Excitement pulses through me as I step toward the front entrance. I take a moment to glance at my reflection and take in the strange sight of me standing on the icy sidewalk. I can't help it. I pinch myself, testing my grip of reality. Nope, I'm not dreaming. *This is actually real. It's hard to believe.*

The smell of coffee and hazelnut assaults my nose as I step through the revolving glass doors. The building already seems different from the day of my interview. Inside, StoneHaven Publishing is a magnificent canvas of black marble stone and polished chrome accents. The lobby area is filled with employees bustling about as they make their way through. I spot an older woman standing behind the front reception desk screening phone calls and handing out visitor passes. Her hair is cut into a short bob with dark grey slivers that run throughout her waves of black. It takes me a moment to realize I've seen her before. She's the woman who helped me the day of my interview. *Her name is Mary.* She looks up and smiles politely as she waves me over.

"Hello, it's you again," she says with a polite smile.

"Hi, yes. My name is Rebecca. I'm not sure if you remember me, but—"

"Of course I do. You're Mr. StoneHaven's new assistant." Mary looks me over with curiosity. "I was afraid you wouldn't be back."

I blush. *Geez, I wonder if everyone heard about what happened.*

"It takes more than that to get rid of me, I guess," I answer, laughing nervously.

I met Mary briefly before my interview with Nicholas's father. I was surprised to find someone so welcoming to an outsider like me.

I've heard horror stories from Carol about some of the people she's worked with in New York when she first came here from California. Mary doesn't seem like the type to go batshit insane on you. In reality, she isn't what I was expecting to find here at all. Maybe it's silly of me to assume that Nicholas would surround himself with young supermodel-type women, but that's exactly what I thought. You know, the kind of woman Nicholas would fuck over his desk. The image of Nicholas bending me over a desk flashes in my mind. *God, Rebecca. Just stop.*

"It's nice to see you again." I smile at Mary as she hands me a guest pass.

"Welcome to the family," she winks. "Please, take a seat." Mary directs me to a row of black chairs adjacent to her desk. "Mr. Stone-Haven will be down shortly."

I gulp at the sound of his name. I'm anxious to see him. I really don't know what to expect. Maybe he'll fire me on the spot. Maybe he's been waiting for me to show up so he can embarrass me in front of everyone. No, his father wouldn't allow it. I might be Nicholas's assistant, but his father is the one who decides if I stay or go. He made that very clear when he hired me. Mary makes a phone call and speaks in low voice. She turns to me momentarily and then turns back, smiling into the phone. She seems a little too enthusiastic. My stomach turns in anticipation. I have the feeling she knows something I don't. *Shit.* I really hope I'm not being fired today. *There goes my promise to Carol.*

———

"Sorry to keep you waiting. It's crazy around here this time of year. My name is Kristy, by the way."

I follow Kristy, a tall brunette down a long hallway toward the back of the first floor.

"I thought Mr. StoneHaven would be meeting me," I say anxiously.

"He is, but Mr. StoneHaven is actually in meetings for most of the day. He ordered me to take you to HR and then show you where your desk will be," she says. Somehow, the words *ordered* sounds dirty coming out of her mouth.

"Thanks," I mutter.

A fter three hours of filling out HR paperwork, I can finally say that I'm officially a StoneHaven employee. I even signed my first non-disclosure agreement. There was far too much technical lingo for me to fully understand, but one thing is clear—going to the press about anything dealing with the company is off limits. As in, do it and your ass is fired and smacked with a monstrous lawsuit. I spent the rest of the day familiarizing myself with my work area.

Kristy was nice enough to show me my desk, which isn't too far from the office of Carol's cousin, Ken Phillips. I'm excited to have my own cubicle. Everything feels so surreal. I even have my own name badge that gives me special access to different levels of the building, and on my desk sits a box of business cards with my name, title, and extension. I gush at the sight of my name programmed into the phone system.

I'm definitely hanging some pictures of Carol and me, and of my mom and dad. My mother has been calling me every night at seven, like clockwork. Most nights she just tells me about her day and the latest gossip in the neighborhood. Dad has even called me a few times. He usually fills me in on what's going on with the latest season of *Game of Thrones*.

Before I know it, five o'clock is just around the corner and it's time to gather my things and head home. I should probably avoid walking home too late, especially when I don't know half the street names around the area.

"Ms. Gellar, welcome to StoneHaven Publishing." My eyes follow *his* mouth as he pronounces each syllable with a mixture of elegance and authority. I hug my dress coat tightly against the crook of my elbow as his voice sends bumps down my skin. Here he is, in the flesh. The dangerously handsome and enigmatic Nicholas Stone-Haven. It doesn't seem like it's been that long, but somehow he looks different. His blond mane is slightly shorter and tousled as if he woke up with gorgeous bed hair. I bite my lip as I try my hardest not to moan at the sight of him in his tailored dark blue suit. I blush as my eyes unconsciously drift down to his crotch. His suit is perfectly fitted in more than just one area.

"Gellar, my eyes are up here," he says, teasingly.

Right. How embarrassing.

"Are you on your way out?" Nicholas watches me as I grab my coat and stuff my badge into my purse.

"Yes, I am."

He gestures for me to follow him to the elevator across the floor. I follow him, partly shaking in my pumps as we walk down the hall. My heart races as we come closer to the entrance of the elevator. It's like déjà vu all over again. This is bad news.

"Maybe I can take the stairs down." I offer.

"Are you afraid to be alone with me?" he asks, as if he's testing me.

"No, I just thought it would be good to get some exercise."

"I have a better way you can burn some calories." Nicholas grabs my elbow and ushers me inside the elevator before I have a chance to slip away. I step back into the corner, trying to put as much distance as I can between us. *I need to make this situation work. I need this job.*

"I don't think you want to climb down thirty flights of stairs just to avoid me," he says, cutting through my thoughts. "Plus, you're my assistant. We need to get used to each other if this is going to work." I'm surprised he's willing to try. I thought he was set on trying to make me leave.

"And here I was thinking I might be getting the boot." I glare at him as he half smiles to himself.

"And who says you're not?" He smirks. *He has to be pulling my leg. My office was set up and everything.*

"I assumed... wait, are you serious? Why the hell would you have me come down here if I'm fired?" I blurt.

"I thought you would want a second chance at getting your job back," he says with a devilish grin. "How far are you willing to go to keep your job, Gellar?" He's toying with me.

"You're an asshole."

"I am, but I'm the asshole who owns you for the next six months," he says flatly.

"Let's get one thing straight," I say, pushing my finger into his perfectly ironed shirt. "No one owns me."

"You're right. No one owns you. Just me," he says, snatching my hand.

"Fuck you," I whisper, pulling my hand from his grasp.

"Not today, Ms. Gellar. But soon. Very soon." Nicholas steps closer, as if to kiss me. He lingers, hovering slightly over my lips, and for a moment, I think he just might do it. He steps back, breaking the strange, heated connection between us and walks out. *What the hell?*

"And Gellar," he says, poking his head back inside the elevator. "I hope you're ready." *Ready? Ready for what?*

13

REBECCA

W hen Nicholas asked me if I was ready, I should've known he had something up his sleeve. My second day on the job was the beginning of my demise. The second I got to work, he sent me on an expedition to bring him a nonfat mocha latte from *Joe's Black Brew,* a small mom and pop coffee house three miles from the office. The lines at the shop were incredibly long. It seemed to be the favorite spot for visiting tourists. To my surprise, when I returned, Nicholas informed me that he had made a mistake and he actually wanted a whole milk mocha latte. He even said he tried to call me from his office phone, but I knew that was a lie. His intentions were deliberate. I could have easily gotten him the same drink at the *Starbucks* on the other side of the street, but I sucked it up and I went again. Each trip took about two hours, mostly because I kept getting lost. By the time I returned the second time, I was exhausted and ready to go home.

The following day, Nicholas sent me to pick up his Great Dane named Otis. It didn't exactly feel comfortable walking around the city with a giant horse dog, but I couldn't really say no, could I? It wasn't until I got back and spoke with Mary that she informed me that Nicholas didn't have a dog. Apparently, he had paid a close friend of his to let him borrow the dog for the day. Thanks to my boss, I went home that day smelling like slobber and of dog breath.

The following week things seemed to calm down a little bit, but I guess that can be attributed to the fact that Nicholas had been called into several all-day meetings to discuss plans for the new fiscal year. It didn't leave him much time to send me on crazy errands. I spent most of Monday replying to his e-mails. Manic Monday is an understatement. Try *'Holy shit, I'm drowning in letters and I'll never survive this apocalypse of mail Monday.'* I hate whoever was Nicholas's last assistant. She left a mess. There's unanswered letters requesting his presence from hundreds of different organizations. The most recent one is Lit for Kids. They're honoring StoneHaven Publishing a week from now and they still need a revised biography and a photo of Nicholas for their program. *I'm sure he can make time to go to this one.*

Nicholas has been on a campaign to get me to leave, but I'm not going anywhere. If he thinks he can just get me to quit by treating me like his own personal slave, he's wrong. Lately, my days have consisted of everything from getting his coffee, cleaning bird shit off his window with a toothbrush to cleaning the scuffs off his shoe collection. I do it all. I think in his head, he holds some twisted fantasy of having me on my knees. I've caught him watching me, and I don't like it. *Okay, that's a lie.*

"Hey, you must be Rebecca."

I turn in my chair just in time to see Ken Phillips standing at the entrance of my cubicle. He stares down at me with his warm honey eyes framed by thick black glasses and a boyish grin.

"Good morning, Ken," I smile.

"Oh, I'm surprised you recognize me."

"I saw pictures of you at Carol's apartment."

It's nice to finally meet you," he says, shaking my hand.

"Thank you for the recommendation. I don't think I would be here if it weren't for you."

"I just forwarded your name," he smiles shyly.

"Well, thank you anyway."

"I'm sure they're glad to have you."

"I'm glad to be here." *Except right now.*

Ken frowns at the heaping pile of work on my desk. "You look overwhelmed," he says, pointing to my desk. "Are you finding everything all right?"

"Oh, no, it's chaotic. I'm pretty sure today is my last day," I say jokingly.

Ken brushes the back of his neck as if he's embarrassed. "I'm sorry. Is there anything I can help you with?"

"No, don't worry. I'm just answering e-mails and trying to get some letters out. I'll manage."

"I don't doubt it," he says with a grin. "When I heard you were hired as Nicholas's assistant, I was a little worried."

"Oh. Why?" *Does he think I can't handle the job?*

"He has a bad streak with his assistants," he says.

"Don't worry. I'm not in danger of falling for Mr. StoneHaven."

"Just be careful. He can be very charming," Ken says with a pained expression.

I was anxious to meet Ken when I was first hired on. From everything Carol told me, he was amazing. I mean, he is amazing. He vouched for me without even meeting me, and within a week of submitting my resume, I had my interview. If it weren't for him, I wouldn't be here. It's funny how similar Carol and Ken are in features. But where Carol is lively and outgoing. Ken seems much more calm and reserved. I guess you could say he's your stereotypical bookworm. In a hot and nerdy sort of way.

"I'm sure you'll be happy to know that Nicholas is out of the office today until five p.m.," Ken says, handing me a note from him. "I ran into him this morning on his way to one of his meetings and he asked me to give you this."

Pick up dry cleaning. Now.

Xx, Nicholas

A flush creeps up my cheeks. *Perfect. Ken must think I'm sleeping with him already. Who just puts X's on their notes? He purposely did this to embarrass me.*

"He didn't even put where to get the dry cleaning. There are probably a million dry cleaners in this part of the city," I say, rolling my eyes.

"Here," Ken says, pulling open a filing cabinet next to my desk. "I'm pretty sure Wendy, his last assistant, kept a list of all of the places Nicholas asked her to go to." Ken retrieves a little black book from a folder and hands it to me.

"Thank you again."

"Oh, I almost forgot. He also wanted me to tell you that he'd like to meet with you in his office around six p.m.," Ken says, as he makes his way out of my cubicle.

Great. I'm supposed to leave the office at five, but now he wants me to stay until six? *Ugh.*

I knew it was coming, but I've been in self-denial about when exactly I would see Nicholas again. Technically, I'm supposed to be like white on rice with him, but it's hard when he's always in private meetings.

"So I'm meeting him alone?"

"Well, yes. I'm assuming alone. He didn't mention anyone else being there," Ken says, laughing. "His office is on the top floor."

"Thanks."

"Good luck," Ken says with an encouraging smile.

———

At a quarter to six, the building slowly grows quieter as employees trickle out to head home. It's only Monday, but I'm ready for the weekend to be here already. I pack my belongings and clean up my cubicle. Ken's desk is empty. The only thing on it is a cup of coffee from this morning. Apparently, he's MIA because I haven't seen him since I got back from picking up Nicholas's suit from the dry cleaners.

As I head to my meeting with Nicholas, I spot Stefan waiting by the reception desk. He's wearing a tuxedo and sporting a fresh haircut. Nicholas must've come out more like his mother because Stefan's hair, aside from the grey, is dark brown.

"Rebecca, working late?" he asks as I stop to say hello.

"I have a few things to do before heading home, and I need to check in with Nicholas."

"I know I haven't had a chance to check in with you, but how do you like things?" The only word that pops into my head is *bizarre*. Stefan smiles, noticing my hesitation.

"This is a great opportunity, Rebecca. I know my son can be a challenge, but he's a good person. He's just lost his way."

"Why did you want me?" I ask.

"I need someone with a good head on their shoulders. It takes a lot of confidence and a little bit of courage to just pick up and move across the country when you've lived in LA your whole life. I also think it takes those same two qualities to deal with this job."

"There was nothing left for me back there."

He smiles. "Well, I'm hoping you'll make New York your new home."

It has to be, because I can't go back to the sad little life I had back in Los Angeles. I spent most of my days crying over Miles and the relationship that I had so much invested in.

I smile. "I feel at home here."

"You're a strong young lady, Rebecca," he says warmly. "You remind me of my son, Alex. He was very spirited like you." *Was?* I knew about Nicholas's sister, Emily, because Ken had mentioned that she swings by the office sometimes, but he never said anything about Nicholas having a brother.

"Did something happen to him?" I ask.

Stefan smiles sadly. "He passed away in an accident."

"I'm sorry."

"Don't be. It's good to remember him. I never understood why Nicholas wanted to bury his memory. As if he dying wasn't enough of a loss."

I can't help but think of my parents in Los Angeles. I don't know what I'd do without them. I never had any siblings, but I always thought having a sister would be kind of cool.

"Well, I better get going. I'm meeting an investor for dinner," he says, checking his watch.

"Goodnight, Mr. StoneHaven."

"Goodnight, Rebecca."

The top level of the building is guarded with an access code. A code that you have to type into the keypad and then have your fingerprint scanned. Each time I make my way up here, it still surprises me that the machine recognizes my fingerprint. I feel like a secret agent on my way to my secret hiding place. The elevator doors usher open, revealing a large office the size of a conference room. My nipples involuntarily pucker as I step out of the elevator. As much as I hate to admit it, I'm not sure if it's from the cold temperature of the room or the thought of seeing him again. *I'm going with option A.*

This isn't my first time being up here, but it feels like it. I don't think I've ever stood here long enough to admire my surroundings. The office is decorated with what seems like furnishings for an apartment with a sofa, a bookcase, a desk, and picture frames. Each frame holds photos of Nicholas, a younger girl, and another handsome blond who I can only assume is Alex. There are even a few of Tristan Knight, Nicholas's best friend who I met at *Riptide*. I walk over to the bookcase centered in the middle of the room. There has to be more than a thousand books here. I trail my fingers over the top row of books and find myself a bit surprised to see so many classic novels— everything from *David Copperfield* to *Sherlock Holmes*. Nicholas doesn't strike me as the type to be a voracious reader, despite his father's company.

I turn to find Nicholas watching me from his desk.

"Ms. Gellar, I'm glad to see you here." I sense a hint of sarcasm in his voice. "There's something I would like you to do."

"Of course, anything."

"The company has our annual gala coming up in January. I need you to submit the insurance documents for the venue, mail the final check payment, and confirm with their event coordinator for the thirtieth of January. We were going to have it on the thirty-first, but I'm leaving for France that day—which reminds me, I need you to book my flight."

"Where is the venue?"

"It's the Museum of Natural History."

"Oh. I'm sure that will be incredible."

"It's one of the biggest events for our company. Please make sure to confirm for the thirtieth. I can't miss this trip."

"I need to speak with you about the upcoming Lit for Kids event next week."

"What about it?" he asks, sounding irritated.

"Well, I went ahead and accepted the invitation. I saw that you were free that night and they called asking for your presence." *More like begging.*

"Ms. Gellar, I would prefer if you didn't accept invitations without directly asking me first."

14

NICHOLAS

I stare at the tablet in front of me as I scroll through my work e-mail. Each morning there's at least fifty new messages that need my attention. For every dent I make, three more e-mails follow. It's like trying to put out a fire by randomly sprinkling water on it. It does shit. I'm happy that Rebecca has exceeded my expectations by at least organizing this monstrous thing. She's labeled everything into folders, but it still requires some attention. I don't know why my last assistant, Wendy, had such a hard time trying to figure out a filter process, but I guess I can't judge her too harshly. I didn't exactly hire her because she was good with computers. I hired her because she was good with her mouth. Speaking of mouths...

My mind instantly wanders to the look Rebecca had when her eyes drifted toward the bulge in my pants on her first day on the job. I'd be lying if I said I hadn't already pictured Gellar's lips wrapped around my cock. *Those lips.* They're similar to the top half of a heart. Perfectly molded into two sultry plumps just waiting to be bitten and teased into submission. If only Rebecca didn't drive me bonkers with her fiery spirit. I can't believe she'd accepted the invitation to the event for Lit for Kids. While I wholeheartedly support the charity and their mission, I don't even want to think about how hard it's going to be to be around people who used to know my brother. It's grueling enough just having to deal with the people at work.

But now, I have no choice. I can't back out of the event. It would be rude and it wouldn't look well for the company. I think Father would say the positive publicity from the event would help counterbalance some of the recent negativity. People want to know that businesses still care about people. That's a legacy I can say I proudly want to be a part of.

An e-mail notification pops up at the top of my inbox, pulling me from my distracted thoughts. I cringe at the sight of the name of Katherine Brown, Executive Director at Lit for Kids. I haven't spoken to her in years. Every year she tries to convince me to attend their donor appreciation event. Most of the time I don't even reply to her e-mails or her invites through the mail, so I'm surprised it took her this long to send me a message. In fact, I haven't received any phone calls from her since Rebecca accepted the invite. Perhaps my she-devil of an assistant figured out that taking messages might help her keep her job.

To: Nicholas F. StoneHaven
      From: Katherine Brown
Reply: Thank you
Nick,
I'm so happy to hear that you'll be attending our event. We've reserved a front table for you and any guests you may like to bring. It'll be nice to see you after so long. It's really been too many years.
Love,
Katherine

It has been too many years, and yet the pain of losing Alex is still fresh. I'm starting to think that this night might be easier with some company than flying solo. Maybe I should ask Tristan to go with me. I haven't talked to him much because he's been so busy with planning the opening of his art gallery. I pull out my phone and dial his number. To my surprise, he answers on the first ring.

"Tristan speaking."

"Hey, it's Nick. I was calling to see if you have plans for next Thursday? I'm attending a charity event and I need a wingman." In the background of the call, I hear what sounds like general noise from a city street.

"Are you asking me on a date, Mr. StoneHaven?" he asks, mocking me.

"No, asshole, I'm asking you to do me a favor."

"You know I would do anything for you, but I have plans next Thursday."

"Plans? Doing what?" It takes Tristan a moment to answer. I check my phone to see if he's hung up, but his name still flashes at the top of my screen. *That's weird.*

"Hello?" I ask.

"Sorry, I, uh, well, I'm going out..."

"Out? Like on a date?" I ask, confused.

"Yes."

"So, who is she?" I ask curiously. Tristan usually doesn't hold information back. He doesn't shove his conquests in my face, but I know he gets his fair share of beautiful women. And I've seen the way women look at him.

"It's complicated, and probably a conversation for another time. I'm sorry I can't go with you. Let's have drinks soon." And with that, Tristan hangs up, leaving me confused as fuck. *What is he hiding?* I redial Tristan's number, but this time it goes straight to voicemail. All right... well, I guess that means I'm going to this event alone. Alison would probably love to go with me, but I have absolutely no desire to entertain her all evening.

My office phone rings and Rebecca's name flashes on the line. *Gellar.* She's the one who got me into this mess. She should be the one attending the event with me. After all, she's my assistant, and I think it's only fair to make her go with me since she didn't even bother to ask if I wanted to attend it. Just as I'm about to pick up the line, it stops flashing. I switch to line two and call Mary at the front desk. She answers in her usual amused voice.

"How can I help you, Mr. StoneHaven?"

"Mary, I need a dress."

"A dress, sir?" I can almost picture the confusion on her face.

"Yes, it's for Ms. Gellar. She will be accompanying me to the appreciation event for Lit for Kids. Can you please contact Melanie Cole from Madison's and ask her to bring some dresses over?"

"Of course. Should I pull Ms. Gellar's measurements from her HR folder?"

"Yes." Thank god, I completely forgot about finding the right dress size. Rebecca's curvier than most of the women I've ever dated... *god, those curves.* I never thought of myself as an ass man, but I can't stop thinking about how good hers felt in my grip. Mary clears her throat pulling me back from my fantasy. Shit. I didn't even realize she was still on the line.

"Is there a certain color or colors you would like Melanie to send?" Mary asks.

"Red." I smile, picturing Rebecca in a deep red dress. The color fits her personality so well. I don't doubt that it would look just as good on her.

15

REBECCA

I shouldn't be surprised to find Nicholas waiting at my desk the following Thursday, but I am. It's late in the afternoon, and most of the office has gone home for the holiday with the exception of the cleaning staff and me. I practically drop the pile of documents in my hand at the sight of him sitting casually in my chair. *Doesn't he have anything better to do?* I suppress a moan as he half smiles at my nervous reaction. It takes me a moment to realize he's dressed in the black tuxedo I picked up from the dry cleaners earlier this week.

"Rebecca, can I have a word?" Nicholas asks, adjusting his tie slightly. I can't help but wonder if I make Nicholas just as nervous as he makes me. He stands, giving me room to squeeze by, so I can set my stack of papers down. Whether it's intended or not, I'm not sure, but he only moves enough so that our bodies slightly touch when I pass him. I catch the slightest hint of honey and mint on him. *Damn him, he always smells so good.*

"Sure, I was just making copies of the financial documents that you asked for," I reply, handing him the second set of copies.

"I need to ask you for a favor."

A favor? "Okay," I say, hesitating. This already doesn't sound good.

"I need a date to a charity event I'm attending tonight."

"A date?" I gulp. "Where's Alison?"

"She's out of town."

"I really don't think that's a good idea. I'm pretty sure if you went alone, the world wouldn't end," I say, crossing my arms.

"Gellar...," Nicholas says in a challenging tone.

"Are you really asking?" I say, exasperated.

"No." he says smirking. "I just thought it would be polite if I tried to first."

"The word 'try' seems to be a foreign concept for you." I roll my eyes at him, trying my best to emphasize my annoyance.

"I'll pick you up at six p.m. Dinner starts at seven," he says, as he turns to leave.

"And if I refuse?"

"I'll drag you, even if it's kicking and screaming."

"Aren't you going to ask for my address?" I ask, annoyed.

"No. I know where you live," he says with a devilish grin. I shiver at the streak of desire coursing through me. Nicholas knows where I live? Somehow, that seems like a very, very bad thing. *Knowledge is power and Nicholas seems to know a lot about me.*

"I don't have anything to wear," I confess.

"I took care of that. Just go home and get dressed," he says, giving me a once over. "No more excuses, Ms. Gellar."

16

NICHOLAS

I don't have a good explanation as to why I asked Rebecca to come with me tonight. No, that's a lie. I need a distraction. I haven't been to this event in five years. Every year the executive director, Katherine Brown, sends me an invitation to come, but I never show and I never accept. If Rebecca hadn't accepted the invite this year, I wouldn't be going. I didn't really need a date. And while the thing I said about Alison isn't a complete lie, she's not technically out of town. She's just gone for the weekend to check out venues in the country for our wedding. She's called me at least five times within the last few hours to tell me about a winery she saw on her way there. It's probably not a good idea if we get married in a place where I can consume massive amounts of alcohol. I'll definitely need it.

"Good evening, Mr. StoneHaven." I turn to find Mary packing away her purse and carrying out the trash from behind the reception desk.

"Mary, you do know we have janitors who do that?" I ask.

"Why have someone else do something that I can do myself?" she says brightly. "Are you headed out to the donor appreciation event for Lit for Kids?"

"Yes, I'm stopping to pick up Rebecca and then I'm off."

"Your brother, Alex, would be proud of you."

I flinch at the mention of his name. Has it really been five years since his death? It seems like just yesterday. "Thank you, Mary."

From my pained expression, I know Mary sees it's better not to bring up Alex again. I've been giving to their organization since my brother Alex passed away. He was the good son and the best brother Emily or I could ask for. Lit for Kids was one of his favorite nonprofits. They promote literacy at schools and they have afterschool programs for children who need help learning how to read. It's a natural fit for our company, and I happily give to it in his memory. Alex was always putting others before himself. He didn't know how to be any other way.

"Mary, can you do me one favor before you leave for the night?"

"Of course," she says, half-smiling.

"Please call and let Rebecca know I'm on my way."

"Done."

"Thank you. Have a wonderful night."

"And you, sir."

17

REBECCA

"I am not wearing that dress."

"Why not?" Carol asks, grinning.

"I have never worn a dress like that."

"There's a first time for everything," she says with way too much enthusiasm.

The dress that Nicholas purchased, which I would hardly call a dress, has a deep neckline that drops and stops just below my breasts. I don't think I can properly wear a bra with it. In fact, I can't imagine how anyone could wear anything underneath it. The fabric is thin and colored a deep satin red. It's formed and fitted like a halter-top, flowing all the way down to my feet and splitting slightly above the knee. It's beautiful, sexy, and seductive, but it's not a dress I would ever wear near my boss.

On top of all of this, it's snowing. I'm going to freeze my lady parts off. I reach inside the black satin bag that the dress came packaged in and find a matching shawl. *At least he's being somewhat considerate.*

"This is what he wants me to wear for a kids' charity event?"

"How old are these kids?" Carol asks, grinning.

"I'm pretty sure not old enough to see my boobs flailing about." I turn to see Carol silently laughing at me.

"You're having way too much fun watching me."

"Sorry, it's like watching a fly try to get out of spider's web."

"I hope you're not implying I'm the fly in this situation," I say, raising my eyebrow at her.

Carol turns me so that I'm staring into her long floor mirror. "You don't look like one, but you're definitely the fly," she says, whacking my ass.

"How was work?" I need to keep Nicholas off my mind.

———

Nicholas drives us from Carol's apartment on Park Avenue down to Lincoln Center Plaza. On our way there, we take a road that runs through Central Park and is peppered with snow. I spot several horse-drawn carriages pulling up on the side. Each one is decorated with Christmas lights fastened to the edges, giving their carriage a fairytale feel. I've always wanted to take a ride in one.

"Have you been on a horse-drawn carriage before?" Nicholas asks, as he catches me staring out the window.

"No, not yet."

"They're a novelty to visitors. You can't go to New York and not take a ride in one. I'll take you on one sometime."

Nicholas's words catch me off guard. I don't say anything, but I can't help but question the motive behind his words. What could I say other than "*why bother?*" Nicholas doesn't owe me anything, but here he is making plans with me. I promised Carol I would enjoy tonight, but it's hard to when I'm already thinking this is a mistake.

Paparazzi stalk the outside of the Lit for Kids donor appreciation event. They snap a flurry of pictures as Nicholas and I step out of his car. A valet attendant takes the keys to Nicholas's car and hands him a return slip. Nicholas grabs my hand and leads me through the front of the Wilkes Library.

The library is a majestic display of architecture. It's like staring at a building straight out of a gothic novel. It's strange to see a building like this in the middle of New York, but it's beautiful. There are even gargoyles protruding from the topside of the building. Each one appears carefully carved with exact details.

96

There's a noticeable shift in Nicholas's attitude as we make our way through the center of the library that's been transformed into a banquet hall. His once confident attitude is now replaced by a more somber one. I watch from the corner of my eye as an older woman wearing a white dress suit approaches us.

"Hello, Nick. How are you?" she says, giving him a quick kiss on the cheek.

"Katherine, it's lovely to see you again," he says with a small smile. "Rebecca, this is Katherine Brown, the Executive Director of Lit for Kids."

"It's a pleasure to meet you," Katherine says, shaking my hand eagerly. "Are you Nicholas' fiancée?"

"His assistant," I say, smiling.

"Ah, you're the one my secretary spoke with?"

"Yes, I am."

"I should be thanking you for Nicholas being here. He never comes to our events."

"Oh, well, thank you for having us."

"I apologize, Katherine. I've been so busy with—" Nicholas stops mid-sentence, and for a moment, I swear I hear a break in his voice. Nicholas squeezes the bridge of his nose as if warding off a headache. "My father has several new developments and we've just been swamped," he finishes his voice barely above a restrained whisper.

Katherine does something completely unexpected. She steps forward and wraps Nicholas in an embrace, hugging him tightly. The almost mother-like display of affection knocks the wind out of me. I stand there feeling awkward, and yet privileged to see such a strange, but vulnerable moment.

"Your brother was a wonderful man, Nick. We're grateful for your generous contributions. I understand why you haven't come, but I'm glad Rebecca changed your mind about tonight," she says, smiling at me over his shoulder.

As Katherine releases Nicholas from her embrace, she whispers something in his ear and then makes her way toward another guest. Nicholas stands completely immobile, frozen by some imaginary force.

"Nicholas?" I call.

It takes a few moments for my voice to register across his face. He slowly turns toward me, as if he's forgotten I was standing only a few feet away.

"Rebecca?" he asks with a look of confusion.

"Are you okay?" He looks down at my hand placed on his arm. I pull my hand away, conscious that to him it might look like something else. Nicholas looks up and stares toward the back room, as if searching for someone or something. His eyes stop on the bar at the back of the banquet room.

"No, but I will be," he says with a look of determination. Nicholas grazes past me and heads toward the bar. In a few short seconds, he returns with a short bottle of whiskey and a glass.

"You're not drinking that whole thing, are you?" I ask shocked.

"Watch me, Gellar," he says, opening the bottle.

———

Nicholas is a grown man. He doesn't need me to babysit him, yet here I am, watching him consume massive amounts of alcohol. We make our way to our dining table, which to my dismay, is toward the front of the room. *Perfect.* So if Nicholas makes an ass of himself, everyone has a perfect view. He seats himself mere inches from my chair and tugs on my hand, pulling me to sit next to him. Seriously, it's like he's five. *Why the hell is he acting so strange?* I remember seeing pictures of Nicholas's sister in his office and a few of whom I assume were his brother. I pull out my phone and open up my Google app. I'm sure I can find information about Nicholas's brother online.

"Rebecca?" I look up to find Nicholas watching me. Pain seeps through his hardened expression.

"Sorry, I was just checking my texts," I say, sliding my phone back into my purse. He sits there silently watching me squirm beneath his gaze. "I think I need some air." After a few torturous moments, I excuse myself from the guests around our table and head toward the outside balcony.

The balcony is lit up with lights stringing down from the roof of the library. The light cascades down, washing me in warmth. Despite the snow stopping, the night air still nips at my cheeks with each passing breeze. It doesn't seem longer than a few seconds before Nicholas joins me outside. He stands beside me staring out into the darkness. He pulls the bottle from earlier out of his pocket and takes another sip of the whiskey from the nearly empty container. I'm not sure what kind of tolerance he has, but this is getting crazy.

"Nicholas, slow down," I say, grabbing the bottle from him. "We can't get home when you're drunk off your ass."

"You can drive," he says, handing me the valet slip.

"I've never driven in New York." Nicholas stares at me, as if I haven't spoken. "I would get us lost." I stare openly at him as he looks down at the bottle in my hand.

"Nicholas, if everyone sees you leaving the party intoxicated, the paparazzi will have a field day." His face is lost in thought. I'm not even sure if he understands the severity of the situation. "They're like ravenous wolves down there waiting to devour the next unfortunate soul that walks out. They know you're here."

"It doesn't matter," Nicholas says, gripping the ledge of the balcony.

"What? Are you insane?"

"I'll give them something to talk about," he says, grabbing the bottle from my hands and tossing it over the edge.

"Nicholas!" I call, as he turns to leave. He doesn't stop until I wedge myself between him and the door to the entrance of the banquet room. He stares down at me in confusion.

"Gellar, get out of my way."

"No." I press my body against his.

"What are you doing?" he asks, oblivious. Despite his questioning gaze, I can feel his erection growing against me. I grind my hips into his and he groans.

"I'm stopping you from ruining both of our lives," I whisper.

I'm not sure if it's the heat of moment, or the idea of losing everything, or maybe just the strange liberating need to do it, but I pull Nicholas by the shirt and kiss him. The shock of the situation is evident in his frozen stature. I run my tongue across his lips and instantly, he melts into the kiss, grabbing me in a haze of lust. He pushes my dress up and lifts me, turning to place me on the cold icy ledge. Nicholas's lips muffle my scream. I grab his shirt using it to pull myself forward. My anxiety of heights is in full effect. "I promise I won't let go," he says, holding onto my waist. *My ass is freezing.*

"You're drunk, Nick."

He stops, looking up at me. "That's the first time you've called me Nick."

I shiver as his eyes search mine.

"I won't take my hands off you," he says, parting my legs open. My heart squeezes at the promise behind his words. He places his hand on my inner thigh sliding it up between the slits of my dress. Nicholas doesn't stop. He doesn't ask if it's okay. He just takes. His hand slows for a moment as he carefully pushes aside my panties. *We shouldn't be doing this.*

I push his hand away, but he entwines our fingers and moves them up to the entrance of my folds. I bite back a moan as he slips two fingers inside me and pulls them back out. He repeats this motion over and over, more vigorously each time. My skin suddenly feels too warm and the outside is too quiet—even for New York. I pant as he stretches me ever so slightly, giving him a deeper angle inside me. Each time I squirm, he squeezes my clit as if commanding me to hold still.

"Nicholas, stop," I beg.

"Do you really want me to stop?" he asks, leaning in.

"Fuck," I whisper.

"I love the little faces you make when you're about to come."

Nicholas's words send me over the edge. I grip the wall behind me as a delicious orgasm washes over me. My pussy convulses as warm liquid seeps between my legs. Nicholas retracts his hand and unapologetically slips one in his mouth. He sucks my wetness off them like he's finishing dessert.

"That's never happening again," I say, trying to still my erratic breathing.

"You don't have to lie to me." *What have I done? This was so stupid.*

He looks down at me with sadness that hurts my insides. I can't quite grasp his mood tonight. One moment he's angry and the next he has this broken look. There's something wrong and I can't fix it, but I want to. *I honestly wish I could.*

"Kiss me, Rebecca." A tear escapes, running down his cheek as he stares back at me with a pleading look.

"Nicholas, what's wrong?"

"I need you." His words are a broken whisper.

I hear them coming out from his lips, but my brain fails to register them as something that's real. "What?"

18

NICHOLAS

The world is spinning. And the only thing I can focus on is the concern etched in each beautiful curve of her face. She steps forward and grasps my hand. *Tonight is a disaster. Why did I come here? Why?* It's just another painful reminder of the pain I've pushed far back into my mind. I pinch the bridge of my nose, sensing another headache coming on. My whole body is shaking.

"Nick, is this about your brother?" she asks, squeezing my shoulder.

Her voice sounds so sweet, but her words send my stomach turning. I stumble toward the balcony ledge and lean over. I can feel something pushing up at the back of my throat. Her cool hands brush the back of my neck as I expel my dinner. She doesn't step back in disgust or even flinch. When I'm done, she pulls my handkerchief and wipes the sweat off my face.

"I'll be right back."

Rebecca disappears, leaving me alone with my thoughts. I take in large gulps of air as I gather myself together. No matter how hard I try, I can't block the painful memories flooding my mind. It's only been a few minutes since Rebecca left, but it feels like an eternity. When she returns, she's holding the keys to my car in her hand. I'm a bit surprised to see her holding them. She must've gone downstairs to the valet.

"Are you ready to go home?" she asks, looking at me.

"Yes, but what about the paparazzi?"

"You're lucky. They're taking photos right now of some of the kids that have benefited from your donations. We'll slip out the back," she says with a tight-lipped smile.

"Thank you, Rebecca."

"You're welcome," she says with a sigh.

———

I wake to my head exploding, or rather the feeling of it exploding within my skull. The room around me is dark, but familiar. I feel my way through the darkness and flip the switch on the lamp beside me. *This is my room.* I recognize the Tuscan colored walls as the light fills the room around me. My body feels warm. I must have a fever. I look down to find myself still wearing my black tuxedo. *What the fuck happened?*

"How are you feeling, sweetie?"

My eyes focus on a dark shape sitting at the edge of the bed. My vision is still too blurry to make out the familiar voice.

"Rebecca?"

"No, it's Alison."

Fuck. What is she doing here? I groan as my stomach rumbles, still angry from the abuse it had suffered last night.

"Where's Rebecca? She was with me at the event."

"Just lie back down. You got food poisoning," Alison says, unbuttoning my shirt. I push her hands away and sit up. *Bad idea.* I grab her shoulders as my head swims from rising too fast. *Food poisoning?* That must be the lie Rebecca told Alison.

"I need to make sure she got home okay." I push back the covers on my bed and stare at the floor trying to focus my vision. *Please stop spinning.*

"I'm sure she's home by now," Alison says, annoyed. "I was here when you guys got here." *We? How does she know where I live?*

"Did I say anything?" I ask, clutching my stomach

"No, you were out of it. Why didn't you answer any of my calls last night?"

"What are you talking about?" I ask. *I think I'm going to barf.*

"I called you about twenty times. Your assistant answered your phone and said you weren't feeling well."

I remember arriving at the Lit for Kids event, but I sure as hell don't remember leaving. Flashes of last night run through my head. I remember Rebecca... Oh, God, I kissed her. I remember the taste of her lips on mine. The taste of her on my fingers. *Fuck. Fuck. Fuck.*

19

REBECCA

The following day, Nicholas doesn't show up at the office. When nine rolls around, I start to get the feeling I won't be seeing him at all. *Big surprise.* I mean, I shouldn't be surprised, right? I've heard Nicholas comes on to his assistants all the time. The memory of his whiskey-stained lips is still fresh in my mind. I want to forget the flavor, but each time I run my tongue across my bottom lip, I taste him.

A pang of guilt hits me. Hearing Alison's voice on his cell phone last night caught me completely off guard. I wasn't thinking when I picked up his line, but after twenty missed calls, I figured it had to be an emergency. Alison didn't seem happy to hear another woman answer his cell. In fact, I spent five minutes trying to explain to her exactly who I was and what the hell I was doing with her fiancé. *That was super awkward.*

Even the drive to Nicholas's apartment was difficult. It took me half an hour longer than it should have to find his place. I think I passed it about three times before I realized it was only a few feet away from us. I guess I shouldn't have been surprised to see that he lives in what looked like a mansion made of limestone. Black cast iron gates and rows of green trimmed hedges surround it. It's not like any apartment that I had ever been to, but that's exactly what he called it. I was genuinely surprised when I didn't see a butler waiting for him at the door. The inside of his place was mostly empty. It felt and looked seemingly abandoned.

Carol was waiting for me when I finally got home this morning at about a quarter to two. It was like high school prom night all over again, except she was playing the role of the concerned parent instead of my mother. She didn't expect me to come home so late, but she definitely wanted the dirty details of what went on. I told her about Nicholas's strange attitude, his drunken stupor, and the heated moment between us. She was happy to hear the play by play as she hung on to each juicy detail.

The other night wasn't what I expected when Nicholas told me I was coming to the Lit for Kids event with him. I don't understand why he needed me to go, but for the first time, I experienced a side of him I hadn't imagined existed. He was vulnerable. A drastic contrast from the cocky exterior he projects around the office. I didn't tell Carol this, but he got to me. The way he practically begged me to kiss him did something to me.

———

By lunchtime, I was starting to feel restless. I can't concentrate on anything, and every time I look at the clock, it's only gone up a minute or so. Time couldn't move any slower than it is right now. I really need to get the hell out of the office. I didn't want to obsess over last night, but every time someone walks near my cubicle, I can't help but hope it was him. I guess I should be happy I haven't heard anything, but his silence has actually annoyed me. *I mean, how hard is it to send me a quick email?* I hate the unwanted feeling of disappointment in the pit of my stomach. It's like I'm in grade school again, waiting for my crush to arrive at school.

Maybe a nice walk would help. The outside streets below still look wet from the overnight rain, but despite the hovering grey clouds, it isn't actually raining anymore. I should text Carol and see if she's free. Like usual, Carol responds within a few seconds. She should just glue her phone to her hand, because she's on it constantly.

C arol: I'm in a meeting. It should be over in five. Meet me at Romero's New York Pizzeria.
Me: Sounds good. Pizza sounds ah-mazing.

S he texts me the address and I pull it up on MapQuest. To my surprise, the pizzeria is only a few minutes from the office. Perfect. Just as I'm about to grab my bag and leave, Ken's voice grabs my attention

"Hey, where are you headed off to?"

I haven't had much time to hang out with Ken, but he's been really helpful with answering any question I have related to our work. Twice I think I've gotten a paper jam in the mail sealer, and he's been gracious enough to show me how to take it apart so I can pull my crumpled envelopes out.

"I'm actually on my way to lunch with your cousin. Do you want to join us?"

"Man, I'd love to, but I'm expecting a call."

"Oh. okay. Well, have a good lunch."

"I actually wanted to ask if you're busy next weekend," he says, pushing up the rim of his thick glasses. He smiles hesitantly, as if he's nervous.

Oh. "Uh, no, I'm not doing anything." A flush stains my cheeks.

"Would you like to go on a date with me?" I don't mean to hesitate, but I'm not exactly sure what to say. It's been a long time since I went on an actual date, if you don't consider the other night one. *Do I consider the other night one? God. It shouldn't matter. Nick is my boss.*

"Sure, I would love to."

"Great," he says, smiling. Ken's phone line rings, drawing his attention back to his office.

"I should probably get that. It's probably the Senior Editor calling about a manuscript. She mentioned she would call around lunch."

"Okay, see you later." Ken waves goodbye as I head toward the elevator. *Oh, man. I have a date.*

————

"You're going on a date with my cousin?" Carol asks with a skeptical look.

"Yeah, is that okay?"

I watch nervously as she pauses to think about my question. She scrunches her nose and then shrugs her shoulders. "It's okay. I just didn't think he was your type."

"So what's my type? Assholes?'

"Becca, everyone can be an asshole. Even nice guys can be assholes."

Romero's New York Pizzeria is packed, but Carol and I manage to slip in front of three off duty firefighters who, to my pleasant surprise, are more than willing to let us cut in line.

"Well, thanks for meeting me for lunch. I needed a moment to get out of the office after this morning."

"No problem. I was actually finishing a meeting with Tristan Knight for the upcoming opening of his art gallery."

"So how did your meeting go?"

"It went great. We're working with a local designer for the inside layout of the studio. Tristan is a perfectionist when it comes to his art, but I wouldn't expect any less."

"He seems a lot more relaxed compared to Nicholas," I say. "A lot nicer, too."

"I guess. He had the nerve to ask me not to take on any more projects until his gallery opening."

"He doesn't think you're capable of juggling projects?"

An annoyed looks crosses over Carol's face. "I think he's an alpha male who likes things done the way he wants," she says flatly.

. . .

When we finally get to the front of the counter to order, it takes me at least five minutes to decide what kind of pizza slice I want. There are too many choices. I can't help but laugh at the name of each pizza. They're unique and some of them are even a little dirty. Like Mike's Meat Load, which is actually a mixture of meats—pepperoni, sausage, ham, and salami. After several eye-rolls from the front cashier, I finally decide on two slices of Lady Liberty, which turns out is just your classic cheese pizza.

The size of New York pizza slices are nothing like the ones in California. I take a bite of my second slice and moan in pleasure at the mixture of flavors dancing in my mouth. I love the taste of oregano, tomato, and mozzarella cheese. It's like the holy trinity of flavors.

"Becca, you sound like you're having an orgasm over there," Carol says, handing me a stack of napkins to wipe the cheese grease off my lips.

"I am," I laugh. "This is better than sex."

"Obviously, you haven't been fucked in a while," she teases. I roll my eyes at her lopsided grin. Sometimes she can be such a brat. "I can't believe you can actually put down a second slice."

"I know! These are ginormous!" I say excitedly.

"That's what she said," Carol says with a shit-eating grin.

"Very funny."

A giant slab of cheese slides off the side of my pizza slice. It leaves a grease spot that travels through the bottom of the paper plate. *I know this is terrible for me, but I don't care.* The best part about New York is definitely the pizza.

"Told you this would cheer you up," Carol mumbles between bites.

"This is pretty good, but I really need to stop eating this stuff. Work has their annual Gala coming up. I need to look somewhat presentable."

"Maybe we can hit the gym together later," Carol says. "Besides, you look great."

"I guess I should be thankful it's a masquerade gala."

"We need to go shopping for your costume. Hey, are you bringing a date?"

"Date?" I ask, almost choking on my slice. *Maybe Ken will want to go with me.*

"Yeah, you know the thing that normal people do when they need to get laid. It might help your mood. Although, if things work out with my cousin, I do not want to hear about your sexcapades with him."

I elbow her side playfully. "I am not that kind of girl."

Her eyes crinkle as she smiles at me knowingly. "That's not what you said last night, baby," she says in her best manly impression, which coincidentally sounds like she's also a chain smoker.

"You're too much."

"That's what she said."

"Does that ever get old?" I snort.

"Never."

"I should probably get back to work." Not that Nicholas is counting the minutes while I'm gone. He's probably still not at the office.

"I think you should take a longer lunch and let me take you to *Demure.* Let's find something you can wear underneath your dress for the gala," Carol says, wiggling her eyebrows. *Demure* is keyword for the hottest lingerie store in town. It's also known for its overly expensive lingerie and the famous customers who are seen wearing it.

"You know, I'm still not sure why they call it *Demure.* Isn't that ironic when nothing in there is shy or reserved?"

Carol laughs as she drapes an arm around my shoulder. "It's their way of luring young girls like you into their store."

"It sounds far too expensive."

"But I get a discount. I'm sleeping with one of the cashiers," Carol says with a wink.

"I guess I won't be missed. Plus, I usually only take a half hour lunch, so sure, let's go."

20

NICHOLAS

After several hours of lying in bed with a massive headache, I was finally able to hold my head up around noon without wanting to puke up my insides. Despite my protests, Alison refused to leave my apartment, and I had to spend hours listening to her as she talked my ear off about our upcoming wedding. After a while, I was fed up, and I told her to go home. She pouted, of course, but eventually, she left. *Thank god.* At one point, she offered to give me a blowjob to help me feel better. While a blowjob usually sounds fantastic, if it meant listening to her gab for the next hour, I would've rather gouged my eyes out. That's even with me suffering blue balls for the past several weeks.

———

As I step into my office, I notice an e-mail notification at the top of my cell phone. It's from my father. Great. I scroll through the message and find myself frowning at his request to *have a meeting to discuss something important.* Panic sets in. What if Rebecca told him about my behavior at the Lit for Kids event? Or worse, what if the tabloids somehow got ahold of a photo of me drunk and out of my mind. *Fuck.* I type my name into the search bar of my phone. To my surprise, there aren't any new articles. Maybe it's not about last night or maybe the tabloids haven't spread their gossip just yet.

I call Rebecca's office line to check in, but it goes straight to voicemail. *I wonder if she's sick.* After checking through my messages, I come to the conclusion that she must be on her lunch break. In a way, I dread having to speak with her about last night. I made a fool of myself because of past memories, and while I'm grateful that she did her job as my assistant, I do owe her an apology. I shouldn't have come on to her. No matter how much I want to do it again.

I make my way through the rows of cubicles toward my father's office. Not a single employee bothers to look up as I pass them. I often wonder if people avoid eye contact with me because they think I'm some kind of monster. In truth, I am a bit of an asshole, but I can't help it.

I find Father typing away at his computer as classical music plays in the background. I recognize the familiar song from my childhood memories. It's the first movement from Beethoven's *Moonlight Sonata.* Our father used to play it on the piano when we went to bed. I loved falling asleep to the slow chord progression. As we got older, the tone of the song seemed a little darker than I remembered. After my mother left, our father would play it into the earlier hours of the morning. I think it was his way of easing his sorrows without touching a bottle.

"Good morning, son," he says. "I'm glad to see you." For the first time in a long time, I notice the fine lines of stress on my father's face. The crinkles at the corners of his eyes have set in deeper. "There's something I think we should discuss." The tone in his voice lets me know that whatever he's about to say is pretty serious.

"If it's about the other night, I can explain—" I start to say.

He raises his hand to stop me. "I heard the Lit for Kids event went wonderfully. I'm happy you're taking the initiative on these opportunities for publicity." He stops for a moment, gathering his thoughts. "It seems everything is working out with Rebecca. I haven't seen anything in the papers to tell me otherwise, and I'm very glad."

"Yes, although she isn't exactly what I was expecting in an assistant," I mutter.

"Rebecca is the last thing you should be worrying about," Father says. "Your wedding should be your number one priority." He turns back to his desk and grabs a document that looks to be at least a hundred pages long. "This is why I called you in. I had our lawyer draw this contract up."

"What?" I ask, as he hands me it.

"It's a prenuptial agreement. Alison's father informed me that you two would be sending out invitations this following week. As soon as I heard that, I met with our lawyer, Eric Hayes. We should've discussed this earlier, but lately, everything has been a little crazy around here. I wanted to wait until things calmed down."

I flip through the document, weary of what all of this actually means.

"It's important to protect the company and this family, Nick. I learned that the hard way when I had to pay off your mother so she would stop going to the tabloids."

I keep hoping that my father will wake up and realize that marrying me off to the highest bidder is another mistake. Alison might not be my mother, but this marriage is just another business transaction.

"Nick, are you listening?" My father sits watching me with an impatient look.

"Yes." I say through gritted teeth.

"How is the wedding plans going?"

"I have no idea," I admit. "I'm sure Alison is handling everything fine."

"I think it would be a good idea if you were a little more involved," he says. The look on his face screams disappointment. "Review the contract and let me know if there's anything you would like to change or add." Prenuptial agreements aren't out of the ordinary, but somehow, this all feels wrong. My gut tells me this isn't the path my life should be taking.

"I don't think I can go through with this." The words are flying out of my mouth before I even have the opportunity to mull them over.

"Go through with what, exactly?" he asks, confused.

"The wedding."

My father circles around his desk to stand in front of me. The tension vibrating off him is unmistakable. I know it's not what he wants to hear, but it's the truth.

"Doesn't my happiness mean anything to you?" I ask. There it is. The question that's been lingering at the surface for so many years. When Alex was alive, my father was all for what made us happy, but that didn't last long after my brother's death. Everything changed for the worst.

"Son, you're twenty-eight. I've watched you these last few years dispose of women without a second thought. Since when have you been serious about anyone?"

He's right. I've never imagined settling down and having children. Just trying to envision any of those things fills my chest with a heavy feeling of despair. For the past few years, I've been ignoring the idea of marriage and drowning myself in beautiful women. It's easier to deal with. I'm not ready to share a piece of my soul with someone and then watch it all burn. I don't want to end up like my father.

"What if I choose not to marry her?"

"Nick, you will marry Alison."

"And if I don't... what then?" I challenge.

"You'll lose everything." The way he articulates each word lets me know that he isn't joking. If I want to inherit StoneHaven Publishing, I'll have to marry Alison Price.

———

"Nick!" I hear someone call as I make my way out of the elevator. My head is still going over the conversation with my father. I turn to see Emily walking toward me with a huge smile on her face. She's carrying her backpack with her. She must be coming from school. The campus is around four miles from here, and I think she takes advantage of it being so close. I often find her hiding out in one of the conference rooms here.

"Hey, big brother. I wanted to stop by to see if you wanted to have lunch with me?"

"Aren't you supposed to be in class?" I ask.

"Bio got cancelled for today, so I thought I would come see you." The sheepish grin on her face makes me think she could be lying.

"Is something wrong?" she asks, encircling me in a quick hug.

"No, why?"

"You're scowling," she laughs. "Who annoyed you this time?"

You have no idea. "It's nothing."

"Are you sure?" Before I have a chance to tell her that my future is hanging in the balance over my impending marriage, Mary, the front desk receptionist, comes scurrying over to us.

"Mr. StoneHaven, wait!" Her flustered expression tells me that whatever she has to say can't wait.

"I have a woman on line one who's calling from *Demure*. She claims she has a lady friend of yours in the store. Should I give her the access code to charge your account?"

"Are you buying bridal lingerie for Alison?" Emily asks. I know Emily's excited at the thought of having a sister, even if it's a sister-in-law, but I don't have the heart to tell her that I'm not sure Alison feels the same.

"No, there's some kind of mistake."

It was a habit of mine to send the women I slept with to *Demure* for lingerie, but since the announcement of my engagement, I haven't even bothered to tell them that I'll be closing my account. Most people know *Demure* as an upscale lingerie store, but clients know them for their discreet business practices. There are plenty of men I know who have accounts there for their wives and mistresses.

"Did she give a name for this lady friend?"

Mary's eyes widen. "She did not. Would you like to speak with her?" she asks.

"Yes, that's fine. I'll straighten this out."

21

REBECCA

*D*emure isn't your typical lingerie boutique—in any shape or form. It's not what I would think of when someone says boutique. It's two stories filled with frill, lace, diamonds, and satin. All of which are way out of my budget. *Two-hundred dollars for a V-shaped thong? You have to be kidding me.* Carol hands me a matching dark green bra and thong set to try on. I'm almost certain that stores like *Demure* don't carry curvy girl sizes. I'm also pretty sure that their fine print reads 'fatties not allowed.' *Okay, I made that last part up.*

"I know who would like you in these," Carol says, wiggling her eyebrows. "It would look great with your red hair." I can almost see the enthusiasm dripping from her lips. I know she's teasing me about Nicholas. On the way over, the subject of the last night came up again, and of course, she had a gleam in her eye when I told her my boss had been MIA all morning. She laughed as I told her how nervous it made me and how I couldn't concentrate on anything.

"Carol, you're really not helping," I say, calling her out.

"He wants you. You're just too proud to let yourself want him back." Her words are so matter-of-fact that I almost want to ask her if she's been secretly talking to him behind my back. Before I have a chance to ask, a petite Asian woman named Lola walks over to us. I couldn't be more grateful for a welcome distraction from this awkward conversation.

"Welcome to *Demure*. How can I assist you?" she asks in a sultry voice. I catch a whiff of Lola's rich perfume and cherry lip-gloss. If expensive had a scent, she's what it would smell like. Carol stops to scan the store. It's as if she's shopping for a car.

"We're looking for something hot for my friend here," Carol says, elbowing me in the side.

"We're just looking," I explain, embarrassed. They're definitely not going to have anything I can wear. Lola glances down at the work badge around my neck and smiles.

"Are you a friend of Mr. StoneHaven?" she asks. Something about the way she says *friend* sends my heart racing. Memories of the last night send a blush straight to my cheeks.

"She is," Carol says, cutting in.

Lola smiles knowingly. "I think I have something that would look perfect on you. Follow me," she says, waving me over.

"Why did you say that?" I whisper to Carol.

"Maybe you'll get a discount," she says, grinning.

"I'm pretty sure I almost saw dollar signs pop out of her eyes," I grumble. Carol laughs as she squeezes my hand and pulls me toward the fitting rooms.

"I'm so excited!" she squeals.

"At least one of us is."

The fitting rooms are decorated with red satin curtains and silver trimming. I sit down on a plush couch that looks more like an over-sized ottoman. Another employee with short blonde hair circles around with a tray of champagne and fresh strawberries.

"Would you like a glass?" she asks. "And some strawberries?"

"Sure," I say, grabbing two glasses for Carol and me.

As Carol patrols the store, I watch with quiet curiosity as Lola gathers some lingerie for me to try on. I'm not sure how many outfits she's picked, but I can see her hanging an assortment of colors on the fitting room rack. I toss back my glass of champagne. It bubbles slightly going down my throat. *Liquid courage*. I have to admit it's a great sales strategy.

An older gentleman sits a few feet away checking his watch. He's your typical Wall Street investor who wears too much grey. I spot a wedding band on his left hand. *He must be waiting on his wife.* On cue, a tall brunette struts out of the fitting room. She's gorgeous and definitely not in her mid-forties. She's gorgeous in the baby doll negligee she's wearing. The pink cream color compliments her long chestnut brown hair. The older gentleman watches with fascination as she prances outside the fitting room. She turns, giving herself a once over.

"*C'est parfait,*" she says smiling.

Carol walks over with a glass of champagne in her hand. "Five bucks says she's not his wife." We watch in awe as the stunning brunette walks over to her companion and whispers seductively in his ear. I only catch a few words, but I don't need to hear the rest to know the meaning of what she's said. She runs back to the fitting room to change as her companion walks to the front of the store and pays. After a few minutes, the two exit arm in arm down the street. I catch a glimpse of her hand as she caresses his shoulder –but there's no ring.

Carol smiles. "Told you."

Lola pokes her head out. "Your fitting room is ready."

"Go get 'em, tiger."

I'm alone in the fitting room, and yet it feels like I'm on stage getting ready for the next *Victoria's Secret* fashion runway. My heart is pounding in erratic beats. I don't do sexy. I do comfy. My idea of lingerie is my tank top and my boy shorts, end of story.

"I'm waiting!" Carol calls. I'm starting to think the glass of champagne is getting to her.

I scan the wide selection that Lola hand-picked herself. The majority of it is a little too risqué for my taste. I finally settle on a gold baby doll top. It shimmers like glitter under the fitting room lights. It's sexy, yet classy. I hold it up under my chin. The soft satin feels wonderful against me. It definitely makes my green eyes pop. I'm not the type to stare at my reflection all day, but I have to admit it looks great against the color of my hair. A bustier catches my eye amid the flurry of lingerie. It's a beautiful nude color with lace that runs up the sides. A matching pair of boy-cut underwear and stockings is attached with it. I press it against me. It's definitely not something I would usually wear, yet I can't help but wonder how it would look on me.

Carol pops her head through the fitting room curtain. "Rebecca, would you just pick something already?" she says, giggling.

"Look, it was your idea to bring me down here. Now you have to suffer," I say, covering my goods.

"C'mon, Becca, I bet you look hot in any of these." I give Carol a 'get-out-already' look and she quickly leaves and closes the curtain behind her.

It's not every day I get to shop for expensive lingerie. Mine usually don't cost more than my monthly rent. Then again, it's not as if I'm actually going to buy any of this. I can't afford any of it. I slip on the nude boy shorts and stockings along with the bustier, and with some luck, I find a pair of garters among the lingerie to complete the piece.

I'm amazed at the transformation. The person standing before me is unrecognizable. It's like I'm naked, except all the wobbly bits and pieces are covered.

"Carol, I think you're going to be happy with this one. Carol?" I peek my head out of the fitting room curtain. Carol is nowhere in sight. *Where the hell did she run off to?*

My eyes scan the room and stop dead as Nicholas StoneHaven makes his way into *Demure*. *Holy shit.* My heart sinks as Lola walks over to Nicholas. Lola's question repeats over and over in my head. "Are you a friend of Mr. StoneHaven?" *Crap. Damn it, Carol.* Lola greets him with a smile and a kiss on the cheek. He must come here often to be so personable with a salesgirl. She ushers him toward the fitting rooms and in my direction. *Double shit.* I slip back inside the dressing room. *I'm going to kill Carol.* A second later, I hear Carol walking up.

"Hello, Ms. Livingston, it's nice to see you." I cringe at the sound of Nicholas's voice. *Why is he here? I thought he wasn't in the office today?*

"Hello... Rebecca is here," she blurts. Gosh, she must be tipsy.

Usually, Carol's a lot better at keeping her cool. A third voice joins the conversation.

"Ah, there you are." It's Lola. She must be referring to Carol. "Is Mr. StoneHaven's friend still in the fitting room?" *I'm screwed.* I hurry, grabbing my clothes and shoes off the floor. I unbuckle the garters from my stockings and pull everything off.

Carol clears her throat. "Oh no, I think she left."

"Didn't you just say Rebecca is here?" Nicholas asks, confused. I freeze. *Oh. My. God. I'm busted.*

"Oh, did I?"

"Excuse me, which friend?" Nicholas asks, directing his attention back at Lola.

I spot Lola's heels standing in front of my curtain. Before I can stop her, Lola pushes open the curtain and gasps. I jump back, covering myself.

"Oh, my, I'm so sorry," she says, embarrassed. "Your friend said you left."

My cheeks burn red as I spot Nicholas staring at me. A look of confusion and surprise covers his face. Even now, I can't help but notice how incredible he looks in his black pants and grey suede jacket.

"Sorry, Becca," Carol squeaks.

I know I'm not naked, but with the nude bustier and matching underwear, I might as well be. Carol looks back at me with guilt written all over her face. I panic as the slow realization hits Nicholas, a smirk creeps up his lips. I was the special 'friend' that Lola had mentioned.

"Yes, Lola, this will do just fine," he says.

22

REBECCA

I don't think I've ever run out of a place so fast, but I left *Demure* in a hurry and quickly headed back to Carol's apartment. I didn't wait for the mortifying conversation that was sure to follow my embarrassing debut, and no one bothered to stop me on my way out. Not even Carol. *I just left her standing there with Nicholas.*

By the time I reach home, it's well past six p.m. I've been aimlessly walking New York City for hours. Going back to the office wasn't an option. I can't see Nicholas right now. He's the reason I left so fast. The way he was looking at me... It was as if I was the juicy thanksgiving turkey waiting to be served to him. I don't know if I would've been able to tell him to stop if he started kissing me. Not that he would kiss me in front of everyone, but I wanted him to.

My purse vibrates against the coffee table alerting me to a new text message from Carol. I don't even know what Carol thinks at this point, but the last thing I saw was the look of shock on her face as I left.

Carol: Did u make it back to our place?

I wait a few minutes to answer. *I should make her sweat.* It's partly her fault for getting me into this weird predicament, but it's hard for me to be mad at her. She was just trying to help.

Me: Yes. I'm sorry I ran out on you.

Carol: OMG. I was so worried.

Me: Just got home.

I shouldn't ask, but curiosity gets the best of me.

Me: Did he ask about me?

Carol: He did, but I didn't say anything.

Me: Good.

Carol: I won't be home until late. I have an emergency meeting with a client.

Me: K. See you later.

I toss my phone back into my purse and lie back on the couch. After flipping through the bazillion infomercials on TV, I finally settle on watching a movie. Instead of ordering out, I decide to grab a bowl of cereal and plop down on the couch. They're playing *Sleepless in Seattle.* It's Friday night, and I'm sure everyone is out partying, but I can't imagine a better way to spend my night than being a couch potato.

A slight brush of fur glides against my leg as I switch on the television. I look down and spot two bright yellow eyes staring up at me. Sprinkles purrs as I scratch the side of his face. As I sit there watching one of my favorite romantic comedies, I start to feel a growing disappointment. Was Nicholas at work all along and just avoiding me? Or did he follow me? It seems too convenient that he just happened to show up at *Demure.*

Just thinking about him brings a familiar heat that stirs me in places I'd rather not have him affect me. I flush at the memory of his eyes trailing down my skin. They were meticulous in their study of my body. No one's ever looked at me that way... My nipples harden at the memory. It's been too long since I've had sex with someone, and the last 'someone' was Miles, my ex-boyfriend. The recollection of Nicholas's hands on me the night before at the charity event flashes through my mind. I shiver at the memory of the need in his voice when he asked me to kiss him. Although, it was embarrassing when he saw me standing in the fitting room half naked, it was as if someone turned up the heat in the room.

My thoughts are interrupted by the sound of my cell phone vibrating again. *Fuck.* I sit up, grabbing my phone in time to see the incoming call that reads *MOM*. I take a moment to clear my throat. God, I hope my voice sounds normal, and not breathless and horny.

"Hi, Mom, I was just about to call you." *Lie.*

"Hi, honey, I was calling to see how your week's going."

"Great, it's going great." *Minus today's incident.* "How's everything at home? How's Dad?" It feels like it's been months since I've seen them. I miss my mother, even if she's a little crazy.

"It's not the same without you." The sadness in her voice is palpable. "That's actually why I called. I have some bad news."

"What's wrong? Is Dad okay?"

"Your father is fine. Physically, at least. He lost his job this week."

"What?" I ask, shocked. *What the hell?*

"His work laid off a hundred of their employees. He was one of them."

"Shit."

"Rebecca, language please."

"Sorry... How's Dad holding up?"

"You know your father. He's a proud man, Rebecca. This has really taken a toll on him." *I can't believe this is happening.*

He's worked for Baron Imports for over twenty years. He wanted to retire, but my parents are still paying their mortgage. They have two more years. Dad was going to retire after that. They had plans to buy a motorhome and travel across the U.S. It's like the new American dream.

"I think you should come back home," mother says. She catches me off guard by her serious tone. Move back home? I'm just getting used to this city.

"What? No, are you kidding me?"

"We need you here." My heart squeezes at the misery in her voice.

"Mom, you guys need my help. I need to stay out here and work. How are you going to pay the mortgage?"

"I'm not sure, sweetie."

"I can send you money as soon as I get paid again."

"Let's not talk about that right now. Let's talk about something happy. Have you met anyone nice out there?" she asks.

Nice? Nicholas's face flashes in my mind. "No, no one special."

The thought of Nicholas meeting my parents turns my insides to mush. My mother's curiosity concerning my love life has always been disturbing. I'm actually surprised she hasn't called me to chat about Miles. I think she's still in denial. Our breakup went public over the Internet. That's the thing with dating movie stars. Your business becomes everyone else's business.

"A certain someone came by today."

"A certain who?"

"Miles."

I freeze. *Miles? As in my ex?*

"He was asking about you. I told him you were off in New York being a big shot at a major publishing company." *Thanks, Mom.* I'm sure he could smell the desperation in her voice when she told him that.

"What did he want?" I ask, annoyed. I really hope he isn't planning to come see me. Just hearing his name makes my hand twitch. I start to feel murderous again.

"I'm not sure, sweetie, but he asked for your information." *Well, so much for anonymity.*

"Ugh. Mother, please tell me you didn't give him my work address."

She laughs. "No, of course not." *Oh, thank God.*

"But I did tell him you work on Sixth Avenue and I gave him your office number."

Damn.

"You never told me why you two broke up." That's a little too tricky to explain. I don't think she would appreciate hearing how I found him balls deep in another woman.

"He's not a good guy, Mom."

"Oh, sweetheart, is that why you left?"

The point is moot. We've been down this road before and it always ends in an argument. "Mother, I have an amazing opportunity here."

"I just miss you," she says softly. "Are you coming home for Christmas?"

"I'm not entirely sure."

"What do you mean? You've never spent Christmas away from home."

"Yeah, but my boss will probably need me."

"He works you too hard."

Try telling *him* that. We say our goodbyes, and I promise her that I'll try my best to be home for Christmas. The conversation leaves me feeling slightly torn. Hearing my mom mention Miles is like ripping old scabs off. They might look healed, but the memories come rushing back and everything feels fresh again. I set the alarm on my phone for work and slip into bed underneath the warm covers.

23

NICHOLAS

I don't remember driving back to the office or taking the time to hang my coat and tie, but somehow, I've managed to undress myself and pour a glass of scotch. When the woman at *Demure* mentioned red hair, I knew it couldn't be anyone but Rebecca, but I had to see for myself. I rescheduled with Emily and promised to take her out to lunch another time. In a way, I'm glad she didn't come, because it would've been a very awkward way to meet my assistant for the first time. Although Emily has been to the office a couple of times, she hasn't had the chance to meet Rebecca.

I toss the glass back as thoughts of her flood my mind. I shiver at the memory of Rebecca's bare skin and the soft curves of her body hidden only by small pieces of lace. Watching her in the fitting room left me floored. *How am I supposed to forget that?* Her hips will forever be engrained into my mind.

I feel like a fucking animal. I'll fuck her until she begs me to stop and then I'll fuck that smart little mouth of hers. I want to be the reason for the blush against her freckled skin. *I've never been so aroused by the mere sight of freckles.* They taunt me as if daring me to kiss each one. I ache to know the feeling of her pussy clenching around me. It's an all-consuming need. And I know I won't get my release until I've buried myself between those gorgeous legs. Maybe then, I can get her out of my mind. Maybe then, I can let her go.

I'm not exactly sure what the hell Rebecca was doing with my account. She ran out of *Demure* so fast I didn't even have a chance to stop her. When I spoke with the woman who called about my account, she didn't know the name of the female shopper who was using my account. The only thing she did know was that she was a redhead. That's all I needed to hear to pique my curiosity. I've never actually dated or fucked a redhead and there's only one redhead I know—Rebecca.

Her friend, Carol, wasn't very informative when I asked her about the incident, and Lola kept apologizing profusely. She even refused to charge my account when I offered to buy the lingerie Rebecca was wearing. She said it was complimentary. *Demure* doesn't give out complimentary items. They don't need to. I'm pretty sure I wasn't supposed to know about Rebecca's little shopping spree. Testing boundaries seems to be the name of the game with her.

The bag from *Demure* is still sitting on top of my bed. I pour another glass of whiskey, hoping to drown my thoughts of her, but I know it's useless. The whiskey only seems to intensify my need to see her. I smile, picturing her spreading her lips apart for me. My cock grows harder at the thought of her running her lips along me.

I think it's time to teach her a lesson. Perhaps, the lingerie won't be such a waste. Rebecca wanted it, right?

This is going to be one hell of a long weekend.

24

REBECCA

The crisp morning and the sound of coffee brewing down the hall wake me from my sleep. I'm drawn from my bed by the smell of hazelnut. As much as I want to stay curled up between the sheets with a good book, I can't. *Wait, yes, I can. It's Saturday.* Relief washes over me as I realize that yesterday was the beginning to my weekend. I won't have to deal with Nicholas until Monday.

The sound of a text message beeping on my phone cuts through my thoughts as I head toward the living room. I search for it in my purse and finally find it hidden beneath my wallet. There's a text message, but it's from an unknown number.

555-580-3000: We need to talk.

I squint, confused at the message. The timestamp reads one a.m. Who the hell was texting me so late at night?

Me: Who the hell is this?

The response is almost instantaneous.

555-580-3000: Your boss.

Shit. He can't fire me through text, right? I guess I shouldn't be surprised that he has my number, considering my staff file is basically at his disposal, but I am a little surprised that he would text me at one in the morning. I close my phone and toss it back on top of my purse.

I'm not dealing with him right now. I want to enjoy the only peace and quiet I have before I have to deal with this disaster waiting to happen.

My purse begins to vibrate. This time someone's calling me. I look over and see his number flashing at the top of the screen. I'm tempted to pick up the phone, but I'm not exactly sure what I can say to make the situation better, and I'm too afraid to know what he wants to tell me.

I spot a note from Carol clipped to the fridge. She must've left it here when she left this morning.

Becca,

I'm sorry about yesterday. I hope today isn't too rough —unless you want it to be. Haha. By the way, the rest of your clothes are back from the dry cleaners. Let's go somewhere fun this weekend. I'll be back around two this afternoon.

Xoxo,

Carol

I search Carol's closet, and lo and behold, my clothes are there. I grab my pencil skirt and white blouse out from the plastic wrapping. After putting away all my work clothes, I decide it's time to venture out and do some more exploring. It doesn't take me long to find the closest bookstore. It's called Books N' Nooks. I'm not sure if it's a play on words because of the e-reader or if it really offers a place for seclusion, but I venture inside anyway.

An hour later, I feel my cell phone vibrate against my palm. I stare down at the text message on my phone.

580-3000: Are you really ignoring me?

He definitely must be mad at me for the *Demure* incident if he's still trying to get ahold of me. It's so hard to read emotion through text.

580-3000: ;)

Wait, did he seriously just use a winky face? *This is weird.*

580-3000: Gellar, you can't ignore me forever.

Maybe I can. I sigh at the reality that there's no way in hell Monday is going to be a normal day.

580-3000: Gellar…

580-3000: Meet me at the coffee shop across from the bookstore in two minutes.

Wait. *What the fuck?* How does he know I'm at a bookstore?

25

NICHOLAS

After debating over several hours of whether I should show up at Rebecca's apartment or not, I decide that if I did, it would probably be pushing it. I've called her at least three times today, and I know she hasn't changed her number or Striker would've told me. Even my text messages have gone ignored. I feel this unrelenting need to talk to her. I don't even really know what I want to say, but I need to see her.

I text her again and tell her to meet me at the coffee shop across from Books N' Nooks. I know she's inside the store. I was on my way to meet Tristan for lunch when Striker called to let me know he spotted her at a store.

As I take a seat beside an open window, a voice breaks my thoughts. "Can I get you something to drink?" It's the waitress for my table. I look up at her for a moment studying her face. She looks about Emily's age, but from the way she's thrusting her tits in my face, I know she's not as innocent.

"No, thank you. I'm waiting for someone," I say, waving her away. She pouts and then leaves me to wait. I look down at my phone hoping there's a text from Rebecca, but there's nothing. Where the hell is she? I peer through the window and search the crowded street for her. It shouldn't be that hard to spot that fiery hair.

I'm just about to get up and walk over to the bookstore when I spot her. She's moving fast down the street in the opposite direction she's supposed to be going. Damn it, Gellar. My cock stirs. It seems she won't be so hard to catch.

My phone pings. It's a text from Striker.

Striker: Looks like she got away.

I can practically hear him laughing at me through the phone. *No fucking kidding.* Note to self—decrease Striker's salary when I inherit StoneHaven Publishing.

———

After finding myself sitting alone in the coffee shop, I decided to meet Tristan for a late dinner. I needed to go to the gym to let off some steam, or rather so I wouldn't go ape shit over Rebecca blowing me off. *God, I wish she would blow me.*

"Nick, if you're going to continue with this grumpy attitude, I'm not going to invite you to the opening of my art gallery." I glance across the table at Tristan Knight and take another sip of my red wine. Somehow, even the company of my best friend is not helping my mood. *She fucking ran away from me. What the hell?* I mutter her name beneath my breath, hoping that it will help ease my irritation. I just want to listen to the sound of it rolling off my lips. *Fuck.*

"You're starting to look like an old man with that grim face."

"What?" My eyes snap up to Tristan's face. I know he's fucking with me because his grin just widens.

"You vain bastard," he says, laughing. "Why are you all worked up?"

I guess it wouldn't be a bad thing if I told Tristan about Rebecca. Maybe talking about it might make me feel better. Probably not, but it can't make it worse.

"My assistant, Rebecca Gellar...."

"I remember her. She's a pretty one."

"I think she's the devil in disguise," I admit.

"It must be the hair."

Tristan pours himself another glass of wine. The room around us is quiet, with the exception of the restaurant staff clearing tables. It's after hours at Mario's Italian Restaurant, but the owner is familiar with my family, and he doesn't ever mind when we stay past closing.

"I'm guessing you're starting to like Rebecca."

"There's just a lot I haven't filled you in on."

"I'm listening," he says, smiling.

Over the next two hours, I fill Tristan in on what exactly has been happening with Rebecca—from the Lit for Kids event up until yesterday. I tell him all the gritty details and I leave out nothing. I even stop to tell him about the conversation my father had with me about marrying Alison and just how depressing the idea is to actually have to follow through with it.

"I think you should tell your father that you don't want to marry Alison."

"I tried and he just threatened to take everything away from me," I say, exasperated.

"But you didn't really tell him exactly why you don't want to."

"What do you mean?" I ask. "He knows I don't like her."

"You need to tell him there's someone else now."

"What? Are you crazy?" My father would flip. Although, he might be surprised to hear I 'like' someone. He's used to me just fucking women. "Who the hell would I tell him about?"

"You know." Tristan says, looking me point-blank.

"Are you talking about Rebecca?" *What the hell has gotten into Tristan?*

"She's definitely under your skin. I can see you grinding your teeth every time I mention her name."

"I just want to fuck her." It's true, I do. God, I do.

"Hmmm. I think it's a little more than that."

"If you keep talking like this, I'm leaving," I say, slightly wobbling as I stand. *I think I had too many glasses of wine.*

"I'll prove it," Tristan promises.

26

REBECCA

The weekend flies by, leaving me little time to actually enjoy my last day off. My mind is still reeling from the multiple text messages from Nicholas. I still have no idea how the hell he knew where I was, but when I got his last text message about meeting him, I booked it. It was the second day in a row that I had run from him. I'm starting to think I should've joined track in college.

Carol and I spent most of Sunday shopping at a nearby antique store for things to furnish the apartment. She thought it might be good if we decorated it together, so I could feel more at home. I was glad to add a few things here or there to the apartment. It made it seem more welcoming. The blank walls were starting to bug me.

I check my phone for any surprise text messages, but thankfully, there are none. I keep hoping the two days off have helped cool the tension between Nicholas and me. All I want to do is get back to work and have everything like it was. Normal. Or somewhat normal. I guess it's time to get ready for work and face the music.

When I arrive at work, I spot Ken standing by the elevators on my way through the lobby. He smiles, waving over to me. It's good to see him. He's a pleasant reminder that not everything is crazy here. At least Ken's attitude is consistent. I don't get whiplash from his emotions changing day to day.

"Hey, how was your weekend?"

"Interesting," I blurt.

"Interesting? How so?"

"Oh, it's nothing."

Ken holds the elevator door open as I step inside. I smile at the small but chivalrous gesture.

"How's everything going with the boss?" he asks.

"It's going. He's a little annoying."

"Just a little?" I smile as his laughter echoes within the elevator.

"No, a lot. Like, really annoying," I admit.

"Are you saying you wouldn't date him?" Ken asks, hopeful.

"What? No, why?"

"Most women find him irresistible." *Ugh.*

"I wouldn't date Nicholas StoneHaven if he were the last man on earth," I blurt.

"Rebecca," Ken winces as he motions to the front of the elevator that's opened.

"What?" I turn to glance at what's so important.

Two fiery blue eyes stare into mine from the entrance. My eyes trace down his face to a pair of lips set in a grim frown. His hair is tousled like he hasn't slept, and I can smell a faint scent of alcohol. *Shit.* I know the world hasn't exploded because he's still wearing a suit, but his tie is missing and the top buttons of his shirt are undone, revealing a light patch of blond hair.

"Mr. StoneHaven, we were just..."

"Save it, Phillips. I already got an earful." His voice is clipped with anger.

I gulp. *I'm in trouble. I so fucked up.* The elevator buzzes as Nicholas blocks the door from closing with his hands. Without further instruction, Ken squeezes past him, leaving me alone. *Damn it, Ken.* I step forward to follow him, but Nicholas blocks me and guides me by my elbow back into the steel cage. Ken stops, realizing I'm not behind him. He turns and heads back to me, but before he can stop the elevator, Nicholas slides his access card and pushes the button for the top floor.

As soon as the door shuts, I feel Nicholas' eyes burning holes into the back of my skull. The air inside the elevator feels paper-thin. The claustrophobia sets in. It's strange the way his presence affects me. Only moments before I felt fine riding up the elevator, but now I can barely breathe. The elevator pings, letting us know that we've reached the top floor. The doors rush open and a blast of cold hits me. *It's always so cold up here.* Nicholas steps out and casually tosses his jacket on a nearby chair.

He disappears for a moment and returns with a glass and a bottle of scotch. He sets the glass on his desk and pours the amber liquid. I watch mesmerized as he tips it back and then sets the bottle and glass down, never taking his eyes off me. *I'm starting to think he might have a drinking problem.*

"What's your problem, Gellar?" he asks sharply, wiping his lips of scotch.

You. I bite my tongue, knowing I'll only make this situation worse.

"Why the fuck did you ignore my texts?"

I can't speak. I don't even know what I would say if I could find the nerve to move my lips and form words. My body instinctively backs away as he stalks over to me. In one swift motion, he corners me against the wall with one hand. He leans in to me and I can't help but drown in the spicy scent of wood and cinnamon. My cheeks flush as his erection grinds into my stomach. A warm sensation fills my lower half. I look away, embarrassed at the sound of my panting. *What is he doing to me? Is this my punishment?*

"What do you want, Nicholas?" I ask, breathless.

His lips graze my ear as he whispers, "I can't stop thinking about your tight little ass in those panties."

He nips the top of my ear and I almost lose control. *Who knew an ear could be so sensitive?* I moan without warning. His warm lips claim mine as his hands go on an expedition. I resist them at first, trying as hard as I can to get away from his grasp. I'm reminded of Carol's metaphor. *I'm just another fly in his web.*

"What are you doing?" I ask, confused.

"What I've wanted to do since Friday."

Nicholas senses my hesitation as he grabs my wrists and pins them behind me. I struggle to get free, but his lips crush against the side of my neck, and the sensation instantly makes me forget why I'm fighting so hard. His hands roam up my shirt and around the side of my back, cupping my ass. He lifts me in the air with one arm and I wrap my legs around him, straddling his waist. Desire pulses through me as I run my hands through his hair, pulling it slightly. Without meaning to, we're crashing into furniture as he carries me over to his desk. His tongue explores my mouth, teasing me into submission. He growls against my lips as I try to pull away for air.

"Shit, woman, you're driving me crazy," he murmurs against my lips.

I silence him with kiss as I bite his bottom lip. He groans, pushing his erection harder against me. I watch with lust-driven eyes as he sweeps the documents from his desk to the floor and then sets me on the cold cherry wood desk. My nipples tighten against my shirt as he fumbles for the zipper of my skirt, my heart pounding wildly as Nicholas unzips it.

Something inside me ignites. There's no turning back now. I want him. I've never wanted anyone this much. I know this is stupid, but I can't stop myself. I'm about to have sex with Nicholas StoneHaven, my boss, and the very man I said would be the last man on earth that I would ever be with. If Carol could see us now, she'd be yelling *I told you so.*

"I'm going to make you remember this," he whispers, kissing my neck. "You'll be thinking about it all day..." He pushes me back onto the desk and positions himself between my hips, slipping his hand up my plaid skirt. "You'll think about me when you're at your desk," he says, running his fingers up my thigh and pushing my panties down. "When you're in the shower..." His fingers slide into me. "When you're in bed..." I gasp as his thumb rubs my already aroused bud. "When you're touching yourself," he says, growling. "I'm going to make you forget everyone who came before me. But first, I'm going to make you come."

Nicholas kneels in front of me, and I can feel my heart palpitate at the sight of him so close to my center. "I want you to watch me," he whispers, staring straight into my eyes. He pulls me to him and then lowers his mouth against me. A rush of pleasure flows through me as his warm mouth encircles me. It feels like heaven. I gasp in pleasure as he starts to suck and nibble.

"Don't stop," I beg, shifting my hips up to him.

Nicholas lifts his head and smiles. "Wouldn't dream of it." He lowers his mouth once again, devouring me without any reserve. His tongue slowly teases me as he flicks my clit, slowly sucking it as if he has all the time in the world. Unsure with what to do with my hands, I bury them in his hair. He rubs his stubble against me in appreciation. I grip the desk, and I cry out in pleasure from the sensation. He slips two fingers inside me, penetrating my center. *I don't know how much longer I can't take this.*

"Nicholas," I gasp.

He changes speed, going from slow to fast as if sensing my need building. I writhe under his touch as I reach the peak of my orgasm. His mouth doesn't let up until I'm gasping for air from the mixture of pleasure and a little bit of pain. Euphoria overtakes me as I feel my heartbeat slow. He kisses the inside of my thigh and then slides his tongue up to my opening. He licks me one last time before standing.

I watch as he pulls out a handkerchief to wipe his mouth. I can't help but feel like we've just finished dinner and I was the main course.

As I reach down for my skirt, Nicholas stops me. "Rebecca, we're not done, sweetheart." He lifts me off the desk and sets me on his office couch. I watch him with curiosity as he slowly unbuttons my blouse. His powerful hands struggle with the small buttons. He smirks at me as I silently laugh.

"Here, I'll help," I say.

Nicholas removes his shirt and pants, leaving only his boxers. My heart hammers against my chest at the sight of his bare chest. There's something sensual about him having chest hair. I usually don't like it on guys, but on him, it's perfection. He smirks, as I openly adore him.

"Like what you see?" he asks.

"Don't get cocky."

"Too late," he says, pulling me against him. It's strange—I thought I would feel embarrassed the first time I was naked again in front of this guy, but the only thing I feel is desire. I push Nicholas back on the couch and straddle his thighs. I reach down, pushing his boxers off. His cock springs up. I hold back the moan dying to escape from my lips. *It's beautiful.* It's strange to think of a cock being beautiful, but his is. I spot a bead of liquid at the tip of his head. I lean forward and take him in my mouth. He sucks in a stream of air as I run my tongue down the side of his shaft.

"God, Becca. I've been thinking about this since the day I met you." *This time I'm taking charge.* His eyes widen slightly as I position myself on his lap. I sense his cock harden even more as I rub myself against him.

"Don't start what you can't finish," he says, challenging me.

"Do you have a condom?" I ask.

He smiles and points me back to his desk. "There's one in the drawer."

I feel him watching me as I walk to his desk and retrieve a condom from it. It's ribbed. *My favorite.* I rip the package open with my teeth and then slide it on him. He moans as I slowly lower myself onto him. A throbbing need builds as he fills me. God, he feels so good inside of me. I'm bursting inside. I hold still, basking in the feeling. Nicholas leans back and moans, slowly moving his hips, silently begging me to ride him.

"I just want to fuck you," he says. "I want to fuck those gorgeous tits." I swivel my hips, grinding myself into him. He lifts his to meet mine, plunging me into an intoxicating state of rapture. I feel his body quake in pleasure beneath me as his hands slide around my ass. He pushes me down against him, guiding me faster.

"That's it," he gasps. "Rebecca, you feel so fucking good."

He reaches up and grabs me, pulling me forward. I watch in anticipation as he places greedy kisses along the side of my breast and then slips my nipple between his teeth.

"Fuck me," I plead.

"With pleasure."

He turns me, flipping my body underneath him. His grunts reflect a sense of a desperate urgency as he plunges back inside me. The fire between us is all-consuming. He moves with determination as he rocks back and forth inside me. I grasp the couch arm behind me and

Nicholas lifts my leg, angling deeper inside of me. I squeeze my muscles around him and he groans in appreciation.

"Keep doing that," he begs. I smile at the sound of his raspy voice.

"This?" I ask, grinning mischievously.

"Yes," he cries out.

"Please, don't stop," I whisper.

"Fuck, you're so tight," he says, slamming into me.

A frenzied feeling of elation builds inside me as he bends my knees against his chest. I can feel him throbbing inside me. *He's just as close as I am.* I yelp as Nicholas slaps against me harder and harder.

"Come for me, Becca." His words send me in a spiral as I combust underneath him, melting into the cushions of the couch. *Fuck.* He lets one last groan out before he shudders in gratification. I gasp as he moves inside me softly. I can feel my wetness trickling down between us. He pauses to grab a napkin from a nearby tray and then dabs at my inner thigh. He grins, obviously pleased with himself. I bite my lip as he leans in and kisses below my navel. I squirm at the feeling of his lips so close.

"That was...." I begin to say.

"Fucking amazing," he finishes. I laugh at his bluntness. Nicholas rolls off the condom and tosses it in a nearby trashcan. For a moment, I'm afraid he might tell me to go. He got what he wanted. Instead, he leans in and kisses me tenderly. The kiss reminds me of the one we shared on the airplane. My heart squeezes at the memory.

As we scan the mess around us, the sound of his office phone ringing brings me back to reality. I sit up, gathering myself together as he grabs the phone from his desk. I don't waste time pulling back on my skirt and my blouse. I should probably go home. I need some time to process everything that has just happened. Nicholas answers the ringing office phone with ease and confidence. The passion that burned in his eyes moments earlier is now replaced with a cool gaze.

"Yes, Mary?" Nicholas swallows nervously as he listens to Mary. He turns to me and I can see panic setting in. *What?*

"Could you ask them to wait for me in the conference room?" he says into the receiver. Mary says something, but I can't hear any of it.

"Shit!" Nicholas exclaims, slamming the phone down. He throws on a white V-neck, slips on his dress pants, and smoothes down the hair that only moments ago I was pulling.

"What's wrong?" I ask.

"My father and Alison are on their way up here," he confesses. "We need to hide you."

Before I can argue, Nicholas pushes me under his desk. What. The. Hell. *How nice, I guess I'm just getting the grand tour today. Lovely.*

He races to the flipped over office chair and repositions it. In a few seconds, he clears the room from any telltale signs that he had just fucked another woman in his office. I hear him walk over to the elevator just in time to greet Alison and his father, Stefan, at the entryway.

27

NICHOLAS

*F**uck. This is not good.***

"Hello, Father..." I greet him and Alison at the entrance of the elevator, hoping to usher them downstairs.

"Nicholas, I didn't see you at the board meeting this morning." The disappointment in my father's voice is palpable. I clench my teeth as he studies the room around him. God, I hope he can't see Rebecca.

"I'm sorry, I got caught up in paperwork," I explain. "Why don't we—"

Alison's voice cuts through my words. "Nick, I was just speaking with your father about our plans for our wedding ceremony."

"I see, well, that's wonderful," I lie. Father briefly gives me a look of annoyance. He knows I'm lying through my teeth. I need to get them out of my office.

"I found the perfect venue. I wish you would've been there to see it," she whines.

"Nick, I'll leave you two alone. I have business to attend to," he says. "Ms. Price, it was lovely to see you." My father kisses her on the cheek before he turns to leave.

The room goes quiet for a moment as he makes his exit. Alison slowly makes her way over to the couch where only moments ago I was with Rebecca. She takes a seat and leans back, opening her legs slightly. I know it's intentional. She's been trying to have sex with me for the past month.

"I'm sorry I haven't been very involved with the wedding plans," I admit.

She crosses her arms, obviously not impressed with my apology. "You told me last week that you would start helping me plan this."

"I will. I've just been really busy with other things."

"Does this have anything to do with that assistant of yours?"

Fuck. Where is this coming from?

"It has nothing to do with Rebecca."

"I don't think she fits in here very well," she says.

"She's a great assistant," I say, deflecting Alison's rude comment.

"Are you serious? Just last week you were complaining that she was the most aggravating employee your father has ever hired."

"She was, I mean she is," I say, flustered.

"Well, which is it?" Alison demands.

"I don't want to argue about this. She means nothing to me." The words are out of my mouth before I've had a chance to think about them. I cringe at what Rebecca must be thinking.

"I'm sorry, baby," Alison purrs. "I've just missed you. I was looking forward to some alone time. I was worried when she brought you home the night of the charity event."

"Nothing happened. And we'll reschedule," I promise her.

"Nicholas, I want you." From the corner of my eye, I see Rebecca watching me. I know she's angry. Furious even. But it's the hurt in her eyes that kills me. She never takes her eyes off me—as if silently wishing for my demise. I push Alison's hand off as I clear my throat for emphasis.

"Alison, not now."

"Why not? I'll let you tie me up," she says, unzipping my pants.

"I have to get back downstairs." I swat her hand away and usher her over to the elevator.

"Why are you in such a hurry?"

"Because I have business to take care of, Alison. Let's talk about this later," I say.

"Come by later?" It almost sounds like a question, but I know it's a demand.

"I'll try," I whisper.

A moment later, she leaves and I wait for the elevator to descend before rushing over to Rebecca. I turn to find myself staring straight into her fierce green eyes.

"Where are you going?" My voice sounds needier than I want it to sound.

"I'm getting the hell away from you."

She's almost to the elevator when I grab her and pull her to me.

"Let me go, Nicholas."

"I can't," I say, pushing her against the elevator door. "We need to talk."

"I think it's better we don't."

Her hips push up against me, my desire pulsing between us, a sinful reminder of the pleasure I gave her only moments ago. I want to bury myself inside her again, wrap my fingers in her locks of hair, and gaze at her beautiful skin. I fight back the desire to touch her. I want her to stay.

"So what, we just pretend like nothing happened?" I ask, frustrated.

"Yes."

"And what if I don't want to?" I ask stubbornly. She shivers beneath my grasp. "You can't deny me." I push back a strand from her face and lean in to kiss her. She pushes me away and hits the elevator button.

"I can," she says.

"You're making a mistake."

"No. I'm fixing one." Rebecca walks past me as the doors ping open. The last thing I see before the doors close again is her beautiful red hair slightly disheveled from where I had run my fingers through it.

28

REBECCA

*S*he means nothing to me. Those five little words play on repeat as I stare at the blank computer screen in front of me. I can't get them out of my head. *I got myself into a really big mess.* I swivel my chair and scan at the office around me. I notice a couple of employees staring my way. I'm starting to feel paranoid like everyone knows. Everyone keeps staring at me like if I've grown wings, which is fitting because, at that moment, all I want to do is fly away. *I'm probably just imagining it.*

A few hours later, I find myself staring at Nicholas's personal calendar. I haven't heard from him, and it didn't cross my mind to see if he's in a meeting until now. Unfortunately, when I pull up the rest of this week, all I see is one name filling up each day—*Alison*.

What an asshole! *I'm so dumb.* I wish I could ugly cry right now, but I can't. *Fuck that. I won't.* I scroll through the next month of January on his calendar and spot a week blocked out from the thirty-first of January until the seventh of February. In the details, it says vacation. I almost forgot that he would be gone. He's probably taking her with him.

I tried to confirm the date with the event coordinator a week ago, but she's been on vacation. I should probably try calling her again. I was able to send the check over to the event department at the

Natural History Museum for the venue so at least there's that. I dial the number Nicholas gave me for the event coordinator, and to my surprise, she actually answers.

"Oh yes, I've been expecting a call from you." The voice on the other line sounds too cheerful for such a shitty morning. "So you wanted to confirm for the thirty-first, correct?"

"Yes, no, wait…" I stare at Nicholas's calendar for a good two minutes. His vacation falls right after the Gala. *But what if it didn't? This is how I get my payback.*

"Yes, we want to confirm for the thirty-first of January."

29

NICHOLAS

THREE DAYS LATER...

Afer spending three days cake testing with Alison, I don't ever want to touch one again. My palate is numb to sugar and I'm pretty sure I have five cavities. That or I'm surely a diabetic now. I have no idea why Alison needed to try so many cakes, but I put up with her just so she wouldn't be suspicious of something going on between Rebecca and me. I still feel like an ass for saying she didn't mean anything to me, but if I had said otherwise, Alison would've known something was going on. Ever since Rebecca dropped me off the night of the charity event, she's gotten it in her head that I'm hiding something—and now she's right.

The hardest part about the past three days was trying to avoid sex. I mean, those two words even being in the same sentence is insanity, but that's what I did for three days. I avoided sex with Alison. The first day I told her I had masturbated too much during the day and my cock was just fucking tired. It was a half-truth. I did masturbate a lot that day, but my cock wasn't tired. No, it was ready and willing, but the problem is the only pussy it wanted to fuck was Rebecca's. *God, it was hard not to think about her at night.*

On day two, I drank too much. Although I was rock hard in my pants, I told Alison my dick was limp, and fortunately, she bought it. Part of me wanted to be a little offended that she thought a bottle a wine would stop me, but I realized after a while that I was being stupid and my pride was getting in the way. I should've been thankful that she believed it, and didn't test her luck.

The third night was the worst. I couldn't use the I-masturbated-way-too-much excuse or the limp dick excuse, so I pulled one out of my ass. I told Alison I had the worst case of diarrhea. The look she gave me was sheer repulsion. I know she's not the type of woman who even goes to the bathroom around me. That night, she booked a separate room. I think she was afraid she would have to deal with the constant smell of shit. I was beyond thankful. Having to stay up pretending to have really bad diarrhea would've been a test for me.

It's good to finally be home. I pour myself a cup of coffee and grab my copy of the *New York Times*. I usually read my news online, but there's something nice about reading an actual paper once in a while. It's the same with books, except I think I prefer the paperbacks to reading it on an e-reader. It takes me a moment to realize that there's an article for the annual Gala is in the paper.

"Finally, the publicity department gets something right."

The words die in my throat as I read over the date of the annual Gala. The thirty-first of January. *What the fuck?* I grab my tablet from my briefcase and scroll through my calendar. I specifically told Gellar the thirtieth. The publicity department didn't even know about the old date. I pull up the week Emily and I are supposed to be gone and my vacation entry isn't there. It was, but now it's not. I scroll through the recent changes, and lo and behold, the most recent change is a deletion. Under 'user' it shows her name—*Gellar.*

30

REBECCA

S on of a bitch. I scroll through my phone to the e-mail notification that pops up at the top. My jaw drops at the real-ization that it's from *him*. Nicholas StoneHaven. For the past three days, I've been blissfully, irrevocably ignorant of his where-abouts. No, that's a lie. I knew he was with her. I just haven't seen or heard from him, but I knew a shit storm was coming.

To: Rebecca Gellar

From: Nicholas F. StoneHaven

Subject: WE NEED TO TALK

Gellar,

My office. Now.

Nicholas F. StoneHaven

Fuck that. I quickly reply to his e-mail, trying to keep my simmering anger to a minimum.

To: Nicholas F. StoneHaven

From: Rebecca Gellar

Reply: WE NEED TO TALK

Good morning,

I am on an important phone conference. I will check in later.

Rebecca Gellar

In less than five minutes, I hear him, or rather, everyone on the whole floor hears him.

"GELLAR!"

From my peripherals, I spot Nicholas as he heads in a straight beeline toward my cubicle. I know just from the scowl plastered on his face that he knows what I've done. I push aside the documents I've been scanning and slip them back into my to-do pile. I'll never be able to get any kind of work done. Somehow, the already heaping pile of busywork I've been given has managed to grow larger.

"What the hell did you do?" he asks.

The one thing keeping me going today is my little slice of heaven —my revenge. I knew it was coming. It was only a matter of time until he figured it out. Not only did I 'accidentally' book the company's upcoming Gala the same night he's planning to leave for his trip, but I also cancelled his airline tickets.

Oops.

Score: Rebecca 1, Nicholas 0.

I think some people forget how much power one little digital calendar can hold. I have access to his schedule. A year's worth in advance.

"Gellar, what the hell is this?" Nicholas asks.

I didn't think this space could get any smaller, but his frame nearly takes up half of it. He waves a copy of today's *New York Times* a mere inch from my face before flinging it angrily on my desk. I almost flinch at the inaudible gasps that are surely travelling down the aisle at this very moment. I'm definitely on his shit list.

I bite back a smile threatening to erupt as he passes one long, manicured hand through his slicked-back mane. The sight of him bubbling with frustration gives me pure satisfaction. His scowl is an ever-relentless reminder that nothing I do pleases him. I keep my eyes in front of my computer as I scroll through my e-mail. *Maybe if I pretend he's not here, he'll go away.*

"Gellar, did you hear me? Are you deaf now? Or are you purposely ignoring me?"

No such luck. It would be easier to ignore a naked man walking into the middle of my office. Have you ever heard of the expression head on? Yeah, well, he invented it. My mother always says, 'kill them with kindness.' but it's obvious that whoever made up that saying never met someone like Nicholas.

"Good morning," I say sweetly. I hope he can smell the sarcasm dripping from my words.

The color of his suit catches my eye. I groan inwardly at the sight of it. He's wearing grey today. I hate when he wears grey. The color contrast brings out the deep blues in his eyes. And it's irritating. Even now, he looks like he should be on his way to a magazine shoot for GQ. *Rich bastard.*

"I asked you, what the fuck is this?" he asks, pointing at the headline that reads *StoneHaven Publishing Company to Host NY Gala.*

"That is... well, you know about the gala. You're the one who asked me to schedule the event."

Just play dumb. Enjoy this. Nicholas has been planning this trip for weeks, but this is payback for saying I meant nothing a few minutes after he fucked me. Apparently, there's nothing cruel about getting belligerently drunk, seducing me into his office, and then pushing me under his desk while he makes plans to fuck Alison. I know she's his fiancée, but it doesn't make it any easier on me.

"Gellar, you know why I'm upset. Why did you schedule the gala on the same night I'm supposed to be out of the country?" he asks as he taps his fingers on my desk impatiently.

"Nicholas, I had no idea that you..."

"Cut the shit, Gellar, you did it on purpose."

If Nicholas hadn't drawn attention to the two of us before, there were definitely some curious stares now. Even Ken is sending 'I'm sorry' glances at me as he types away at his computer. His office sits directly in front of my cubicle. The only thing dividing us is a walkway to the elevators. Thank God he's so close. I could use the moral support right about now. Nicholas takes a seat on the edge of my desk, crossing his arms in an effort to intimidate me.

"Why did you cancel my tickets? And don't fucking toy with me." My silence only makes him angrier. "What do you have to say for yourself?" Nicholas asks, almost growling.

"I'm sorry. I got the gala dates mixed up. Would you like me to call the event coordinator and the museum?"

The date of the event is already public. Changing it would only confuse people or make them suspicious, but Nicholas knows that.

"I'm not sure what you'd like me to do. The papers won't print any retractions." I smile inside. I've won this battle, but the war is definitely not over.

A smirk creeps up Nicholas's face. He stands, and in one swift motion, he spins my chair, pulling me to him. I squirm under his scrutinizing gaze. His hands hold my chair in place as he leans in, closing the space between his face and mine. *What is he doing?*

The memory of being underneath him as he fucked me flashes in my mind. My body betrays me as I melt under his gaze. His breath is cool with the faintest smell of cinnamon. It's enough to draw me in. *There's something wrong with me. I just know it.* My brain says go away, but my cheeks flush at the sight of him wetting his bottom lip. He smirks at me as he catches me staring at his lips, but he doesn't stop. I can almost feel the warmth of his lips against mine. The way his tongue felt sliding across my skin. It's a moment of pure bliss. And a moment I've been trying to forget the past few days.

"Touché, Rebecca, but remember, Christmas is just around the corner and you just gave me all the ammo I need to keep you from flying back home," he says. He pulls back slightly and stops to gaze at my lips. His eyes trace them as if claiming them for his own.

Oh, My.

"I'll have you all to myself," he says softly. "You better believe I'm going to make you pay for making me miss my trip."

Somehow, his words sound more like a promise than a threat. A strange static charge dissipates between us as he releases me. His gaze is wild, but his outward appearance is restrained and calm. He adjusts his tie, and right before he turns to leave, he smiles. And it's one of those 'oh-my-God-I-just-came-in-my-panties' kind of smiles. *Why does it always have to be the gorgeous ones?*

A moment ago, I couldn't wait until he left, and now, well, now I just feel like putty in his hands. You have to focus, Rebecca. Remember, he's your annoying, over the top, 'I-just-want-to-murder-him-slowly' boss who said you meant nothing. *Repeat after me, you will NOT sexually fantasize about him doing you in the elevator. Ever. Not even just a little bit.* Okay, maybe just a little bit.

"What an ass," I mutter as I grab my pile of manuscripts.

Ken walks over, grinning. "Man, Rebecca. You really get under his skin. What did you do?"

"I messed up his plans for sunbathing on the French Riviera."

"Oh. He's been talking about that vacation for months," Ken says.

"I guess he'll have to get over it," I say, trying not to sound too crabby. "God, why are New York men so annoying?"

"Not all of us are like Nicholas." Ken grins. "I hope you're still up for that date tonight?"

"Yes, definitely." I smile.

Fuck Nicholas. I need to forget him. I need to remember why I wrote my 'Run-Like-Hell' List. The really frustrating part is things never seem to work out the way I plan.

31

NICHOLAS

She's getting under my skin. That crazy redhead is going to drive me insane. Today's fiasco was yet another reason why my father hiring her was a mistake. She has some nerve. I've been planning this trip for months. After seeing her smug little smile, I had to restrain myself. I just wanted to bend her over her desk and fuck her right there. I don't care if the whole office watched. I can't help it—the more she fights me, the more... God, I'm going to burn in hell. I need to stop fantasizing about her. I thought finally having a taste of her would fulfill my craving, but it didn't—I just want her more. She's my employee—and at the moment, she's the thorn in my side.

Thanks to her, the trip I have planned with Emily will need to be postponed. For the past five years, my sister and I have taken the same week off from school and work to travel. Each year, it's somewhere new. It might sound somewhat odd, but our brother used to have a list of places he wanted to visit before he died and he never was able to finish the list. Emily and I decided as homage to his memory, we would finish it. It's easier to deal with the idea of him being gone when we have other things to focus on, but now it's ruined.

32

REBECCA

Here I am again. For some reason, I wanted to go to *Riptide.* I think it's partly because this was the beginning and end of any real relationship I could've had with Nicholas. This is where I found out he had a fiancée. The club is bustling with New Yorkers as Ken guides me to a booth far enough from the dance floor. The closed-off corner lends itself to a very intimate setting. We slide in the booth and I order a Midori Sour, my favorite.

"Thank you for inviting me out," I say as our waitress leaves.

"You're welcome." Ken smiles and rests his arm at the top of the booth. "I'm glad you accepted."

"I needed a night out."

"Good, I was afraid Nicholas was going to fire you."

I want to tell Ken everything, but there's no easy way of explaining it—if there's even an explanation. "Ken, there's something I need you to know."

"Oh, no, he didn't fire you, did he?"

"No..." My heart squeezes at the memory of Nicholas's hands on me.

Our waitress returns with our drinks and I order another. I'm going to need a couple more drinks to get through this conversation.

"Something happened between Nicholas and me."

Ken looks at me as if I've gone insane. "What do you mean something?"

"Well, the other day when we were in the elevator..."

"You did something in the elevator?"

I laugh nervously. "He took me to his office, and at first, I thought he was going to fire me, but then he started kissing me."

Ken's mouth drops open. "I thought I told you to be careful," he says, shocked. "I didn't know you were actually interested in him."

"I'm not," I say defensively.

"But you guys kissed?" Ken argues.

"Yes, and it went too far."

Ken's eyebrow arches. "How far?"

"We... we had sex." I blush. This was a bad idea. How can I ever look at him again without thinking of this awkward conversation? I take a sip of my Midori Sour, hanging my head in shame.

Ken's expression makes my heart ache. "What's wrong?" I ask.

"Sorry, Becca, I just thought you were better than that."

Ouch. I don't even know what to say to that...

"I'm sorry, I'm being an ass," Ken says, rubbing my shoulder.

"Why would you say that?" Tears slip out from the corners of my eyes. I can take most people thinking I'm a floozy, but Ken thinking it is not okay. I look up to him. I like him.

"Becca, I'm an idiot. I'm sorry. I've liked you since I met you, and I know you don't feel the same, but I want you to know... you're amazing."

Ken's revelation nearly knocks the wind out of me. *You like me?*

I wish my heart could sort out my feelings. I know Ken is a great guy, but the reality is—I can't get Nicholas out of my head. I'm sure I would be happy to be with a guy like Ken. He's caring, smart, and although he's a little shyer than I am, I know that doesn't mean he's not a tiger in the sack. I pull Ken in an embrace and kiss him on the cheek.

"Thank you, Ken. You're amazing, too."

"Thanks." A small blush traces his cheeks. It's adorable.

"Thank you for being my friend."

"Always." Ken raises his class and clinks it against mine.

As we sit there quietly observing the crowd of people around us, Carol's words about Ken not being my type slowly resurface. *Why can't I be attracted to a nice guy?* It's like I'm bound to always fall for the asshole.

"It must not be your night," Ken says.

"What do you mean?"

"Your Mr. Tall, Blond, and Dangerously Gorgeous just walked in with his fiancée," Ken says sarcastically as he nods toward the club entrance.

"Huh?" I turn and look over my shoulder to see Nicholas walking in with Alison on his arm. Her creamy pink Chanel dress reminds me of a more contemporary version of Jackie Kennedy's dress. But even Alison doesn't compare to the way Nicholas looks tonight. The jeans and plaid shirt he's wearing hugs his muscular frame. I can't help but remember his warm hands trailing down my skin. I squeeze my knees together, fighting off the desire between my thighs.

We watch as Nicholas and Alison make their way to the second level of the club reserved for VIPs.

"Are you sure you want to stay?" Ken asks.

I look back at him. "I know you're worried about me, but I'm okay."

"Let's get a couple drinks in us and get on the dance floor," he offers.

After yet another Midori Sour, I'm starting to feel unstoppable as we head to the dance floor.

"You're a really good dancer," Ken yells over the music.

I feel a warm sensation creep over me as we move to the music together. The drinks are starting to kick in my system. I usually have a high tolerance, but tonight, I'm really feeling the alcohol. I giggle in excitement as the DJ starts playing "I Feel So Close to You" by Calvin Harris. The club comes alive as bodies flood the dance floor in groups.

We spend the next five minutes laughing as we try out new dance moves. I show Ken my infamous running man move, and he shows me how to do the water sprinkler. Ken might be shy, but he's just as fun as Carol. We make our way over to the bar, and just as I'm about to order another drink, Tristan Knight appears only a few feet away.

He heads toward Ken and me as we bounce to the music, waiting for the bartender to pay attention to us. It's a little surprising to see him here. He wasn't with Nicholas when he arrived at the VIP section. I wave to Tristan, wondering if he'll remember me. The last time we were at *Riptide* seems like ages ago.

His face breaks into a smile as he spots me. He's wearing a sharp blue shirt and dress pants. *He must be coming from work.*

"Do you know him?" Ken asks.

I smile. "I do." Tristan gives Ken a once over as he passes by another couple to get to us. He doesn't seem too surprised to see me here.

"Hi, Rebecca," Tristan says, slightly bumping as someone passes him from behind. He ignores the stranger and keeps his eyes trained on me.

"It's nice to see you again."

"It's great to see you. How are plans going for the opening of the art gallery?"

"Wonderful. Carol is very talented."

"She is," I say. Ken clears his throat, reminding me that I haven't introduced him. I step back and introduce the two gentlemen to each other.

"This is Carol's cousin, Kenneth Phillips."

"Nice to meet you." Tristan's smiles briefly before turning his attention back to me. The crowd on the dance floor disperses as the DJ changes the track to a slower song. John Legend's voice bellows out across the dance floor as the DJ plays *All of Me*. A handful of couples make their way to the center of the room. It's like Jr. High all over again. Slow dances were the awkward moments where I spent most of my time being the wallflower in the room.

"Ken, do you mind if I dance with your date?" Tristan asks.

"If she doesn't mind," he says with some reluctance.

"I would love to." I'm surprised Tristan would want to dance with me.

I turn to Ken and he looks just a little disappointed, but it doesn't stop him from encouraging me to have fun. He takes a seat at the bar and orders another drink, leaving me alone with Tristan.

"Shall we?" Tristan offers me his hand and we head to the dance floor. Unlike me, Tristan seems confident on the dance floor. He gently grabs my hand and twirls me in a graceful motion. I feel the air knocked out of me as he pulls me in close so that our chests are touching. My nerves are going haywire. It's hard enough being around one gorgeous man, but two is just overwhelming. I sneak a quick glance up at him. His hair falls back in waves of black and his shirt makes his hazel eyes lean more toward blue.

"Nicholas tells me you're doing a wonderful job at the company." Tristan smiles as he catches me looking at him. I'm sure Tristan knows he's handsome, but you could never tell from his demeanor.

I look up to find Nicholas watching us from the VIP section. By the scowl on his face, he isn't happy to see Tristan dancing with me. *What's his problem? He's here with her.* Alison sits beside him, engaged in a conversation with a waiter.

I laugh. "I'm surprised he thinks so."

Tristan follows my gaze. He chuckles, ignoring the glare Nicholas shoots down at him. There's a silent exchange of words between them. My heart flutters as Nicholas grips the rail of the second level.

"Nick can be an asshole when he wants to be. But he's under a lot of stress."

"I'm sure," I say, unconvinced. Tristan grins as I roll my eyes.

"His father wants him to marry Alison because it means being able to keep their biggest investor." The thought of Nicholas not marrying Alison had never crossed my mind until now.

"And if Nicholas chooses not to?"

"He'll lose everything." Tristan's words shake me to my core. The few times I've talked to Stefan, he's always seemed agreeable, charming, and extremely fair. It surprises me that he would even think of doing that to his son. *Who else would he give the company to?*

"I grew up with Stefan. He was a wonderful father to me. He took me in and adopted me as his own, but he always had certain expectations of Alex, Nick, and Emily. When Alex died, it tore our family apart. Nick wasn't himself after that. He was always getting into trouble with the paparazzi. For a good long while, he didn't even want the company. He didn't want to be the one to replace his brother."

"That can't be a good feeling," I say.

"No, but I think he's come to terms with reality. He's not replacing his brother. He's helping keep his memory alive by taking over the company. It's as much a part of the family as he is."

"He doesn't really talk about his mother."

A dark, clouded look crosses Tristan's face. "She was poison. She married Stefan and then gave him hell. When Alex died, she sold the story to the tabloids, only she lied and trashed his memory. She said he was on drugs when he had his accident."

"Wow, she sounds like a bitch."

Tristan's eyes connect with mine as he nods his head in agreement. "She was leaving Stefan and she wanted money—as much as she could get. It didn't matter who she hurt. Every year around the same time that she had left, she contacts Nicholas and Emily, hoping they'll send her money." *Wow.*

"That's pretty heavy."

"It is. I'm not trying to make excuses for Nick, but I know he cares about you."

"He does?" I ask. *He sure has a fucked up way of showing it.*

"Yes, whether it's something he wants to admit or not." Tristan spins me out and then into his arms. "Is he still looking?" he asks.

I look up to find Nicholas still watching us. I hate to admit it, but I wish he were down here dancing with me. "He's still watching."

"Good. I wanted him to see this."

"What?"

Before I have a chance to move, Tristan dips me and then pulls me back up. The gesture seems innocent, except when he pulls me back up he kisses me straight on the mouth. For a few brief seconds, our lips are locked. I can't say the kiss is bad. In fact, if I had never kissed Nicholas, Tristan would be a runner-up.

"Sorry, Rebecca. I needed to do that."

"Why?" I ask, breathless.

"For Nick." His statement is so strange that I find myself frozen in place. My mind races to unravel the puzzle before me. I don't understand. Tristan squeezes my hand and thanks me for the dance. The crowd suddenly breaks as I spot Nicholas speed-walking over to us.

Everything happens so quickly that I hardly have a moment to breathe, when Nicholas punches Tristan straight across the jaw. The crowd of gasps echo from all around us.

Holy shit. Tristan stumbles slightly, but quickly regains his composure. He smiles, wiping the split in his lip. I'm not sure why he finds it funny, but it's as if he was expecting it to happen.

"Don't you ever touch her again, you piece of shit," Nicholas says, steaming with anger. He turns toward me and grabs my elbow, practically lifting me off the floor.

"What were you thinking?" he growls.

I snap out of my shock. One minute Nicholas is punching Tristan in the face, and the next he's talking to me like he owns me. *Like I did something wrong.*

"What do you mean, what was I thinking?" I maneuver out of his grasp and push his hand away. Tristan takes the opportunity to walk away, but Nicholas turns and punches him again.

"You fuck." Nicholas hits him just below the eye, sending Tristan spiraling to the floor.

"What is wrong with you?" I yell, turning on Nicholas.

From the corner of my eye, I spot two bouncers quickly approaching us. It doesn't matter if I'm with two VIP members—they aren't going to put up with a fight breaking out. A moment later, I spot Alison making her way over to us. Apparently, she saw everything go down, too.

"Nicholas, what the hell?" Her voice rasps against her throat. "Why are you fighting with Tristan?"

"Alison, take the car and go," he says without any explanation.

She stares at him, openly shocked. He doesn't even move or flinch when she pushes past him in a huff of anger. Her angry glares sear me with hate.

"Jesus. Tristan, are you okay?" I lean down to help him up.

"I'm fine," he says, half-smiling. "I told you, Nick."

"What?" I ask.

"I told you I would prove it to you." Somehow, I think I'm missing out on something in this weird conversation. *And why isn't Tristan angry?*

"Leave him," Nicholas commands. "We're going." He dusts off his shirt and grabs my hand as he ushers me toward the front door of the club.

"I'm not leaving with you!" I say, fighting the pull to be near him.

"Oh, but you'd leave with him?" he asks, pointing to Tristan. "My best friend?"

"Fuck you," I blurt.

"You wish, sweetheart," he says, laughing. "In fact, why don't I take you to my car right now?"

"I'm sure Alison would love to know her fiancé is cheating on her." I know it's a low blow, but he's ruined my night. He doesn't answer me. He just stares at me in a way that I'm unsure if it means he wants to fuck me or fight me. Maybe both. "Yeah, exactly. Fuck off."

When I exit the club it's raining, and by raining, I mean pouring. I stand on the sidewalk, silently cursing every taxicab that speeds by. It seems all the cabs are taken for the night. The night is cold and my nipples are now cold, hard, and in pain. *Fuck, I forgot my dress coat.* I turn to go back into the club to retrieve it, and I smack face-first into *him.*

"Let me take you home," Nicholas says.

I look up to find him getting just as wet as I am. He holds a coat over his head as he approaches. Fuck me, he still looks gorgeous, and I can't think of a moment where I've hated him more. Where I've wanted him to fuck me more... His tight-fitting shirt hugs him, and beneath the cotton, I can see his perfectly sculpted abs. His hair looks longer wet, and it's still a bit tousled from the scuffle. How can he be so goddamn annoying and yet so irresistibly fuckable?

"Don't be stubborn," he says curtly. "I told Ken I would take you home."

Shit, Ken. I wonder if he saw everything. I didn't even bother to say goodbye. I just ran out. I'm such a bitch.

"Just leave me alone." I turn back to street, hoping a taxi will finally stop before the heavy rain washes me away.

33

NICHOLAS

"Y ou're the most stubborn woman I have ever met," I mutter under my breath. "You're going to catch pneumonia."

"I clearly said fuck off, Nicholas."

I don't take no for answer. I pull her to me, crushing her body against my frame. She looks up, watching drops of rain drip from my hair, down my lips, and to the ground. I fling my jacket down. I don't even give a shit if it gets ruined. I just want her in my arms. I need her.

"It drove me crazy," I say, tugging her hair loose from its band. Rebecca's curls cascade down in one swift motion. She watches me as I take a single strand, pull it between my fingers, and then watch it spring back. I smile, amused by the simple motion of her hair.

"Even your hair defies me," I whisper, staring at her lips.

"What?" she asks.

"I loathed watching him kiss you. Watching him touch you," I say, stepping closer as I cup her face. "I wanted it to be me. Only me..."

She gasps at the feel of my erection sliding against her.

"Don't you remember?" I say, nibbling her bottom lip. I trail hot kisses up to her ear. "You're mine."

I lift her and push her back against a nearby brick wall. I pull her panties off and they fall to the gritty ground. Before she can protest, I hush her with my lips. "I'll buy you twenty more where that came from."

She moans against me as I grind into her. She pushes her hips to meet mine and it sends a rush of heat through me. It would be so easy to fuck her here. It would feel so good. "I think we should move this somewhere else." I grab her hand and move it to the bulge in my pants. I'm rock hard for her. I growl as Rebecca rubs her hand up and down the front of my pants.

"If you keep doing that, I'm going to take you right here against this wall or over that trash can," I say, nodding to a nearby alley.

"Yes," she pleads

"You little vixen," I chuckle. "Don't tempt me."

34

REBECCA

Nicholas hails a cab, and together we step inside. He doesn't ask if I should go with him, and I don't say anything. We just get in and he gives the driver my apartment address. When we finally arrive, it's a little after ten. I'm sure Carol will be surprised to see me home so early.

We step out of the cab and Nicholas hands the driver a hundred dollar bill and tells him to keep the change. The neighborhood around us is dark with the exception of the flickering streetlights flashing down from each lamppost. It's still raining, but at this point, it doesn't matter anymore. I'm already soaked through, and so is Nicholas. I'm actually surprised the cab driver didn't charge us an extra fifty just for soaking his seats.

Nicholas grabs my hand and we walk in silence toward the apartment. I don't know what we're doing, but somehow, his fingers entwined with mine feel right. He stops me just before we get to the front entrance of the apartment complex as leans in to kiss me. The kiss is soft and slow, and so very different from other times we've found ourselves in each other's arms.

"Rebecca—" he says, pulling back.

"Please don't say anything," I ask, pushing my fingers to his lips. "Just kiss me and let's say goodnight."

Nicholas leans in and captures my lips in a heated rush. I run my fingers through his hair and he growls in appreciation as he grabs a handful of my ass. It takes us several minutes to pull apart, but when we finally do, he wraps his coat around me.

"Goodnight, Ms. Gellar."

My heart flip-flops at the way he says it. I've only ever heard him say it when he's mad or when he's telling me what to do, but I like the way it sounds when he's happy.

———

After a long, dramatic night, the only thing I want is to drift into sleep and dream about a world where things aren't so complicated. I'm halfway down the long corridor to our apartment when a familiar voice from behind stops me.

"You look good, Becca."

It takes me a moment to put my finger on the familiar but condescending tone. I turn to face him and gasp at the sight of his tanned, brawny face and brilliant smile. The one person I thought I would never ever see again.

Miles Storm.

PART III

PROLOGUE

NICHOLAS

Six Years Ago

"Fuck! I can't get this stupid thing right," my brother Alex, roars as he tosses yet another sheet of paper away. For the past hour, he's sat hunched over his office desk writing and re-writing a letter. Each time he grows angrier and angrier, flinging crumpled up sheets of papyrus paper across the room or over his shoulder. The floor is engulfed with beige little balls. It's as if he's trying to cover the entire goddamn floor.

I watch him from the door as he wipes his ink-stained fingers across his forehead. He's a mess of blue blotches, hands, face, neck, left arm, and even his clothes. Physically and emotionally, he's not much better. *What is his problem?* I don't think I've ever seen him this way.

"Do you need some help?" I take a cautious step into his room hoping there's something that I can do.

"No, Nick. I'm just trying to write Nina a letter." *Ah, Nina.* The girl Alex has been chasing for the past year. At first, they were just friends when she and my brother met in college. They even graduated together. They've been friends since the first day they met at freshman orientation. I always thought they would end up together, but Alex never made a move, and neither did Nina. Then this past summer she got engaged and Alex went ballistic. He's never been much of a settle-down-and-marry-her kind of guy, but I think my brother's finally realized that he could be that guy for her.

"Is there anything I can do?" I ask. I know there isn't, but I feel like I should ask anyway.

"Actually, there is one thing," he says, turning toward me.

"Shoot," I say, taking a seat on his bed. Alex pulls his chair over by me and sits so we're face to face. He pauses, inhaling and then exhaling a long, overdrawn blow of air.

"One day, you're going to love someone more than the fuckin' air you breathe, and when that day comes, I want you to remember to tell her. Tell her the moment you realize you do. Don't wait, even if you think it's one-sided. Tell her anyway."

"I will," I say. The favor seems easy enough.

"Promise me." A look of despair crosses my brother's face as he reaches out and pats me on the arm. I know he wishes someone could've made him do the same thing.

"I promise."

35

NICHOLAS

It's only been a few minutes since I left Rebecca's apartment and I already regret leaving. *I'm such a stupid fuck.* This night is a fucking disaster, *and* it's raining. I'm halfway down the block when I realize that there's no way in hell I'm going back home. *Fuck being a gentleman.* I thought it would easier to let her go and give her space to think about things. Hell, I need space to think about things. Each time I'm near Rebecca, the desire to touch her, to drown in those curves, hits me like a freight train. That woman stirs something fierce inside me. Even her familiar green eyes leave me spellbound. *God, those eyes.* Tristan is right—it's not just about the sex. Although, I would be lying if I said I wasn't thinking about it every time Rebecca opens her mouth. *That mouth has a way of bringing me to my knees.*

I stop just beneath a street lamp as the rain slowly stalls to a light drizzle. White puffs of air rise from my mouth as I exhale. It's cold as fuck outside, but I know that fiery assistant of mine could keep me warm. I should just go home, but I need to talk to Rebecca. It's killing me to not know what's going on between us. I've never second-guessed myself, but now I'm second-guessing everything with her.

I thought I could avoid the complication of caring about some-one. It's not like I have the best of luck with the people I love. *Love.* There's that word again. I've carefully navigated my life to avoid that word, but there it is, knocking on my door, scraping at it, trying to claw its way through. One innocent kiss had a major fucking snow-ball effect. I never thought Rebecca would be my undoing. And now, here I am, standing in the middle of this fucking wet city, pining over the woman that was just supposed to be my assistant. *Who am I kidding?* Pining doesn't properly explain what I'm feeling at this moment.

I need to keep moving. I can't just keep standing here, arguing with myself. What's the point? Rebecca and I could never be together. At least not without some major fucking consequences. *I could lose everything.* But even money and a comfortable life don't make up for the amount of pain I would feel if I lost Rebecca. There are times where she pushes my buttons and I just want to shove my cock in her smart little mouth, but most of the time, she amazes me with her wit and personality. She's fun to be around and her smile is infectious.

A sharp pain vibrates through my fist and I'm left with an over-whelming ache that spreads across my knuckles. I look down surprised to find them turning purple. I'm sure I'll have some ugly bruises in the morning. *Shit.* I should be happy I didn't break or frac-ture any of my fingers. They're sore as hell, but I can only imagine what Tristan's face must look like by comparison. *Tristan. That fucker.*

In all the years I've known him, I don't think I've ever cocked him across the face. Sure, we fought occasionally when we were younger, but it was never anything more than wrestling. I have a feeling I'm going to have some explaining to do when Emily and my father see him. It's not that he didn't deserve what was coming. That kiss between Rebecca and him nearly killed me. I wanted to maul him, and then throw Rebecca over my shoulder, and stomp out of *Riptide* thumping my chest like some enraged, primal beast. There was only one consistent thought racing through my head—*she's mine.* And I wanted to sear Tristan's kiss off her lips the moment he placed it there. I knew my best friend had something up his sleeve, but I never imagined he would be planning something like that. *I should've known.* I squeeze and release my grip, hoping the pain will subside, but it only grows stronger.

Maybe I should call him... I check my phone and grumble at the sight of Alison's name flashing across the screen. She's called three times, and now there's even a text message from her.

Alison: Nicholas, where are you? We need to talk. Now.

I lock my phone and slip it back into my slacks pocket. It's getting harder and harder to pretend like everything is going to be fine. The thought of actually marrying Alison gnaws at me like a plague, but this all just seems like one really bad dream. I know I'm in denial, and the only thing that keeps me from panicking is that there's still time to sort everything out. There's still some time to talk to my father and beg him to understand that his ideas about my future marriage are archaic, and the exact opposite of what I need at this point in my life. No, marrying Alison is not even close to what I need in my life.

My phone vibrates in my pant leg and I know without a doubt that it's Alison again. She's persistent, and while I usually admire that in a female, I find it aggravating in her. I'm dreading the conversation that's bound to happen when I finally make it home. I know she's probably pissed that I told her to leave without me, and I can only imagine what she must be thinking right now. I don't want to hurt Alison, but I need to make her see that going through with this marriage is a mistake. I've made plenty of stupid decisions in my life, but this one would be monumental. I don't want to live the rest of my life with someone I don't care about. My father risked it all with my mother and he got burned, but he loved her. A feeling that I cannot conjure for Alison.

No, the one person who even comes close to evoke any feeling in me is the one person I shouldn't have feelings for. When I'm near Rebecca, it's like she sets my nerves ablaze. I can't stop the rush of emotion and the amazing feelings of sensory overload, like a shot of adrenaline coursing through me. I can't go home tonight feeling the way I do. *I want and need to see her. I have to see her.*

I turn and make my way back toward Rebecca's building. I might be fucking everything up by doing this, but I don't care anymore. I don't fully understand what's happening between us, but I do know that, whether we're fighting or fucking, I want to spend my time with her.

173

36

REBECCA

oly shit. What the hell is he doing here? Miles steps toward me, and I step back as if we're in some awkward dance. He cracks a smile, and the sight of it sends my stomach spiraling into a nosedive. I think drinking all of those Midori Sours was a really bad idea. I should've eaten something more substantial before drinking, because I can feel those same drinks trying to make their way back up. I watch as he slides his duffle bag off his shoulder and lets it drop to the floor. *I have to be imagining this, right?* No, I'm not. He's standing here, plain as day, in New York City—waiting for me outside my apartment. Miles Storm, the man who tore my heart from my chest and carelessly tossed it aside. The memories of that day still give me a sick feeling that builds with each passing second that I stand here staring at him.

I find myself analyzing each detail in his features, as I try to process what I'm seeing. He looks the same, except his once familiar brown hair doesn't curl at the top of his collar anymore. It's cut short and combed forward in a messy wave. His honey colored eyes scan mine as he slowly saunters toward me. He's going to touch me. The feeling of dread that washes over leaves my airway constricted. *Breathe.* I force myself to inhale and exhale slowly. I'm having a panic attack. *He shouldn't be here. Why is he here?* He's so close I can almost smell the ocean breeze lingering on his leather jacket. My heart squeezes and I silently curse it for doing so. I hate that he still has an effect on me. He shouldn't matter. He doesn't matter. He's an asshole. I close my eyes for a moment, and chant the words over and over in my head until I can muster enough strength to take another step away from him.

I turn, but I'm too stunned to make an escape, and then I feel him before I hear him step behind me. He wraps his arms around my waist and he hugs me, crushing my back to his chest. The motion sends a wave of shock through me, and his embrace unleashes so many all-too familiar feelings inside me. I'm helpless, immobile, and physically exhausted all at once. His skin is warm, despite the obvious cold draft wafting through from the outside. His closeness and his touch used to make me feel secure and loved. Now, it's just another reminder of his betrayal. *He didn't love me enough.* The smell of him fills my senses. It's an earthy scent mixed with leather. I used to love the way he smelled.

Time seems to have gone by so quickly and yet it doesn't feel like it's been enough. They say time heals all wounds. No amount of time could make me forget how humiliating it was to find him with another woman, and worse, how she had laughed in my stunned face. The memory of Scarlett's haughty smile ignites a fire inside of me. I wish I could punch her in the face all over again. It would be so worth it.

"NO! *Let me go!*" I seethe, pushing Miles's hands off me.

"Becca, I missed you," he whispers against the back of my head. I feel his lips graze my hair. He breathes me in and exhales me out. After several awkward moments, I think he's going to reluctantly let me go, but instead, he turns me and leans in to kiss me. His contact with my lips is brief, but it turns my stomach. I push away from him, trying to put several feet between us. At this moment, I don't think three-thousand miles is far enough away for me.

"Why are you here?" I ask, pulling out my apartment key from my bag. *I should just get inside and close the door. I don't have to stand here and deal with him.*

Miles stands there for several moments, staring at me in confusion. "I came here for you." Bright red stains his cheeks as he shifts his stare past me at the apartment door. I watch as he swallows slowly. The silence between us is deafening. He digs his hands inside of his pockets as if to keep them from finding their way back to me. I've never seen him act like this. It's almost as if he's nervous. *Miles nervous?* He was never nervous. At least not with me.

"I didn't ask you to come," I blurt.

He nods his head in agreement, wincing at my tone. "I know, but I came here to tell you that I made a mistake. I took everything for granted. You. Us. Everything. And I'm sorry."

I let the words settle over me like dust before quickly shaking them off. I'm going to kill my mother for giving Miles my contact information. He found my apartment information somehow, and I have no doubt she gave it to him. My mother could never tell him *no.*

"Why now?" I ask.

"What?"

"Why now?" I say again more firmly.

"I realized I made a mistake. What we had was special. After you left, I kept hoping you would come back. I didn't want you to leave. I called your mother almost every week asking to see how you were. I knew you wouldn't answer my calls if I called your cell. I called your office a few times, but you were always out, and I was always too afraid to leave you a message. It wasn't until I saw your picture in the paper that I knew I needed to come out here."

"You saw my picture in the paper?" *How the hell did it get in the paper?*

He pulls a newspaper clipping from the pocket of his jeans and hands it to me. It's worn, as if it's gone through a couple of washes. I slowly unfold it, fearful as to what it might say. My breath catches at the sight of the photo within the article. It's a photo of Nicholas and me walking into the Lit for Kids event. The paparazzi must've snagged a photo before we got inside. I completely forgot about the photographers waiting at the entrance of the event. I know they didn't take any of us when we left because we slipped out the back, but there's definitely at least this one of us walking in. I wonder if Nicholas has seen this.

"I got lucky and I landed a role in a miniseries that's filming here in New York. I took a chance because I wanted to see you," Miles says.

I smile at the sight of my arm looped through the crook of Nicholas's arm. He looks so good. I fight the itch to take the news clipping inside with me. I bet Carol would nag me to death about it. God, I have to tell her about what happened tonight. She won't be surprised. In fact, I think she'll enjoy rubbing it in my face.

"Are you guys together?" Miles's voice breaks through my thoughts. His face is shrouded in disappointment.

"Excuse me?"

"You just seem pretty close in that photo. Are you seeing him?" He shifts uncomfortably, waiting for my reply. *No, but right now I wish I were.* I wish I could rub Nicholas in his face and show Miles exactly what he missed out on by cheating on me. *You're such an asshole.*

"I don't see how that's any of your business," I say. My heart skips as a familiar scowl appears down the hallway of my apartment building. *Nicholas StoneHaven.* It's as if the gods have heard my wish. His suit is still lightly dripping from the rain as he steps out of the shadows. His blue eyes stare back, assessing Miles, and then me. *I thought he left.* Nicholas slowly walks toward me, only pulling his gaze away from me long enough to give Miles a stony glare. *He probably heard our conversation.* His frown reaches all the way to his eyes.

"Nick?"

Miles turns and his eyes widen at the sight of Nicholas. I can only imagine what's going through his mind.

He looks back at me and reaches out for my hand. "Can we go inside and talk?"

I hesitate, wondering if Nicholas is going to start a fight with him. In all the years I dated Miles, I don't think I've ever seen him fight anyone, but I have seen Nicholas in action. I know he could take Miles out any day of the week. Nicholas is a few good inches taller than he is, and there's muscle behind those expensive suits. *Lots of it.* Not to mention the look on his face could easily be described as murderous.

"I think you should go, Miles." My nerves jump as Nicholas walks past him. To my surprise, he treats him like he's invisible. A startled expression passes over Miles's face, but it quickly turns to annoyance. He eyes the back of Nicholas's frame, as if trying to size him up. *That would be a very stupid move.* Miles looks to me as Nicholas walks up and seizes my elbow. He wastes no time tugging me backwards toward the door. Confusion fills me as Nicholas flashes me an angry look before his lips crash against mine. The action startles me and yet excites me tremendously.

The warmth of his lips has me melting in his arms. I suck in a moan as he glides his hand down my ass and pulls me to him so I'm basically straddling his leg. A mixture of annoyance and satisfaction rushes through me. I hate but love that he's so animalistic sometimes. It takes me a few moments to break the kiss, but I do after remembering that Miles is still standing in the hallway only a few feet away.

"I thought you left?" I ask, breathless. Nicholas leans in, kissing the top of my head briefly. It feels like the tip of a feather gliding over my skin as it sends shivers down my body. My nipples perk up in desire. *Damn you, body.*

"I did, but I couldn't stop thinking about being inside of you." My breath catches at the bluntness of his words. *Did Miles hear that?* From the smug look on Nicholas's face, I know he purposely said it loud enough for him to hear. *Sneaky bastard.* I want to kiss the smirk right off his face. He tugs a curl and leans in to kiss me again, but the sound of Miles's voice stops him.

"Becca, can I talk to you... alone?" I turn to find Miles standing only a few feet away. He shoots Nicholas a wary look as he steps forward and tries to grab my hand. The desperation in his voice stings my heart. A piece of me feels guilty at the thought that I put it there, but I quickly squash the feelings. I have no reason to feel guilty. Before I have a chance to respond, Nicholas steps in front of me, and the words that come spiraling out of his mouth sound like a growl.

"She's done talking to you," he says. Nicholas turns back to me and pulls my key from my hand. He unlocks the door in one swift motion and pushes me inside. Miles watches in shock as Nicholas slams the door in his face.

37

REBECCA

I stand off-kilter from the scene in front of me, my heart still lightly beating. *Did that really just happen?* I feel Nicholas's hands grabbing me and pushing me up against the door. He pulls me into another kiss, but this time, there's urgency behind it. I don't fight him. I'm too tired, too weak, and too lost in the sensation to ask him to stop. He traces his hand over my neck and then down the side of my shoulder.

When he finally breaks the kiss, my legs feel like they're about to fail me. The expression 'weak at the knees' has a whole new meaning for me. Nicholas reluctantly lets me go and walks over to the panoramic windows just beyond the living room of the apartment. The night sky looks ominous with storm clouds looming low over the city landscape, and the streets below are illuminated in bright hues of red and white. It's twelve a.m. but the city is just waking from its daylong sleep. The one great similarity between Los Angeles and New York is they're both always vibrant with people flowing in and out of the streets.

Nicholas wanders across the room, surveying the furnishings around him. He stops to stare at a framed photo of my mother, my father, and me. The apartment looks small around him. I can only imagine how puny it must be to him compared to his giant mansion of a place. Carol would be thrilled to know that he's here. Knowing her, she would be sending me mental winks from her bedroom. Speaking of, where the hell is she? I thought she would be home by now. *That woman is never home anymore.* I'm starting to think she has a boyfriend on the side that she's not telling me about. *Carol is* going to be shocked when I tell her about *Riptide* and about Miles coming over tonight. Although, it might be better if I don't bring up the Miles situation just yet. Carol might go looking for him to kick his ass.

I set my purse down and fling off my heels, watching Nicholas walk as he quietly continues to stare out into the darkness of the city. His perfectly sculpted shoulders sag slightly as if he's upset. A strong need to comfort him pulls me toward him. I'm only a few feet away when he whips back toward me. There's heat behind those stark blue irises. A primal heat that tells me his mind is being occupied by something deliciously dark.

"Rebecca, I need you. I need you underneath me. I need to be inside of you. Right now, it's the only thing that makes sense to me in this world." His words both flatter me and concern me. I don't want to be someone's escape, but even though my feet are firmly planted in reality, I need and want the same from him.

"I don't want to see you with anyone else."

"Are you asking for exclusivity? That doesn't exactly work when you're engaged to another woman," I retort.

Nicholas pivots on his heel and heads back toward me. There's a look of exasperation written all over his face. The calm and collected Nicholas I'm used to is now replaced with an anxious demeanor. He rakes one hand through his messy wet mane and then looks up at me.

"I don't know what I'm asking. You don't even know how much I wanted to beat the shit out of that fucker," he growls. I don't doubt it and I would be lying if I said it didn't turn me on. *It totally does.* "Why are you wasting your breath on him?" Nicholas asks in a serious tone. I'm taken aback by the anger seething from his words. There's a slight accusation in them. By 'him,' I can only assume he means Miles. *But I never told him Miles was my fiancé.*

"How do you know who he is?"

Nicholas smirks, giving me a look of mild irritation. "It isn't that hard to figure out that you didn't want him near you."

"You're avoiding the question."

Nicholas shrugs his shoulders in a noncommittal gesture. "I found out about him when I had you investigated."

"What?" I ask, shocked by his revelation. "You had me investigated?"

"I don't let just anyone work with me. I wanted to know more about you."

"You couldn't just ask? I did a regular background check when I submitted my paperwork to HR. You had no right to snoop into my private life," I say, irritated.

Nicholas steps closer and his eyes wash over me with interest. "No, I couldn't just ask because, to be frank, at the time, I was going to use any information I could to get you to leave."

Ouch. The words hit me with a painful intensity that sends my heart racing through my chest. *Get me to leave?* I guess I shouldn't be surprised. It's not like Nicholas made it a secret about him wanting me to go. Sending me off on crazy errands was a pretty good indication, and yet over the past few weeks, his actions and words have said otherwise. I'm not so sure he wants me gone anymore; though I'm not sure that his reasons for wanting me to stay are any better.

"So is there anything you don't know?" I reply with a mouthful of sarcasm.

"Rebecca, I'm telling you this because I want to be honest with you."

"Thank you for your honesty," I say, circling around to the front of the door. "But I need you to leave." I hear a bell jingling and spot Sprinkles, the cat we've been babysitting, heading over toward me. He stops just short of me to smell Nicholas's pant leg. *Shit, he's going to pee on him.* Part of me wants to watch this train wreck, but before I have a chance to shoo Sprinkles away, he starts to purr and rub himself on Nicholas. *Weird.*

Nicholas reaches down and picks him up. Sprinkles nuzzles his head against Nicholas's palm. *That damn cat peed on my clothes and now the little traitorous bastard is cuddling him?*

"That's so weird."

"What?"

"He never likes anyone," I admit. "He didn't even like me when I first got here, but he seems to love you."

"That's because I know how to handle a pussy," he says, with a twitch of his lips. Really? *Ugh, arrogant ass.*

"Rebecca, I came here to talk to you," he says, placing Sprinkles back on the floor. I sigh at the stubborn look that crosses Nicholas's face. He's not leaving unless I throw him out.

"I don't want to talk."

"We don't have to talk," he says with a smile.

"Please. Leave," I say, pointing to the door.

"I'm afraid I can't do that," he says, loosening his tie. My stomach tightens at the sight of his fingers pulling at the topknot. He steps closer, grabbing my waist. "You want to know what I found out? I found out you were engaged to an actor named Miles Storm. I found out he cheated on you. But more importantly, I found out that he never deserved you, and if I had my way, I would have no problem making him disappear off the face of this planet."

Nicholas's words strike a chord inside of me. Without any warning, I feel my eyes burn with tears. It's really hard to be angry with him when he says things like this. It just makes this whole situation so much more confusing. He reaches out and cups my face with his hand. The feeling of it spreads a warm tingling all over me. I shouldn't want or need him, but I do. He wipes a tear with his thumb and then leans in. I close my eyes anticipating a kiss but he doesn't kiss me—at least not yet. He trails soft kisses from my temple to my chin, and then he does the same on the other side of my face. When he's done, he places one more at the corner of my mouth, and I immediately smile at the sensation.

"There's that smile," he murmurs.

"What smile?"

"The one that makes me feel like I'm free-falling."

"That sounds horrible."

"It's not. It's a rush."

38

NICHOLAS

My eyes flicker open to a familiar darkened bedroom. After a few seconds of repeatedly blinking like an idiot, my blurry vision eventually subsides and I realize exactly where I am. Warm, soft curves are snuggled in beside me as Rebecca lays curled up against my chest. We're lying on her bed, still fully clothed. It's hard to hide my disappointment at the realization. I wish we were naked and underneath the covers. Rebecca must've been exhausted because she's still wearing her dress from the club, minus the heels. I push the red strands of hair from her face and she nestles her cheek against my chest. My cock instantly grows hard from the feeling. *God, she feels so good against me.* I can't think straight when I'm hard for her. I wish I could just stay here and hold her, but I know I need to get back to my apartment and deal with Alison. She's probably livid, and she's going to be even more so when I talk to her about our engagement.

I slide out from beneath Rebecca's hold and gently shift her so she's lying against a soft while pillow. Despite the ache in my knuckles, I don't fight the temptation to run them across her cheek. Last night would've been a record for me. First, I punch my best friend for touching her, and then I almost punch that other motherfucker in the face. Miles Storm. *I can't believe he showed up here.* I have to make a mental note to send Striker here to make sure he doesn't come back. *Ever.* And if he does, I'll break his face with my own goddamn hands. My chest aches at the memory of Rebecca's face when he was talking to her. It was slowly killing me to watch the pain fill her eyes and to hear the hitch in her voice when he touched her. I know Rebecca can handle herself, but I was so close to just putting that fucker through the ground.

Rebecca was pissed about me looking into her background, and I can't say I blame her, but I don't regret it. I needed to know more about her past. I just hope she'll forgive me for it. After arguing with her for more than half an hour, she finally conceded to let me stay to *talk*, except she didn't want to talk about us. Every time I brought the subject up, she avoided it completely. I'm starting to think she's afraid of there being an *us.*

I check Rebecca's room for my cell phone and find it sitting on top of the nightstand. To my dismay, there are another ten missed calls from Alison and two from my father. *Shit.* The numbers on the dashboard of my phone let me know that it's well past nine a.m. *Great.* I've managed to sleep most of the morning away. Thankfully, as I slip out of Rebecca and Carol's apartment, it isn't raining anymore. It's time to set things straight and figure out what the fuck I'm going to do about all of this. My world right now is one giant *clusterfuck*, but I know one thing for certain—I'm going to make Rebecca mine. *Forever.*

———

Dread fills me as I pull up to my apartment and spot Alison's white convertible Porsche parked in front of my apartment. Even worse is the sight of boxes piled into the backseat of her car and the movers unloading furniture into my place from the moving truck parked illegally on the side of the street. No, she didn't. *What the fuck is going on here?* I nearly startle one of the dipshits unloading a dresser from the truck as I tear across the icy street. The short man's eyes widen as I sidestep in front of him, blocking him from going inside. He looks two times older than I am, but I have no problem throwing his ass out of my way.

"Hey, what the hell is all of this?" His partner, a fit balding man, looks me over and continues to unload the truck. "This is private property. What the fuck are you doing?" I ask.

At the sound of my voice, Alison comes hurrying out of the building in a long pink coat. She's dressed down in sweats and her hair is tied up in a bun—glaring evidence that she's been moving her shit into my apartment. *What the fuck is she up to?*

"Oh, good, you're here."

"What are you doing here?" I ask.

The look on her face would have most men crawling under a rock. She spreads her hands across her hips, a mixture of impatience and irritation radiating off her. She doesn't like my question, but I don't give a shit. It's hard to believe that the movers would just show up and start moving her things in.

"I tried calling you several times, baby," she says in a sardonic tone. "When you didn't answer, I thought I might as well go ahead and go forward with the move-in plans." She blows a strand of blonde from her face and bats her long eyelashes at me. I know behind that innocent expression is a stone cold businesswoman. Alison is cut-throat when she wants to be.

"What move-in plans? We didn't even talk about this."

She pulls me to the side. "Keep your voice down, Nicholas. People are watching." Alison nervously brushes away a loose strand from her face as she quickly checks to see if there are still people walking nearby.

"Does it really look like I give a shit?" I growl. We could be in the middle of Times Square for all I care.

"Well, you should. You've already been in the papers enough." *Bullshit.* I haven't gotten any bad press since Rebecca was hired. In fact, I think the company has had a lot of positive exposure since the Lit for Kids event. I know Rebecca has been working her ass off trying to answer the flood of emails in my inbox since.

"Alison, you're not moving in." I head toward the move-in truck when I hear her shrill voice.

"I am moving in, because I'm not letting my fiancé run around New York City with his assistant. You've been fucking her behind my back, and Friday night was proof of that. You can go ahead and treat me like I'm an idiot, but I'm not blind."

Her words hit home for me. I'm tired of lying to everyone, including myself. I'd rather Alison know the truth about how I feel. I want Rebecca to know the truth first, but I think this charade needs to end.

"Yes, I fucked her," I say, grinding my jaw. Alison winces at the words tumbling out of my mouth. She gasps as if shocked and angry all at once. I know it's not what she wanted to hear. Sometimes it's easier to accept a lie than the truth, but I'm sick of lies. I'm sick of the deceit.

"Why?" Tears breach the corners of her eyes and she quickly wipes them away with her hand.

"Alison, I was forced into our engagement. I never wanted any of it."

"But why do you want to be with her?" she cries. "She isn't anyone important."

"You're wrong, she's everything to me." And there it is—the frightening truth of my feelings for Rebecca. She fucking means absolutely everything to me. I was just too stupid to see it only hours ago. Now it's right there, in plain sight. I can't wrap my head around why I hadn't seen it before, but my brother would probably laugh his ass off right now if he were here. *God, I miss him.* Life seemed a lot simpler when I had him to go to for advice. He probably would've punched me if he knew I was engaged to Alison.

"So you're in love with her?" Alison looks up at me with a cold disappointment.

"When I first met Rebecca, I couldn't get her out of my head. I thought I could move on if I had one night with her."

"But it didn't help, did it?" she says, practically spewing the words.

"No, it didn't."

Alison steps toward me with determination. She quickly grasps my hand and places it on her hip. The touch is unexpected and her lips catch me completely off-guard when she quickly presses them against mine. Before I can pull back, coldness overwhelms me. The sensation is a shock to my system, but I quickly recover, pushing back away from her. Anger vibrates off Alison as I break the kiss, and her face distorts into a furious gaze. *I would be lying if I said I felt anything for her.* The warmth that I've become so accustomed to with Rebecca is completely absent with Alison.

"I don't want to continue with this facade anymore."

"But it isn't one for me," she says.

"I'm going to schedule a meeting with your father and mine this week."

"No, please don't do this."

"Don't make this any harder than it needs to be."

"We're meant to be together."

"Alison, I can't marry you," I say, practically yelling. The movers shuffling furniture across the way freeze as they overhear our heated conversation. Alison blushes in embarrassment, but she quickly recovers from the shock of my words. She looks down at her feet and then back up at me before turning on her heel. Relief washes over me as she tells the movers to pack up her shit and put it back into the truck. It takes them several hours, but they finally have all of Alison's furniture back into the truck by eleven o'clock.

I sit on the steps in front of my apartment and wait for her to finish stuffing the rest of her items back into the Porsche. Despite my need to break off our engagement, I hate seeing her cry. She pulls her soft blonde hair from her ponytail and walks over to me. I bite the inside of my cheek at the sight of her puffy red eyes. Seeing any woman cry is like a punch in the gut.

"Nicholas, I just want to make you happy," she sniffles. It's not easy telling someone that they could never make you happy. It's a cold, hard truth, but some things just need to be said. False hope can eat you alive, and I don't want to leave Alison with a shred of it.

"You were a one-time thing for me. I never thought it would turn into this shit storm. Before we slept together, I told you that if this weren't a one-time deal for you, then I would leave. I never wanted it to be more."

"But somehow, everything is different with your assistant?"

"She's different," I say.

"She's nothing."

"Alison, leave." A streak of anger pricks at my nerves. "This mess will all be over soon. If you won't convince your father to break the arrangement, then I'll tell mine that it's over."

"If you think that your father is just going to let you throw everything away over her, then you're wrong."

"It doesn't matter. One way or another, it's over."

As I watch Alison get into her car and leave, I realize that this battle is just beginning. She won't let this go without a fight. She didn't give up on trying to buy Tristan's painting when I met her, and she won't give up on the idea of us being together. I know it hurt her pride to know that I'm choosing Rebecca over her, but she was never a viable option to me. She's just a woman obsessed with getting what she wants at all costs, and I was stupid enough to sleep with her.

39
REBECCA

Saturday morning, I wake to Nicholas's name on my lips and the memory of his kiss imprinted on my skin. I turn in my bed, soaking up the feeling of it. I wish I could just lie here forever and bask in the memory of his touch, but life seems to get in the way of everything. I rise from my bed just in time to hear my phone buzzing from my nightstand. It vibrates twice before flashing red to let me know I have a text. I pick it up, hoping that it isn't from Miles. *That would be the last thing I need.* Nicholas's number flashes across my screen. I still haven't saved the number on my phone, but I know it by memory now. My fingers linger above *add new contact.* I know it must be silly, but there's something symbolic about adding someone to your contacts. It might be better if I don't add him. The disappointment might be easier to handle.

Nicholas: I can't stop thinking about you. Xx

My breath catches at the sight of his text. I stare at the timestamp and it says it was sent only five minutes ago. Damn, it's already one o'clock in the afternoon. *Way to sleep the day away, Becca.* I needed the rest, though. Last night was exhausting.

After telling Nicholas off about digging into my personal life, I finally agreed to let him stay so that we could talk. Everyone dreads having *the talk,* but the funny part is we're not in a relationship. He's engaged, for fuck's sake. And yet, every time he's near me, it feels like we should be. It's as if I'm fighting an inevitable pull that he has on me, and I can't seem to stay away.

My evening didn't exactly end the way I thought it would. Seeing Miles standing in front of my apartment still feels like a really bad dream. The kind of dream where you wake up with an ache in your chest that you can't seem to shake off. *Why did he have to come here?* I should've punched *him* in the face instead of Scarlett. *How could he ever think that I could forgive him?* I didn't know what to tell him, and there wasn't really much I wanted to say to him. I wish Carol had been there last night. She always has a way of knowing just what to do, although she might've just ended up decking him in the face, too. I should probably avoid telling her for a little while.

After several minutes of debating on whether I should get up or not, I finally manage to roll out of bed and exchange my wrinkled dress for my Garfield pajama bottoms and a regular shirt. Carol's smiling face greets me as I open my bedroom door, and I spot her hand mid-air as if she was just about to knock. She stands there looking flawless in her pencil skirt and matching blazer. It's as if her outfit came hot off the press. Unfortunately, she puts my disheveled appearance to shame. I'm pretty sure I still have dry slobber crusted to my face. *Yum.*

"Hi, girly, how's it going?" Carol says, eyeing my frizzy hair. "Did you wake up on the wrong side of the bed or something?"

"No," I laugh. "I just woke up and I haven't had a chance to fix my hair."

"You kind of have the whole Orphan Annie thing rocking," she says, smiling. I would probably be hurt if I didn't know she's actually just teasing me.

"Carol, that is the meanest thing anyone has ever said to me," I say, pretending like my feelings are hurt. I give her my sad puppy face, and she just starts laughing.

"It's cute. Maybe we can put little bows on your head and then it would be perfect."

"You're such a bitch."

"Yeah, but you love me."

"Where were you last night? I didn't see you come home."

Carol's gaze slides over my face with a nervous smile. "I was just going over some documents at the office. So anyway, I came in here to tell you that someone sent you some very pretty flowers. I put them in the kitchen."

"What?" I ask, confused. I'm not enthusiastic about Carol's reluctance to answer my question, but the word flowers quickly steal my attention.

"Yeah, there's like two hundred roses... and they look expensive."

"From who?" I ask.

A slow, cheeky smile spreads across her lips and immediately, I know they're from *him*. Who else do I know that would send me flowers? *No one.* Miles certainly never sent me flowers, and I highly doubt they're from Ken. Carol would've said something if they were. No, this is none other than the doing of *Nicholas-fucking-StoneHaven.* Carol stops me as I try to walk past her. "Now, who would buy you roses, I wonder?" Her tone is playful, but I know she's genuinely intrigued by this sudden surprise. Just wait until I tell her about what happened at *Riptide.* She'll never let up on teasing me about Nicholas.

"Don't you have better places to be?" I ask. "Like work, maybe?"

"Ouch, kitty has claws. Weekends are off limits. I've been trying my best not to work 7 days a week."

"That's good, I miss seeing you around here... Can I see who the roses are from now?"

"Wouldn't you like to know," she says, waving a small white envelope. I know she can see the wheels spinning in my head. She doesn't wait for my response as she turns on her heel and dashes down the hallway. *Damn it.*

The bright red colors of the flowers stop me in my tracks as I enter the kitchen. They're beautiful—breathtakingly beautiful—and each one looks like it's just been picked from an outside garden. The bushel of long-stemmed roses is sitting in a large vase on the kitchen counter. To most people, red roses are symbolic for romance, but I've learned that Nicholas has a subtle and yet not so subtle way of saying things. He picked red roses because of his new fascination with the color.

Carol walks around the kitchen and slides the giant vase toward me. I didn't think they made vases big enough to fit 200 roses, but apparently, they do. Carol waves the small white envelope that came with the roses in front of my face. Her taunts are working and the more she waves it front of me, the more I need to read it. I try to snatch it out of her grasp, but she's too quick.

"I think I'll read it first," she says, taking a seat on one of her three barstools. My grumbles only encourage her to keep going.

"Let's see what your mystery man has to say," she says, wiggling her eyebrows. I watch as Carol grins at the message in the card. Her eyebrow quirks and she lets out a low, dramatic whistle. "Damn, Becca. Someone has it bad."

Desperate to see the note, I quickly grab the card and open it.

B*ecca,*
    I love waking up next to you.
Xx,
Nicholas

M y cheeks burn. *Fuck.* Carol is going to think we slept together again.

"Was he here last night? Is something going on between you two that I didn't already know?" she asks.

I need to come clean and tell her about the drama at *Riptide* last night. I'm sure she'll be surprised to hear that he punched his own best friend in the face because of me. The memory of last night's craziness hasn't left me. I don't think I've ever had such an eventful day—from going on a date with Ken to finding my ex fiancé waiting for me by my front door and now this.

"Becca?"

Before I can answer, I sense something vibrate in the pocket of my pajama bottoms.

"It sounds like someone's calling you," Carol says, eyeing my pocket. I pull my cell phone out and Nicholas's number sits under my missed calls list. A warm rush of heat pools between my legs, and I inwardly sigh at the thought of his body hovering over me. A familiar ache pulses through me. Just seeing his name makes me hot and bothered. I clear the missed call and close my phone.

"Is it him?"

"I have no idea what you're talking about."

"So it is?" she asks with a gleam in her eye. "Your boss seems to be calling you a lot lately. And now he's sending you flowers after sex..."

"We did not have sex," I argue.

"Sure, you keep telling yourself that."

"We didn't. It's just that a lot of stuff went down last night."

Carol jumps off the barstool and walks over to me. I could die of embarrassment at the pure excitement shining on her face.

"Spill," she commands.

"Well... I went on a date with your cousin and we went to *Riptide*."

"Okay, weird, but go... Wait, does he even dance?"

"He does," I laugh. "So the next thing I know Nicholas and his fiancée show up."

"Uh, oh."

"Yes, which was fine. I was fine. Until Tristan showed up and he asked me to dance." Carol's eyes widen in confusion but I continue. The best part of the story is coming.

"Okay, and..."

"And then he kissed me," I blurt.

"What the fuck?"

The words fall out of my mouth in a sudden rush. "Yes, he full on kissed me and Nicholas saw him. Everything happened so fast, and well, he punched Tristan in the face."

"Wait—is Tristan interested in you now?"

"No, I'm under the impression he did it on purpose to make Nicholas mad."

"Geez." I watch as Carol deconstructs my words in her head. It takes what seems like a two good minutes before she can form words.

"Rebecca, can I ask you something?" She fiddles with her hands like she's nervous about what she's about to ask.

"You know you can."

"Do you think he's... you know... in love with you?"

Now it's my turn to be speechless. Her words hit me like a bomb exploding inside my chest. My insides are torn by the idea of Nicholas and the word *love* being in the same sentence. *In love with me?* I take a moment to let her question settle inside of me. There is no way he could feel that way about me. I honestly don't know if he could feel that way about anyone. As much as I would like to think that Nicholas is capable of it, it seems like he's been a player most of his life. No, I'm convinced what he feels for me is fleeting. He's just used to getting what he wants and I'm just another woman to chase.

"I ask because no one punches their best friend in the face over a girl they're going to toss the next day." Carol stares at me with a firm look. She knows what I'm thinking, but I can't help but feel insecure about how Nicholas really feels about me. Sure, he's intense when we're together, and he has no problem telling me that he loves to fuck me, but if he actually loves me... that is an entirely different monster.

"To be honest, sometimes I'm not sure what he's feeling."

"How do you feel about him?" Carol asks.

I've been so afraid of feeling any way about him. The last time I loved someone it didn't end so well. I know I'm strong, but your heart can only take so much before you just lose yourself. Although there are times when I think losing myself with him wouldn't be so bad. I swallow the growing lump in my throat as Carol reaches over and squeezes my hand. I want to believe that everything will work out. That life will have some fairytale ending for me, but after everything that's happened—fairytales just seem like bullshit now.

"Sometimes I feel like we've known each other for a long time, and other times I feel like I hardly know him at all," I admit.

"I think it's safe to say, sometimes even knowing a little bit about someone has us falling." Carol's words are reassuring, but they still don't take away the uncertainty that clouds my thoughts of a future with Nicholas.

"Since when did you get so wise?" I say, half smiling.

Carol laughs, wrapping her arms around my shoulder and giving me a quick squeeze. "I've always been wise."

"The Carol I remember from college was always too busy getting banged by frat guys to remember to give me such sage advice." I laugh at the memory of watching Carol chugging beers just to show that she could hang with the guys. She was a force to be reckoned with during college parties. I never had the balls to walk up to a guy and tell him to fuck me in the supply closet, but there were several times where I watched Carol do just that.

"So are you going to call him back?"

"I don't really know if I should." Maybe Nicholas was just calling about something work related for Monday.

"Of course, you should," Carol says.

"I can't just start a relationship with him."

"Becca, I think it's too late to pretend like there isn't something already there between you guys. Haven't you learned yet?"

"There is something there, but I refuse to be the woman on the side."

"Who says you would be?"

"I don't see him dumping his fiancée any time soon."

"Well maybe that's why he wants to talk to you."

Her words shake me. Nicholas breaking off his engagement with Alison would be a *very* big deal. I know Carol wants me to believe that he cares about me enough to do that, and it seems that Tristan wants me to believe it too, but breaking off his engagement would mean more than just not getting married. According to Tristan, it would mean losing his company and disappointing his family. I know now what family means to Nicholas. I've seen the pain in his eyes every time someone even mentions his late brother's name. As much as I want to be with him, I could never ask him to give all of that up for me.

"I'm just going to ignore it," I say.

Carol looks at me with a sadness that seeps into her smile. "Okay, Becca. Okay."

40

REBECCA

Monday morning, I wake up feeling terrible. The building pressure behind my sinuses sends a throbbing pain across my forehead, temples, and behind my eyes. After taking an extra twenty minutes just to get ready, I'm finally able to dash out of the apartment and head to work.

At the office, I find Ken standing near my cubicle. He stares at the wall with a cup of coffee in one hand and the other nervously drumming against the top of his thigh. I don't think I've ever seen him so anxious, but I can guess that he's probably waiting to tell me off about this past Friday. I feel horrible for ditching him on our first date. I don't doubt that he saw me leave with Nicholas. As much as I was enjoying my time with Ken, it was probably stupid of me to accept his offer to go on a date. It also would've been really awkward with Carol. She didn't seem to jump for joy at the idea of me dating her cousin.

I make my way down the walkway between the wall and the rows of cubicles. I really hope Ken will forgive me. I would hate to have things be awkward between us. Especially when I have to work in such close proximity to him, plus he's Carol's family.

"Good morning," I say, hopeful.

Ken turns toward me, and to my surprise, his face breaks into a smile. Rebecca, there you are," he says, almost sounding relieved. "I need to speak with you." Ken leads me into his office and closes the door.

I raise my eyebrows in confusion as he locks it. *What's going on?*

"Nicholas's fiancée, Alison Price, is looking for you," he blurts.

She's looking for me? Despite the frigid looks she always seems to give me whenever I'm in her presence, I've never actually talked to her for more than five minutes. Although Friday night did nothing to put me in her good favor. At this point, I wouldn't be surprised if she thought I was screwing Nicholas. I mean, how do you justify getting angry and punching your best friend for kissing another woman who isn't you fiancée?

"Can you tell me why she's looking for me?" I ask feeling exhausted at the idea of having to talk to her when I'm not feeling well.

"Honestly? I think she's here to talk with you about the other night at *Riptide.*"

"What exactly makes you say that?"

"You should've seen her leave the club. She made a scene on her way out. She practically threw a tantrum—knocking over anything in her path. If she wasn't a VIP member, I'm pretty sure they would've thrown her out."

"Is she in the office?"

"She's in the building. I had Mary keep her downstairs until I got ahold of you. I thought it might be bad news. Mary said Alison is in a mood."

"Does Nicholas know she's here?"

"He's probably locked in his office working on the budget for the new fiscal year."

"Okay, well, I guess there's no hiding from her."

"Use my office," Ken says. "It will be more private than your cubicle."

"Thank you."

"Rebecca, I also wanted to tell you that I understand what went down at *Riptide*. I don't like it, but I know you just see me as a co-worker, and I'm not about to compete with Nicholas StoneHaven over you unless I have even the slightest chance of winning you," he says, searching my face. "I just don't want to see you get hurt like the other women who've worked here. Don't get caught up in his allure. Don't be like all of the other girls. You're different, and I mean that in the best possible way."

At first, I thought Ken's words would annoy me, but after every-thing he's done for me, I've realized some people have different ways of showing you they care. For my mother, it's bugging me about grandchildren; for Carol, it's hounding me about my feelings; and for Ken, it's warning me whether I want the warning or not. I should be thankful to have so many people who do care.

"I know you mean well, so thank you for worrying about me, but I'm okay. I can take care of myself," I say, taking his hand and squeezing it. "Thank you for caring enough to unnecessarily worry about me."

———

I t don't think it would've mattered if I would've accepted Ken's offer to use his office for privacy. Every head turns as Alison struts down the hallway toward my sad little corner cubicle. She flips her hair back and it flutters as if suspended momentarily by some imagi-nary wind. She must've been a model in some other life because she looks like one. Alison has the tall slender frame you would expect from most models, and she wears couture as if she were born into this world with it sewn to her body.

"Hello, Ms. Price. It's lovely to see you." *Lie. She's the last person I want to see.* In fact, I would be in heaven if she turned around and took her toothpick legs with her. "Nicholas isn't available at the moment. I believe he is in a meeting upstairs. Would you like me to take a message for you?" I really wish he was down here to take care of her himself. It's not like Mary couldn't call him to come meet Alison. She's usually good about calling him if she can't get ahold of me.

"I know he's unavailable because he's still in bed." The words are said with a sneer. Who knew something so ugly could come from someone so beautiful?

"Is he all right?" I feel stupid for not even knowing where the hell he is. I hope he's not sick. I'm starting to get chills and even my muscles are starting to ache. I knew one of us was bound to get sick wading through the heavy downpour from Friday night.

"He's fine. We were just discussing our wedding plans. We've decided to get married a few weeks after the gala in February."

Any words I might've said died in my throat at the sting of hers. *So much for Carol's theory that Nicholas wanted to talk because he's breaking off his engagement.* He probably wanted to talk to convince me to be with him despite his impending marriage to Alison. Nicholas never said he didn't want to be with me, and he never promised that I would be the only woman in his life. Deep down I knew this was coming, but I never expected it to hurt so much.

"So then how can I help you?" I ask, holding back tears. *Did he send her here to humiliate me?* Alison quirks a pristine eyebrow at me as she drops her bag onto my desk and steps so close that she's only a few feet away from me. The loud thud echoes down the hall like a small explosion going off. A sudden silence takes over the normal sound of shuffling and typing across the office. Without looking, I sense heads popping up from the cubicles behind me. My cheeks flame as all eyes turn to us.

"You can help me by staying away from my fiancé." Alison steps in front of my face and corners me in my cubicle.

"What the hell?"

"I won't have him distracted by his desperate-for-a-man assistant," she says.

My blood heats at the venom in her words. I bite the inside of my cheek, trying to hold back from saying something I'm bound to regret. *Keep your cool, Becca. Don't do anything to get you fired.* I feel light-headed as anger ripples through me. Ken steps into my fuzzy line of sight and I shake my head to warn him to stay away. The fury coming off Alison isn't aimed at anyone else but me, and I don't want Ken getting on her radar. I could've guessed that this awkward conversation was coming. Nicholas blew Alison off and told her to go home without an explanation. What woman wouldn't assume that something strange was going on? What I didn't expect was for her to come down here and treat me like trash. Any guilt I felt for sleeping with her fiancé is gone.

"We have a professional relationship. Nothing more."

"I've seen the way you look at him," she huffs. "If you think you think you can take him away from me, you're wrong."

For the first time since I met Alison, I actually feel sorry for her. She's childish and immature. Nicholas is her shiny new toy, and I can't help but wonder if she'll throw him away when she tires of him. I guess she's a woman who's used to getting what she wants, but she already has him, so I'm not sure why she's come down here to try to intimidate me. *She's already won.* My heart squeezes at the thought of Nicholas getting married so soon. I should be happy for him, right? Except I feel like my heart's being torn from my chest. I knew they were going to get married eventually, but it didn't feel real until now. Now it feels too real.

"There's nothing going on between your fiancé and me. I am his assistant, and that's where our relationship begins and ends."

"I will ruin you," she says, seething with anger. "Not only will you lose your job, but I'll make sure you don't ever work at any other publishing company in New York again." I don't doubt Alison for a second. She doesn't seem the type to make idle threats. Losing my job is out of the question. I'm not going to let her fuck everything up for me. I'm just beginning my career here and getting familiar with our departments, and on top of that, I need the money to help my parents.

"Is there something else I can help you with?" My patience is definitely wearing thin with this monstrous bitch.

"Stay out of our lives and we won't have a problem," she says, grabbing her bag.

"Believe me, I will."

Holding my temper as Alison sashays down the hallway takes every ounce of control I have. She leaves a bitter taste in my mouth that I immediately want to spit out. I really thought I was going to explode on her. That would've been lovely. *Oh, sorry, Nick. I didn't mean to punch your bitchy fiancée in the money-maker. Or did I? Yeah, I totally did.* Ken pops his head in my cubicle just in time to catch me flipping off Alison's back.

"I hated seeing her talk to you like that," he says, squeezing my shoulder.

If Alison's father is such a big investor for the company, then I can only assume pissing his daughter off would not be good for business or our own jobs.

"Alison can go choke on a dick."

Ken laughs. "But how do you really feel about her, Rebecca?"

"Sorry, she really got me going."

"You should've let me step in."

"It's better that you didn't. I'm sure if she wanted, she could have you fired."

My computer pings on my desktop, notifying me of a new e-mail. *Fuck.* It's an email from Nicholas. Irritation fills Ken's face at the email, but he shrugs and leaves me alone to open the message. My heart flutters at the subject line.

To: Rebecca
From: Nicholas F. StoneHaven
Subject: I want you for dinner.
Rebecca,
Meet me in the lobby. I'll pick you up at 5:30 PM.
If you don't show, I'll find you.
Xx,
Nicholas

Damn you. Damn those Xs—they get me every time. He's an idiot if he thinks I'm going out to dinner with him when his fiancée just badgered me for the last fifteen minutes. *No way in hell.*

Let him look for me. He'll be lucky if Carol doesn't call the police if he tries to come to the apartment. She's never going to let him near me when I tell her what happened with Alison. I delete the email and then permanently delete it from my trash. I'm just going to pretend like I never saw that.

41

REBECCA

By the end of my workday, I'm ready to go home and sink into my familiar quilted top mattress. I thought lunch would help get rid of the strange nausea that has assaulted my stomach, but it has only made it worse. *I'm sure I'll feel better with some sleep.*

Convinced that I'm over the worst bump in my day, I'm startled to see Miles Storm walking through the lobby of StoneHaven Publishing. He has some balls showing up here. I watch him from the elevator as he approaches Mary, the front desk receptionist. She eyes him, checks her clipboard, and then she does something that I've never seen her do to anyone. She tells him to *please* leave. I've heard of Nicholas putting paparazzi on the *No Access* list for the building, but I didn't think he'd put Miles on there. I'm guessing he didn't want him showing up here.

The elevator doors buzz at me as they try to close. *Move, woman.* Miles turns at the sound of the elevator ringing. I gulp as he immediately spots me. He waves at Mary and points over toward me. I hear him tell her that he's here for me. Miles ignores Mary's calls as she tells him to wait.

"Hey, Becca. I was hoping to catch you." My stomach rolls as his face breaks into a smile.

"What are you doing here?" I ask. From the corner of my eyes, I can see Mary running over to interrupt the conversation.

"I'm sorry, Ms. Gellar, but I've been strictly told not to allow this man in the building," she says with a frantic look.

"It's fine, Mary. He was just leaving."

Mary looks from me to Miles with an expression of uncertainty. She nods and heads back over to the reception area. Without hesitating, I make my way across the lobby and out the door. I know Miles is following me because I can hear the *swish* sound his jacket makes when his sleeves rub against his side, but I don't care. I don't want to deal with him tonight. Or any night, really.

I race out the front doors of StoneHaven Publishing and out into the bitter night. I'm still getting accustomed to having to wear a coat everywhere I go. Even a cold winter in Los Angeles is nothing compared to the temperature out here.

"Becca, wait!"

"What do you want?" I ask, pivoting toward him. Miles steps back, startled by the anger in my voice. He puts his hands up as if surrendering. People bustling by on their way home turn toward us with their curious stares as if waiting for a fight to break out. My cheeks flame in embarrassment. I don't want to deal with this anymore. I'm over it.

"I wanted a chance to speak with you..." He looks at me with an innocent countenance. "You know, without your overly possessive boyfriend hanging around."

"He's not my boyfriend."

"That's not how it seemed," he says. "Although, I'm not sure why you're interested in him at all."

"Miles, leave me alone. Go back to California or stay here. I don't give a care anymore." I need to get home. I'm starting to feel dizzy again.

"I'm just worried about you." Miles grabs my hand and pulls it to him. I shiver at the touch of his lips, but not in pleasure. His affection used to turn my world upside down, but now it's an ugly reminder of the years I wasted. Miles and I were together for so long that sometimes I forget he was a whole other person. He became an extension of me. We were two souls intertwined, until the moment we weren't and everything became a lot less clear and a lot more broken.

"I've done my research on this guy. He has women all over him. He's not someone you want to settle down with." The irony is that Nicholas is going to settle down with someone, it's just not going to be me. That reality hurts. Even if I don't want it to, it does. Nicholas draws me in like no one else. Every time I'm near him, my Run-Like-Hell list just flies out the window.

"But you're saying that you are?" I ask, rolling my eyes.

"Becca, I want to build a future together. I'm not like this guy." *Yeah, you're definitely not like him.* I'm beginning to realize that Nicholas falls under his own category. He doesn't fit in a box and I like that. "I made a mistake, but I love you. I want to marry you," he pleads.

"I don't love you anymore."

"What?"

"I don't love you anymore," I repeat.

"But I love you, and I'm willing to fight for us to prove it to you," he says. "I think if I could prove just how serious I am about us, you could let yourself love me back."

To my horror, Miles gets down on one knee and pulls out a black box. He opens it, and in the middle sits a beautiful pear cut diamond. A slow panic creeps up my chest and into my heart. My head begins to swim and my body goes weak as I sway to my right, barely catching myself from falling flat on my face. I hear Miles calling out and the feel of his fingers gripping my arm, but his voice is muffled. A slight ringing pierces my ear and then everything goes silent. The last thing I see is a shadow and two bright blue eyes blazing with anger in front of me. *Nicholas? Where did he come from?*

42

REBECCA

Two days later...

The rays streaming through the window blind me with an overwhelming gush of sunlight. My head pounds as I slowly sit up in a bed that seems vaguely familiar. I brush my hand along the side of my face and my temple aches beneath my touch. I grimace at the pain that shoots along the side of it. My skull feels like it's on fire. I survey the room around me, taking in the pastel colors and pictures adorned on the wall. It takes a moment for my foggy thoughts to clear, but not long after. I realize I'm in my room. *What happened?* It even hurts to think.

"How are you feeling?" I hear Carol's voice before I see her walk into my bedroom. "I've been so worried." The sight of her hits me hard. Her eyes are slightly watery like she's been crying.

"I feel like I got taken down by a sumo wrestler."

She laughs, causing me to wince as I smile back.

"You passed out."

"I passed out?"

"You don't remember?" I close my eyes, trying to recall the last thing I can remember, but everything feels fuzzy.

"I remember going to work, Nicholas's bitchy fiancée coming to the office, and then seeing Miles in the lobby... oh, god, I remember him proposing to me."

"Yeah, and somehow you forgot to tell me that he was even in New York, missy." Carol looks at me with disappointment, and immediately, I know I messed up by keeping it from her.

"I'm sorry, I just wanted to forget that he was here," I say, rubbing my face. Carol takes a seat on the edge of the bed beside me.

"You missed out on some drama. Your butt fainted when you were talking to Miles. Apparently, Nicholas was looking for you when he saw the whole thing go down. He thought Miles did something to make you fall and so he ended up punching him in the jaw."

"Holy shit."

"Yeah... The good news is your doctor said that you most likely fainted because you were upset and your body was already working overtime, trying to fight off the flu. Becca, I'm really surprised you didn't dent the damn sidewalk with your head."

"I'm glad I didn't. But it's true that I hadn't been feeling well all day."

"Yeah. You'll be fine. It does look like you'll have some bruises for a while. By the way, were you avoiding Nicholas? He mentioned that he asked you to dinner."

"Yes," I moan.

"Okay, why didn't you want to go?"

"Because I was afraid he would ask me to be with him."

Carol smiles. "And that's a bad thing... why?"

"His fiancée came to the office to tell me they're moving up the wedding and to stay the fuck away from him."

Carol rolls her eyes at the mere mention of Alison. I know if she's ever in the same room with her again, it's going to be a clash of the titans, but I don't doubt that Carol will knock the bitch out.

"What happened after I passed out? Did someone take me home?"

"Are you kidding me? Take you home? We were afraid that something was terribly wrong. Nicholas called 911, then he called me, and when they weren't coming fast enough, he took you to the hospital himself. We were so worried, until the doctor saw you. He told us you would be fine in a week or so."

"I feel like I've been asleep for days."

"You woke up a couple of times, but the pain medication that they gave you for the fall kept you knocked out."

"Did I say anything?"

"You spoke to Nicholas."

"I did?" I ask.

Carol winks and then laughs. "Yeah, you called him an asshole but I think he was just happy to see you wake up. Poor guy, he was such a wreck. I swear, he's nuts about you. He stayed with us at the hospital until they were ready to release you, and then he helped bring you home. I think the staff at the hospital got so tired of him complaining that they weren't moving fast enough, so they expedited the waiting process."

I blush at the thought of Nicholas making such a fuss over me. He does some unexpected things that are so sweet that I can't help but want to kiss and punch him all at once. I look down the open hallway, secretly hoping to see him.

"He's not here." Carol grins. "He did mention that he would try to stop by later this week to check on you. I told him it was probably better if he stayed away for a while. I don't think he likes that I told him what to do," she grins.

"That sounds like him."

"I forgot to tell you. Miles also stopped by."

I sit up, sending my pillows flying to the floor in one hurried swoop. "He was in our apartment?"

My memory after Miles showed up is a blacked-out blur of anxiety. I remember seeing his smiling face and feeling the familiar suffocation of being around him, but everything else was engulfed into a black abyss.

"I left him for a moment," Carol says, eyeing me wearily.

"What did he say?" I ask.

"Aren't you going to ask what I said?"

I look up at her with curiosity. *Shit, now I'm worried.* "What did you say?"

"Well, first I said he's lucky I don't punch him in the face. Fortunately, Nicholas already did that for me. And then—"

"Nicholas punched him?"

"Oh, yeah," she laughs. "I forgot to tell you that part. He decked him in the face after Miles let you fall. But between me and you, he probably did it because he saw him proposing to you."

"Great." He probably thinks I'm getting back together with that jerk.

"So, anyway, I laid into Miles for a while. I told him that he's an asshole for cheating on you and that he totally doesn't deserve you. He doesn't even deserve to breathe the same air as you. I also told him that he's lucky I wasn't there when you found him, or else he would've gotten kicked in his balls," she says, grinning.

"You said all that?" Tears form at the corners of my eyes. I never thought threatening someone with bodily harm would sound so sweet, but somehow it does coming from Carol.

"Of course. Do you think I'm going to let some douche treat my best friend like she's just some toilet he can shit all over?"

"Nice metaphor," I laugh.

"I love you, Becca." Carol leans in, hugging me. "You deserve better."

43

NICHOLAS

After a week of being unable to see Rebecca, I'm desperate to even catch a glimpse of those familiar red strands and hypnotic green eyes. I call Mary, my receptionist, to let her know that I'm going to be late to the office. I need to make a quick stop to see how Rebecca is doing. I hope she's still not feeling sick.

After repeatedly harassing her best friend, Carol, I'm finally able to convince her to let me come by. I'm relieved to know that I have something to look forward to today. For the past few days, I've been worrying that Rebecca wouldn't come back to work. Or worse, that she'd come back only to tell me that she's moving back to Los Angeles and getting back together with her ex. I've contemplated having Striker keep watch at her apartment just in case Miles comes back, but I'm confident it won't do anything to calm my nerves. I know I would spend my day calling Striker to see if he's shown up, and that's probably not the best use of my time.

My heart pounds like a jackhammer as I step out of my car and head toward the front of Rebecca and Carol's building. Outside, the air is chilly, despite the large coat that I'm wearing, but as I step inside the apartment building, I feel a rush of heat bloom over my skin. I'm all nerves. *Fuck.* I can't think of the last time I felt butterflies in my stomach like this. *Is this how she feels when I'm around her?* I can only hope. To be honest, I can't think of a better way to welcome the weekend than seeing Rebecca, especially following such a hellish week.

I knock twice and Carol opens the door with a curious stare.

"Hi, Nicholas," she says, welcoming me in. Her eyes drift suspiciously to the box of chocolates in my hand. I wanted to bring her something and I'd already sent flowers, so I stopped by a local chocolatier shop to pick something up. I wasn't sure if Rebecca was the dark chocolate or milk chocolate kind so I got a mixed box of truffles. I'm just hoping she isn't allergic to anything in them.

"They're for Rebecca." I hand her the box and she quickly places them in the kitchen.

"I'm sure she'll love them," she says, walking back toward me.

I glance around the apartment hoping to see my fiery assistant, but my excitement fades when I realize that she's nowhere in sight. I know Rebecca is probably resting, but I was hoping to see her up and about. I've been worrying all week.

"She's in her room," Carol says, reading my expression. "I'm actually glad you came when you did because Miles just stopped by." The sound of his name has me grinding my teeth. *That son of a bitch. What the hell was he doing here?* Carol smiles smugly at the sight of me clenching my fists.

"That was an ugly split lip you gave him," she says, as she gestures for me to take a seat on the couch.

"Yes, it was," I grumble.

I'm going to murder him. In fact, I'm fairly certain I would have the night I found him proposing to her. The only thing that stopped me was the sight of Rebecca falling. Seeing her lying on the ground brought me back to memories of my brother connected to a respirator and lying unconscious in a hospital bed all over again. The anger I felt overpowered any clear thoughts I had. Miles never saw me coming and I took advantage of it. I had been on my way out of a meeting when Mary warned me that we had a visitor in the building by the last name of Storm.

The blood that had spewed from Miles's mouth is just one of the ways I wanted to hurt him. Watching his hands all over Rebecca unleashed a rage inside of me. It was just his bad luck that he was standing between us.

"Would you like some coffee?" Carol's voice draws me back from my murderous thoughts.

"That would be lovely, Ms. Livingston."

She heads back toward the kitchen and I watch anxiously as she pours two cups of coffee. The thought of seeing Rebecca feels just like Christmas coming early. I can't stand being away from her any longer. It's killing me just sitting here knowing that she's in the other room. *Has she missed me as much as I've missed her?* Either way, I don't intend to be away from her any longer. The past week has been torturous enough.

"Here you go." Carol places a mug onto the coffee table between us and slides it to me.

"Thank you."

"Would you like some sugar?" she asks, studying my face.

I lean over the table and take the mug. Usually, I'm more than happy to have a cup of coffee, but I get the feeling that an awkward conversation is destined to follow this cup.

"No, thank you. I like mine black." I watch as she sits herself directly across from me as if I'm an interviewee and she's the one who's here to determine if I'm worthy of hiring, or rather, if I'm worthy enough for her best friend.

Carol's glare pierces me for a two good minutes before she decides to set her cup down and break the awkward silence. I watch as she sweeps her long brown hair from her face and crosses her legs. I can only imagine what kind of boss she would be. Firm? Easy to anger? Or perhaps confident and relaxed. Either way, I understand now why Tristan hired her. She's a woman with a backbone of steel.

"What's going on with you and Rebecca?" I can hear the patience slowly draining from her voice as she begins her interrogation. To be honest, I'm not even sure if Carol likes me, but my guess is that she at least pities me enough to let me come see her best friend. Not that I would even let her keep me from seeing Rebecca.

"That's something I need to speak with her about," I say, shrugging off Carol's watchful gaze.

"If you hurt her, I will cut your balls off."

My eyebrows shoot up in surprise at the threatening promise in her words. *Talk about brutal honesty.* I didn't expect Ms. Livingston to lay her cards on the table right off the bat, but I guess I shouldn't be surprised. She doesn't seem the type to take any bullshit. She's shrewd, but not in a bad way. I think most business people would consider that a quality of a successful person. *My father sure would.*

"I have no intention of hurting Rebecca."

"What are your intentions?" Carol asks, crossing her arms.

"Things are complicated right now."

"So un-complicate them."

"I wish it was that easy."

"I think it is," she says in a challenging tone.

I smile. She's persistent. I'll give her that. I hold back a chuckle as she drums her fingers on the top of her leg, waiting for my response.

"How are plans going for the art gallery?" I ask, trying to focus her attention on something else.

"Don't even try to change the subject."

"Is that your way of telling me that I need to start talking?"

"Precisely," she says with a quirk of an eyebrow.

Carol is stubborn in nature, but so am I. I think she's genuinely surprised when I stonewall her during her little interrogation. After several minutes of having her give me her best death glare, she gives up.

———

I find Rebecca lying asleep on her bed in her dimly lit bedroom. The long strands of her red hair are braided into one long mass that's pulled back from her face. A pang shoots through my chest as I spot small bruises on her arms. They must be from the fall. The marks are yellowing like they're almost healed, but the sight of them makes me ill with worry. My mind goes straight to the memory of punching Miles. *I didn't hit that fucker hard enough.*

I roll the black office chair from Rebecca's computer desk to the edge of her bed. The chair screeches and I wince at the thought of waking Rebecca. She probably needs all the rest she can get. Just when I think I'm safe to sit, she moans softly and rolls to her side so that she's facing me. I suck in a shaky breath as I reach over and trace my thumb across her lips. *I miss her. My little fire goddess.*

44

REBECCA

His raspy voice calls to me in the middle of my sleep, and I wake to find Nicholas sitting mere inches from my bed. My chest instantly aches at the sight of his disheveled appearance. *What's going on?* The large circles under his eyes stand out even in my darkened bedroom. I look down to find his tie and jacket missing from his usual ensemble. Today, even the fitted gray shirt and black pants he's sporting look off, and his hair is styled in a ruffled mess. Despite the shock on my face, Nicholas just smiles in appreciation as his gaze slides over me. I blush. My raised nipples tell me that my sheer nightie doesn't stand a chance under his heated gaze.

His cool fingers reach out and brush my cheek with tenderness sending a rush of adrenaline through my body, and it immediately feels ten degrees hotter. His gesture reminds me of the moment when I first met him. My skin heats at the memory of not being able to keep my hands off his face. *He must've thought I was so strange.*

"You're here," I mumble as I force myself to sit up from the bed. Nicholas leans forward, helping to place a pillow behind me for support.

After talking with Carol about what went down the night Miles came by the office, I can't help but feel that nervous tick in Nicholas's presence. He punched Miles in the jaw, and I'm not really sure how to feel about it. It thrills me more than it should that he cares enough to physically fight-off unwanted attention. But I'm also worried that he's in too deep to safely keep a handle on the reality of the situation. I'm not sure I'm fairing much better.

"I wanted to stop by before going to the office. How you are feeling?" he asks.

"I'm okay. My body still aches something fierce." I immediately regret the words as a grim look spreads across his face. I want to laugh and reassure him that I'm fine, but I have a feeling that it would only anger him.

"How's everything at work?" I ask, hoping that the change in subject will erase the frown on his handsome face.

"It's strange not having you around..."

His words remind me that it's been over a week since I've been to the office. While the time away from the office, at first, seemed like a blessing in disguise, I can honestly say I miss being useful, even if it means menial tasks like answering emails, making photocopies, or running errands for Nicholas. I'm starting to get cabin fever trapped inside this apartment. I can only watch so many daytime dramas before I want to poke my eyes out. But I'm stuck for at least another few days. The doctor insisted I fully recuperate before returning to work, but I don't know if I'll last another day.

Nicholas shifts to sit on the edge of the bed and I wince at the sudden movement. His eyebrows lift in concern and I quickly smile, hoping to ease his tension.

"Are you sure you don't miss me because you just enjoy telling me what to do?" I joke.

"No, it's more than that." I watch as a slow grin reaches his electric blue eyes. *Liar.* He loves telling me what to do. My mind drifts to wicked memories of him bending me over his desk. I hate to admit, the thought of that happening again excites me.

"When you get back, we have to talk about the gala," he says.

"Yes, of course." I'm thankful to have something to look forward to working on. I know it's going to be difficult working side by side with Nicholas, considering his fiancée threatened to get me fired if she even thinks that something is going on between us. It crushes me knowing that his actual wedding date has been set. I know it shouldn't, but it does. I can't picture him marrying a cold fish like Alison.

"Do you know what you're going to wear to the gala?"

"I don't know. Maybe a red devil?" I laugh.

"Very fitting, Ms. Gellar."

"And you?"

"I'm thinking Poe's *The Red Death*."

"How very gothic of you."

"It fits my mood as of late," he mumbles.

Carol's words about Nicholas punching Miles in the jaw comes rushing back to me. Why exactly did he punch Miles? He wasn't hurting me physically, though he did make me feel horribly uncomfortable. He's probably pissed that he showed up where I work. I still can't believe Miles tried proposing to me in the middle of the sidewalk, or that a flood of New Yorkers didn't scream at him to move, let alone push him out of the way.

"Rebecca, there's something else I need to speak to you about."

"Okay..." I look up to find Nicholas staring at me intently.

"I don't want you seeing *him* anymore," he says in a commanding tone.

I know exactly who 'him' is. I shouldn't be pissed off that he's saying this, because in reality, I have no intention of seeing Miles ever again. But it still annoys the hell out of me that Nicholas thinks he has the right to demand anything of me in regards to my personal life. Maybe I should tell him that I don't want him seeing Alison anymore. Right, like that would do any good. It would just get me fired and Nicholas disinherited.

But still, he has no right asking me not to see anyone. I might have a head injury, but I didn't magically forget about Alison showing up at the office to tell me that they're getting married after the gala. What's even worse is she threatened me about my job in front of the entire office floor. Why would he think he has any say in whomever I see? He never made threats toward Ken, and it was obvious Nicholas plans to go through with his marriage to Alison. I just need Nicholas to forget about us. I need to forget about us. So if he wants to think that there's something between Miles and me, then let him.

"I will see who I want to see." His eyes widen in surprise at my words. A look of disappointment and then sheer anger floods his face.

"Why do you want to continue to see that fucker?" His words come out clipped. "He cheated on you and fucked someone else."

"No one's perfect," I point out.

"No, but anyone who treats you like he did doesn't deserve you."

"It's really none of your concern."

"Where were you going with him?" he asks.

"Nowhere."

"Is that really how we're going to play this?"

"No, Nicholas, I don't play games. You do. I'm tired of all of this drama. You want to treat me like I'm yours, but I'm not. Please just go. Don't worry. I'll be back at work as soon as the doctor releases me."

Nicholas stands, looking wounded from my words. His gaze pierces me for only a moment before he turns and strides across the room. I watch him stop at my door as if poised to say something, but then he seems to quickly change his mind and leaves. I hear the front door slam slightly and the sound of Carol's heels scurrying over toward my room. She was probably listening to our whole exchange.

45

NICHOLAS

My whole world has deflated to a miserable existence. I leave Rebecca's apartment fuming with anger. I feel like a giant asshole. Instead of just telling her how I feel, I fucked it all up by telling her I didn't want her to see her ex. The worst part is now I'm starting to think that Rebecca still has feelings for him. *Why?* How could she be so naïve to think that he would care for and respect her after he broke her heart? It kills me to think that she still thinks about that fucker, and I could kick myself for leaving her apartment without working things out.

The main lobby in our building is quiet, despite it being so close to the holidays. Fridays are usually chaotic with calls about the company printers breaking or our network in the building going down, but today, everything seems calm.

"Good afternoon, Mr. StoneHaven," Mary says, greeting me from behind the front reception desk. She hands me a copy of *The New York Times,* a cup of black coffee, and my meeting schedule for the day. Her eyes flicker up in surprise at my unkempt appearance.

"Sir, are you all right?"

"I'm fine, Mary. I just need this day to be over."

"You'll be glad to know your schedule isn't overbooked," she says.

I'm grateful for the small break from all the department meetings

I've been swamped with this week. My father insisted that I attend each one, and I have, but they have been nothing but exhausting. On top of everything else, I haven't really had the time to sit down with him to discuss breaking off my engagement. It's not something I can just email him about or catch him on the way to a meeting. No, this conversation needs to be well thought out and structured.

I think I've had an easier time preparing for a business proposal than preparing myself for this conversation with my father. The few times I've run into him, he's been on his way out or into a meeting. I never realized how little I actually see of him during the week. At least I know I'll see him for our pre-Christmas dinner that we have at my apartment. That should give me some time to speak with him. The offices will be closed so this might be the best chance to talk to him. Plus, it's closer to Christmas, the season of peace and joy, though I have a feeling that my father is not going to be too forgiving.

"Is my father in by chance?"

"No, sir. He's actually in a meeting with Mr. Price. He asked me to tell you to stop by his attorney's office to discuss your marriage contract."

That damn contract. Has Alison said something to my father?

"Also, this came in the mail today." Mary hands me an ivory envelope. My heart slams against my chest at the sight of Alison's and my name written in cursive on the front of it. *What the hell?* I flip it over and find a candlewax mold of the letter S sealing the envelope closed. Is this what I think it is? I rip it open, nearly destroying the contents inside. To my utter horror, a wedding invitation sits inside.

Mr. and Mrs. Grayson Price
request the honor of your presence
at the marriage of their daughter
Alison Lee Price to Nicholas Fitzgerald StoneHaven
on Saturday, the twentieth of February
at six o'clock in the evening.
Plaza Hotel
New York, New York

Reception to follow.

"Sir? Are you all right?" Mary asks, stepping over toward me. "You look pale."

"Has Ms. Price called?" I barely manage to get the words out without exploding from anger. Alison sent out invitations to a wedding that I told her would never happen. Now half of New York thinks I'm getting married, and what's worse, I know she did this to spite me.

———

"Alison, what the fuck is this?" I ask, trying my best not to scream in the middle of the damn sandwich shop. She flinches at the irritation in my voice. Her eyes briefly scan the area around us like she's expecting someone to join us. It didn't take as much convincing as I thought it would for Alison to agree to meet me for lunch. When I brought up the invitations over the phone, she feigned ignorance, blaming the company that was in charge of printing them. I know better than to believe her bullshit excuse. She knew exactly what she was doing.

"I thought I made myself perfectly clear." I grip my knee to keep myself from slamming my fist across the table. I'm livid, to the say the least. Every time I try to take one step forward in moving past all of this, something has to go and mess it all up. I'll be lucky if Rebecca doesn't somehow receive an invitation.

"I'm not giving up on us." Alison runs one long manicured fingernail across my arm. I flinch beneath her touch and she immediately pulls her hand away, offended by my abruptness. "You obviously aren't ready to give up on us either. I know you haven't spoken to your father," she huffs.

It's not because I haven't tried. "My father is coming over this week," I say.

"She doesn't love you. Not like I do," Alison pleads.

"This needs to stop. I don't want to hurt you, but—"

Alison snakes her arms around my neck and pulls me into a kiss. My first instinct is to pull back, but she grips my neck tightly, squeezing me to her. A flurry of white flashes showers us before I'm finally able to pull away from the kiss. Her face breaks into a smile as I spot a group of photographers on the outside of the entrance to the restaurant. *Fuck! Did she call the paparazzi?*

"What the hell is this?" I seethe.

"I'm just clearing up some loose ends, sweetie. You can forget about your trampy little assistant when she sees those pictures in the paper. Once she's out of the way, maybe you can finally manage to get yourself back on track with our plans."

46

REBECCA

"Wake up. Now. You are going to stop being so damn depressed."

"I am not depressed," I moan, rolling in bed and burying my face in my pillow. It's Sunday, a day dedicated to rest and moping around in nothing but PJs, but Carol still denies me the privilege of sleeping in until my heart's content. She wakes me at nine a.m. with a rough shake and the rich smell of freshly made donuts. *Damn it, Carol.* I sigh inwardly at the knowledge that my best friend could be a fairly awesome assassin if she wanted. She knows my kryptonite —fluffy maple donuts. I'm sure she sent her driver, Steven, for them.

I'm tempted to toss her butt off my bed, but I can't resist the sweet smell of deep fried dough. It calls to me.

"You are deeply depressed. I brought you maple donuts and you're not even tackling me to the floor to get them. I know you're still pissed over Nicholas."

"Ugh."

She's right. I was glad to see Nicholas on Friday, up until the point where he demanded that I not see Miles anymore. It is just another reminder that Nicholas and I shouldn't be anywhere near each other. There's far too much at risk for the both of us.

"Here," Carol says, shoving a greasy white donut bag in my face.

Wait a second. I must look pretty bad if she bought donuts. I made Carol promise to help me lose a few pounds before the gala, and she said she would if I stuck to her 'diet' — a.k.a. her horrendous version of juicing. I don't know how, but Carol always finds the smelliest veggies to mix in our shakes. It probably doesn't help that she's been mixing them with prune juice. I'm really surprised I haven't shit my pants yet, although I think I may have come close a couple of times.

"You know you want some."

"Damn you for tempting me," I say.

Carol places the greasy bag on my nightstand and pulls back my bed covers, baring me to the cold room.

"Now eat your sugary dough and get dressed. We're going shopping before all of the tourists steal all the good deals on dresses."

"And why am I buying a dress?" I complain.

"Well, you're going to Tristan Knight's gallery opening. It's in a little over week, and you still don't have a dress for the gala for work."

"Shit. You're right, but I don't think I'm up for shopping."

"C'mon, Becca. It will help get your mind off him."

I sigh. "I'm not so sure anything is going to help."

———

"Wow, you look great!" Carol says, telling me to spin around. After four hours, my feet are exhausted and most likely covered in blisters from walking in circles at *Macy's*, but I'm happy to admit that Carol was right to suggest going shopping. The dress I bought for the gala is a beautiful crimson fabric embroidered with crystals that look like diamonds.

Carol was dead serious when she said we were going shopping. So serious, in fact, that Steven had to help us carry her twenty-something bags in from the car. As for me, I was as frugal as I could be with the limited amount of money I have left in my checking. I'm actually surprised I found a dress for the gala and for Tristan's event. With Carol's help, I picked out a forest green swing dress for the opening of the gallery. It's perfect and definitely, something I would wear again.

"Are you sure the red one looks all right?" I ask as Carol riffles through her bags of dresses. She looks up with a sneaky smile.

"Yes, I'm sure. You are going to look gorgeous. By the way, it's good you didn't buy any heels, because I have some that will go perfect with your costume."

Carol walks over to her room and reappears a moment later holding a silver shoebox. "A client of mine gave them to me. She bought them in Paris."

I watch in anticipation as Carol removes the glass-like heels encrusted with white crystals. I slip the pair on and they fit snuggly on my foot. *It must be meant to be.* They're going to look perfect with my dress.

"It sounds like your phone is going off in your purse," Carol says, waving over to my purse on the other end of the couch.

I scramble over just in time to pick up the call on the final ring. A smile breaks free from my lips as my father's phone number flashes across the screen.

"Rebecca? Are you there?"

The sound of his voice and the familiar warm tone immediately makes me homesick. It's been far too long since I've seen my parents. This Christmas will be the first one I'll spend without them.

"Dad, is that you?" I smile into the receiver at the sound of his hearty chuckle. It's the kind that effortlessly fills a room with cheer. I can almost picture him sitting in his La-Z-Boy chair, wearing the tattered UCLA pajamas I bought him, and flipping through the television stations looking for something gory to watch. I used to love watching cheesy seventies horror flicks with him. Our favorite was George A. Romero's *Dawn of the Dead.*

"It's me, cupcake. It's good to hear my little girl. You sound so different."

"Different? A good different or a bad?" I ask with curiosity.

"Good. Really good. I guess living away from your mother probably helps." I know he's joking, but in a way, I think he's right. Living on my own, or at least with another roommate near my age, has given me a taste of real independence.

"How's mom treating you?"

"Oh, fine, you know... she thinks I'm depressed," he grumbles.

"Are you?"

"No. It's just finding a job isn't as easy as it used to be, but something will come up."

Guilt plagues me, eating away at my conscience. Here I am, just coming back from a shopping spree, when my parents aren't even able to pay for their house. I've been tempted to take a part-time job at the *Books N' Nooks* store, but I'm not sure how I would have the energy. I want to help my parents, but I'm not sure if I'm even making a dent in their problem.

"I get paid in a couple of days. I'll send you guys a check." I try my best to sound reassuring, but by the exasperated sigh, he can probably tell I'm exhausted.

"Becca, that's actually why I called, I don't want you sending us money anymore. I wish I would've known sooner about your mother taking the money, but she said it was money she was pulling from her 401K."

"You guys need it," I argue.

"And so do you. I don't even know how you're eating. Are you eating?"

I have been eating somewhat healthy, thanks to Carol. She refuses to let me eat the forty-one-cent noodles from the supermarket for meals. Sure, I can't afford fancy dinners or visit all of the places that I want to see in New York, but there's still time for all of that. In a few months, I'll have a permanent position at StoneHaven Publishing with an incredible salary, or so it's been indicated on the employee job portal.

"Rebecca?" he warns.

I laugh at the worried tone in my father's voice. "Yes, Dad. I'm eating."

"I don't want you wasting your money." As much as I would like to be saving my money, I don't want to see my parents lose my childhood home.

"What are you and Mom going to do?"

"Let us worry about that." I hear the faint sound of my mother's frantic voice filling the background. My father's voice is muffled for a moment, but I can hear him yelling over to my mother. "Your mother is back from the grocery store. I'll call you later, cupcake."

"Okay." From my father's long sigh, I can tell he's just as reluctant to hang up as I am. *I miss seeing them.* "I love you, Dad."

As I end the call, I notice a new text message in my message inbox. My breath hitches at the sight of Miles's text. I thought Nicholas punching him in the jaw was enough to deter him from bothering me again, but I was wrong.

Miles: Becca, I'm sorry for what happened. Can I please see you?

47

NICHOLAS

Tristan greets me at the front of the *CrossFit* gym with the promise of helping me clear my head for at least an hour. For the first forty minutes, he makes good on his promise. We hit the weight machines, and the only thing that fills my thoughts is the pain that courses through my muscles each time I push them just a little further. We're almost near the end of our session when Tristan screws it all up by bringing up Alison's name.

"So I got your wedding invitation." Tristan glances sideways at me as I do another rep of arm curls.

"Alison sent them. I didn't." I groan as I let go of the handle for the arm curl weights. Thinking about Alison just makes me furious. She's only made the situation worse by using the paparazzi against me. Calling off the wedding won't be easy, and now that the invitations are out, people will be expecting an actual wedding. It isn't just a rumor anymore.

"I sort of figured since the last time we talked you were punching me in the face for kissing your assistant."

I finish with my arm curls and walk over to a nearby squat machine. Tristan stares at me waiting for my acknowledgement, but I simply ignore him. I know I owe him an apology, but I've realized that if he was so sure of my feelings for Rebecca, he shouldn't have touched her. He should've known what was going to happen. We grew up together and he knows my temper, and yet he still provoked me.

"So let me guess, you came to your senses and you realized you're in love with her." Tristan grins as he adds more weights to my squat machine.

Okay, now I'm starting not to feel so sorry for punching him in the face. When I called Tristan to see if he was free to meet me for a quick workout, I thought it might be time to put what happened at *Riptide* behind us. Not that we haven't spoken, he's the only person I called, besides Carol, after I took Rebecca to the hospital, but for the most part, he's been giving me my space. I guess it helps that he's been busy preparing for the opening of his gallery, too.

"You make it hard to feel bad about punching you." I grit my teeth as I bend my knees and lift the bar onto my shoulders.

"Is that finally your apology?" he says, amused. "Took you long enough."

After two weeks, Tristan's bruised eye is nothing more than a faded memory. Somehow, he managed to avoid an awkward conversation with my father and sister, and for that, I'm grateful. I'm already nervous about telling my father about calling off the engagement, and I still need to figure out what the hell I'm going to say to Rebecca to tell her I'm sorry. I don't need to add anything else to that already heaping pile.

"That's probably the best you'll get from me," I admit. "Especially when you patronize me." I lean into another squat and slowly rise back up. Tristan stands nearby to spot me.

"It was worth it," he laughs. "How else were you going to realize how blind you were?"

"It doesn't matter anymore. She's with someone else." The words spill bitterly from my mouth. Tristan helps me place the bar back in the holder behind me and I clear the machine for the next person to use. He walks over and hands me bottled water from his gym bag.

"Who? Is she with one of your employees? Is it the guy that was with her at *Riptide*?"

"No. An ex fiancé from back home." I take a swig of water and then head toward one of the treadmills. Maybe some running will help get the sinking feeling out of my chest.

"Hold up, so she told you she's getting back with her ex? The ex you told me about who lives in California?"

"Yes, well, not exactly. He's in New York right now."

"What exactly did she tell you?"

"Something about it being none of my business." I wipe off a trail of sweat that runs from my neck across my back with my gym towel.

"What did you say to make her say that?" he asks.

"I told her I didn't want her seeing her ex-fiancé anymore."

Tristan chuckles and I'm tempted to punch him in the face again. This is definitely *not* funny.

"Nick, you should know by now that she's not the type to be told what to do. Even I can see that, and I haven't been around her as much as you have."

"I don't want to see her with that idiot. He was trying to get back with her the night I took her to the hospital."

"She's not stupid enough to go back with him. On top of that, she's in love with you."

Tristan's words fill my chest with warmth. I want to believe that she is, but Rebecca is confusing sometimes. There are days when I think she hates me, and then there are days that I'm almost certain she feels the same way I do.

"I wanted to tell her how I feel, but I fucked up."

"That just means you better buy her a really nice gift for Christmas," Tristan says, grinning. "She'll forgive you. I don't think she's used to being loved by someone like you."

"What are you saying?" I scoff.

"You love fiercely." Tristan smiles as he pats me on the shoulder. "But it's one of your best qualities."

48

REBECCA

It's two days until Christmas, and the office is a chaotic mess of employees scrambling to finish their work before the holiday. My work has been an endless chain of emails, filing of paperwork, and replying to press inquiries for our upcoming gala, which is little over a month away. Over the past several days, I've received more than 100 calls on my office line asking for Nicholas. It seems that everyone is waiting until the last minute to call him with their inquiries, and he's been too busy with company meetings to get back to anyone.

"Ms. Rebecca Gellar?"

I look up to see a pretty brunette wearing a gray blazer and skirt standing in front of my cubicle. She wears a badge with the name *Selene* on it, but it looks nothing like the ones we wear at work. I shove aside the stack of papers on my desk before giving her my full attention. She must think I'm a pig with my cubicle looking like it was hit by a windstorm. I can't blame her.

"I'm sorry if I'm interrupting you," she says warily.

"No, it's fine. Can I help you?"

"Yes, I was given instructions to give you this." She extends her hand, holding a single red bag toward me. "Merry Christmas."

She flashes me a smile before walking away heading toward the elevator. I stare at the bright red bag that has a single gold letter: R. *Who would get me a gift? Carol?* No, I told her not to get me anything when we went shopping at Macy's. *Oh, god. I hope it's not from Miles.* I haven't seen him since the *incident* and I couldn't be happier about it, although that's not to say that I haven't gotten more text messages from him. This morning he sent me two more asking if I would go with him to a party for New Year's Eve. I immediately deleted his texts. Later tonight, I'll have to figure out how to block his number.

I call after the pretty brunette, but she walks through the elevator doors before I have a chance to catch her. After staring at the bag through my lunch break, I decide to take a peek at what's inside. Buried toward the middle of the bag I find a card with eerily familiar handwriting. *Shit. Is this from Nicholas?* I rip it open, to find only two words written in heavy print:

Merry Xx-mas.

If the card was from anyone else, I would laugh at the misspelling of the slang for Christmas, but I know who this gift is from, and I also know that he didn't accidentally misspell it. No, Nicholas has a thing for his double X's. I slowly remove the pink tissue paper from inside. *What if there's something embarrassing? Frilly Lingerie? Dildos?* Okay, Nicholas wouldn't buy me a dildo, but it could still be something embarrassing.

At the bottom of the bag is a long, white box with my name engraved in shiny gold lettering. I slowly remove the top, holding my breath in anticipation. To my surprise, there is a white Venetian mask in the middle of it, shining brightly up at me. I lean back in shock at the flawless beauty of the mask and its encrusted frame. *Holy shit, are those real diamonds?* It sits there taunting me, begging me to try it on. I don't think I've ever had anyone give me such an expensive gift. This must be his way of apologizing for being an asshole.

"Whoa. Who bought you that?" Ken asks, walking into the break room.

"No one," I squeak. I close the box and throw it back into the bright red bag.

"Okay... I'm glad to see you back at the office. We missed you around here."

"We?" I ask, looking at the empty lunchroom around me. I barely speak to anyone on the floor so I'm pretty sure no one missed me.

"Okay, I missed you," he says, blushing profusely. "You sort of brought the color out in the office. Without you, it's sort of just…"

"Gray?" I offer. What is it about New Yorkers and their gray suits? Everywhere I go I'm surrounded by masses of gray, whether I'm walking down the street or taking the subway. I guess after almost two months, I'm still not used to the absence of colorful Los Angeles.

"Exactly." Ken smiles and hands me an envelope. "So what are your plans for our time off? Any special plans for Christmas or New Year's Eve?

"I'm not sure. I would like to visit my parents, but I don't have the funds to fly to Los Angeles, and Nicholas said he was going to have me working through the holidays because I messed up his vacation plans."

"I think he was bluffing," he laughs.

I know what my plans are for tonight. I'm going straight over to Nicholas's apartment and returning this damn gift. It's far too expensive, and I'm pretty sure his gifts aren't the kind that comes without strings attached.

———

After work, I find my way back to Nicholas's massive limestone mansion, or as he calls it—his apartment. Snow peppers the hedges that line the majestic building behind the black cast-iron gates. Somehow, the upscale neighborhood that surrounds it looks desolate, despite the slew of tourists and holiday shoppers that have invaded the icy streets of New York. Perhaps most of the residents here are on holiday vacations. *I wouldn't doubt it.* Anyone who lives here must have more money than God if they own an apartment in this part of the city.

To my surprise, a festive snowman flickers inside Nicholas's apartment window. I didn't take him as the type to put up holiday decorations, but then again, I didn't expect him to get me an early Christmas present, either. I knock on his door twice and wait, half expecting to see Alison's bitchy face. My heartbeat quickens at the sound of his muffled voice coming through the door. I look down at the small, red gift bag in my hand, and for a second, I regret coming here. *This is stupid.* I should've just left it on his desk or something. I hesitate a moment longer before turning to go back home.

"Rebecca?" Nicholas's voice calls to me and I turn to find him standing at his door.

The smell of freshly baked cookies wafts through the door. The sight of Nicholas in a snowman apron over a crisp, white dress shirt and black slacks hits me full force. He looks like he just stepped out of a role-reversal from a 1950's catalog.

49

REBECCA

I bite back a laugh as I spot the red oven mitt on his left hand. His blue eyes go wide in surprise and his mouth opens as if he's about to say something, but nothing comes out. A faint rush of red kisses his nose and cheeks. I don't think I've ever seen him look embarrassed. I'm guessing he doesn't usually wear things like this at home. He looks down and spots the red gift bag in my hand. I shove it into his hand and then focus my attention at the empty space behind him.

"I just came by to return this to you. It's too much, and I can't accept it."

"It was a gift. I—"

"Who is it?" A petite blonde woman with striking aquamarine-colored eyes pops into view, cutting Nicholas off. For a moment, disappointment fills me at the sight of another woman in his apartment, but it quickly evaporates as a familiar smile lights up her face. *I know her from somewhere.* Her gaze washes over me in curiosity before looking up at Nick. We wait for him to say something, but Nicholas keeps his eyes trained on me as he grips my present.

"Well, obviously she's not Tristan," she says, smiling as she elbows Nicholas. *Could she be his sister? She seems to be very comfortable with him.* Nicholas's silence is starting to make me feel uncomfortable. I can sense an awkwardness filling the space. *Why is he being so quiet? This is already embarrassing enough.*

I find myself apologizing for no reason. "I'm sorry. I didn't mean to intrude... I... just wanted to drop the gift off on my way home." *Lie.* It isn't a gift for him and his apartment is out of my way. It's actually past Carol's and my apartment.

"Come inside, please? We were just about to have dinner," he says, giving me an apologetic smile as he holds open the door.

"Uh." *Fuck.* "I should probably go." If Alison sees me here, it will only cause more trouble for me.

"I insist that you stay," Nicholas says, as he grasps my elbow. "And this was a, gift. I'm not taking it back." He hands me back the red gift bag and I suppress my embarrassment as I shove it in my coat pocket.

"The dining room is this way." The pretty young blonde gestures for me to come inside, and the only word I manage to get out before I'm steered in is, *"Okay."*

"This is my sister, Emily," Nicholas says, motioning toward the young woman. That explains the familiar model-like features. "Emily, this is my assistant. Rebecca."

She takes my hand and shakes it with vigor. "It's nice to meet you." A wide grin lights up Emily's face. "I've heard so much about you."

I blush. Nicholas has probably told her how I'm a big pain in the ass. "Thank you, it's lovely to meet you, as well."

"Come inside, Nick was checking on our chocolate chip cookies." *He bakes?*

"Here, I'll take your coat." Emily says, grabbing it and hanging it in a nearby walk-in closet.

"Thank you."

Emily and Nicholas lead me through the limestone mansion toward the dining room. I swallow the lump of nerves in my throat as Nicholas follows closely behind me. The air inside this apartment suddenly feels very thin. He brushes up against me, and I'm immediately caught off guard as he rests his hand just above my hip. The sensation strikes me with the memory of dragging him home from the Lit for Kids event. My cheeks heat at the need that fills my lower half. I haven't been able to forget the night of the Lit for Kids event and the way he slipped his fingers inside me and rocked me to an orgasm on the icy ledge of the balcony.

Something happened that night that propelled us to this moment. This awkward moment where we try to tiptoe around the giant-ass elephant in the middle of the freakin' room. God, I miss the feeling of being ravaged by him. Nicholas squeezes my hip and then releases. I exhale and hope to God that I didn't just say that aloud instead of just thinking it.

We step into the dining room and my eyes are immediately drawn to the walls. They're textured stucco and painted a Tuscan-orange with brown accents. The color is rustic and lovely and warm, and coincidentally, it reminds me of home, and the feeling of digging my toes in warm sand. That's probably the thing I miss the most about California, and I haven't had a chance to go to any of the beaches out here. Not that they would be any fun to go to in the winter.

In the center of the room is a round, wooden table surrounded by five cream-colored chairs. Above the table hangs a black cast iron chandelier completing the rustic character of the entire room. Whoever designed this room put a lot of love and care into what they wanted it to look like. I can't help but wonder if Nicholas designed it himself, or if he had someone else do it.

Nicholas clears his throat, and I turn to find myself inches from his father. Stefan's salt and pepper eyebrows shoot up at me in surprise. He walks over from the kitchen and greets me with a warm smile and a quick handshake.

"Hello, Ms. Gellar. I'm surprised to see you here." A curious look crosses his face and I'm not sure if he's pleased or annoyed to see me here.

"I came by to..."

"She came by to drop off some files. I invited her to stay," Nicholas says.

"Well, it's nice to see you, Rebecca."

I smile to myself. "Thank you."

He wasn't expecting to see me, and I definitely wasn't expecting him. This can't be good. I hope Alison hasn't told him anything about what went on with Nicholas and me. No, I doubt he would be greeting me so warmly if that were the case.

"Is Alison joining us for our Christmas celebration?" Emily asks.

Nicholas looks over at me. "No, she had a family obligation to attend to." I sense a feeling of dissatisfaction from Nicholas's father.

"You celebrate Christmas the day before Christmas Eve?" I ask, hoping to lighten the tension.

"We always celebrate Christmas the day before," Nicholas explains. "It tends to slip by us if we don't."

Emily sighs. "Dad and Nick are always busy at the office."

Nicholas smiles. "We try to catch up on as much work as we can during the holidays."

The sound of knocking echoes throughout apartment, interrupting us.

"That must be Tristan," Stefan says. "Emily, why don't you get the door so your brother can bring dinner?"

"Sure," Emily says quietly. Her easy smile is replaced with a nervous one. I watch her get up and quietly walk down the hallway. Just before she disappears around the corner, she stops to smooth out her dress and hair. Her nervous gesture piques my curiosity. Tristan is Nicholas and Emily's brother, but not by blood. In fact, I'm not even sure when he was adopted into the family, but it must be strange growing up with a good-looking adoptive brother.

———

After dinner, Stefan and Tristan wander into the living room with talks of single-malt scotch and the fireplace while Emily follows them in under the guise of putting finishing touches on the Christmas tree.

"Let me help you clean up," I offer to Nicholas.

We head toward his kitchen as I help him clear the dining room table of dinner plates. The meal he prepared was simple, yet probably the most delicious thing I've eaten since I've been in New York. The baked honey-glazed salmon went well with the rosemary and garlic potatoes. In fact, I'm pretty sure I made a fool of myself when I practically licked my plate clean. It was definitely better than the microwave-friendly food I've been eating.

"Where did you learn to cook like that?"

My stomach flutters as Nicholas flashes me a smile and then winks. "I have my secrets," he says as he moves the cookies from the cooling rack onto a plate.

"Don't let him fool you," Tristan says, interrupting us as he walks into the kitchen. He sets an empty salad bowl on top of the counter and pats Nicholas on the back. "He learned from the best."

"Who's that?" I smile.

"Me."

Nicholas throws him exaggerated eye roll. "Tristan taught me one dish and ever since, he's claimed the title of being my teacher."

Tristan laughs as he takes a bottle of Moscato from Nicholas's wine cooler, pops the cork, and pours a glass. He offers a glass to me and I sip it slowly, savoring the sweetness.

"The one thing I can't take credit for is his baking skills," Tristan says. "You should taste one of these." Tristan grabs a cookie and plops it in his mouth before excusing himself. Nicholas stares after him in look of mild irritation as he walks back into the dining room.

"Did your mother teach you how to bake?" I ask.

"I taught myself," Nicholas says, smiling sadly. "We don't have a lot of traditions, but we try to keep the ones we do have. My mother used to make the best chocolate chip cookies for Christmas, and Emily loved them but after she left, the tradition went with her."

"When did you decide to learn then?"

"After my brother died, there weren't a lot of memories to make this season bright for us. So two years ago, I decided to try to resurrect some of our old traditions. This is one of them."

"It's a good tradition." I smile.

"Here, try one." He holds one to my mouth, and for a second, I hesitate. The thought of anyone hand-feeding me makes me feel like a little girl. He holds it closer and I lean forward, taking a bite from the cookie. Warm chocolate oozes from the piece as it fills my mouth. *It's heavenly.* Somehow, Nicholas baked the cookie to the perfect texture. It's not too hard or too soft. I quickly move my hand to wipe my face of the chocolate that stains the corner of my lips, but Nicholas stops me.

I look up and his piercing blue eyes scan my face as he reaches up and lightly wipes the chocolate off. My lips part and I pucker them, kissing his finger. I can't explain why I did it, but my body responds before I have time to think about the repercussions of my actions. His pupils dilate and his breath goes shallow. He steps forward, never taking his hand from my face. I feel myself slowly back toward the sink. His hips lean into mine, and I can feel him growing hard against me. My heart beats chaotically as he presses harder against me. I know what's coming, but I don't have the willpower to stop him.

50

NICHOLAS

Rebecca gulps and it takes all my strength not to chuckle at her nervous response to me. I close the space between us, letting her feel the effect she has on me. She kisses my finger, and immediately my body aches to be against her. Her green eyes widen as I place my thumb at the entrance of her mouth. She parts her lips once more and I slip my thumb in. Without asking, she sucks it. *Fuck.* Her eyes close as her warm mouth envelops my thumb. My cock throbs as a moan escapes her lips. *I can't take it anymore.*

"Rebecca, you're killing me. My family is out there waiting for dessert." My voice is probably strained from all the blood rushing to my cock. I'm going to have to wear a cone to hide my erection.

"I'm sorry. I don't know what came over me," she admits, pulling back from me and trying to step around me. Her face is flushed in embarrassment.

"I know. It's the same thing that happens to me every time you walk in the room." I grab her waist and kiss her. Her lips are hesitant at first, but she opens up, letting me run my tongue along her bottom lip. I slide my hands up her dress and she gasps as I run my tongue down the side of her neck, trailing kisses on my way back up. Rebecca's soft moan and the feel of her nails digging into my hair only encourage me.

"Nicholas?"

Her voice brings me back to my senses. "What is it, Becca?" I pull back, peering down at her flushed face and the desire mirrored in her eyes.

"Nothing. It's nothing."

Her eyes trace mine as I push back a lovely red tendril from her sweet face.

"I never thanked you for bringing me to the hospital," she blurts. "Carol said you were the one who drove me there, and I didn't properly thank you for doing that."

"Shhh."

"Are you trying to shut me up?" She laughs.

"I can think of a better way of getting that job done."

"I bet," she says with an eye-roll.

"Nicholas? Rebecca? Are you guys bringing the desser–oh hey, uh...?" A sheepish grin spreads across Tristan's face as he stumbles in on us. "Your dad and Emily are waiting on dessert. They're starting to threaten mutiny." Tristan rubs the back of his neck, apparently not knowing what else to say.

Rebecca blushes and I reluctantly drop my hands from her. It seems like every time we get a moment alone, it doesn't seem to last. I watch as she straightens out her dress and grabs the tray of cookies from the countertop. Tristan holds open the door that divides the kitchen and dining room for her as she heads out.

"Nick, next time you might want to wait until your dad and sister are gone before you seduce your assistant," he winks.

"Have I ever told you that you're an asshole?"

Tristan laughs. "Love you, too, buddy."

———

My father's gaze glides over me as I enter the dining room carrying a pitcher of milk. Without saying a word, I sense a strange tension emitting off him. His glance sways to Rebecca and then back toward me. Panic filters through my chest, as his face turns red. *He's angry.* I set down the milk next to Emily and take a seat on the opposite side of my father. His eyes never stray from mine.

"Nick, you're not going to have any of these cookies?" Emily asks.

"He's already had his dessert," Tristan says, piping in. From the corner of my eye, I can see Rebecca's cheeks flaming red at his words. *Fuck.*

"Nicholas, can I speak with you in private?" My father clears his throat and the room goes completely silent as all eyes turn to me. I watch as he rises from his chair and exits the dining room in a few quick strides. Tristan stares after him in shock before turning toward me with an apologetic frown. I expected to speak with my father about my feelings for Rebecca, but I wasn't prepared for him to figure it out on his own.

I find my father standing inside my study, surveying the stacks of books I've collected over the years for my own personal library. He turns as I step into the room, and the look on his face is enough to tell me that this conversation is not going to end well.

"What's going on with you two?" father asks, glaring at me with suspicion.

The words hang in the air for several minutes before I'm able to put my scattered thoughts together. I've been waiting more than two weeks to speak with him, and now I have my chance.

"I love her," I confess. There it is. The words I've been longing to say to her, except here I am confessing them to my father. He stares back at me in confusion as if the thought of my loving someone never occurred to him.

"You can't be in love with your assistant, Nicholas. You're engaged to Alison Price." He paces the room as if trying to grasp what's been going on around him, stopping only to shake his head in exasperation.

"I'm only engaged to Alison because you forced me into it. I have no desire whatsoever to marry her."

"Nicholas, this is ridiculous. If you told me you had an affair with your assistant, I would understand. But you're not breaking off your engagement over this," he says, throwing up his hands.

"Even if she makes me happy?"

"Alison could make you just as happy if you let her. Do you even know if Rebecca feels the same way about you? You're risking an awful lot for a woman you barely know."

It's true. I haven't known Rebecca as long as I've known Alison, but I've been around Gellar enough to know that I'm crazy about her. Maybe I'm an idiot and this is all one colossal mistake, but I'm taking a risk on someone that would make me happy and that I could make happy.

"Here's what it comes down to, son. Either you marry Ms. Price, or I will disinherit you, and you will lose any claim you have over this company."

The cruelty of his words sends my head into a tailspin. The loving father who used to play Moonlight Sonata for us as children is gone, replaced by the cold and unyielding man standing in front of me. Perhaps my mother is to blame for his destructive attitude on life, or maybe this is just the result of his love for money.

"I'll give you until the new year to decide. And Nick, just remember that your life isn't the only one being affected by this choice."

He leaves without another word, and it isn't until I hear the front door slam that reality sinks in. I just gave him ample reason to fire Rebecca. His words plague me as I stand inside my study. If Rebecca doesn't feel the same way about me, I just ruined her career. And if she does, I'm about to lose everything I've worked for these past five years. I never thought loving someone would cost so much.

51

REBECCA

wkward. It's the only word that comes to mind the moment Tristan walks in on our heated embrace. Worse were the words tumbling from his mouth when we sat back down in the dining room. I know they're meant as a jest, but from the abrupt way Nicholas's father leaves the room, they must have triggered something in his mind. Or maybe my expression gave something away. Nicholas has a way of affecting me even without my consent. The angry glare that flooded his father's face left me with a feeling of suffocation. I'm afraid to know what is going through his head. It can't be good.

Alison's words come rushing back to me. *'I'll make sure you don't ever work at any other publishing company in New York again.' Did she tell him something?* Perhaps my presence was just confirmation of his suspicions. Either way, I shouldn't have come here. There isn't a work-related explanation as to why I'm here tonight. In reality, I just wanted to return the gift Nicholas bought me before going home. While it's lovely, it's not something you give to a woman who's just supposed to be your assistant. And it's certainly not something you give to a woman who isn't your fiancée—at least not in my mind. In the kitchen, I let my emotions get the better of me. After hearing about Nicholas' mother, I couldn't help but feel an overwhelming sense of loss for him. I understand now why the holidays seem to be so difficult for him and his family.

Even after so many years, it seems the wounds he carries are still fresh. It's a startling reminder that I need to keep my guard up. Wounds aren't so easily healed. Not when your heart is involved.

"What's going on?" Emily asks, looking over at Tristan. The muffled voices coming from Nicholas's study increase in volume by the second. I'm thankful I can't make out the content of their conversation, although from the look on Tristan's face it's undoubtedly about me.

"I'm not sure." He glances toward me.

"I think I should get going," I say. "It's getting late." I don't know Tristan as well as Nicholas, but I'm pretty sure he doesn't want to say anything in front of me.

"I'll drive you home," he says, standing.

"Thank you."

"It was lovely meeting you, Rebecca." Emily slips several cookies into a plastic container and hands it to me. "I hope to see you soon."

"She's coming to my gallery opening." Tristan flashes me a dazzling grin. "Aren't you?"

"I am," I say, mustering half of a smile. Emily's arms wrap around me as she gives me a quick but hearty embrace. The welcoming warmth that radiates from her fills me with a strange sense of comfort. I've always been disappointed at being the only child in my family. My parents had me and I guess they were satisfied with one kid, although I think it would've been nice to have a sister, or even a brother. I can only imagine how fun it must've been growing up with older brothers like Nicholas and Tristan.

At the front door, Emily helps me slip on my coat. We're nearly out the door when the sound of their father's voice startles the three of us. The door of the study swings open and I turn to find him striding toward us. Stefan stops in front of me as if ready to say something, but instead, he swiftly kisses his daughter goodnight and nods a goodbye to us before rushing out the door. I flush at the awkward scene before me. *He must know now.* And if he does, I'm surprised he didn't fire me on the spot. Maybe the conversation was related to something else. I know I'm being naïve, but I'm still hopeful that I'm right.

My gaze drifts back toward the study and my heart nearly crumbles at the sight of him hunched over his chair with his head in his hands. An intense pang shoots through my chest rendering me breathless. I want to go to him, but it would be a tragic mistake for both us. Emily clears her throat, excusing herself as she walks to Nicholas in the next room.

"Tristan, could you take me home now?" I ask. He looks at me with a questioning gaze before reluctantly nodding *yes.*

As soon as Tristan grabs his coat and keys, I practically sprint out the door to get away from the scene inside. The ride home from Nicholas' apartment is silent with the exception of the classical music Tristan plays in the background of the car. Several times, I catch his glance swaying over toward me before finally returning to the wet streets in front of us. The anxiety he radiates is nearly palpable, and it eats away at my soul. He doesn't understand what's happening between Nicholas and me, and I can sense his disappointment at choosing to leave rather than staying to talk to Nick about what happened between him and his father. I should've stayed with him, but I just can't get any more involved.

————

B ack at home, I find a voice message from Miles waiting for me on my cell phone. His tone in the voicemail seems impatient, even agitated. I haven't bothered answering any of his texts. I don't see the point in talking to him when I have no desire to revive what we had, but it hasn't stopped him from trying to contact me.

Becca, where are you? I've tried calling you several times. I've even stopped by the apartment, but you're either gone or working. I need to see you. Can we get together over Christmas? Maybe we can go see the Rockefeller Center Christmas Tree? You used to talk about wanting to go there. Call me.

52

NICHOLAS

THREE DAYS LATER...

Emily walks into my study with a worried expression fixed across her face. I haven't left my apartment in what seems like decades. In fact, I'm resolved to spending the rest of my life reading in my library, as long at the liquor cabinet is replenished, but Emily seems to have other plans for me. She's been trying to get me to eat, and she refuses to leave me alone, despite my reassuring her that I'm perfectly fine. I guess the several glasses of whiskey aren't very comforting.

She winces at the sight of me splayed out across my leather couch. I must look like I feel. *A fucking mess.* She sets down the tray of food and takes a seat next to my feet. She stares at me as she waits for me to acknowledge her.

"Nick?"

"Yeah, Em?" I roll to my side as a wave of nausea rushes over me.

"Why are you torturing yourself? What did Dad say?"

I turn toward her, and the sight of her sad expression hurts like hell. My sister is lucky. She's yet to experience the cruelty of my father's expectations. He's always been so lenient with Emily. She chose to major in Journalism at NYU, and my father didn't bat an eyelash.

"He gave me an ultimatum. He said if I don't marry Alison, then he'll disinherit me."

"This is probably a dumb question, but you don't love her, do you?"

"It's not dumb, but no. No, I don't."

"Is there someone else?" she asks, hopeful.

"Yes," I groan. "You met her the other night."

A funny little smile plays across her lips. "Your assistant? I thought so."

"Is it that obvious?" I slowly sit up, hoping the new position will help alleviate the growing ache in my head. Emily gives me a quick hug and a grin frames her mouth as she pushes back my messy locks of hair.

"You look at her the way Alex used to look at Nina."

My brother would probably be so disappointed in me right now. He worked with my father to build StoneHaven Publishing, and now we might lose one of our biggest investors because of me.

"Stop it," Emily says, nudging my shoulder.

"Stop what?"

"I can hear you blaming yourself."

"How can I not?"

"I don't want Dad to disinherit you, but you should be able to love whomever you want. If she's worth the risk of losing everything, you should ask her to marry you."

"I think you've just always wanted a sister, even if she's just a sister-in-law," I laugh, groaning inwardly at the building pressure spreading across my forehead.

Emily giggles. "Well, I can't deny that. It would be nice having another female in the family to talk to."

"I'm sure the two of you would get along well."

"She seems really nice and if she makes you happy, that's all that really matters. I think you guys look good together."

"The problem is she won't have me." The thought of Rebecca rejecting me sends a surge of dread through me. Over the past few days, I've convinced myself that maybe it's better if I keep my distance from her. Since I've met Rebecca, she's been pushing me away. I know the situation with Alison has probably had a large hand in that, but I can't help but think that maybe she doesn't feel the same way about me as I do her. *Could my father be right about her?* I've never been one to doubt myself with women, and yet I find myself doubting every step I take with Rebecca.

"You'll never know, unless you ask her."

———

An hour later, I find myself wandering by the front of Tiffany's contemplating my future and the woman I'm desperate to have to be a part of it. If I asked Rebecca to marry me and she says yes, then I'm destined to start my life all over again. While that means being cut-off financially from the company and my family, it doesn't mean we'll be desolate. I learned enough from my father to invest in companies that are worthwhile. In fact, if I wanted to, I could start my own independent publishing company. Of course, it would be minuscule compared to my father's empire, but all companies have to start somewhere. The alternative is living the life my father has mandated for me, and marrying a woman that I feel absolutely nothing for.

"Good evening, Mr. StoneHaven." A young, blonde associate greets me at the front of the sleek gray Tiffany & Co. building. Her broad smile widens, telling me that she's more than just a little excited to be helping me. I can only guess what kind of commission she makes on engagement rings. When I spoke with her over the phone and she heard me say my name, she practically squealed with excitement.

"Thank you for staying open late."

"Of course, we're more than willing to go out of our way for our customers." Her eyes trail over me with an uncomfortable degree of interest. "My name is Stephanie and I will be the one assisting you tonight."

"Perfect. I'm here to purchase an engagement ring for my fiancée."

"Is there a specific cut you're interested in?"

"I was leaning toward an emerald-cut." After doing some quick research online, I'm convinced that an emerald-cut diamond would be the perfect shape for Rebecca. She seems to be a fan of old-fashioned styles, and I think it would suit her beautifully.

"A very elegant choice. Let me show you the different types we have on display," she says, leading me toward the back of the store.

After an hour of looking at rings, we've narrowed my selection down to two different rings. The first is platinum solitaire with a large emerald–cut center diamond. The second is an emerald-cut center diamond with a diamond border and several diamonds running down the sides of the band. I'm starting to regret not asking my sister to come choose the ring with me. She probably has a better grasp on which ring a woman would want more.

"Is your fiancée the flashy type?" Stephanie asks.

"No, she's hard not to notice, but she doesn't purposely draw attention to herself."

"Can I make a recommendation then?" Stephanie asks.

"Of course."

"Take the first one. The emerald cut is simple but classic with a single platinum band. You can't go wrong," she says, winking.

"Actually, I think it would be great if I had my assistant come to your store after the holiday and take a look at the rings. I would love if you could get her opinion on them."

"Of course, we would be more than happy to."

I leave the store feeling hopeful that when I ask Rebecca to marry me, she'll say yes. I don't think I can go back to my life if she doesn't.

53

REBECCA

Over Christmas, Miles calls me several times before finally getting the hint that I'm not interested in seeing him. Or at least it seems that way until he shows up at the apartment on Saturday night, drunk and staggering. To my dismay, Carol is out shopping for groceries when I find him waiting outside, mumbling to himself.

The shameless smile on his face tells me he's more than forgotten the incident that happened the last time I saw him, but I can't say the same. He pushes his way inside my apartment before I have a chance to tell him to leave.

"Hey, baby, it's good to see you again," he says as he sways slightly toward me.

"Miles, what are you doing here? I need you to leave. Now." He resists me as I try to push him back out the door. A panic creeps over my skin. I've been alone for the last half hour and Carol still isn't back. She said she would be in and out of the store. "Please. Go."

"You're only saying that because that other asshole is trying to get in between us." His words run into each other in one long slur.

"There is no *us*," I say, exasperated. His eyes perk in surprise at my anger.

"Do you think you could be happy with him?" Miles stalks toward me and he grabs my waist in a painful grip. It's not the loving touch that I'm used to feeling when Nicholas puts his hands on me.

"Carol will be here any moment, and if I don't call the police, she will," I warn.

"I just want to talk. You've been avoiding me for the past several weeks and your boyfriend has banned me from visiting you at work."

"He had every reason to," I fire back.

"So he is your boyfriend?" Miles smirks at me. "I bet you didn't see him sticking his tongue down another woman's throat."

I flinch at his words. "What are you talking about?"

Mile sneers at me as he removes a folded up article from his jacket. "I saved it because I thought you might need proof that he doesn't give a shit about you." He hands me the clipping and I unfold it to find a picture of Alison and Nicholas kissing at a restaurant. My eyes water at their passionate embrace and the way Alison's hands are wrapped around Nicholas's neck. Miles is wrong. It's not just some woman. It's his fiancée. There's nothing wrong with this picture, besides the fact that I wish it were I with him, not her.

I feel a cold shiver as Miles wraps his arms around me and pulls me into an embrace. He leans in, pressing a sloppy kiss against my lips, and I recoil in disgust. Suddenly, I realize that the man I used to love, my college sweetheart and the handsome young actor with brown locks, has been replaced by a less than pleasant version. He's a sloppy version of his former self. *What did I see in him? Why was I so in love with the idea of us?*

"Let's go in the bedroom and rekindle what we had, Becca."

I roll my eyes at the cheesy words that sound like a one-liner from one of his TV shows. "You're an idiot."

"You're such a bitch now. You let New York change you. Your mother said you worked at some big publishing company, but I bet she doesn't know that you whored your way to the top."

His words send a violent flood of anger through me. I pull out of his grasp, but he grabs my wrist and drags me back into him so that my bottom is pressed against his pelvis. My father once taught me that if a man attacked me from behind, the best thing to do is jam my heels in between his toes and then aim my elbow toward the groin.

"If you don't get the fuck out of my apartment now, I'm going to break your face," I say, pushing back.

"Oh, really?" he says, laughing at me. The feeling of his hand slithering down my hips is the last straw. He shrieks in pain as my heel connects with his foot and my elbow hits him right in the groin. The feeling that pulses through me can only be described at pure elation. That and adrenaline. Miles immediately hunches over as he clutches himself and whimpers in pain.

———

"Oh, my god, Becca. Are you all right?"

Carol runs over to me, throwing her hands around my shoulders as the police officer finishes his notes on my statement. She nearly tosses the bag of groceries on top of him, but he steps back just in time to avoid being hit in the face.

"I saw the police car outside the building. I thought something horrible happened."

"Don't worry. You won't be seeing my story on *Law and Order: SVU*."

"Did he hurt you?" she asks.

"Minor bruises, but I'm okay."

I knew hitting Miles in the balls wouldn't be the end of his harassment. Lucky for me, it seems he had already racked up some complaints from women who lived in the same building where he was crashing. I wasn't the first woman he'd harassed tonight, but I am glad I'm the last.

"Did they already cart that asshole away?" I get the feeling that if I hadn't finished the job, Carol would've been more than happy to kick his ass.

"Yeah, he's being booked as we speak."

"That probably won't be a pretty headline in the papers. I would hate to be his publicist."

"Yeah," I sigh. "Tomorrow I should probably file a restraining order."

"Do you want me to get you something?" Carol says, rubbing my shoulder. "You seem really tense."

"I'm okay, I'm just exhausted."

"I could call Nicholas if you want." I smile at Carol's attempt to make me feel better. If there is anyone I want to see, it would be him, but after seeing the newspaper clipping of him and Alison kissing, I think it's better to maintain my distance. Maybe once they're married it will be easier to let go of Nicholas and focus on moving forward in my career.

54

NICHOLAS

I t's New Year's Eve and the city is overrun with tourists. When Carol calls asking if I can drive Rebecca to the opening of *Trinity*, I jump at the chance to have a moment alone with her again. Over the past week, I haven't stopped thinking about her. I know that I'm going to ask Rebecca to marry me, but I'm not sure that any time before the gala would feel right. I don't want to rush asking her if my attention is needed on the upcoming gala.

With the offices closed for the holidays, I haven't been able to see Rebecca, making my anxiety about the situation that much worse. I could've followed through with my threat to have her work through the holiday with me, but I realized it's probably not a good start if I'm trying to fix things with her.

I'm eager to tell Rebecca how I feel, but I'm also dreading the possibility that with one word, she can either shatter my world or make it complete. I've thought about how I'm going to ask her and what I'm going to say, but it seems any words that I come up with pale in comparison to how I really feel about her.

I sit anxiously in my car outside of her apartment building, waiting for her to step out. Every minute that passes feels like an eternity as my heart thunders against my ribcage in anticipation of just being near her again. Just when I think I'm mentally prepared to see her again, the sight of her in a dark green dress and her hair in cascades of majestic curls knocks the wind out of me. *How am I ever going to get through tonight?*

55

REBECCA

I step out of my apartment building to find Nicholas waiting for me. My body hums as I take in the rich sight of his coat and dark blue suit fitted against his tall, muscular frame. He leans against the top of his sleek, red Ferrari as if he's posing for some millionaire's sports magazine. His hair looks wet and combed back like he just stepped out of the shower. Images of his naked torso flash through my mind and heat my blood. I have no idea who tailors his clothes, but they certainly know what they're doing.

Carol said she was sending Steven to pick me up to take me to the gallery opening, but he's more than fifteen minutes late. Something tells me she may have been lying about who was going to pick me up.

Nicholas looks up from his phone and a slow smile spreads across his face as he spots me. He slips his black driving gloves in his pocket and walks toward me. My nipples prickle at the way his eyes wash over me. I'm wearing my dark green swing dress and a shawl but he makes it seem like I'm standing in nothing but my bra and panties.

"You look beautiful," he says, offering his arm as I step down the stairs in front. Despite my best attempt to not go weak at the knees by his mere presence, I fail miserably, almost toppling over.

"Careful," he says as he steadies me before I fall face first onto the sidewalk. The presence of his fingers around my waist only makes my thought process even fuzzier.

"Thank you. What are you doing here?"

"Carol said you needed a ride and she had already given her driver the night off, so I offered to pick you up." That makes perfect sense. No one wants to spend his or her night driving someone around, at least not on New Year's Eve.

"Shall we go?" he asks, gesturing to his car.

"Sure."

Up close, the red Ferrari is a magnificent specimen of machinery. I've never actually seen a Ferrari this close up. Usually they were whipping past me on the 101 Freeway when I lived in Los Angeles. I know from overhearing Miles talk about cars that just to buy one is over two hundred grand. I can only imagine how much it costs to maintain a car like this.

"Is this new?" I ask.

Nicholas smiles. "It was a gift... Come on, I'll let you drive." He walks over to the car and opens the driver's side. My breath catches as it lifts open like a butterfly wing. I peer through the open door to the inside. It's covered in beautiful tan Italian leather.

"I can't," I say.

"You don't know how to drive stick shift?"

I smile at his question. Having a truck driver for a dad has its perks and learning how to drive stick shift is one of them. In fact, growing up it was one of his requirements when it came to learning how to drive.

"Oh, no, I do. I just can't drive this. What if something happens to it?"

I've never driven anything so expensive. I don't even want to know how much it would take to repair if I accidentally bumped it or scratched the paint. I'm sure Nicholas could afford to buy several more of these cars, but I would rather not be the reason he has to.

"Are you always such a good girl?" Nicholas teases. I find myself laughing at the mischief behind his eyes. He lifts an eyebrow at me as if daring me to say yes.

Yes. "No."

"Get in."

I roll my eyes at his commanding tone as he extends his hand and helps me into the car. The first thing that hits me is the smell of leather and the lingering scent of his cologne. An image of riding Nicholas flashes in my mind. I shift in my seat, squeezing my knees together as I will the image away. He slides in the seat beside me and suddenly, the car seems way too small. The seats recline back, giving the illusion of being in a space ship. I can't help but feel a little claustrophobic as the doors close shut.

"Rebecca? Are you all right?"

"I'm fine," I murmur.

"You're gripping the steering wheel like it's going to fly off and your eyes are closed."

"I'll be okay. Give me a minute." I inhale and exhale slowly, willing my nerves to calm. Delicious warmth spreads over my knee as Nicholas's hand squeezes it. I open my eyes and my heart flip-flops at the closeness of his mouth to mine. He leans forward as if to kiss me, and for a moment, I freeze. I stare into two mesmerizing blue eyes. His gaze never strays from mine as his hand slides over to the steering wheel. I hear keys jingling in the background, and the sound of the car starting. It's a faint zooming sound.

I look forward and try my best to steady my breathing. Nicholas leans back into his seat, but he doesn't take his eyes off me.

"Cold?" he asks, half smiling. *Well played, Nick.* I exhale, trying my best not to pay attention to the tingling sensation progressing up from my knee. *Is he testing my boundaries on purpose?* I shiver as he slides his hand down my shoulder. *Focus, Rebecca. If you crash this car, Nicholas will probably never forgive you.*

"I'm fine."

"Good, I wouldn't want you to be uncomfortable."

"Does your car have a name?" I ask, quickly changing the subject. He looks down thoughtfully and then back up at me.

"Her name is Red."

I laugh. "That's a color, not a name."

"Well, I like it," he says, resting his hand behind my seat.

"Why is it a *she* anyway?" I say, trying my best to ignore the closeness of his hand near my neck.

"Because she purrs like a pus—"

"I get it," I say, silencing his lips with my fingers. He seems to like throwing that word around. A chuckle erupts from Nicholas as he grabs my hand. I blush at the sound and at the look on his face. I'm sure he revels in the thought of making me uncomfortable. His hold is warm and soft, and I'm not sure I even want him to go.

"We should probably head out before it starts raining again," he says, letting my hand go but not before placing a soft kiss just above my knuckles.

"That's a good idea," I stutter. "I hate driving in the rain."

"You'll be fine. The gallery isn't too far. Plus, I promised Carol I would get you there in one piece. She threatened to chop off my balls if I didn't."

"She is a little overprotective." I laugh at the image of Carol impatiently waiting in front of *Trinity* for me to arrive.

"Just a little?" he says with a smirk. I'm sure Carol would be proud that her protective nature has Nicholas walking on eggshells.

We head down the wet street of Park Avenue toward SoHo. I drive slowly, trying my best to avoid pedestrians darting through the congested traffic. I'm glad we left an hour early because the streets are jam-packed, and many are even closed for the festivities as visitors and New Yorkers flock toward the New Year's celebrations in Times Square. I am a little bit envious of them. I've always wanted to stand in that crowd during the final countdown and watch the ball drop. It's not the same just watching it on TV. There's something magical about everyone's gleeful expressions, even in the freezing weather that always made me want to go.

I smile as Sam Smith's *Stay with Me* starts playing on the radio. It sounds crystal-clear coming through the premium audio system of the sleek Ferrari. I've always been a fan of piano-heavy songs.

"Rebecca?" Nicholas's husky voice interrupts my thoughts. He leans over and turns on the defroster. The windows of the Ferrari are fogging up with the cold outside and the warm heat on the inside.

"Yes?"

"Thank you for letting me take you tonight."

I smile. "Well, I guess I sort of needed a ride anyway."

———

It's beginning to rain like it's the end of days, and the road ahead is starting to look like one giant ocean of black. We've been driving for nearly 40 minutes in almost complete silence and each minute has been torturous. There are so many things I'm bursting to say, but all of them involve ending the night in Nicholas's arms. Just as I'm about to give up hope of ever finding this damn gallery, it appears on my right. I swerve, barely missing another car as I try not to completely pass the entrance. *Shit.* Nicholas watches me with a smile.

"Sorry."

"You're cute when you worry." Nicholas laughs.

"Are you making fun of my driving skills?"

"Not at all." From the corner of my eye, I can see Nicholas grinning. He's totally making fun of my driving. *Jerk.* I would cry for an eternity if someone scratched or dented my two-hundred-thousand dollar car.

I pull to the front of the building, silently praying that it will give us a shorter run to the front entrance. The gallery is an elegant space that sits smack in the middle of several other glass-like structures. Surprisingly, the surrounding shops on the street are lively, despite being only a few short hours from the New Year.

"So have you been here before?" I ask, hoping to break the silence between us.

"This is my first visit. Tristan's kept everything under wraps. He refused to let me see it before the opening."

"I'm surprised he didn't want your opinion."

"He knows I would've given him a hard time about the location."

"I don't think we're going to make it inside without getting drenched."

"Hold on, I have an umbrella somewhere." Nicholas reaches behind his seat and pulls out a giant black umbrella. "Give me second and I'll come get you."

"Okay, sure." The passenger door of the car lifts open and Nicholas immediately jumps out and runs over to my side. For a moment, I'm caught in the rain as he lifts open the car door. Water splashes inside, wetting the bottom of the car. *Oh, shit.*

"Nicholas, the inside of the car is getting drenched." Nicholas appears at my side to help me step out of the car.

"Don't worry about the car," he says, covering me with his umbrella. A trickle of pleasure overwhelms me as he pulls me up toward him. For a moment, everything goes still, and the only sound I hear is the frantic rhythm of my heart and his ragged breath. I'll admit that staying away from Nicholas hasn't been the easiest, but I wonder if it's been just as hard for him. Nicholas places a hand to my cheek and caresses my skin. He doesn't say a word, but his eyes give away everything. He takes his thumb and trails it across my bottom lip. His eyes never move from my lips and I shiver at the heat coming off him. A crack of thunder slices through the tension and he immediately releases me and pulls away. A flood of disappointment and then relief washes over me. I've often wished I could just flush him out of my heart, but he always seems to find his way back in.

"Let's get inside before we're drenched," he says.

"Sure." I pull away, leaving enough distance between us so that we're not immediately touching.

Carol stands just inside the entrance of the gallery, greeting guests as they make their way inside the glass palace that is *Trinity Art Gallery*. Her face beams with exuberance as we walk through the entrance adorned in white crystals. She's wearing a beautiful plum dress that flows all the way to the floor, and the color makes her tanned skin glow. I smile at the way her hair is done in an up-do. She took my advice and went to have her hair done. Ringlets flow down the side of her face, reminding me of one of Jane Austen's characters from the Regency Era.

Tristan appears at Carol's side holding an information pamphlet with his picture on it. The man is breathtaking in an impeccably tailored black suit with an open-collared shirt. From the top opening, I can see a hint of his toned chest. His dark hair is combed forward giving him a youthful look. I never realized how long his eyelashes were until now. They frame his eyes perfectly.

"Rebecca, I'm so glad you could come celebrate the opening of my gallery," he says, embracing me with a warm smile.

"Thank you for inviting me. It's beautiful."

"Nick, glad to see you, as well." The two men shake hands before turning their attention back to us.

Carol steps forward, giving me a quick hug. "Are you okay?" she whispers in my ear.

"I'm fine." I smile.

We step past them and join the rest of Tristan's guests inside the gallery. From the number of people here, I think it's safe to assume the opening is a success. I'm shocked that at least half of the people in attendance are women. I guess I shouldn't be surprised that the single women of New York would be attracted to a gorgeous artist who's probably on everyone's most eligible bachelor list.

My breath catches when I finally get a first look at a few of Tristan's paintings. They're nothing like what I imagined they would be. I thought he was painting landscapes or maybe some weird contemporary art. But no, these are something entirely different. Each room inside the art gallery is privy to a different painting. The paintings are dark and erotic. The first is a painting of a black-winged man penetrating a young woman wearing a white collar. In the description, it says the painting was done with oils and a mixture of bodily fluids. *Oh, my.*

I'm a bit taken aback by the description. *Um, body fluids?*

"You look just as surprised as I feel," Nicholas mutters from the side of his mouth close to my ear so no one will hear.

"Has he always painted stuff like this?"

Nicholas stares at the painting for a few moments as if trying to recall old memories.

"One time, when Tristan was home from college, my father caught him painting something like this in his bedroom. My father threatened to stop paying for his classes if this was the type of stuff he was learning in school. He never really approved of Tristan studying art. He thought it was a waste of time and money."

"Looks like he was wrong. They're beautiful. Although they're not exactly something I could hang in my kitchen."

"It would probably look better in a bedroom," Nicholas says, his eyes glittering with humor.

"Rebecca!" A flurry of long, wavy blonde hair and bright blue eyes descends on us before I can place the face of the young, petite beauty.

"Hello, Emily." I smile. It's actually nice to see another friendly female face and have someone else to talk to besides Carol. I'm not sure what I did to warrant such warm affection from his sister, but I don't mind it in the least. Emily's charming disposition is magnetic and endearing. If I were to have had a younger sister, I would have wanted one like her. It's too bad Alison is the one who gets to spend time with her.

As the evening wears on, I start to sense a growing tension from Emily. Every time I look in her direction, she's watching the growing crowd of supporters clustered around Tristan. I can't help but wonder if she somehow feels left out. She and Tristan obviously seem close, but I think there might be something going on between them.

"Nick, I think I'm going to go outside for some air," Emily says, kissing her brother on the cheek. "It's a little crowded in here."

"All right, don't stay out there too long. It's still raining buckets."

"I'll be back. You two enjoy," she says, flashing me a smile.

56

REBECCA

I try my best not to stand too close to Nicholas throughout the evening, worried that Alison will make an appearance and cause a scene. There's something slightly dangerous about staring at erotic paintings all night while standing next to Nicholas and having to appear like everything is normal and not act on the overwhelming urge to touch him. It doesn't help that every time I try to secure some distance between us, he goes right back to standing mere centimeters away from me. I'm not sure how much longer I can take this.

"Are you all right," Nicholas asks.

"Fine." I swallow back the nervousness that trickles over me. Nicholas watches me with a look of concern.

"Do you want to circle back around? You seemed to like that first painting," he offers.

"Actually, I think I'm going to find the restroom." I quickly leave him, forcing myself not to look back. I'm starting to unravel as I walk through a random black door ready to combust at any moment. A warm desire overwhelms me as I stare at the room around me decorated with extravagant office furniture. This must be Tristan's private office.

The sound of footsteps echo in the hallway behind me, and I turn to find Nicholas with a look of frustration on his face.

"Why did you leave?" he asks, stepping closer toward me.

"To get away from you." I try to push past him but he blocks my path.

"What's wrong?" Exasperation is evident on his face as he grabs me and pulls me close. "Did I do something wrong?" *No, I just can't stop thinking about you.*

"Just let me go," I blurt.

"Rebecca, is that really what you want? I think we know how this game ends." He grabs me, capturing my lips in a searing kiss that would probably send most women into explosive ecstasy. The thought of Nicholas's mouth on me overtakes me and my legs turn to jelly. Try as I may, I can't seem to shake the desire to be with him. The problem is I want to be more than just someone on the side.

"From the moment I met you, I've wanted nothing more than to make you mine."

My cheeks flush at the sweetness of his words. His rich chuckle sends shivers through my body, causing my nipples to tighten beneath my dress.

"I don't want..."

"There's no need denying it. I'm going to make you mine, even if it's the last thing I do," he promises.

I'm tired of being the one who unravels at his touch. I'm tired of feeling weak. His gaze shifts to the dip in my dress and his hand slides up, cupping my breast in a tight squeeze. A warm sensation crawls down my belly, and I know my lace panties are growing wetter by the second. The world seems to shift as Nicholas throws his jacket on the floor and unbuttons the top of his shirt. He rolls up his sleeves and something inside me caves as I watch him slowly undo his watch. I breathe in, holding back my jaw from dropping at the sight of his chest and forearms. He unzips his pants and then unbuckles his belt with slow but torturous precision. My whole body goes weak from the desire coursing through me.

I need him, just one more time. After that, I'll let go. I'll forget about the allure that drives me toward this beautiful man. This isn't about love—it's about regaining control over my body and my emotions. *Or at least that's what I'll keep telling myself.* I'm glad I chose to wear heels tonight. It's given me the extra confidence I need to play this game. I slowly unzip my dress in the back, letting it fall to the floor, pooling in one fluid cascading ripple of silk. His breath catches at the sight of my pronounced nipples beneath the transparent lace of my demi-cup bra. To his surprise, I'm wearing a pair similar to the ones I tried on at *Demure.* He licks his lips as if he's going to devour me whole. And I can't deny that it would be an incredible way to go.

Nicholas may have a hold over me, but I've come to realize that I know how to push his buttons, too. Mustering all of the courage I have, I step to him and pull his hands and wrap them around my hips. I take my time running my hands down his chest and abs, savoring the feel of him. *Is there some kind of hot-as-fuck-diet that only he seems to be aware of?* He smirks as I trace my finger along the top of his pants and impatiently tug his belt from the loops. His pants slide to the floor and he kicks off his shoes to get them off.

I'm so fucked. My confidence dwindles at the sight of his cock bouncing out of his pants. He's not wearing any underwear. He grins at me as I force myself to tear my gaze from the sight of him in all his glorious perfection. It beckons my lips to suck and tease it.

"Like what you see?" he asks.

"I've seen bigger," I bluff. *It's a lie.* While I know Nicholas isn't abnormally big, he's bigger than any man I've even been with. He flashes me an angry *nice try, but you're so fucking lying* look.

"If you keep this up, I'm going to fuck you until your legs are numb." He crushes me up against his frame. "You and I both know how much you love it when I slide my cock inside you." Nicholas leans in and nips the bottom of my ear, sending a shiver through me. He's right, but I also love the way his voice goes hoarse when he talks about being inside me. A piece of me almost breaks at the thought that I will never do this again. In a month, he'll be married to someone else, and this moment will just be a passing memory in his mind.

Nicholas bends me over the desk as he wedges his knee between my legs, spreading them wider. His fingers trace from the inside of my knees, up the inside of my thighs, over my hips, and then up my sides to my breasts. He squeezes my nipples between his fingers and pulls on them until they're puffy and sore.

"Are you ready for me?" he says, pushing me against the desk. The anticipation makes me wild with excitement. Before I can answer, his hand slaps my ass cheek. I yelp at the sting ringing off my skin. *Fuck! I'm in trouble.*

"Hold still," he says, pulling my hair and slipping two fingers inside me. He slides them in and out of me, stroking my clit each time. An animalistic growl erupts behind me like he's about to annihilate his prey like he's been starving. And I know when I wake up tomorrow morning that I'll have bruises all over me. But I also know it will be well worth it. I feel his mouth on me as he kisses and sucks his way down until his tongue slides across my core. I jolt at the shift from cold air to the heat of his exquisite lips. His fingers spread my cheeks, giving him better access to my center. He licks me up and down as if lapping cream off me. I push back against him and he stops.

"I think we're done playing games, sweetheart. It's time to show you why I always win when I play." His hand comes down hard on my ass, sending another divine sting over my exposed skin.

"Fuck me." The words escape my mouth as I bite back the moan from the loss of pleasure and heat radiating from my center.

"Not until you beg," he warns. His words send a rush of goose bumps over my skin. "You like it rough, baby?" *Yes.* I try to turn, but he holds me down, spreading my legs farther apart.

"Are you ready to come for me?"

"Fuck off."

This is the game. I fight and he pushes back harder. I feel him pull back and I hear the sound of a wrapper ripping open. Before I have a chance to stand, he slams into me and I whimper at the abruptness of the impact. He rams into me sending my heart into my throat.

"Is that all you have?" I gasp. I look over my shoulder to find him smirking at my words. He chuckles, tugging harder on my hair.

"Not even close."

"We'll see," I taunt.

"Mmm, I love that mouth of yours."

"Why don't you let me show you how much it likes you?"

"Not just yet..."

Nicholas slams into me again, pulling me tighter and tighter against him each time. I try to inhale and exhale to steady my breathing, but it's no use. Nicholas is relentless. With each thrust, I find myself falling further into a whirlwind of an orgasm. His grunts only drive me further to the edge. *I love the sound of him fucking me.* He grips my hips, tugging me against him. I cry out from pleasurable pain as I unravel beneath his hold.

"Fuck," I moan.

"Are you giving up already?" he asks, taunting me.

My eyes snap open and I realize my mistake in this seduction. I've let Nicholas use his body to trick me into forgetting the purpose of this game.

"Never."

I pant as he drags his index finger in and out of me. "You're nice and wet," he whispers, leaving a bite mark on the edge of my hip. "I think you want this more than you let on." I have to hold back as desire ripples through me. I want him to go back to fucking my brains out. He slides his hands over my hips, and before I know it, his fingers are caressing my center. I've always loved his hands because they're thick and long. *Like something else.* I've heard some of the females working on my floor joke about having an orgasm at the mere sight of them. I guess I can't blame them. They don't disappoint, and I find myself thinking about them often.

I turn to face him, and he doesn't waste time as he sits on top of Tristan's desk and pulls me on top of his lap. His breath hitches as I readjust myself so I'm rubbing against him. Nicholas moans at the pressure of my center against his cock. I lean in and tease his head, slowly taking it inside me before pulling away as he growls and bucks his hips. His hands grasp my waist to overpower me, but I push back.

"You like driving me insane, don't you?"

"I do," I smile. "But you love it."

"No, but I do love your tits," he says, chuckling. "And I'd love them more in my mouth."

"Did I say you could talk?" I ask, pulling his face forward and placing my breast to his mouth. I almost explode at the sensation of his tongue encircling my nipple. He murmurs a sound of approval and I lean back, enjoying the mixture of pain and pleasure as he bites and sucks me.

As much as I don't want to give in, I can't fight the urge to have him inside me again. Nicholas cradles my back as I slowly lower myself onto him. He moans as I grind against the base of his cock. The sensation is intense enough to make me orgasm, but I exhale, trying my best to relax and calm the building sensation. I'm so consumed by the exquisite feeling of him inside me that it takes me a moment to realize that our frantic fucking has suddenly shifted to something far more intimate and sensual. But I know better than to think this thing between us could ever be called lovemaking.

"Becca," he moans, as the thrust of his hips meet mine. His fingers entwine in my hair and he pulls me into a kiss. We sit there, our breaths ragged from trying to outdo the other. Nicholas lifts me and leans me against the wall for support. He moves inside me with slow, sensual thrusts. It only takes a few moments before he's convulsing against me. His breathing is strained and I can feel the heat of his breath spreading over me as he rests his head against the curve of my breasts. I steady my breathing, but my heart still beats as if it's on crack. Nicholas pivots his hips, and I moan at the feeling of him still half hard inside of me.

"Nick," I moan.

"Don't move."

"Why?"

"I want to remember this feeling for the rest of my life."

His words overwhelm me and confound me all at once. The truth is, even if I wanted to forget the memories of being entangled with him, I can't.

57

NICHOLAS

Each time I'm with her, I lose a piece of myself. Her body goes rigid at my words, and I quickly remove myself from her body and give her space. Rebecca immediately stands, attempting with one arm to shield her breasts from my view. Her nipples are pink from being in my mouth only moments before. I would do anything to have them in my mouth once again. The look on her face sends a streak of fear through my heart. I stand and she steps back, obviously uncomfortable at my nearness. The sudden shift in her mood has my mind spinning. *What did I do? Was it what I said?*

"I can't do this anymore. I can't pretend like this doesn't mean anything." The honesty in her words sends hope shooting through my chest.

"Who says it doesn't?" I confess.

Her eyes go wide with shock as if she's never thought about the possibility that I might feel the same. I've never actually said the words to her, but it doesn't make them any less true. I'm in love with Rebecca Elizabeth Gellar. The funny thing is—I can't seem to breathe without her being near me. I'm not sure how I did it before or how I lasted so long without her, but I need her now. I can't imagine living another month without knowing that she'll be mine. Forever.

Before the words are said, the office door swings open and Carol walks in with Tristan trailing just behind her.

"There are some extra pamphlets that I put..." Carol's eyes go as wide as saucers as she stops and looks from my naked body to Rebecca hiding herself behind me. Her shocked expression is quickly replaced by a sly but embarrassed smile.

"Rebecca? Nicholas?" Tristan turns toward us with a look of puzzlement.

"Sorry, Becca, I didn't know we were interrupting," she says, almost snorting.

58

REBECCA

reat. I can't even imagine what's going through Carol and Tristan's heads. No, actually, I can, and I'd rather not think about it. I'm sure Carol's probably jumping for joy because now she can rub my Nicholas-shame in my face. The look on her face is of sheer satisfaction at the scene before her.

"Carol, it's not what it looks like," I say, grabbing my dress off the floor and covering my goods.

Nicholas walks over to the front of the desk and picks up his shirt, pants, and tie. He's completely nude, but he moves like he walks around naked all the time. He doesn't even mind that Carol is openly staring, or that Tristan is standing only a few feet away. In fact, there's a pretentious smirk on his face that I would love to slap right off it. I watch as Carol's eyes dip below Nicholas's waist and then back up to his face. Her eyes sparkle with mischief.

"Well, we better... we better go," she says, giving Tristan a look. The two of them quickly leave the room, but Carol stops just in time to throw me a knowing wink. *Damn it, Carol. If you weren't my best friend, I might punch you.*

Their exit leaves behind an awkward silence that sucks the air out of the room. I stare down at the office around me. The room smells like sex. I smell like sex. And Nicholas, well, he looks like sex-on-a-stick. He watches me as he slowly dresses. He doesn't have a mirror, and yet, he does his tie up perfectly. I guess that's what happens when you've been wearing suits most of your life. I keep waiting for him to say something, but he just stares at me with those very distracting blue eyes.

"Why don't we get back out there and enjoy the evening, and we'll talk about this later," he finally says.

I can't do this. There's too much at stake and too much to lose. How could I ever live with myself knowing that Nicholas lost his family's company because of me? Alison warned me about being around her fiancé, although I don't think I can take the entire blame for this situation. I didn't ask Nicholas to pick me up tonight. I didn't ask for my body to overpower my need to stay away from him.

"Whatever *this* is, it's over," I say. Nicholas looks at me in surprise.

"We can't just make love and act like it's nothing. We're meant to be together. I tried fighting it. You tried fighting it. But we have to stop. It's useless. Give in. I have."

"We just fucked, Nick." The words come fumbling out of my mouth. "It doesn't mean anything. You're getting married in less than a month. You should just go back to your fiancée."

"So is that all I am to you?"

"Yes," I lie.

"This is more than just a fleeting fuck, and you know it."

"No, this was just my way of forgetting you."

"So that's it then?" His eyes pierce me with an unwavering intensity. "You're just going to walk away from me and pretend like there's nothing between us?"

"Yes." I lean in and kiss him hard on the lips before picking up my purse and walking away. *I love you.*

———

"What are you doing here?" Alison's shrill voice catches me off guard as I shift through the gallery, trying to find Carol. She glides through the sea of guests toward me in a black dress that dips far too low. Her gaze darts back and forth across the room, as if searching for someone. I'm guessing that someone is Nicholas. Her presence is a disaster waiting to happen. I was hoping I wouldn't see her here. *Why didn't Carol warn me?* Perhaps she didn't check in at the front. I doubt her entrance would have gone unnoticed.

"I'm here for Tristan. My friend, Carol, is the PR person for his event."

Alison's eagle-like gaze studies my face as if trying to ascertain if I'm lying. She steps toward me, closing the space between us. I'm almost certain that the coldness emitting from her could freeze hearts.

"Just remember, if I see you anywhere near my fiancé, I'll have you fired. Nicholas won't do it, but his father will." She leaves me with the nauseating feeling that I might not survive the next few months. Tonight's event is just getting started, but I find Carol in the hope that she can somehow get me home.

———

On our way back to the apartment, Carol doesn't say much. She just holds me as I cry into her shoulder in frustration at the world. I know she'll have to go back to the gallery once Steven drops me off, but I'm still grateful to have her to lean on. Several times, I catch Steven tearing his gaze from the road to check on us. I feel horrible that Carol had to call him to drive us home, but there was no way that I was getting back in the car with Nicholas, and Carol refused to let me take a cab.

A steady stream of tears continues to flow for the entire length of our ride home, no doubt leaving horrific smears of mascara across my cheeks. At one point during the ride when a fresh wave of sobs overtakes me, Steven offers to stop at a McDonald's to get me a milkshake. It's comforting to know that he cares and wants to help somehow, but despite my love of soft serve and candy, my appetite is nonexistent at the moment.

It's really time to let go of Nicholas StoneHaven.

59

NICHOLAS

Three weeks later...

T he weeks that pass seem like years, and each one drains the life from me further. I've been ignoring all of the calls to my cell phone, especially the ones from Tristan. After my conversation with Rebecca, I'm convinced that my feelings must be one-sided. She made it perfectly clear that what happened between us is just physical. If I could turn off the ache that I feel every time I catch a glimpse of her at the office, I would. But I'm afraid that even that wouldn't help me forget her. If only it were that easy.

After she left the gallery opening, I couldn't muster the strength to actually enjoy the evening. Instead, I stood in the shadows, licking my wounds and keeping my distance from the general crowd of people.

"Good evening, Nick," a voice says from the corner of my office. I look up to find Striker standing a few feet away. He walks over to my desk with an impassive look on his face.

"I didn't hear you come up."

"I took the stairs," he smirks.

He slides a blank manila envelope across my desk, tapping on it twice to grab my attention. The last time I asked him for a favor, he was following Rebecca for me as she made her way to a local book-store in the city. I promised myself that would be the last time I asked him for anything regarding her. He had a good laugh at me when Rebecca fled from me, and now I'm sure my father has explained to him the details of our relationship, or lack thereof. I wouldn't be surprised if he has Striker watching us both.

"What is this?" I ask, irritated.

"You wanted me to inform you if there was anything new that came up with your assistant's file." I tear my attention from the stack of checks that I'm signing for the accounting department to peek over at the folder.

"Did something come up?" *Are there skeletons in Rebecca's closet that I don't know about?*

"It's about her parents," he says, taking a seat in front of my desk.

"Well, what about them?"

"It seems her parents are having some financial problems. The father lost his job some months back, and they might lose their house." I shouldn't care about financial troubles of Rebecca's family, but I do. The bitterness that has been seeping its way into my heart has yet to ruin my feelings for her.

"How bad off are they?"

"According to their lender, they're behind a few months."

"Thank you for bringing this to me, Striker."

"Goodnight." He nods and then turns to leave. "Oh, one more thing."

"Yes?"

"Your father loves you, Nick, and he just wants the best for you..."

"I know," I grumble.

"You didn't let me finish," he chuckles. "The thing is parents don't always know what's best for their children. They think they do, but sometimes they're just stubborn assholes." Striker's words surprise me, considering it's probably the most he's said to me in one conver-sation since I'd first met him. He's an unusually quiet man, and I don't think I've ever heard him say much about my father, and I've certainly never heard him speak out in disagreement with anything ordained by the almighty Stefan StoneHaven. And while I don't see how they can help the situation, I find his words comforting.

"Is that your way of telling me he's wrong about my impending marriage?"

Striker looks down at me with a strange smile, as if he's remembering something funny. "Marry the redhead. She'll make you happy. Plus, any woman who has the fortitude to kick you in the balls is definitely worth fighting for."

Ass.

60

REBECCA

Whoever claims that being an event planner is fun has no idea what the hell they are talking about. It's the week of the gala, and I've spent the past several days running all over New York City like a madwoman trying to make sure everything is going right. After speaking with the event coordinator Stone-Haven Publishing has contracted with, I'm convinced, despite the amazing caterer, photographer, and live performers that are booked, there's still probably a thousand ways this event could go wrong. My anxiety had gone from mild nerves to full-blown panic mode.

I've been given strict instructions to follow up with the event coordinator nearly every day this week. I know that my general paranoia that something might go wrong isn't uncommon, so I'm glad that I'm not the only one worrying about such a large public event. Work *seems* to be back to the normal routine with Nicholas if you call him avoiding me for days and only communicating with me via email normal. I hate to admit it, but I miss the days where we were so caught up with each other that everything else seemed insignificant.

After the gallery opening, I was convinced he would scream or yell when I showed up at work, but he's been painfully quiet. It's become quite a juggling act to accomplish all that I need to and manage to avoid crossing paths with him, especially when my job responsibilities mostly revolve around being his assistant. I guess I should be thankful that he's not sending me on wild goose chases with a Great Dane this time, but the whole avoiding each other thing hasn't helped with the awkward situation of working with him. If anything, it's been a constant reminder of my glaring mistake the night of the gallery opening.

Carol was right when she told me the other day that I've been acting strange. I haven't been myself since that night. In fact, I've been someone entirely different. I've turned into the pathetic woman who watches romantic comedies in her pajamas all weekend and spends the entire night eating frozen yogurt and crying for the heroine who just can't seem to find the *one*. I wish I could pull myself out of this funk, but I know that only time can do that for me.

"Rebecca... I mean, Ms. Gellar?" My heart squeezes at the sight of Nicholas standing outside of my cubicle. His facial hair seems longer this week, giving him the appearance of a scruffy outdoorsman in a well-tailored suit. His gaze trails over me before quickly focusing back on the paper in his hand. "I was hoping you could help me with Friday night's speech. You seem to have a better gift for flattering words. Do you think you could look over this welcome speech?"

"Of course," I say, taking the paper. My nerves have gotten the better of me, and I can't stop my heart from racing as he runs his hand across the second paragraph of the speech.

"I'm having some trouble here. Feel free to make any notes."

"I will."

I smile and Nicholas flinches slightly. He steps back, letting his gaze linger over me once more before clearing his throat and excusing himself. "I should be on my way. If you need me for any reason, please call my cell phone. I'll be out of the office."

Things are definitely not okay between us. His meetings out of the office have become more and more frequent. Anytime I have a question, he offers to meet me somewhere public. I'm torn between thinking that he's afraid of being alone with me, or that he's avoiding me because of Alison.

"I'll email you my revisions," I offer.

"Thank you. Goodnight."

My gaze lingers over Nicholas's frame as it grows smaller and smaller as he makes his way across the building. I grip my chair as I try to hold back the startling need to run to him and feel his arms wrapped around me.

––––––

"Hey, Becca, are you ready to party Friday?" Ken asks, as he does the beginning of the electric slide out of his office. I laugh, unable to contain my amusement at his sudden outburst of energy among the overly quiet office. I don't normally see Ken so lively during the middle of the week. Most of the time he's too busy fretting over deadlines and meeting with angry or overzealous authors, but after a rather depressing week, his cheesy smile is a welcome sight.

"Definitely, I'm sorry I haven't stopped in your office to chat," I say.

After the incident at *Riptide,* I left our friendship on a rather strange note, but I'm hopeful that Ken and I can still be friends.

"I hope you don't think I've been ignoring you."

"No, I figured you were busy, and the holidays are always a weird time to catch up with people," he says with a polite smile. "Are you going to bring a date to the gala?"

My heart clenches at the thought of Nicholas. "No, are you?"

"Actually, I am," he grins, blushing slightly. "I met someone over the holiday break. I didn't want to say anything until after a few dates."

"That's great," I say, trying my best to muster a smile.

"Single women can be so crazy here. You never know if you're secretly dating a hoarder or a woman who likes to rub mustard on her tits during sex."

"What? You're telling me yellow-stained nipples don't turn you on?" I say, pretending to be shocked. I'm pretty sure that's the first time I've heard Ken say the word tits.

"I'm guessing, probably as much as you like a man who wants you to wrap him in an adult diaper and read him a bedtime story."

"I don't know," I laugh. "That sounds a lot less complicated than my love life right now."

———

When I first get to my desk from lunch, I find an email in my inbox with instructions that sends my stomach turning in violent knots. I stare at the screen with watery eyes as I re-read the words in Nicholas's email.

To: Rebecca Gellar
From: Nicholas F. StoneHaven
Subject: Pick Up Ring
Gellar,
Please head over to Tiffany & Co this afternoon. I need you to help me pick out Alison's engagement ring. The sales associate has two rings on hold for me. I need your opinion on which one would be the better choice. I've told Mary to have a cab ready to pick you up when you return from lunch. Have the driver bring you home when you're finished.
Thank you,
Nicholas

My world implodes. I should be happy, right? This is exactly what I wanted. I wanted him to stop bothering me and move on with his marriage to Alison. I guess I just wasn't expecting to be caught in the middle of it again. I'm tempted to email Nicholas back and tell him no, and that I can't help him pick out his fiancée's ring, but what would that prove? Nothing. It would only tell him that I still have feelings for him. I can't let myself get emotional about this. This is my job, and as Nicholas's assistant, I'm supposed to be fine with this. *I have to be.*

It only takes me five minutes inside the cab to realize that I'm not fine. I'm on my way to pick out Alison's engagement ring, aka the catty bitch who's marrying the gorgeous man who has occupied my thoughts for the past several months. It's hard to imagine coming into the office and seeing her here. I'm sure once they're married, she'll be itching to have me leave. The thought of not being able to see Nicholas feels like my insides are being torn apart.

The drive through downtown traffic takes a lot longer than expected. By the time we reach Tiffany's, I've called and convinced Carol to postpone a lunch engagement to meet me.

Carol's eyes nearly pop out of her head as she stares in shock at the two giant rocks that sit displayed in front of us. I couldn't fight the temptation to try one on, but I immediately regret doing so. While it's nice to live in the moment and imagine what it would feel like to be engaged to Nicholas, it's also extremely painful. *Geez.* Both of these rings cost more than my college education.

"Holy balls, they're huge," Carol says with wide eyes. I'm tempted to crack my usual *that's what she said* joke, but the sight of the two emerald-cut diamonds has me teetering into a jealous guilt. Having Carol here with me has helped ease some of the pain, but nowhere near as much as I had hoped.

"Both are really breathtaking," I admit. Carol's critical gaze washes over me with annoyance. She's still irked at me that I told Nicholas that what happened was just fucking. For the first time since I've known her, she's genuinely disappointed in me. It only makes me feel that much worse.

"Which one would you choose?" she asks.

"I don't know..." Panic starts to set in. "I can't do this," I say, backing up from the display of sparkling diamond rings. "I need to get out of here."

"Becca, breathe, you're okay."

Carol wraps her arms around my shoulders, trying her best to reassure me, but the world around me feels everything but okay. Any moment, I'm going to break into a thousand little fragmented pieces and I will never be able to recover from it. I'll never feel complete because there will always be a piece of me missing that has been carelessly swept under the rug, never to see the light of day again.

61

NICHOLAS

"You did what?" Tristan asks as he stares at me in astonishment as he practically throws his hot cup of saké at me. The sound of his booming voice nearly stops the traffic of the restaurant as everyone turns to watch the spectacle before them. A couple nearby whispers in hushed voices as they turn and stare at us, waiting to see what happens.

"You sent Rebecca to pick out Alison's ring?" he repeats.

"I have my reasons."

"Which are what? Being a prickly asshole? I can't believe you're marrying her."

I smirk at the underlying anger in his words. If I didn't know any better, I'd say Tristan cares about Rebecca a little too much for my liking. After leaving the office to get some air, or rather to distance myself from her, I decided to take a stroll through Central Park. It was on my way back that I got a call from a frantic sales associate from Tiffany's. After dealing with several minutes of the woman apologizing, she informed me that Rebecca had left without choosing a ring.

"The ring is for Rebecca, not Alison," I say, with an exasperated expression as I push away the Hibachi steak on my plate. Tristan taps his fingers on the table as he impatiently waits for me to explain.

"So you tricked her into thinking it is?"

"I wanted to know if she still cares about me. If what's happening between us is *just fucking,* as she says, then she wouldn't have freaked out and fled the store."

I watch as Tristan sits back, rubbing the side of his face in contemplation. "If you weren't my best friend, I would take you outside and kick the shit out of you." He pops a single shrimp into his mouth and continues to stare with an irritated, but amused look on his face.

"Any day, buddy," I challenge with a grin, hoping to lighten the mood.

"I still owe you for the black eye." His lips twitch into a half smile.

"So did you pick a ring? When are you going to ask her?"

"I did on my way over here," I say, pulling out the emerald-cut diamond. "I was thinking of taking her with me to France and asking her there."

"Alex would've been proud of you."

My heart throbs at the mention of my brother's name. If there is anything I'm certain of, it's that Alex would've been happy knowing that I married someone like Rebecca. I'm positive that wherever he is, he's smiling down at me and shaking his head at the beautiful mess I've gotten myself into. *I'm keeping my promise, Alex.*

Tristan holds up his saké cup like he's about to give a toast. "To your upcoming marriage."

"You're rather optimistic," I grumble.

"Don't forget, I better be the best man at your wedding," he says.

"You will be, but first she has to say yes."

"Just make sure you don't tell her about tricking her with the ring before she agrees," he says, laughing at me. "She might end up kneeing you in the balls."

"Well, we all know it wouldn't be the first time," I laugh. "Thank you for the lovely reminder."

"Anytime." Tristan grins.

62

REBECCA

I'm almost ready to leave for another day of work when my cell phone emits a shrill ring through the apartment, commanding my immediate attention. I scurry over to my purse just in time to catch the call before it goes to voicemail. I smile at seeing my mother's name flashing across the screen. I haven't talked with her for weeks, and I can only assume that she probably isn't very happy that I didn't come see them over Christmas. Despite my dad's protests that I don't send them money for their house payment, I've sent them a check with a note to my mother that specifically says not to tell my father. I don't care what kind of lie she comes up with—I'm not letting my parents lose their house.

"Hello?"

"Rebecca? Are you there?" I can hardly make out her words, but I know it's my mother. In the background, I hear someone telling her to shut off her phone. *Where the hell is she?*

"Sweetie, I have a surprise to tell you." I can hardly make out her words, but the excitement in her voice surprises me. The last time I heard her so excited was when she found out that Miles had proposed to me. I bet she's going to be surprised to hear that he was arrested for harassing me. *He's damned lucky I didn't tell the officer just how much he was manhandling me.*

"Mom, I can barely hear you."

"We're coming to visit you!" she squeals.

"What? You're coming to New York? When?" I never imagined that my family would be able to come visit me. *How is this possible?* They're losing the house. They don't have money to fly to New York.

"We'll be there in a few hours. We had a stop in Houston."

"Mom, how?"

"Your boss invited us! He's so lovely. He said he felt horrible about keeping you from visiting over the holidays so he wanted to fly us out there to visit."

"Nicholas?" He didn't keep me from flying back home. My lack of funds did, and I'm pretty damn sure I didn't mention either to him.

"Yes, that's him." I hear another muffled voice come over the phone. "Sweetie, I have to go. We're getting ready to board the plane."

"Do I need to get a cab for you guys?"

"No, your boss said he has everything arranged. We'll call you when we land."

He has arranged everything? I haven't spoken to Nicholas since I left Tiffany's without picking up Alison's ring. *Why would he do this for me?*

"I'll leave work early and we'll meet for dinner," I suggest.

"Sounds wonderful! See you soon."

As I exit the bathroom, I hear my mother's rich laughter fill the restaurant dining room. She must be enjoying the champagne she ordered just a little too much because she's starting to snort. It's still hard to believe that my dad and mom are in New York. I didn't think I would ever get them to come visit me. The only downside to having them here is that I'm not exactly sure how much more I can take of my mother asking me about Miles. She knows he's here in the city, but she's yet to mention that she was the one who gave him my address. I could kill her for telling him.

I wish I could thank Nicholas for bringing them here, but that would feel like I was breaking our unspoken-ceasefire agreement, and I just don't want to disturb what has become relatively calm waters.

My chest deflates as I return to the dining room. Nicholas is standing in the middle of the restaurant dressed casually in jeans and a dark blue shirt. His hair is combed back in messy wet strands of golden silk. Tears burn at the corners of my eyes at the sight of him here as I slowly make my way through the dining room back to our table. I shouldn't be crying, but I can't stop the threat of tears from choking me. I'm in agony, and he's standing there looking normal and confident and so freakin' gorgeous.

He grins as my mother fawns over him. I stifle a chuckle as my father grips my mother's hand as if she might take flight at any moment. I think even my dad can tell that Nicholas has a way of smooth-talking the ladies. My mother looks up and waves me over to the table. Anxiety eats away at my insides as I reach our table. I probably look like a mess. I inhale and then exhale, willing away my watery eyes.

Nicholas turns just in time to spot me heading their way. He half smiles at me, but his expression seems uncomfortable, maybe even pained.

"Rebecca?" The way he says my name makes my knees quiver. I try my best not to flush in front of my parents. My mother can sniff out butterfly nerves.

"What are you doing here?" I ask.

"I wanted to stop by and make sure the restaurant was taking care of you guys."

"Do you own it?" I ask, quickly scanning the room.

"No," he says flatly.

"Oh."

"The owner is a family friend. We come here often." Nicholas lifts his hand as if to reach out to touch my face, but he quickly pulls away. "Well, I hope you have a wonderful time. I should go."

It's the sound of my mother's voice that stops Nicholas in his tracks.

"Please stay and have lunch with us."

"Thank you, Mrs. Gellar..."

"Call me Patricia."

Nicholas grins. "Thank you, Patricia, but I really must get back to the office."

"Oh, no, I insist that you stay," Mom says, pulling out a chair next to her. It takes all my strength not to laugh at the way she's practically drooling over him. It seems even my mother isn't immune to his charms, and by the frown on my father's face, he isn't too happy about it. Nicholas looks over at me, and I know without a doubt that he's wondering if any of this is making me uncomfortable.

"Please, stay," I say. He hesitates and then nods before pulling out my chair for me. Nicholas takes the seat between my mother and me.

"It's so nice that Rebecca is working for such a wonderful man," Mom says practically gushing. I look over at my father and his face turns a deeper shade of red. *Poor Dad.*

"Your daughter is a wonderful employee. In fact, she's one of the best we've had at StoneHaven Publishing." Nicholas reaches for his water and I notice a slight tremble in his hand.

"Are you feeling all right?" I ask in a hushed voice.

"Fine. Just nerves."

"Nerves?" I ask surprised.

"Yes."

Nicholas is nervous? I look over at my mother, who's wearing a frilly top, jeans, and open-toe wedges, and then at my father in his trucker hat, faded jeans and well-worn shirt. *Why the hell would he be nervous?* It's just my parents. If anything, he should be embarrassed to be here. My mother isn't exactly the most well-mannered person. A young waiter with spiky black hair comes to take our orders. I wait for my mother and father to order, carefully listening to their choices. *I have no idea what the hell I want.* Mario's Italian Restaurant is supposed to be known for their lasagna and their fresh cannoli's. I flip through the menu and suddenly, everyone's eyes are on me. Nicholas half smiles and then turns to the waiter.

"She'll have the meat lasagna, extra cheese. I'll have the crab raviolis. And we'll take a bottle of Sori San Lorenzo Barbaresco please." Without even thinking, I pass my menu to Nicholas and he hands them to the waiter.

There's a strange silence as my mother's eyes turn on me. I can feel her eyes glued to my face. *Nicholas just ordered for the two of us.* It seems like a normal thing for him, but I can tell by the confused look on my father's face that this has a completely different meaning to them. Ordering for another person is usually a sign that you're in a relationship. I'm pretty sure I even saw that in Cosmopolitan's latest issue. *Great.*

"So, do you two go out often?" Mom asks. Her question is seemingly innocent, but I know what she's really asking is how long we've been sleeping together. I take the opportunity to steer the conversation away from us.

"Mom, how long do you guys think you'll be in New York?" My mother looks at me with a dissatisfied expression. She was probably hoping to find out that my ovaries aren't full of cobwebs anymore. That's all I need. Pregnant by my engaged boss. *How lovely.*

"We're thinking of staying another week," my father says, piping in. "Would you like that, cupcake?" I blush at the overly affectionate nickname my father calls me by.

"Of course, Dad. That would be great."

"Feel free to stay longer," Nicholas says. "I would be more than happy to call The Somerset and let them know that you will be staying another week."

"That's so sweet of you," Mom chimes in.

"Nicholas, you don't have to do that," I whisper.

He turns to me and smiles politely before quickly squeezing my hand beneath the table. "It's fine."

Warmth spreads over my hand and just as quickly dissipates when he removes it. I want to reach out to him and tell him that I miss him, but I don't. *It's too late.* I have to forget the way he makes me feel and to forget the feelings I am struggling to pretend aren't real.

After two hours of sitting and listening to my mother drone on and on, we finally leave Mario's. It doesn't surprise me that Nicholas immediately takes the bill and tells the waiter to charge it to his account. I think it's the icing on the cake for my mother. She's head over heels for him. At one point, she even tells Nicholas that she would love to see me with someone with his old-fashioned good manners. I stop her before she embarrasses me any further, but the words are already out there, and I can sense a growing tension between Nicholas and me. The words he said to me back at the gallery opening repeat in my head like a broken record. *We're meant to be together. I tried fighting it. You tried fighting it, but we have to stop. It's useless. Give in. I have.*

I'm not sure how Nicholas put up with my mother's barrage of questions, but he did, and he never looked annoyed. The only time he seemed to fidget was when my mother asked him about Alison. For the most part, Nicholas kept his calm and cool demeanor, but he definitely avoided questions about her. And when he couldn't avoid the question, he quickly changed the subject once he'd answered it. It didn't bother me that he didn't want to talk about her. In fact, I was grateful. I didn't want to hear him talk about her. It's already hard enough pretending like I'm okay.

"Thank you for lunch," I say as Nicholas holds open the door for me.

He looks down at his cell phone and then back up at me. "You're welcome."

I can't help but wonder if he was texting Alison.

"Thank you for putting up with all of my mother's questions."

"She's sweet. I like her," he says with an honest grin.

"I should've introduced you two sooner," I joke.

Nicholas stops for a moment. "I should probably go." I sigh internally, knowing the moment wouldn't last. He's still angry with me, and I don't blame him.

"I'll see you tomorrow morning, then for the gala." Nicholas hands me a card and I notice the name The Somerset on the front with a delicate swan imprinted on the front.

"Please let your parents know I set up a room for them."

"I will."

Before leaving, Nicholas takes my mother's hand and kisses it. I watch in amazement as she nearly swoons at his feet. *Oh, my God, Mom!* There's something about this man that makes women melt in their panties, and the worst part is, he totally knows it.

"It was such a pleasure to meet you," she says, blushing. "Rebecca never mentioned how handsome you were." After a few minutes of watching them back and forth, Nicholas finally manages to break away, apologizing for having to return to the office. He quickly shakes my father's hand, and I have to bite back a laugh as my father tightens his grip on him. A sharp pang hits me at the memory of my father doing the same gesture with Miles. I don't think my father ever really liked Miles, and I always thought it was because he flinched when my dad gripped his hand. He always used to tell me you could tell a lot about a man by his handshake. The air is silent as the two have a stare off. Nicholas keeps his cool, and after a few moments, my father finally breaks the awkward silence.

"Thank you," Dad says. "Take care of my daughter."

I nearly die of embarrassment, but Nicholas's strained voice sends an electric shiver up my spine.

"Always," he says. A strange feeling blossoms inside me, though it takes me a moment to recognize what the feeling is—*hope.*

63

REBECCA

W e're halfway to The Somerset when my mother pulls me to the side. She points out a pair of Manolo Blah-niks and waves over to my father, letting him know that we're going inside the upscale boutique store. She's never been into expensive shoes, so I know this is just a detour so that she can get me alone and interrogate me about Nicholas. She ushers me into the two-story building and then toward the back of the posh-looking store filled with expertly-placed white, antique chandeliers, a white faux bearskin rug, and red wall accents. This hardly looks like a place that my mom would be drawn to, so I know her sole mission is to corner me about what she witnessed back at the restaurant.

I'm dreading every second leading up to this awkward encounter.

My mother has the talent and ability to read me like an open book. And unfortunately, this is a chapter in my life that I wish I could close. It's hard enough dealing with the raw emotions I feel every time I see Nicholas. I shouldn't regret telling him to stay away because it was the right thing to do. *Right?* I don't want to be the other woman. I deserve better than that, and it would only serve to slowly destroy us both. *So, why is it that I can't help but feel like it was the worst decision I've ever made?*

A lovely petite sales associate walks over and asks us if we need help, but my mother just waves her off as if she's an annoying fly. I silently pray for strength and patience as my mother furrows her brow like she's trying to telepathically extract information from my brain. It's not hard to see that she's annoyed from the way she purses her lips. I scan the room, doing my best to avoid eye contact with the woman. She's like a T-Rex—if I don't move, maybe she won't see me. I wish in this moment more than any other time in my life that I could just fade into my surroundings and avoid detection, but she grabs my hand before I even have a chance to thwart her inquiries.

"Are you sleeping with him?" my mom asks, eyeing me suspiciously, as if horns might sprout from my head.

"With who?"

"Rebecca Elizabeth Gellar, you know exactly to whom I'm referring."

"Actually, I don't," I lie.

"Your boss.

"No."

"Are you sure?" she asks.

"Mother, don't you think if I were sleeping with a man, that I would know?"

Obviously exasperated, she presses on. "I think you're lying to me." There's a slight tremor in her voice that tells me her feelings are hurt. I hate lying to her, but she's far too inquisitive. And anyway, what does it matter? It's in the past. He's getting married, and we'll never have anything more between us. Wanting desperately to end this line of questioning, I look over at a pair of red heels with crystals embedded on the front. They would fit perfectly with my costume for the gala.

"These are beautiful," I say, trying to distract my mother from asking any more impertinent questions, but she quickly catches on.

"I wouldn't blame you if you did. He's very handsome and very sweet."

"I'll let him know you think so," I mutter.

"What?"

"Nothing."

"I just want you to be happy," she says. "I think he's in love with you." She grabs the red heels from my hand, forcing me to look at her.

"What?" *In love with me? No.*

She reaches out and cups my face. Her eyes start to water, but she quickly wipes the tears away and fixes the collar of my shirt. There's something she's not telling me. My mother isn't normally one to cry.

"What is it?" I ask. "Why are you crying?"

My mother desperately tries to wipe away the tears welling up in her eyes. "It's nothing. I just think you should go fix things with him."

"I've been so stupid, Mom," I moan.

"You're not stupid."

"I told him what was between us was just physical."

"So you have been together?"

"Mom..."

She laughs. "I'm sure he'll forgive you."

"It's too late. It's always been too late. He's engaged to someone else and he's going to marry her. It's just complicated with the way things are now, but there's no changing it."

"But he loves you?"

No, Nicholas must think the worst of me, and that's probably why he's been so distant. I need to talk to him and apologize for what I said. This visit with my parents is another reminder that he's done so much for me. He flew them out here, paid for our lunch, and he's putting them up in a hotel. He's gone out of his way to make sure that they have been well attended. It's too much. *And why? Why did he do all this for people he doesn't even know?*

"Mom, I need to go. Can you tell Dad that I will talk with you both after the gala?"

"But, Becca, I..."

"Please, Mom. I just really need to be alone for a little while."

I slip out of the store before my dad can spot me and I head back to the office. It's a long walk, but I need the time to think things through.

64

REBECCA

"A woman like her always has a price."

The sound of Nicholas's father startles me as I head past one of the conference rooms on my floor. The bitter words come out in a hushed voice just loud enough to prick my ears. I peep between the cracks of the conference room door and spot Nicholas sitting in one of the chairs with his hand poised against his face. He taps his stylus on the edge of his tablet with a look of impatience and irritation.

"What are you talking about now?" Nicholas asks, throwing up his hands in exasperation.

"I found these in your desk." I watch as Stefan takes a seat next to Nicholas and slides over a manila folder, opening it in front of him. Nicholas stares at it with a surprise glance. I peer in closer trying to make out what the folder says, but I'm just too far away.

Stefan watches his son with a critical glare and a surprising amount of hostility. "Do you have an explanation for this?"

"Not one you're going to like," Nicholas says.

"She played you for a fool, son."

"I willingly wrote the check to her parents."

My heart palpitates at the words: *check* and *parents*. What the hell is he talking about? Why the hell would Nicholas write a check to my parents? Is he sending my parents money to get rid of me? My stomach turns at the thought of him wanting me to leave. No, my mother would've said something if he was trying to get me to leave. Instead, she encouraged me to talk to him about my feelings.

"Why would you do something like that? For that amount of money?"

"Isn't it obvious?" Nicholas says.

"No, it really isn't. I hired her to help keep you on track, but now she's become an overwhelming distraction, and she's costing this company money."

"You're not firing her." Nicholas says with a look of sheer contempt.

I step back from the door trying my best to hold in my tears. *Be strong. Don't cry.* My dreams of working at this prestigious company are quickly disintegrating. As I turn to leave, I hear Stefan's angry voice rising in pitch.

"I'm giving her the opportunity to leave on Monday morning, and I want her letter of resignation on my desk by the end of the day," he commands.

"Why are you doing this? Why are you making me choose?"

Nicholas' voice fades into the background and the last thing I hear is his father.

"She's just a gold digger... your marriage to Alison is worth more than her weight in gold."

The office floor is deserted as I gather my belongings from my cubicle and file them into a white storage box. In a way, I'm thankful for the absence of employees. This situation could be a lot more humiliating if I had to worry about prying eyes watching me sob as I box away my dreams. I text Carol asking if Steven can give me a ride home.

I check in my ID badge and drop it in HR's overnight drop box. The thought of walking away from all of this is devastating. I thought Miles cheating on me was about the worst feeling in the world, but it doesn't compare to this feeling. I'm tempted to find Nicholas and tell him goodbye, but I'm torn at the thought that it might just make things worse. *Maybe this is better.* Nicholas won't lose the company his family built and he can honor his brother by making it greater. I know it's selfish but in a way, I wish I were important enough to sacrifice everything for.

––––––

W hen I arrive home to our apartment, I'm filled with the bittersweet sadness of finding Carol waiting for me in the kitchen. Her bright smile exudes happiness as she holds up two different shots—one tequila and the other vodka. She grins, gesturing for me to take my pick. I muster a sad smile, taking the shot of tequila to numb my pain. It burns all the way down my throat, leaving me with a warm pool in my stomach.

After several minutes of listening to Carol talk about her day, I muster the strength to tell her that I'm leaving New York. The look of betrayal in her eyes squeezes my heart.

"You can't be serious?" she asks. Carol circles around the kitchen and grabs ahold of my arm. "You're not leaving. Like ever." I know me leaving probably isn't what she wants to hear right now, but I can't stay. By Monday, I won't have the job I moved three-thousand miles across the country for and the man I've fallen for over these past few months will soon be married to another woman.

"He can't just make you leave," Carol says, tapping her fingers against the kitchen counter.

"He owns the company. Of course, he can."

65

REBECCA

A bittersweet sadness fills me as I make my way toward the front of the *Natural History Museum.* The gala has turned out better than I could've ever anticipated or even imagined. A flurry of paparazzi crowds the red carpet trying to capture candid shots of guests walking into the event. Everyone seems to be here. I even spot several of the authors we have contracts with Stone-Haven and a slew of celebrities, and city officials lined-up for their photo-ops on the red carpet.

As I walk into *The Cullman Hall of the Universe,* the outstanding beauty of the room awes me. The ceiling of the cavernous room is painted a deep, dark blue and speckled with tiny lights that look like clusters of stars. The low-lighting gives off the illusion that we're sitting outside underneath the stars. It reminds me of when I used to drive up to the mountains near my home in California. It was probably the only place you could still see the stars beyond the horrible Los Angeles smog.

The farther I walk through the hall, the more tables I spot decorated in red silk tablecloths, tall centerpieces of golden candelabras, and statues of angels and demons. Somehow, the event coordinator has managed to make it feel like something straight out of one of Edgar Allan Poe's stories. The gothic ambiance is a perfect setting for the string quartet that plays on the main stage just in front of the massive dance floor.

When I've finally taken my fill of the beautiful ambiance, appreciating the way all of my work and planning have helped make this event come together, I direct my gaze to the guests that mix and mingle in cheerful conversations. A strange flutter of excitement washes over me as I realize the anonymity that I feel walking into a room with a mask.

I enjoy my time watching guests sip champagne and devour the assortment of hors d'oeuvres that waiters carry on antique trays. As I gently pass through the clusters of guests toward the front of the room, I spot *him* standing in the middle of the dance floor greeting guests and making small talk.

His red cape hangs only inches from the floor and the top-half of his face is hidden behind a skillfully-crafted skull mask. My heart throbs at the sight of his smile peeking out from beneath it. It's hard not to notice that behind that grim mask is a beautiful man. I study him from a distance, hoping to capture this vision of him in my memory forever. I smile when I realize his blond hair is styled and combed in one slick wave, much like the first day I met him on the plane. True to his word, his extravagant costume depicts The Red Death—intriguing, alluring, and ominous. I didn't actually think he would go through with it.

Just as the string quartet strikes up another song, Nicholas turns in my direction, and suddenly, there's no room in the air. Everything halts in some form of suspended animation. I understand now when people say *it's like no one else is in the room.* There are over fifteen-hundred people here, but everything else just falls away, leaving us locked in each other's gaze. His blue eyes pierce through me, and I find that I have to remind myself to breathe.

Remember, you came tonight to say goodbye to Nicholas. He quickly leaves his party and crosses the room, pushing past the flood of guests filing in through the front entrance. His hands touch me before he even opens his mouth, and a warm shiver invades my senses.

"Please, say you'll dance with me?" he asks with a faint smile and intense gaze. *How could I refuse him?* The memory of Nicholas's conversation with his father threatens to unravel me, but I quickly squash the feeling.

"Yes," I reply. If this is the last time we touch, then I want to savor the moment.

Nicholas takes my hands and wraps them around the collar of his red cape. Despite the thick layers of my red dress, the pressure of his hand warms my skin with an alluring sensation. He pulls me toward the middle of the dance floor and we take off in a whirlwind of turns and spins. His grin warms my heart as he dips me and then pulls me close so that our chests are meshed.

I don't want the feeling of his arms around me to stop, but as the song ends, I feel him step back taking the air from me. A pang of guilt fills me as our eyes connect and he smiles.

"Do you want to step outside?"

"Okay. I could use the air."

The breeze flowing in through the open balcony surrounds us with the faint smell of burning firewood. I lean against the doorway, my eyes lingering on his lips. The slight trail of stubble just beneath his bottom lip has me itching to feel it with my lips, my tongue. The mask might fool most, but I know beneath that haunting facade are lips so sinfully-skilled that the memory of them on me has me rooted where I stand as Nicholas stares back at me.

Something inside me wants to reach out and touch him, but I know it would be wrong. There's nothing left to say but goodbye. I give him a faint smile that doesn't betray the sorrow stewing inside me, and I turn to leave. A hand wraps around my wrist before I can put any more distance between us. His other arm snakes around my waist as he pulls on my wrist until I turn to face him again. I look up into his face as he hoists me up to plant a kiss firmly on my lips. My hands instinctively go to his face but the mask is in the way. He releases his grip on me only long enough to remove his mask. My breath leaves me in a whoosh when his face breaks into a dazzling smile. Black paint circles his eyes—a stark contrast to his brilliant, electric blue irises.

God, I could love this man. I've never felt this way about anyone. Not even Miles.

"Becca, there's something I need to tell you." It's too easy to fall back into our familiar reactions to one another, but I have to stop it before that happens. I can't be with him if it means he loses everything. *I have to go.* I pull away from him and the smell of his cologne follows me. I love that smell, but it threatens to break me. Tears swell in my eyes as I turn to leave. I try to muster up the courage to tell him that I've loved him all this time, but his father interrupts us, calling Nicholas back inside.

"Nicholas, are you going to welcome our guests?" Stefan asks, letting his piercing gaze slide over me before turning back to his guests. He doesn't know that I heard every word he said to Nicholas. The ugliness of his words repeats in my mind as I let my gaze drift from him back to his son. *She's just a gold digger.*

"I... I'll be back," Nicholas says, grabbing my hand and placing a kiss just above my knuckles. My hand trembles beneath his touch as the warmth of his kiss spreads across my skin. He doesn't know that I'm leaving New York and I'm not coming back. Nicholas's eyes pass over me with concern at my silence. I look past him at the flurry of guests laughing and drinking without a care in the world. Knots form in my throat as he squeezes my hand.

"Wait here. I'll be right back, okay?" He waits for me until I acknowledge his request.

"Sure," I say forcing a smile.

Tonight is a lot harder than I ever thought it would be. I wait for several moments for Nicholas to return, but the sight of Alison showing up sends my emotions into a panic. Alison approaches Nicholas and she wraps one long, manicured hand through the crook of his elbow. I watch her smile at him with her flirtatious touch. I wanted to stay until the end of the event and say a proper goodbye and a thank-you to Nicholas, but I can't stay here and watch them together.

How did I get here, heartbroken, a second time in mere months? I don't think I can take much more. My soul feels broken. Saying goodbye is going to be impossible. I know he won't want to let me go, and I don't want to leave, but there's no point in putting this off any longer. Come Monday morning I'll be gone, and he'll have no idea that I've left until he shows up at the office. By then, I'll be settled back in California, and hopefully, I'll have enough distance from all this to process everything without the temptation to run back. I love New York City, but everywhere I look, I see him. It breaks my heart to know that I'm not just losing Nicholas—I'm losing the promising life that I was building here in the city. I'm leaving behind my best friend, and it feels like I'm losing her, too.

Carol did not take the news well when I told her I quit my job at StoneHaven Publishing. I hate hurting her, but how can I stay? I love my friend and the life we have here. I know she's angry because I'm running, and I don't blame her, but I'm on the verge of shattering. *I'm not the strong woman I once thought I was.*

———

I find Ken and his date in the crowd of partygoers as I make my way back through the hall. I don't think I would've ever spotted him if it weren't for the fact that his mask only covered part of his face. Ironically, he easily spots me by my red hair as I almost pass by him.

"Rebecca, you look beautiful," he says, taking in the sight of me. Ken steps away from the group he's with, and we walk over to a corner of the hall. He looks at me with a beaming smile that quickly fades as he registers that something is wrong

"I'm leaving."

"Oh, all right. I guess I'll see you Monday?" he smiles.

"No, I mean I'm leaving New York." Ken's expression falls and a look of concern fills his eyes.

"Is everything all right?"

No.

I explain my plans to him and quickly thank him for his friendship and ongoing support. He's hesitant to let me go, but after a few moments, he gives in and kisses me sweetly on the corner of my mouth. I think he knows that I'm barely holding it together, because he takes pity on me and doesn't say any more. We say our goodbyes with promises to keep in touch, but deep inside, I know I can't keep my promise. I need to leave this all behind me.

I make my way down the marble staircase toward the main entrance, and for a moment, I think I hear a voice cry out after me. *Nicholas?* I turn, hoping to see him standing at the top following after me, but instead, I see Tristan Knight. There's a torn look on his face and it tears at me. I have to get out of here. I can't stand to be here any longer. Tristan races down the stairs after me as I turn and hurry across the museum lobby. I can't let anyone change my mind because I know he'll try.

"Rebecca, wait!" he calls frantically. "Don't leave!"

The edge in Tristan's voice sends tears to my eyes. Somehow, he's figured out that I'm leaving without Nicholas. I can hear Tristan behind me just as I reach the door. Guests walking through the entrance stare as Tristan calls for me to stop. This is so embarrassing. Tears stream down my face, and for once, I'm thankful for my costume because the mask hides my face.

"Becca, where are you going?" His words slice through me, but I keep moving. I jump into a waiting cab and tell the driver to leave. The night feels colder than ever as the taxicab pulls out of the circle drive to leave. I tell myself not to look back, but I can't help it. I watch Tristan slowly grow smaller and smaller as we drive away. He doesn't move. He just stands there in the middle of the street watching me drive away.

"Where to, miss?" the cab driver asks.

66

NICHOLAS

A breathless Tristan comes scrambling into the hall. There's a look of utter panic on his face as he walks over to me, still trying to catch his breath. His hair is a mess as if he's been running, and he swipes his mask from his face as he reaches me. *What the hell is wrong with him?*

"She's gone, Nick."

"Who's gone?" I ask, utterly confused.

"Rebecca."

"What do you mean she's gone? I'm on my way back to see her. She was waiting for me on the balcony." Panic starts to set in.

"Nick, listen to me. She's leaving New York. I overheard her talking with one of your employees. The one I met at *Riptide*. She told him she was leaving tonight."

"Why the fuck would she do that?"

Tristan squeezes my shoulder as anger rips through my chest. "I'm not sure, but we need to go if you want to catch her."

Alison steps into my line of sight as I head toward the exit of the hall. Tristan tries to usher me past her, but she quickly blocks my path. I watch as she pulls the overly extravagant half mask from her face. She looks at me with a questioning gaze. Irritation swarms me as a sickly sweet smile crawls over her lips. She looks from Tristan to me before assaulting my ears with her whiny voice.

"Where are you going, sweetheart?"

"To find Rebecca."

"She's not coming back. She already got what she wanted," she says.

"What the hell are you talking about?"

"Nick, don't listen to her," Tristan says. "We need to go." He tries to push me toward the door, but Alison's taunt draws me back.

"How does it feel being taken for a fool by the woman you love?"

Anger filters through my senses, and for a moment, I'm trapped by the desire to throw Alison on her ass outside. *Spoiled brat.* She doesn't even know what the fuck she's talking about.

"You know what your problem is, Alison?" I say.

"No, enlighten me." she says, rolling her eyes.

"You're just a shitty person. I feel sorry for any man who's willing to throw his life away for you... but if you think that's me, you're wrong." *Damn. If I weren't so panicked about finding Rebecca before it was too late that would have felt really good.* I pivot on my heel and rush outside the hall entrance. I'm done with Alison. I'll be happy if I never have to see her again.

Tristan hails a cab with a wave of his hand and pats me on the back in a silent wish of good luck.

"Did Rebecca say where she was going?" I ask, stepping inside the cab.

"She's going to the airport," Tristan says, popping his head through the window. "Did she mention which one?"

Tristan grimaces. "No."

"Do you have Carol's number?" I ask.

"Yes, I'll call her."

———

Tristan: She's flying from JFK via American Airlines. Her plane leaves in a few hours. You should catch her in time.

"Kennedy airport," I growl, sliding inside the filthy taxicab. My stomach turns at the smell of sweat and stale water that lingers in the backseat. I do my best to avoid having to take a cab, but I didn't have time to wait for the valet attendant to bring my car. The driver of the dilapidated death box weaves through traffic, narrowly missing a group of tourists trying to cross the street. He rushes over to the on ramp, almost completely missing the freeway.

My cell phone buzzes and my father's number flashes across the screen in bright white numbers. I almost don't pick up, but the temptation of telling him off is far too much to ignore. *I'm sure Alison told him that I was leaving.*

"Nicholas, where the hell are you going?"

"To the airport. Did you really think that I would just let Rebecca go?"

"It's better this way," he says.

"For who? For me? Or for you?"

"She's using you. She's just like your mother!" he shouts into the phone. "I'm trying to save you from the heartache of finding it out too late."

"She's nothing like her. I told you in the conference room that if you're going to make me choose between this company and her... I'm choosing her."

"Nicholas, don't do this," he warns.

"Goodbye, Dad."

67

REBECCA

John F. Kennedy Airport

"I'm sorry, miss, your bag needs to be checked-in. It's doesn't meet the requirements for a carry-on," the petite flight attendant says as she scans over my frazzled appearance with curiosity. In my rush to leave, I forgot to clean my face. I must have mascara smeared under my eyes. I can only imagine how bad I must look.

"Isn't there anything you can do?" Frustration consumes me as I lean my back against the front of the check-in center.

"I'm sorry, but we'll need to check it in."

"Fine," I mutter. "Just take it."

I turn back to take my seat in the waiting area of the terminal when the sight of Nicholas running through the airport knocks the wind out of me. His mask is off but he's still wearing his red costume and cape. Despite his strange appearance, no one seems to notice or care that he's walking around the airport in this getup.

"Nick?" I call.

He turns at the sound of my voice and closes the space between us. "You left before I could catch you," he states, his tone furious. He takes a hesitant step toward me. A few of the passengers in the boarding area turn to stare in curiosity at the scene before them.

"I can't stay. I can't stay here and ruin your life. I heard what your father said about me in the conference room the other day."

"Why didn't you talk to me before you left?"

"I knew you would try to convince me to stay," I admit. Tears threaten to pour out of me as his hand reaches up and caresses my cheek.

"Damn right."

"I can't stay, Nick." I look up and a small smile plays at the corner of his gorgeous lips.

"Why?"

"Because."

"Tell me why, Rebecca," he begs.

His thumb trails across my lips and my heart contracts almost painfully at the sudden contact. I've missed his touch and the way it always heats my skin.

"I need to hear it."

"I fucking love you—that's why!" I scream. It's the first time I've ever said the words aloud and hearing them now sucks all the air from my lungs. This beautiful, arrogant man captured my heart and now I have to let him go. On top of everything, he's going to walk down the aisle with someone else and the thought of it is enough to fracture my heart irreparably. I'm not a masochist.

"You can't leave," he says, grabbing me with a look of determination in his eyes.

"I have to. I don't want to ruin your life, and I can't watch you marry her."

"That's where you're wrong," he says.

"Please, Nick, don't do this." Nicholas grabs me pulling me out of my seat and leading me toward the exit of the airport. No one stops him. In fact, several passengers stare in fascination.

"I'm not going with you," I cry in frustration as I pull myself from his hold.

"You are, or I'll carry you out myself." I pivot to go back to the waiting area, but Nicholas is too fast. He lifts me over his shoulder as if I'm a weightless sack and carries me through the terminal. It isn't until we're near a customer service station that he sets me down.

"Come with me," he says, practically dragging me to the service desk.

"Hi, how can I help you?" the cheery attendant with bright red lipstick says. She looks from Nicholas to me and her smile widens.

"I need two tickets to Paris for today," he says.

"What?" I squeak. "Nicholas, what are you doing?"

"Great, give me a moment and I'll look for the next available flight."

"Nicholas, what the hell are you doing?"

He turns toward me with an impatient look. "Gellar, I don't want to do this here."

"We sure as hell are doing this here. I can't have you give up your father's company for me. And I'm not leaving with you when your fiancée is waiting for you at home." The words start out as a whisper but quickly crescendo to a yell. My cheeks burn as several travelers passing by, including the customer service rep, turn toward us, eyes gaping in shock.

"Excuse us for a moment," Nicholas tells her as he pulls me to the side. An impatient look crosses his face as he maneuvers us past a group of waiting travelers.

"Nicholas, I can't bear to stay and ruin your future, and I'm not going to be the other woman," I say when we're finally at a safe distance and out of earshot of the waiting passengers.

"So what you're saying is you won't be my mistress," Nicholas asks, smirking.

"You are such an—"

"Before you call me an asshole, listen. You left the gala before I could tell you that I broke off my engagement with Alison. I told my father that I was coming here to find you. If I'm going to be running his company, then I think I deserve the right to choose whom I'm going to marry. If he can't accept it, then I don't want any part of it. I want to be with you. I know you think that I'm giving up everything, but you haven't realized that... you mean everything to me."

"I do?" My eyes scan the area around us as a cluster of passengers watch in fascination. It's like we're putting on a TV show over here.

"Yes, I love you." Tears fill my eyes at the shock and raw beauty of his words. I never thought I would hear those words coming from his lips.

"I really didn't want to do this here, but…" I watch as Nicholas slowly lowers himself to one knee, pushing back his red cloak as he pulls the familiar little turquoise box from his pocket. A grin spreads across his face as he opens it. My breath catches at the sight of the emerald-cut ring. This asshole led me to believe I was picking out a ring for Alison, but it was for me all along? *He loves me? He's asking me to…*

Nicholas takes my hand and kisses the center of my palm. My center instantly heats at his touch.

"Rebecca Elizabeth Gellar, my fiery red goddess and the some-times thorn in my side, will you do me the honor of becoming my wife? I can't promise the future won't be rocky, but I *can* promise that I will love, cherish, and fuck you every opportunity I get." He takes the sparkling diamond ring and slides it on my finger.

I blush at the gasps that escape from people around us.

"I'm all yours," he says. "Will you have me?"

Mine. I never in my wildest dreams imagined that this would happen. When I first met Nicholas, I thought he was just another gorgeous face with an enlarged ego. This man has tested my patience, my sanity, and has stretched me nearly beyond my breaking point. It seems that these weeks of agony and despair have been in vain. Instead of fighting to stay out of his arms, I've won my way into them.

"Yes."

Nicholas scoops me up and crushes my body to his. "I love you so much, Rebecca." His lips claim mine in a ravenous kiss that makes my toes curl. For several seconds, all I know is the feeling of his lips against mine.

"Does this mean I have to share my side of the bed with you?" I laugh.

"Sweetheart, I can promise you there won't be much sleeping when we're in bed."

"I'm going to hold you to that."

"I think we'll have to reschedule our flight for tomorrow," he growls.

"Why?" I ask, confused.

"Because I have to take you somewhere right now and fuck you. I can't wait four hours. I need to be inside you, right now." Nicholas nips my ear and it takes all of my control not combust right here in the middle of the airport terminal.

"Yes, let's go."

EPILOGUE

68

REBECCA

*P*aris, France

My mind drifts to thoughts of Nicholas and I entangled in bed sheets as he walks back into the hotel room carrying a bottle of champagne, and one long stemmed rose. My eyes trace over him, anxious to begin my exploration.

"What dirty little thoughts are running through your head, Ms. Gellar?" Nicholas asks as he scans my face. My cheeks warm at the low rumble of his knowing chuckle and the slow twitch of his lips. I hate and love that he now always seems to know what I'm thinking. I bite my lip, feeling a boost of courage shooting through me.

"I'll show you," I say, flashing him a cheeky smile as I pull him to the bedroom. The mixed look of shock and desire on his face is priceless. He grabs hold of my nape and pulls me into a tantalizing kiss. His lips are soft, even with the slight abrasion of his five o'clock shadow. His hold on me grows urgent as I mold my body against his. A trickling sensation builds between my legs. It's a need that only he seems to be able to fill. Nicholas palms my bottom, pressing me firmly against him. I love when his hands are on me.

I pull at his tie and run my hands through his hair. The soft moan that escapes his lips only makes me bolder in my attempt at seducing his clothes off—although at this point, he's not really putting up a fight. He stops me then and proceeds to shed his tie, shirt, and pants. I marvel at the way his boxers ride down on his hips, revealing a light trail of blond just below his navel. My lips itch to kiss and lick the sexy muscular lines of his hips. Nicholas pulls his boxers down and steps out of them. I hold back the gasp that threatens to escape from the sight of his hard cock. Nicholas's gaze smolders as he watches me slowly and seductively pull my dress over my head. I've always felt silly stripping in front of guys, but somehow, with him, he always manages to make me feel like this is one really hot show. There's no room to feel self-conscious about the way certain things jiggle or bounce when I move, and in reality, there's no need to, because Nicholas doesn't seem to mind.

A smile plays on his mouth as I throw my dress at him. He tosses it to the floor and saunters over.

"I can't seem to get enough of you," he chuckles. There's a deep timbre in his voice, and for a moment, I can't help but think that there's a double meaning to those words. I don't want him to have enough of me because I can't seem to get enough of him, and it thrills me that those feelings might not ever change.

"You could try..." I say with a smirk.

He sits down, admiring my naked form from the edge of the bed. I watch his eyes trace the curve of my hips and then down my belly. I step forward with confidence and he grabs me, pulling me close to straddle his lap. Each movement replays in my head in slow motion. His hands wander down my back to knead the flesh of my bottom. He grips me firmly, pressing me against his hardness. A hiss escapes his lips as I grind my hips against him.

"Rebecca." His voice comes out tight and raspy.

"Yes?" I ask, panting. I feel him purposefully pressing into my thigh.

"I'm going to show you how much I've missed this pussy of yours," he warns. My insides clench in desire at his words. Nicholas cups my breasts and pushes them together into his mouth. The scorching pressure of his tongue sends me into a tizzy.

He slowly grinds his hips up toward me as if warning me not to move. My underwear and bra aren't even off, but I can feel an orgasm building inside me. I hear a popping sound as Nicholas pulls my nipple from his mouth. They tingle from the sensation of going from warm to cold. Just as I'm about to sink down onto Nicholas, he flips me on my back, landing me softly on the Egyptian cotton from the hotel bed. His body easily covers mine as he scoots me back against the top. I watch him with lust as he pulls off my panties and unclasps my bra with ease.

I'm calm until the moment he pushes open my legs and pulls my bottom toward him. The tension in the room suddenly feels unbearable. Nicholas looks down at me as if marveling at the sight before him. I close my eyes and enjoy the warmth of his body leaning into me. One moment I feel him gently pressing against my entrance, and then in the next he's thrusting inside me. There's a slight pain as my body adjusts to him. The pain quickly subsides as he rocks into me in slow strides. Tremors radiate throughout my body.

"Nick!" I gasp.

"I love the way my name sounds on your lips."

His speed and rhythm climbs to a different level of intensity. I arch at the slapping sound of skin on skin as he drives deeper into me. He grabs my hands and crosses them above my head. I don't fight him. I just let him take control and revel in the thought that simultaneously he's giving back that control he so desperately needs. His grunts grow heavier as his hands roam down to the top of my chest.

Each time he enters me, a tidal wave of pleasure swallows me up. I've never done drugs, but I'm pretty sure the *high* that people talk about feels something like this. In this moment, I'm suspended between life and death. My limbs feel too good to move, and every time Nicholas whispers sweet nothings into my ear, I come a little closer to melting into the sheets. I clench around him and he nips my earlobe in appreciation.

"Keep doing that," he begs.

I smile at the sound of him begging me. I reward Nicholas with another clench, but this time, I hold myself tightly around him. He pants and growls and it's as if someone let a tiger loose in my bed. He lifts my right leg, giving him a deeper angle. I cry out as he drives into me. It only takes three thrusts before the shockwaves take over and my insides liquefy beneath him. A second later his body slumps against me. I giggle at the feeling of his blond mane tickling my now overly sensitive skin. He brushes his growing facial shadow against my breast, and before I have a chance to moan he leans up and captures my lips. I shudder as he runs his tongue lazily across mine.

EPILOGUE

69

NICHOLAS

aris, France
My eyes snap open and the first thing I see on my right is red. Silky red curls splayed out across white bed sheets. I exhale in relief at the sight of her lying beside me. I was so afraid last night wasn't real. *She's still here with me.* The sunlight trickles in through the hotel window, illuminating her skin in warm sunlight. It must be well into the morning already. I scan the room for a clock, but find none. Last night felt too good to be real, but here she is, snuggled up inches from me. I can still smell myself on her. The smell is a sweet mixture of her flowery perfume and my sweat and cologne. *She looks so peaceful when she sleeps.* I reach out and trace my hand across the curve of her hip. Her skin is soft beneath my fingertips. It takes every ounce of strength not to turn her over and restart what we had last night. I glide my hand down her stomach until I'm only inches from her pussy. I want to feel her go wet for me again.

As if sensing the pressure of my hand, she moans and juts her hips up. My body immediately responds to the sound. My head says *go to sleep,* but my cock has other plans. I watch her stretch and roll toward me. Her breasts sway, brushing against my chest, and the sensation sends a pool of heat down my body. I pull her to me and she immediately lays her head against my chest. Just as I'm about to close my eyes and let sleep overtake me, I hear her soft voice.

"You're poking me," she whines. She shifts her body and I feel my erection rubbing up against her.

"What?" Rebecca's hand slips under the covers and she wraps it around my cock. *Fuck. That feels so good.* I groan as I thrust into her palm.

"Either my remote control found its way in your pants, or you're just really happy to see me." I chuckle at the wicked look on her not so innocent face.

"I'm just really happy to see you," I admit.

She bats her eyelashes and a beautiful smile breaks across her face. I rub off the mascara that is lightly smeared underneath her eyes. Most women would freak out if I saw them without their makeup being utterly flawless, but Rebecca seems to have this adorable take-me-as-I-am attitude. She covers her mouth with the bed sheet just as I'm about to lean and kiss her.

"Stop hiding your lips," I rumble.

"We haven't brushed our teeth." A bright blush stains her cheeks. If she thinks her comment offends me, but it doesn't.

"Are you afraid of my morning breath?"

"No," she starts to say.

"I'm not going to stick my tongue down your throat, sweetheart. But if you don't let me kiss you, I'll be forced to pin you down." Before she has a chance to turn away from me, I pull the cover from her face and seize her lips with mine. It isn't the open-mouthed kiss that I crave, but it's still a gorgeous reminder of how good it felt to be inside her hours earlier. I break the connection just long enough to roll her underneath me. Her eyes go wide as I plant myself between her luscious thighs and position my cock inside her warm center. Her back arches as I lean in and thrust. I'm greeted with the familiar blissful sensation of her warmth.

Rebecca's head goes back and she swerves her hips with me. "Nick, mmm, ohhh, God."

"I'm not a god, baby, but you sure make me feel like one," I say. Despite the urgent need to fuck her senseless, I take each thrust slow.

Her fingernails dig into my ass, pushing me to drive deeper and harder, but I hold back and shoo her hands away.

"I'm going to fuck you slow, baby. The more you claw my ass, the slower I fuck you."

"Please," she begs. "Faster."

My restraint is unraveling. From the desperation in her voice, I can tell she's close to her release. I would do anything for this woman. She's the fire in my life, the kick in the balls I needed, and the love I've always craved. She's my everything.

I can't wait for us to begin our forever.

ALSO BY VANESSA BOOKE

Bound to You: Volumes 1-3

Bound to You: Ever After

Drawn to Her

Drawn to You: Volumes 1-3

Filthy Beast (Filthy Fairy Tales, Book 1)

Grade A A$$hole (ABCs of Love, Book 1)

Her Russian Bodyguard (Intl. Lovers, Book 1)

BOUND TO YOU: EVER AFTER

Get ready for Nicholas & Rebecca's wedding story!
NOW AVAILABLE ON All RETAILERS.

I, Rebecca Gellar, am doing the unthinkable. I'm marrying a man who hits every category on my Run-Like-Hell list...
1. Arrogant.
2. Dangerously Handsome.
3. Brooding.
4. Domineering.
5. Possessive.
6. Playboy.
The funny thing is I couldn't be happier.

DRAWN TO HER

Can't get enough of the Millionaire's Row Series? Check out Drawn to Her and Drawn to You: Volumes 1-3 featuring Tristan Knight & Emily StoneHaven. Flip ahead to read a chapter preview. Be warned, this preview is extra steamy.

EMILY

IT'S A NEEDY moan that startles me awake. The soft sound of her voice vibrates through the air ventilation and into my room. My eyes flicker open and I stare into the darkness of my bedroom. *It's happening again. He's down there with another one.* I hold my breath as I strain to hear their voices. My heart races as their cries fill me with a lustful warmth, and I flush at the wicked thoughts that flood my mind. Thoughts of him touching me, thoughts of him spreading me open and taking me from behind. Thoughts of me being the naked woman entangled in his sheets.

A gasping voice calls out his name. Tristan! I hear his deep, throaty roar and the sound of her moan desperate for release. This isn't the first time I've heard him take a woman down to his room. There have been many nights I would lie here wondering what it must be like to be on the other side of that vent. I shouldn't be having sexual fantasies about Tristan. He's not my older brother by blood, but it doesn't make the situation in the pantry any easier to swallow. Even the kiss we shared on the stairs blurred the lines between us. I don't know how I should look at him anymore. Brother? Friend? Or something else entirely?

I turn over and try my best to go back to sleep, but their voices draw me in, and before I realize it, I'm panting with them. I grow wet at the touch of my nail gliding across my bud. If he only knew how many times I've pictured him touching me. I close my eyes and imagine his hand inside me, pressing up against me and rubbing me at a slow, torturous pace. I arch at the warm sensation that starts at my center and builds its way up. My nipples harden as I roll one of them through my fingers.

I'm so close. After several minutes pass, my hand grows tired. Frustration consumes me as the image of Tristan touching me dissipates. I lie there annoyed at the lack of release in my life. Most of my high school friends lost their virginity long ago, but I'm still stuck with mine. My best friend has reassured me that there's no need to rush into anything, but when everyone around you is doing it, it makes me wonder if she's just saying it because she feels bad.

After several minutes of tossing and turning and doing my best to drown out the sound with my pillow, I muster the courage to get out of bed and walk down the long set of stairs to Tristan's bedroom. I've always wondered why he chose to take one of the bedrooms downstairs. They're usually reserved for guests. From the bottom step, I spot a cascade of light seeping out from his bedroom door.

The scene before me sends a rush of heat straight to my center. I clench in arousal at the sight of Tristan's long, muscular frame kneeling between two lovely legs adorned around his shoulders. I've never seen anything like it. I can't see her face, but I hear the way her voice grows tight with each lick. Her body trembles as he kneels back and inserts two long fingers inside of her. I can feel myself dripping at the sound of his digits sliding in and out of her quickly.

I'm so lost in the haze of it all that I don't realize I've moaned aloud. Tristan stops and turns on his knee. His hazel eyes grow wide at the sight of me standing there as I watch the intimate session between two lovers. His lips part as if he's about to speak, but he says nothing. Embarrassed at being caught, I turn and flee from his watchful eyes. They burn into my mind, threatening to unravel me.

I'm halfway up the stairs when I feel someone grab at my heel. I turn and nearly tumble down, but warm hands are there to catch me. Despite the overwhelming darkness of the house, I know that it's Tristan. His fingers are slightly calloused from the constant pressure of the drawing pencil in his hand. I'd recognize those hands anywhere. His body hovers slightly over mine as he stares down at me. I can feel the cold steps of the stairs digging into my back.

For a moment, the only sound I hear is the ragged breath as it flows in and out of his shallow gulps. My breath hitches as I watch the reflection of the moonlight catch his face. His hair is ruffled into a mess and there's a strong shadow of facial hair spread across his jaw and cheekbones and around his lips. I subconsciously reach out and touch his face. His skin burns beneath my fingers. If it weren't for what I had just seen, I would be worried that he's getting sick.

Although the darkness of the house cloaks his frame, I know he's fully nude. In his haste to catch me, he must've forgotten to cover up. It isn't until I feel his erection pressing against my stomach that I sense a strange shift in the air between us. Without a word, Tristan positions himself between my legs. The world slows to a halt as his hand glides up my nightie. His warm fingers slide across me, leaving a trail of heat behind them. I tremble at the sensation. It's like nothing I've ever imagined. It's better. I feel him watching me as he pushes up the soft fabric of my nightgown and positions himself at the opening of my center. I writhe against him as he rubs his cock at my opening.

I moan, and in one quick movement, his fingers wrap around the front of my mouth. He stops for a moment, listening for the slightest movement upstairs. My frantic thoughts return to the memory of the woman whose legs were wrapped around his shoulders only moments earlier. Where is she?

Tristan loosens his hold on my mouth and leans in, letting out a harsh whisper against my ear. "You're so fucking wet."

It's the first and only words out of his mouth before I feel him thrust inside me. A sharp pressure hits me, and I immediately push back against him. This is what my friend Ceci had warned me about. Tristan slows to a stop as he sees discomfort etched across my face. I flush as concern and then disbelief fills his eyes.

"Fuck," he says, gritting his teeth. Without another word, Tristan pulls out, leaving me shivering against the stairs. The sudden shift in temperature from his warm body leaves me aching for him to envelop me once again.

"Emily, I didn't know…"

His words crash over me, and I'm left with a devastating feeling of regret. In one thoughtless decision, we've changed everything between us.

THANK YOU!

Dear amazing reader,

Thank you for taking a chance on this story and me. So many of you have reached out to me asking for more of Rebecca and Nicholas and to be honest, that's probably the best compliment any writer could ask for. I'm so glad that so many of you have fallen in love with this story. It really means the world to me.

If you have a moment, I would greatly appreciate if you would consider leaving a review on Amazon, B&N, or Goodreads. I hope you've enjoyed this story as much as I've enjoyed writing it.

Thank you,

Vanessa Booke

Want notifications when I have a new release? Sign up below:
MAILING LIST SIGN UP

ABOUT THE AUTHOR

Vanessa Booke is a USA Today Bestselling Author of the Millionaire's Row Series. She loves writing about strong curvy women who fall in love, alpha males with filthy mouths, and sex scenes that don't fade to black. When she isn't writing, you can find her listening to true crime podcasts, watching PBS, or reading Scottish Highlander Romances. She's also a huge fan of traveling.

CONNECT WITH VANESSA ONLINE:

www.VanessaBooke.com
VanessaBooke@gmail.com

Made in the USA
Las Vegas, NV
22 April 2021

21868080R00190